MONEYBAGS

MONEYBAGS

A NOVEL

Tulley Holland

Library of Congress Control Number:		2007901315
ISBN:	Hardcover	978-1-4257-5700-7
	Softcover	978-1-4257-5699-4

This book was printed in the United States of America.

To order additional copies of this book, contact:
Xlibris Corporation
1-888-795-4274
www.Xlibris.com
Orders@Xlibris.com
36610

FOR

SUSAN

Acknowledgements

This book is dedicated to my wife, Susan, who has been my greatest supporter and my most constructive critic for over forty-two years. After spending far too much time trying to write *Moneybags* and a nonfiction book, *Impolite Dinner Conversation*, she advised, "Pick one and finish it; otherwise, you never will." She was right. I hope to finish *Impolite Dinner Conversation* later this year and begin a sequel to *Moneybags* next spring.

Thanks to my editor, Linda Cashdan, who was very patient with me as she led me through the entire process. I learned so much from her. Also, a great deal of credit goes to Carl and Judy Napps, who held many dinner parties and asked me to read chapters as entertainment for their guests. Each dinner gave me encouragement, and the meals were Epicurean in style, taste, and presentation.

Several friends read drafts and offered valuable advice: Ed and Sally Gripkey, Bryant Nickerson, Paula Newcomb, Lynn Holland, Finley Glaize Kuhner, and Arthur H. Bryant II. My children, Katie and Chris, were especially insightful with their focus on grammar and content. Many other people were helpful just by asking, "How's the book coming?" They served to offset my natural tendency to procrastinate. Others asked, "Am I in the book?" They indicated their interest, and I tried to use as many names as I could by mixing first and last names of different people. However, I would remind them that if they saw their name, it would bear no resemblance to the truth. This is a total work of fiction. It is my imagination, and I even had to repeat that to my wife, who wondered at some of the sex scenes.

Lastly, I must thank my mother and father, though both deceased, their positive influence lives on. Dad was a small-town newspaper editor and publisher. Mom was a contributing writer, mostly on local social goings-on. Both were avid readers and gave unlimited love and guidance.

Tulley Holland
2007

Chapter 1

Gabriella Alverez was a familiar sight on the C&O Canal towpath. Every day at dawn, no matter the weather, she could be seen with five other runners winding their way through Georgetown, heading toward the river and its adjacent towpath. The run was the first priority of Gabriella's disciplined life that included daily exercise and meditation. The other runners rarely interrupted her thoughts as they proceeded like lemmings on a mission, going up the towpath to the Cabin John Bridge, turning around, and heading back, never changing their routine.

As usual, the runners noticed the Potomac River in all its majesty. It was rising and swift, overflowing from heavy snow. Tree branches, bottles, and an accumulation of riverbank debris bobbed on the muddy current, cascading toward the Chesapeake Bay.

Unlike the river, the runners' movements appeared unhurried and graceful. Gabriella was the only female in the group, and she dictated their speed and their route. It was always the same. She ran in the middle, and the others would adjust to her stride. She was a superb athlete whatever the challenge, and she was accustomed to the company of men. Most women just couldn't compete with her aggressiveness and skill.

With a final half mile to go, Gabriella increased the pace of the run, stretching her powerful legs to the limit. The other five automatically sped up.

In spite of the cold, beads of perspiration ran down Gabriella's forehead, wetting her cheeks and blurring her vision. She wiped her face on her sleeve and grinned when Key Bridge came into view. She focused on the bridge traffic as it poured into Georgetown imagining the city coming to life, people rushing to work, trying to achieve their dreams.

The man beside her, Ashley Sheppard, had dreams of his own. He was a medical student at Georgetown with a very busy schedule. Yet, he relished every minute in her company. As usual, he was determined to match her pace; but her legs were longer, so he had to take extra steps to keep up with her final burst of speed.

Across the river in Virginia, horns blared and tires shrieked as anxious drivers jockeyed for position on the crowded George Washington Parkway. Commuter traffic on the parkway was always heavy at this time of day, and the loud noise seemed normal.

Her friend was oblivious to traffic sounds and everything else, except the woman beside him. He was in love, and someday, he hoped to have Gabriella all to himself.

But there were always four others: two leading and two trailing behind. These men were related to Gabriella and very protective of her. Each of these protectors was identically dressed, and all were armed with automatic pistols carried in holsters under their windbreakers. Normally, they would be closer, but when she was with her friend, they allowed Gabriella some privacy and personal space.

Except for the men working ahead of them, in Potomac Edison uniforms, the six runners were the only people near the towpath this early in the day. In another hour, the place would be crowded, a popular spot for runners, hikers, and bikers.

A sudden snow shower blew across the river, further dropping the temperature, whipping the wind and reducing visibility, but the change didn't faze the runners. It was usual Washington winter weather, and it had been this way for weeks.

The workmen leered at Gabriella as she went by, her breasts bouncing up and down in her Georgetown sweats. She wore a bulky sweater under an oversized sweatshirt and her sports bra as tight as she could stand; yet still, they bounced with every step. One of the workmen was about to say something to Gabriella, but he held back when he saw the look of the two men behind her.

It happened all the time. She was graceful and statuesque: a cover girl's face on an athlete's body. Her posture was aristocratic, her head held high, and proud. She was blessed with long eyelashes surrounding big green eyes, high cheekbones, and lips that were perpetually pouty. A patrician nose gave her the look of Spanish nobility. Yet sometimes, she looked like the girl next door, with her jet black hair pulled back into a ponytail under her baseball cap.

Gabriella was in her finishing stride when she saw another group of Potomac Edison workmen ahead of her, not far from the tunnel to Georgetown. She was wondering what Potomac Edison could possibly be doing on the towpath when she heard the unmistakable sound of automatic weapons being fired. Instinctively, she ducked and turned to see what was happening. The workmen behind her had drawn guns and were firing at her friends.

Pop, pop, pop, pop, pop, pop, pop, pop, pop, pop, pop, pop, echoed all around her, and she saw the workmen in front begin shooting too. They were firing at the two runners ahead of her. She watched her running companions dodge and turn, trying to avoid the workmen's bullets, but they fell in a heap, unable to avoid the furious assault.

A tall, thin man, wearing Potomac Edison coveralls, calmly walked up onto the towpath, leveled a shotgun at two of the downed men, and finished them off. Sounds from the twin blasts reverberated across the river. The tall man and the four other "workers" with him turned toward Gabriella with guns raised.

Her friend bravely shielded her while frantically looking for an escape route. There was no place to go. All around them, the shooting had stopped.

Surrounded by the flood-swollen Potomac River on one side and armed workmen on all other sides, the two raised their hands in the air. Ashley stood protectively in front of Gabriella and begged them not to shoot.

"You in the wrong place at the wrong time, lover boy!" the tall man said, shooting him in the face with a pistol as he pulled him away from Gabriella. It took two shots at close range to bring the young man down. The first bullet pierced the top of his ski cap, going through the Georgetown Bulldog emblem. As he was falling, a second bullet entered his open mouth and exited just below his right ear.

Ashley's blood splattered Gabriella's face, and she bent down, trying to help him, screaming, "Stop! Oh dear God, please STOP!" Her frantic request was almost ignored, but the man with the pistol didn't shoot again. He just stood over the two of them, waiting to see if her companion moved. Then other attackers grabbed her by each arm and pinned her face down on the ground. Roughly, they frisked her, their hands conveniently fondling her breasts, crotch, and legs, supposedly searching for hidden weapons.

"Okay! Enough feeling her up! We got to move out!" The tall one yelled at his men. They then forced her to stand and held her mouth, trying to muzzle her hysterical sobbing. They half-dragged her to a large tool cart, stuffed her in, and wheeled her to the street.

On Canal Road and nearby MacArthur Boulevard, commuters in a variety of vehicles competed to reach Georgetown before traffic came to its normal standstill. No one seemed to notice the Potomac Edison van as it entered the flow of traffic going into the center of the city.

Slowly, the van crept through Northwest DC, and ten grinning, "Potomac Edison workers" inside continued to congratulate one another with high fives. The one who seemed to be the leader turned to Gabriella as the van hit a pothole.

"We all biznessmen here, we mainly peaceful, but this's our town, and we got a problem. Try to scream, call for help, or try to escape, and we goin' to help ourselves to yo' beautiful ass. Be a good girl, we goin' to respect you. You understand?"

Gabriella nodded, unable to speak, tears of despair haunting her eyes. Her breathing became difficult, coming in quick gulps. She was on the brink of hysteria.

After an agonizing twenty minutes of stopping and starting through DC's morning rush hour, the van slowed through a quiet neighborhood. Traffic was light as a police car coming in the opposite direction flashed its lights. Gabriella looked up; a spark of hope brightened her face. The van didn't stop. Instead, both drivers waved in recognition and raised their fists in a familiar salute. The police car went on. Soon after, the van pulled through a wrought-iron gate into a hidden driveway. Once inside, two men closed the gate, and the van pulled to a stop.

They had arrived at an old slate-roofed brick mansion in Adams Morgan. The very private-looking home was secluded from the street, surrounded by a high wall covered in ivy. Inside, the wall was lined with vines and shrubs. A wooden rake was upside down against the wall next to a pile of dead leaves.

When the van stopped, everyone became quiet, and the tall, thin man put a burlap bag over Gabriella's head. Then the van doors opened, and one of the men helped her up and guided her out through the door. When her feet hit the ground, she lost her equilibrium and vomited. The bile covered her sneakers and the splatter reached some of the shoes worn by her captors.

"SHIT!" Was all she heard; the speaker more concerned about his appearance, ignoring her nausea.

She stayed down for a while to catch her breath and regain her balance. She tried to notice where she was, hoping for any information that might prove helpful. But all she saw were someone's shoes being wiped off with a handkerchief, the bottom of a chain-link fence that looked like a dog pen, and a green asphalt driveway that was covered here and there with melting patches of snow.

In downtown DC, a popular nightclub was as quiet as a church. The bar had long closed, the band shut down, and the 152 patrons had staggered home. Dishes and glassware were piled high on tables and in the sink, waiting to be washed. Lights were out; partially hiding the trash-littered floor, still sticky from the evening's spilled drinks. Ashtrays were full, most to overflowing, and a stale smell of marijuana hung in the air.

Only three men remained in the club, and two of them were nodding in their chairs. They were in the largest of the back rooms that served as an office for the club. One man sat at an old partner's desk, tapping his fingers and pretending to read a *Sports Illustrated* magazine, when one of the two phones on the desk broke the silence. Before the first ring ended, the red phone was picked up. "Well, how'd it go?"

"Total surprise! Took 'em all down in less than a minute! Piece o' cake; just like we called it."

"Any damage to our girl?"

"She's okay, a little shook, scared, and wonderin' what's next, but lookin' good! Reminds me of a movie star, Sophia Loren, only taller. She got a full rack, Boog. Stickin' out, real proud, ya know?"

"I'll take your word for it. You bein' an expert in anatomy. Just you be sure she's treated like the queen of England an' leave the rest t' me."

Chapter 2

Driving south on the George Washington Parkway, across Key Bridge, Will MacKenzie moved slowly in late-morning traffic. Like others ahead of him who had slowed to gawk, he couldn't help noticing all the lights and sirens over on Canal Road.

Will was on his way for a luncheon meeting with a very small group. There were only three members, and they called themselves the Ignorant Assholes. But when they were with outsiders or in public, they tended to refer to themselves as just Ignorants. The name came from an all-night binge in a Saigon nightclub. They were all rip-shittin' drunk, singing every song they could think of. They'd planned to go from the bar to the airport for their ticket home when a group of marines complained about "those loud-mouthed assholes." A club-clearing brawl was avoided when the "assholes" started singing, "From the Halls of Montezuma, to the shores of Tripoli . . ." After that, the marines bought the drinks, and they almost missed their plane.

Today's luncheon meeting was unusual. Normally, they met for dinner—either in New York, Philadelphia, or Washington—and would wind up drinking and partying all night. This was their twelfth "official" annual meeting, remaining true to the pact that they'd made in Vietnam.

The three of them, different from one another in almost every way, considered themselves blood brothers, all part of a very special, elite group. Together through thick and thin, for better or for worse, "'til death do they part," and after death, the ones who remained alive would remember their dead.

Today's meeting was going to be a major change from the past; they were going to be on their best behavior. When they'd met the last two years, Will MacKenzie had become so sloppy, so depressingly drunk that the other two had to carry him back to his room. They had been asked to leave restaurants because of Will. Sadly, they'd watched Will's depression ruin his marriage, his job, his social life, and his health. He'd spurned their frequent offers to help. Nothing had worked. Will had been on a self-destructive path that had steadily worsened in recent years.

But Will MacKenzie was smiling today as he turned off M Street onto Wisconsin and parked in the Georgetown Mall garage. He was anxious to show his friends he had recovered. Sober for months now, he had exercised hard every day. He'd become a new man as he worked to improve every aspect of his life: physically, mentally, and spiritually.

The recovery had begun almost one year earlier. After two weeks of binge drinking, he'd finally reached bottom, as low as he could go without killing himself. Drowning his troubles in bourbon, he grew to hate himself.

His savior was a dog, always with him, no matter what. Waking up with another headache from hell, lying in his own vomit, he realized that his dog, Watson, was licking the bile off his face. The dog was looking into his eyes with a love so deep and trusting Will finally found a reason to live.

He surely felt alive today as he quickened his step. He whistled to himself, heading for the restaurant, anxious to see their reaction.

Several drivers had heard the shots and called 911 shortly after passing by. Soon after the first call, three DC Metropolitan Police cars converged on Canal Road at a spot adjacent to the C&O Canal where the anonymous callers had reported shots being fired. No one had seen the shooting.

Eight minutes later, the police found what looked like a war zone and called for backup and ambulances. The crime scene stretched over a hundred bloody yards of the towpath. After first checking to see if anyone was alive, the officers called homicide and were extra careful not to disturb anything, especially footprints and spent shells, which seemed to be everywhere.

Gabriella's friend was unconscious, but the only one still alive. He carried no wallet and could not be immediately identified. The medics gave him a shot of adrenaline supplement, a head bandage to slow the bleeding, and then gently placed him on a stretcher, not sure he would live through the ambulance ride. Georgetown Hospital's emergency room was close by, less than five minutes away.

Homicide detectives Joy and White of the Georgetown Precinct arrived within minutes after the radio call from the first patrol car. Police photographers, crime scene investigators, and support personnel were quick to follow. The detectives' first instinct focused on getting a feel for the action, trying to "see" what had happened. They then began to try to identify the bodies. By this time, over fifteen patrol cars were on the scene, their emergency lights blinking, their occupants busy with familiar routines, some were directing traffic, others were marking off the perimeter with yellow tape.

Television crews had also arrived.

When a photographer from the *Washington Post* broke through and began taking pictures of two of the dead men, the flash caught the attention of Detective White.

"Get that son-of-a-bitch outta here!" He shouted. "Who let him in?"

The photographer backed into the growing crowd and seemed to disappear.

Detective Joy was checking the pockets of the dead men, bagging every item.

Detective White faced the crowd. "Anybody here see anything?" He got no response. All had arrived after the police.

The two men nearest the Georgetown tunnel could not be positively identified with the driver's licenses in their pockets because their faces had been blown off.

The passports, empty wallets, and other personal items that all four dead men carried indicated they were foreign nationals, Colombians specifically. All four had been armed. Only one had managed to pull his weapon. They all lived in DC, and they had all entered the United States three years earlier.

Over two hundred cartridge shells were recovered, including four shotgun shells. Investigators were able to identify each of the weapons that had been fired. Later, footprints revealed that at least eleven people, other than the victims, had been present and that one was certainly a female. From the footprint locations, it appeared that the female had been taken. Her trail led from the path to a place where cart tracks began, which led to the road. From the path to the cart, her feet appeared to be sometimes dragging, sometimes just touching the ground as if she were being carried between prints of two of the assailants, one of whom was wearing boots.

Clyde's wasn't too busy yet, so Will MacKenzie was able to get a table by the window. As he watched the students, shoppers, and honking cars outside, he thought back to the first meeting of his closest friends.

It had been 1968, just after TET, and all hell had broken loose in Vietnam. Will was a squad leader waiting for replacements at a firebase near the Cambodian border. Something big was about to happen, and the entire battalion was on alert. Intelligence was coming in from everywhere that the enemy was up to something.

His future friends came into the bunker at the same time, a big black man and a wiry Jew, remnants of another unit that had been shot to pieces. You could tell from their eyes and the way they looked around that they didn't trust anybody, certainly not the new lieutenant who had just come grinning and strutting out of battalion headquarters. The lieutenant was bringing bad news. He'd just volunteered to lead their reinforced rifle platoon on a special mission.

Will's memories were interrupted by the sight of his old comrades, coming down M Street. They looked like Mutt and Jeff but hadn't changed much. Twelve years older, of course, faces hardened, but to Will, they looked great, and he smiled in anticipation. A tall Champ Lewis, clad in a brown leather full-length overcoat, dwarfed Steve Beinhorn, in his lawyer's pinstriped suit and red tie. They were laughing, both talking at once, as they came toward the restaurant door.

Off to the left, another police car, siren blaring, whooped by, heading for Canal Road.

Will stood up, almost knocking the waitress over as he rushed to greet these warriors. After bear hugs, sarcastic remarks, and vigorous handshakes, the three realized they were blocking the door and moved to their table.

Normally, they would look one another over and let loose with the insults. Today, the other two congratulated Will on how great he looked. He did too. Almost as tall as Champ but much fitter, he seemed ten years younger than the last time they'd met. Champ and Steve glanced at each other again and swore that after seeing such a huge change in Will, they were going to get back to the gym. They couldn't stop staring. What a change in such a short time. Will's hair was still full and brownish blonde. He was all muscle.

Champ's head was shaved to the bone. It looked like a mahogany bowling ball, with a flat nose and recessed eyes, sitting on a heavyweight wrestler's body.

Steve Beinhorn was the same compact size he'd been twelve years ago, only now he had thinning hair and a bald spot on top and circles under his eyes from too many hours of late-night reading.

Before they could say another word, the waitress, a cute Georgetown student wearing a low-cut blouse and short shorts, introduced herself as Diane and got their attention. They all ordered iced tea, out of respect for

Will, and stayed quiet while all eyes followed the waitress as she sashayed back to the bar.

"Wow! Would you look at that." Mumbled Champ

"She reminds me of a candy bar—good and plenty," growled Steve.

Champ sighed, "Good enough to eat."

"You assholes never grow up," Will announced. "She's too young for you old farts." But the distraction didn't last. They always remembered old times, rehashed events of the past year. What on earth had brought about the change in Will? He tried to joke about it, but it didn't work. His friends knew the marriage was over.

"It was my dog. I woke up one morning, after a binge of I don't know how long, and there he was on top of me. It was as if he was going to do mouth to mouth on me an' I knew where that mouth of his had been." He made a sour face as he said it.

His friends grinned, but they all knew how bad Will's drinking had become.

"I guess I owe you guys an apology. Thanks for sticking with me. You're the only ones." Will started to choke up, but he cleared his throat and forced a laugh.

Champ patted him on the shoulder. "Shit, Will, you don't owe either of us an apology. We're just glad you're recovered, that's all. We knew you'd get back to your old self."

"When we promised 'til death do us part, we meant it in spite of this asshole's treatment of you last year," Beinhorn said, looking at Champ with a grin.

Will shook his head. "I don't even remember. I'm sorry. It seems like I don't remember many things that happened in the last two years."

"Some things are best forgotten, but Champ's the one who should apologize. We were having drinks at the Marriott when you got a little out of hand. Champ picked you up and carried you out over his shoulder with your ass staring down the whole bar. You were a true Asshole." Steve pointed the finger of guilt at Champ.

"You dropped your drawers, and I didn't know what you were going to do, but you weren't gonna do it in front of everybody in that bar," Champ said, looking at Will, trying to explain.

"Thanks, thanks to both of you." Will tried to change the subject. "Enough about me. I'm anxious to hear about you guys." He turned to Steve. "What's happened in your life? How's the job at Justice going? Catch any bad guys lately?"

Steve ignored the question, too interested in Will's remarkable transformation. He wanted to hear everything about Will's status, and his tone became serious.

"How about it, Will? Did Sue Ellen's lawyer leave you with anything?"

"I got a house, a car, a dog, about 200 K in the bank, and no debts. Not much compared to what I had, but I can keep bread on the table." Will did not mention a cabin in the mountains of West Virginia. He never mentioned his private sanctuary.

"That dog of yours likes steak, not bread. Didn't you have a lawyer in divorce court? You had several million according to the papers." Beinhorn showed off his law school training.

"I just signed what her lawyer drew up. I didn't deserve anything after what I'd become."

And the talk went on. Close friends, so close they could share any subject, no matter how personal. How were MacKenzie's kids doing in New England? Did he ever talk to Sue Ellen?

Champ looked across the table at Will. The last time he'd seen Will look so fit was at his sister's funeral over three years ago in Philadelphia.

A loud group of six, ushered to the adjoining table, temporarily interrupted their conversation. Champ started to say something but stopped when he saw who they were.

One of them was a priest, and they all were marked with ashes on their foreheads. It reminded Will that today was Ash Wednesday. He remembered an Ash Wednesday joke he'd heard and began recounting it to his friends. "It seems a man was walking in a park alone, and suddenly, a robber jumps out of the bushes and demands the walker's wallet. The walker opens his coat to get the wallet, and the robber sees that the man is a priest wearing a clerical collar. 'Excuse me, Father,' says the robber. 'I didn't know you were a priest.' Then the priest, feeling relieved, asks the robber if he would like a cigarette and talk things over. The robber shakes his head and says, 'No, thanks, Father, I gave up cigarettes for lent.'"

Champ broke into a big grin.

Beinhorn just shook his head. "You and your Catholic jokes!"

Chapter 3

The conversation turned to sports, then politics. They spent a good five hours eating, talking, arguing, laughing more, and remembering old times. And then, finally, as always, they talked about the event that had brought them together. These were soldiers who'd been there and done that. Every time they got together, they'd relive their Vietnam experience as a way of pinching themselves, amazed at their good fortune. It was years ago, yet it always seemed like yesterday.

The news wasn't good, but it wasn't all bad. Intelligence reports were conflicting: the enemy was probing, the enemy was moving, the enemy was reinforcing, and so on. The battalion commander, Colonel Joe Conly, had ordered every precaution, adding new rows of concertina wire projecting ever outward from the base. Artillery concentrations were fired, and coordinates were checked and rechecked with headquarters. Conly requested reinforcements and close air recon. He cut down trees and brush and extended fields of fire to three hundred meters. Foxholes were dug deeper, and overhead cover was constructed. Extra listening posts were dispatched and more frequent patrols were ordered, but it wasn't enough. Colonel Conly had to know what was going on beyond the river and Lieutenant Hannock raised his ass-kissing hand sooner than any of the experienced officers, who all knew better.

Lieutenant Hannock had been in camp one week, and in Vietnam, only one month; and this was a chance to prove himself, earn a medal maybe, and advance his career. A career totally focused on the army, he'd been a military school student since the age of ten. He was only five-nine, but seemed taller due to his built-up boots and ramrod straight posture. Wherever he went, he insisted on being saluted by enlisted men and demanded all privileges of his rank. His uniforms were custom-tailored, and his boots glowed from hours of spit shining. The reinforced, ranger-trained rifle platoon was his first real combat command, and he was eager to show that he knew everything about military warfare.

The plan called for a secret river crossing into Cambodia before splitting into four squad-sized patrols to determine enemy location and strength. Sergeant Will MacKenzie's squad was on point when they reached the river and stopped moving. He sensed that something was wrong; it seemed too quiet. Normal jungle sounds were absent, just the sound of river current lapping against rocks in the stream. Normally, the correct tactical maneuver in such an open danger zone would be to send a small squad across, recon the area, and secure the other side before exposing the full platoon. But Sergeant Mac was so concerned that he didn't want to risk a single soldier, much less his whole squad.

He was well qualified to know what was going on. He'd grown up in the woods of West Virginia and Virginia, learned to hunt before he was twelve. His uncle had taught him how to track an animal, how to survive in the forest. He'd been in Vietnam for ten months, had experienced many encounters with the Viet Cong (VC), and was wise of their ways. He knew they were out there. He could feel it in his bones.

He waited and waited, looking up and down the river, hesitant to cross. The river was muddy from persistent rain. It rained every day for periods lasting fifteen minutes to two hours. Then, just as quickly, the sun would shine through, and the foliage would seem to grow right before your eyes.

Lieutenant Hannock had promised headquarters a report as soon as they crossed the river, and the patrol was moving too cautiously for Hannock's expectation. The lieutenant felt confident, knowing they had the extra firepower of a reinforced platoon and were far better equipped than their enemy. Furthermore, they had sole control of the skies. Lieutenant Hannock was livid with the unnecessary delay. Hannock stormed to the column front and demanded to know the cause of the holdup.

McKenzie didn't waste words and didn't address his lieutenant as sir, and he failed to salute his lieutenant before he spoke. Hannock stopped him before he could finish explaining. First, he chewed out Sergeant MacKenzie for being disrespectful to an officer, and then he accused him of cowardice. He refused to listen to the sergeant's concerns and didn't want to discuss plans for an alternate crossing.

Both the lieutenant and the sergeant were angry following the brief argument. However, Sergeant Mac would not give up; risking a court-martial, he insisted on the need for a small team to secure the far side before allowing the main body to cross. Again, Hannock refused to listen. To show the troops who was in charge, the lieutenant made a big deal out of sending MacKenzie and his squad to the rear and proceeded to lead the river crossing himself.

The river, only knee-deep at the crossing, was approximately two hundred meters wide, with a swirling, muddy brown current. The crossing itself was cleared and marked by a well-worn trail. Both sides of the crossing were rutted and cluttered by years of ox-driven wagons, carts, and foot traffic. Hannock's timetable had been delayed too long, and he didn't allow debate in his army. Speed and decisiveness won wars, and he refused to stay any longer. He urged his men to move at the double through the crossing with rifles at the ready and eyes alert for danger.

Hannock's pace was quick, his eyes sparkled, and a grin formed on his face as he led his men through the water. Almost all of the troops were in the water. Then the river exploded with merciless machine-gun fire from the western riverbank. The Viet Cong had set the trap, and with Lieutenant Hannock's help, the Second Platoon, Eighth Battalion, 3d Infantry, ceased to exist three minutes after the first shot was fired. Just as he was about to step up on the far bank, his chest filled with pride, Hannock's confident grin was obliterated when his cheekbone shattered below his left eye. The back of his brain exploded as the bullet made its exit. His death was instantaneous even though he was struck at least six more times before his body hit the water.

The thunderous fusillade continued long after every single soldier in the water was hit and hit again. Downstream, the river turned a brownish red. Screams could be heard over the roar of gunfire. Cries of "MEDIC!" went unheeded and were quickly, but literally, drowned in a combination of blood and waterlogged coughing. Not one single shot was fired in return; so lethal and devastating was the ambush.

At the rear of the column, Sergeant Mac's reactions were a series of automatic reflexes. He and five other members of his squad dove for cover among fallen trees and tall grass that surrounded the eastern bank of the crossing. Even so, four of the six were wounded, and the radioman, Corporal Steve Beinhorn, had his breath knocked out of him. Two VC bullets had simultaneously blasted into his tactical radio, which was strapped to his back. Beinhorn was knocked to the ground almost on top of Privates Fetler and Vaugan, who had dropped their weapons in a mad dive for cover.

Corporal Champ Lewis saw it all in disbelief. Minutes earlier, he had stopped to take a dump while the column was halted; and he was just rushing up the rear when all hell erupted on the river. A stray bullet tore the remains of a handiwipe from his left hand but miraculously grazed only two fingers. The sixth and last survivor, Kit Muldoon, was covered in blood. He was the last man in the water and was shielded in front by bodies that were torn to shreds in seconds. He managed to crawl into the reeds next to the shoreline but was shot three times in the process. Only one bullet did any damage, entering the fleshy part of his right buttock as he hit the water. The back of his boot was almost shot off his left foot, but aside from a throbbing heel, he could walk. A third bullet splattered his canteen and creased his ribs. He was covered in so much blood that he would have been left for dead had he not been moving.

Fetler and Vaugan watched the slaughter as if it were a play staged for their entertainment. They had dropped their weapons and were frozen in shock. In a lightning move, MacKenzie slapped them back to their senses. They started to run but stopped as Sergeant Mac ordered them to grab their weapons. Beinhorn managed to shed and then slip back into his backpack. He retrieved ammo and an M-60 machine gun from fallen comrades who never even made it to the water's edge. Muldoon was playing dead until he heard familiar voices on the bank. One of the voices started to pick up Muldoon's rifle, and that's when he moved. The voice was Vaugan's, and he literally shit his pants when the bloody ghost looked up and asked him, "What the fuck was he doing?" All along the river, things were intermittently quiet except for an occasional moan or groan from wounded men, who somehow survived the wall of gunfire. These groans were succeeded by another burst of bullets, which would rain down on every soldier near the helpless sound.

Finally, there were no more sounds, but the Viet Cong stayed put. Nobody on the west bank moved. Bodies bobbed in the water, some floating downstream, leading a scarlet wake.

Beinhorn and Lewis were old Vietnam hands. Old in Vietnam was more than six weeks in the field, in combat. Like Sergeant Mac, they did not have to be told what to carry. They took only the necessities: water, food, weapons, and ammo. Beinhorn, a Jew from New York City, was the other nonofficer college graduate in the platoon. He had all three essentials for survival in Vietnam: courage, common sense, and a respect for the enemy; and he didn't volunteer for anything.

Lewis was not college educated, but he knew the art of survival, and he'd been in gunfights long before he came to Vietnam. He was serving his second tour and was, by far, the most seasoned combat veteran in the platoon. Lewis had learned hard lessons on the streets of Philadelphia's toughest neighborhoods. He'd had some problems following orders in his first tour and had been "volunteered" for his second. Both Lewis and Beinhorn respected MacKenzie's judgment, a common respect that was earned over time in a variety of firefights with Viet Cong.

Time was measured differently in Vietnam. It went slowly because everyone knew their tour was one year, 365 days. Every day was counted, and every day remaining was a day closer to getting out of hell. You were either bored or scared, but either way, time moved too slowly, always delaying the remaining days of your tour.

This time, the survivors weren't thinking of days; they were focused on this minute, and they all knew that time might be running out. They began to hear voices on the other side of the river. All shooting had stopped. There was still no movement on the other side. Smoke still hung heavy in the air as MacKenzie got the survivors headed back toward camp. They each moved silently and quickly for the first two hundred meters. Vaugan and Fetler had recovered their wits and were supporting the arm of Beinhorn who was carrying one of the M-60 machine guns and who was wounded after all. A bullet had entered his open mouth, chipped a tooth and exited cleanly through his right cheek. Mud from the riverbank had covered the wound and had helped stop the bleeding.

Muldoon was having trouble keeping up with one good foot and only half a boot on the other. His mind wandered, worrying about what was causing his heel to throb. Initially, this slowed his pace; and he fell behind, but he picked it up as adrenaline numbed his pain.

Once past the bend in the trail, they ran, crashed into, and dragged each other for a quarter of a mile. Once they stopped to regroup, Sergeant MacKenzie got another one of his "feelings." It was more of a foreboding, a premonition of danger that resulted in a "feeling." MacKenzie wondered why no one was following. *Why was there such a delay in movement from the western bank?* The answer, he determined, had to be another ambush. The Viet Cong, patient as always, were surely waiting up the trail for stragglers on their return trip to home base.

Without a sound, Sergeant MacKenzie held his hand up, stopping all movement. He placed his forefinger across his lips, and everyone knew to keep silent. He motioned them off the trail, gradually turning downriver away from the crossing and away from the suspected second ambush. Moving slowly, halting every few yards, they listened for any pursuit. Finally, they made their way back to the riverbank, only to be saddened. The entire river was reddish brown with blood and debris from the slaughter upriver. MacKenzie stealthily worked his way back to the bend to try to assess their situation while the others formed a defensive perimeter and tried to become invisible. Looking at the battle scene, Sergeant Mac realized they could have shouted and screamed and would not have been seen, such was the commotion being made over the defeated American platoon.

The silence after the ambush was now replaced with every Viet Cong talking at once, and all were shouting to be heard. Each body was being stripped of everything down to gold fillings in their teeth. The Viet Cong were laughing over every body. Unbelievably, one soldier was still alive, managing a grunt in protest as his watch was being pulled from his wrist. Briefly startled, the wrist grabber dropped his prey and fired a burst at point-blank range, tearing off the entire top of his captive's head.

Victory was total; not one shot was fired in retaliation. The only VC casualty came in the form of a first-degree burn from grabbing an overheated AK-47 assault rifle. The injured VC ignored his hand and went about the business of collecting chocolates and personal items from waterproof bags.

Subconsciously, Sergeant MacKenzie knew that safety lay in the opposite direction of where they would be expected to go. That direction meant Cambodia, across the river, going north toward Me Fing, a known Viet Cong hamlet and resupply point. Lewis and Beinhorn immediately endorsed this plan over strong objections from Fetler and Vaugan. Muldoon was still in semi shock and had no opinion. MacKenzie also felt that speed was nearly as important as stealth, but even so, they crossed the river one at a time. Once across, they immediately turned north along the Black Trail, which paralleled the river. This trail was not as wide as the infamous Ho Chi Minh trail but served the same purpose, moving troops and supplies into South Vietnam.

The survivors were approximately one mile south of the crossing, yet they could clearly hear squeals of delight as their enemy found some new treasure from the bodies of the doomed patrol. Hoping that the Viet Cong feeding frenzy would hide their movement, Sergeant MacKenzie headed north until they were within several hundred meters of the crossing. There, they turned west into jungle to avoid any chance of contact and turned north again until they could no longer hear voices of the victors. Finally, they circled back to the trail where they could make good time heading toward the enemy stronghold of Me Fing.

After what seemed like an eternity, the six paused to rest and bind their wounds. The most serious was Muldoon's, but he was still numb. All others mainly had flesh wounds, which cost blood but would repair easily enough with attention. MacKenzie assessed their situation: the radio was lost, so hope of calling in choppers was out of the question. On the bright side, he was sure the Viet Cong would be looking for survivors on the other side of the river. Plus, every one of his troops carried an automatic weapon and a good supply of ammo. Beinhorn's M-60 machine gun provided an extra degree of firepower. Lewis carried a half-full duffle bag of extra ammo and two Claymore antipersonnel mines. They could hold their own in a fight, at least for a while. Surely, Colonel Conly would send another patrol, if only to find out what happened to Hannock's command.

Just before dawn, Sergeant Mac came to a decision, one that had been nagging at him ever since he viewed what the Viet Cong were doing to his fallen comrades. An eye for an eye, ambush for ambush, was what was on his mind. Realistically, he didn't like their chances of going further north with no radio. He checked the operations map. The trail to Me Fing was through heavy jungle except at an intersection at the road to Qui Li. From that intersection, the trail became more of a road than a trail because four-wheel drive trucks could, and did, make it to this point with supplies from North Vietnam. The intersection was as good as they would find to mount a counter ambush. MacKenzie figured their attackers would surely return back, up the trail with their booty and plenty of soldier stories to tell. One advantage that the intersection provided was a small hill at the northwest corner, which provided a clear field of fire on the trail for almost three hundred meters. Their target would be exposed for several minutes before the trail reentered the jungle overgrowth at the northern end.

It was just after sunup when they arrived at the intersection. To be effective, the ambush required crossfire between the hill at one end and a pile of rocks and downed trees at the other. Both positions offered tactical cover with a sweeping view of the trail. They could fire directly into the VC unit from above and at ground level.

Sergeant MacKenzie placed his two Claymore mines on the west side of the trail. The ambush was a "classical box" about halfway between his two positions where he could detonate them remotely, using a hardwired, handheld trigger device. The Claymore is an awesome weapon. If it were better known, it would be classified along with nukes and napalm as too evil to use, even in war. It sits low to the ground and resembles an electric heater except for the camouflage. Packed tightly together in front of the composition C-shaped explosive charge sit hundreds of steel balls, each the size of a small marble. At detonation, the force of the shaped charged explosion sends the balls spraying in an ever-widening swath, obliterating everything in its path for sixty meters. The result is total devastation, a force powerful and cruel, maiming as effective as killing.

Muldoon took the M-60 and dug in as high as he could on the hill with Lewis and Fetler. From this vantage point, he would be able to provide overlapping fire within a two-hundred-meter killing zone. Sergeant MacKenzie, Beinhorn, and Vaugan hid below at the pile of trees and rocks, where they planned to let the enemy pass until they were exactly halfway through the intersection. Their signal to fire was just after the Claymores let loose. Sergeant MacKenzie controlled the Claymores from his ground-level position. Quickly and quietly, they went about the tasks of digging in, laying out extra ammo, camouflaging their positions, and clearing vines and limbs that obscured their view. They were ready. Now, they waited.

The wait was interminable, not knowing when, or if, the Viet Cong might come. Combined with heat and humidity, the anxiety created a sauna like effect. Sweat soaked through their clothing, and MacKenzie began to have second thoughts. Insects of every description invaded their lair, in the stillness, feasting on dried blood. Then came sounds of movement, sounds of men, but not from where they expected.

Even though they were separated by some distance, all six survivors heard the noise at once. Several voices talking, laughing, and some singing.

Unfortunately, the sounds were coming from the wrong direction, from Me Fing. It was five minutes from the time they heard voices to the time the voices took shape. A small squad of eight soldiers, mainly dressed in black, and fully armed, was heading south. MacKenzie prayed that Muldoon would let them through. There was no way to communicate with Muldoon or Lewis, and this was something they had not planned for. But they were now totally committed and had agreed that no one would shoot until the Claymores fired. They were supposed to wait until all enemy troops made it to the halfway point.

It was difficult to understand the careless attitude of the enemy troops. The VC made no effort to maintain silence. Obviously, they felt safe in their Cambodian sanctuary. After all, everyone knew that the Americans were not supposed to bomb or pursue the enemy into Cambodia. Certainly, American soldiers were not supposed to be there.

MacKenzie wiped the sweat from his eyes and waited. He'd already given the sign to Beinhorn and Vaugan to hold fire and lay low. Fortunately, Lewis had done the same on the hill because at the first sound, Muldoon looked at him for direction and saw a silent signal to remain still. Their hearts seemed to pound harder, fingers softly caressing freshly oiled triggers as all eyes followed the Viet Cong heading south. A mosquito landed on Vaugan's arm. Later, he was to describe it as so big it could fuck a turkey.

Slowly, ever so slowly, they came. It seemed to take an incredible amount of time for the troop to travel the intersection, and Sergeant MacKenzie breathed a sigh of relief when the unruly band of soldiers made it through without detecting their position. And so they continued their wait.

It was about ten o'clock in the morning, two hours later, when they heard the first sounds of many men coming from the south. They too were moving slowly and noisily without a care in the world. Two observations went through MacKenzie's mind as the enemy approached. First, he was surprised at their number: only twenty-five troops and these included the eight who had passed earlier. He couldn't believe that seventeen Viet Cong had wiped out a well-trained, superbly equipped fighting force of almost fifty army rangers. Three of the enemy were women! All three had apparently come from the river crossing ambush as they were fully armed and loaded down with American weapons and supplies picked off the dead bodies.

Mac's second observation was the continued careless attitude of this black-clad, ragtag group that seemed to have no leader. They were euphoric! They were superior to a so-called superpower's troops. They were victorious: they had their spoils and souvenirs to prove it! Virtually every weapon, every ammo belt, every item of clothing and supply had been recovered from the river. Each soldier seemed to be smiling and laughing and talking all at once, carrying much more than was comfortable. Some of them were smoking American cigarettes and arguing over who had spotted what first.

MacKenzie's heart was pounding like thunder. He was so close; he could almost spit on the enemy column. Adrenaline poured through his system. All senses were on fast time. He had never been more alert. Their hideout of bamboo, brush, and vine was perfect for ambush. No one could see in, but they could see out. Finally, the last man filed by.

But to Mac's surprise, he wasn't a man after all, but a boy of barely fourteen. He rattled when he walked from a necklace of dog tags and appeared to be carrying a lode of booty bigger than he was.

Sergeant MacKenzie prayed again that Lewis's group would be patient. They were not to fire until the entire enemy had filed past the southern ambush point. Once past, MacKenzie would unleash the Claymores and prevent any kind of retreat.

To his horror, one of the women soldiers left the trail and headed directly toward their position.

He relaxed when she nonchalantly dropped her trousers and proceeded to pee. She was only ten meters from their position when the main body reached the center of the intersection, and then she looked directly into MacKenzie's face. Her mouth was forming a warning shout when the Claymores erupted! The Viet Cong troops were spread out all along the intersection in twos and threes, but MacKenzie had no choice. He had hoped for a more bunched up target, especially for the Claymores. Too late for moral judgment, MacKenzie shot the woman first. She was bringing her

AK-47 up to fire even with her pants down. The explosions threw her aim way off, and she took three bullets before pulling the trigger and falling over backward.

The surprise was total. It was over in minutes. Just as at the river, not one true shot was fired in retaliation. The Viet Cong commander's error was greater than that of Lieutenant Hannock's ranger patrol because not one of them got away. Two Viet Cong were wounded, one being the woman who almost spoiled the ambush. She was crying, and her eyes begged for help. As MacKenzie bent to check her out, he spotted the chain of freshly cut ears around her neck. Some of the blood was still oozing from the ears. Without hesitation, he blew her head off. The savagery of this act seemed to ignite all six of them, for they quickly shot every fallen Viet Cong soldier with a burst of bullets.

The Americans then proceeded to re-arm themselves from supplies dropped from, and strapped to, every dead Viet Cong. They were delighted to find a radio that appeared to be in good shape. They ripped U.S. dog tags hanging from lifeless necks and tried to recover every personal effect of their fallen comrades that had been scavenged by the VC.

Sergeant MacKenzie's last act before leaving was to bury the ears that hung from the bloody stump of a neck that remained on his first victim. Lewis had to pull him away because he seemed to be losing it. The victorious survivors then headed south and soon discovered that the radio didn't work after all. Beinhorn was their radio expert, and he tried everything he knew, but the radio had taken on too much water and remained silent. Now they knew their trip back to camp would be much more difficult. Surely, the enemy based at Me Fing had heard the explosions and shots at the intersection and would now be on the move.

Retracing their route back, they moved silently and slowly, with Lewis on point. As they approached the fateful river crossing, they became especially vigilant. Their caution was rewarded because four enemy soldiers were carelessly searching dead bodies and checking the river battleground for anything their comrades might have left. Frustrated with their lack of booty, these four were sitting ducks in the water just as Hannock had been. Their weapons were slung, and they too did not return fire. Muldoon kept wading in and firing long after all four were down. His blood lust was unrequited until he expended every round in every clip. No one else had entered the water, and Sergeant MacKenzie had planned to go farther south before crossing. But no enemy returned fire from the eastern bank, and Muldoon noticed that two of the Viet Cong were carrying U.S. dog tags around their necks. Apparently, these four Viet Cong had set up another ambush on the route back to camp to catch any stragglers that escaped the main ambush. MacKenzie's earlier hunch had been right; the decision to go into

Cambodia saved their lives, at least to this point. It was not surprising that he didn't recognize any of the names on the dog tags. Many of the men in the platoon were brand-new—like the lieutenant.

The trip back to camp took two more days as MacKenzie was convinced that there were enemy positions all along the trail. Moving slowly through the jungle, staying clear of well-used paths, they saw no more Viet Cong. Finally, they reached the outskirts of base camp. Relief turned into exhaustion, and they almost broke down until a shot fired over their heads brought them back. Down on the ground, they became instantly alert.

Could the VC have overrun the camp? thought MacKenzie. Then they heard an American voice with an Alabama accent ask, "Password, y'all know the password?" But they didn't know the current password.

A chorus of four-letter words from six vocal throats ending with "Fuck you and Westy too!" convinced the guards that they were on the same team.

Within the safety of their battalion base camp, the six met with Colonel Conly to provide a briefing about the ambush and an estimate of enemy strength and location. Sergeant MacKenzie provided map coordinates of enemy unit locations. Colonel Conly ordered air strikes and multiple artillery barrages, followed by air recons that didn't respect the Cambodian border. No more patrols were sent out; instead, the battalion hunkered down and waited.

MacKenzie and the other five survivors tried to drink the battalion's entire supply of liquor and beer. Later, they were awarded Purple Hearts and Medals of Valor. Lieutenant Hannock was briefly considered for a medal, but Sergeant MacKenzie's report was too damning and the matter was dropped. Within weeks of the ambush, all six rotated back to the United States and out of the army.

Only MacKenzie, Lewis, and Beinhorn returned on the same plane. They made a pact, born in blood and nurtured in booze and beer—to get together often, to stay in touch, to be there for one another. They remembered what the marines had called them, Assholes. Liking the term, they decided to amplify it to Ignorant Assholes because they used the term so often to describe everybody else.

They often wondered whatever happened to the other three that had survived the Viet Cong ambush: Fetler, Vaugan, and Muldoon. They could be Ignorant Assholes too, had Will and his buddies not lost touch with the three of them after Vietnam. Beinhorn vowed to use the FBI and Justice Department files to track them down. It didn't seem right not to have them included.

"I'll bet Vaugan's a mortician," said Champ. "He was heartless, and death didn't seem to bother him."

Beinhorn disagreed. "Nah, wherever he is, he's with Fetler. The two acted half-married to each other all the time. Did you ever see one without the other? They're probably running a driving range somewhere. They were always talking about who was the better golfer."

"What about Muldoon?" Will asked. Where do you think he is?"

"Probably selling drugs. The son-of-bitch always had some scheme going. Remember when he sold fried chicken?"

"That wasn't fried chicken. Maybe fried rat or fried dog, but it wasn't chicken," said Beinhorn.

"Everybody ate it up though, especially you, Steve."

"Assholes! You are rat Assholes, both of you."

"Do you all want dessert?" The question brought them back to the present. The waitress, who flirted with a natural ease that never failed to positively impact her tip, batted her eyes and bent over the table, opening up another two inches of cleavage.

Will, determined to stick to his fitness training, declined and switched from iced tea to water. Champ Lewis couldn't resist the giant ice cream brownie. Steve Beinhorn ordered some more onion rings in place of desert. As usual, Beinhorn had eaten twice what the others had eaten, and he never gained a pound.

Chapter 4

At the Budget Motel on South Route 1, Alexandria, the two Hispanic men were confused. Their English was limited to a few words, and the desk clerk could not understand them. One thing was clear though: the three other Hispanic men they were seeking that had come a week earlier were no longer registered at the motel.

The taller of the two, Julio Mendez, the one with the knife scar down his right cheek, had driven their rental car all over Alexandria with his brother Carlo. They were looking and looking and looking. But no sign of their friends could be found. It was as if they had dropped off the earth. No note, no forwarding address, and no evidence that they'd been here except for the guest register.

Julio pointed to the names in the register and made hand signals so the clerk would know they were trying to find these men.

The clerk, a balding, fat man with a mustard stain on his tie, did remember the other three. But those three spoke English as well as Spanish. The clerk remembered them all talking at once; they seemed to be excited about things. "They're gone. Left in the middle of the night without notice."

But Julio and Carlo didn't understand. "*No comprendemos.* English bad."

The clerk waved his hands and then raised his voice as if the volume would help with the interpretation. "Out. Gone away. No here."

Julio pointed to the lobby phone.

The clerk pointed to him and then to the phone. "You want to use the phone?"

Mimicking the clerk, Julio said, "*Si.* Use the phone, *si.*"

Julio then gave the clerk a note with a phone number and, by hand signals, asked him to dial the number.

But the clerk said, "No can do. Long distance. Costs money." He pointed to his wallet, repeating "money" while increasing the volume of his voice for emphasis.

This Julio understood. He gave the clerk a hundred-dollar bill. "Okay?"

"Okay." The clerk smiled and carefully dialed the number. At the first ring, he handed the receiver to Julio.

The number was a very private emergency number that a man named Diego Estrada had established for his DC operation. Diego himself always answered this phone. Estrada was surprised to hear from these two. He didn't think they could even make a local phone call in the United States, much less a long-distance one.

The first three men that Diego had sent were expected to handle most of the talking. They were all educated at Catholic schools and fluent in English.

Julio and Carlo were mainly muscle, backup in case there was trouble from the locals. Diego asked questions, but Julio could only give limited answers. Diego told him to put the clerk on the phone.

Diego's English was perfect. "Hello. My friends are looking for three of my employees who checked into your motel earlier this week." His voice was polite but authoritative.

"Oh yes. Right. Yes, sir. I remember all three. Their names were pointed out on the register. Your friends here spotted their names right away. They left without checking out. Only spent two nights, and they had paid for the whole week. We rent by the week here."

"Did they leave anything in their rooms? Any luggage, papers, trash, notes, keys, anything?"

"No, sir. Didn't leave an empty can or anything. Their beds were slept in though, so it looks like they got some sleep."

"When did you last see them?"

"Well, I didn't actually see them the last night they were here, but I know they were in 'cause their beds were unmade. We make up the beds every day, and we often have to change the sheets. In case they're messed up, you know. They just never showed up for the third night. We kept the room open for 'em all week though, in case they came back, you know."

"They never came back?"

"No, sir, they never came back."

"Did you notice any strange cars or people around?"

"Well, yes, sir. Almost all the time, there are strange people here. The only ones we recognize are the ones who spend several nights or who have been here before. Even them we don't know too well."

Diego asked several more questions and then asked to speak with Julio again. He gave Julio instructions to stay put at the motel until he could find out where those guys were.

Outside the motel, two sedans with DC license plates were facing the lobby with their engines idling, trying to stay warm. Inside each sedan were four black men.

Dessert was offered and rejected in the elegant dining room of the massive Spanish-style villa outside of Cartagena, Colombia. At the head of a long table, Don Alverez had little appetite due to the quantity of drugs and radiation he had taken to treat his cancer. All he wanted was to hear from his only daughter. She usually called every day around breakfast, just after her morning run. She hadn't called this morning, and the Don was disappointed.

Although the table could seat twenty diners in comfort, only two other people were having lunch with the Don. The three men looked lost in the high-ceilinged room, sitting at one corner of the otherwise empty table. The room was elegant and formal, with two sideboards, one with a dazzling display of silver, the other serving as a base for a series of shelves that held row upon row of rare china. Proportionately placed on the table were three tall sterling silver candelabras and, as a centerpiece, a huge china bowl of yellow roses. A uniformed waiter stood next to the kitchen door, ready for any command from the head of the table.

Small and thin, Don Alverez was a very sick man, yet he sat erect, regal in bearing, wearing an open-collared silk shirt under a blue blazer. To his right was his second in command, Paul Xavier, who resembled the Don greatly and was rumored to be his bastard son. A much larger man sat to the Don's left, Diego Estrada, a nephew. Both subordinates wore dark suits, white shirts, and black ties, which was their custom for formal meetings with their don.

They were deep in conversation, and some repetition was necessary because the don's attention span wasn't what it used to be. Every day, usually over lunch, they would brief him on the activities of his many businesses. Today, they were discussing coffee prices around the world. It usually took a day to get through each business segment: banking, ranching, emerald mining, importing, exporting, and so many other businesses that they had organized groups of companies into separate conglomerates.

Normally, he would have many questions, but today, he seemed impatient, disinterested, interrupting the business report from Diego and turning to Paul. "Paule, was that the phone? Did you hear the phone?"

"No, Padrone, that must have been from outside."

"I'm expecting a call from Gabriella. She usually calls before now. Where could she be?"

"I'm sure she will call soon, Padrone. You know how carefree the young are, especially in America."

"Diego."

"Yes, Padrone?" Diego blinked, nervous now, looking into Don Alverez's eyes with apprehension, wanting to get back to the subject of today's meeting. "Shall we raise the coffee prices, Padrone?"

"I cannot think about coffee prices right now. I'm concerned about Gabriella. What's going on in Washington?"

Diego hesitated. "Did the question refer only to Gabriella, or was it broader?"

"It's your territory. Does she have a boyfriend, Diego? Why would she not call? She calls every day. I look forward to that call. Is something wrong? What is the name of our senior representative in Washington DC? I know you have him checking on her."

Since it was his territory, Diego was expected to know everything. Because he was especially interested in Gabriella, he knew more than he could say, but because he had something to hide; he had to be very careful with his answer.

"She doesn't have a serious boyfriend, but she has a good friend. His name is Ashley Sheppard. He's a medical student. They're just friends."

"Why hasn't she called, Diego? Is there something else going on that I should know about?"

Paul Xavier was enjoying watching Diego, fidgeting and shifting in his seat as he answered question after question. Diego was a large man and often used his size to bully others. Physically, he could crush Don Alverez in a bear hug, but he had always been afraid of the Don. Diego was jealous as well as nervous, especially of the Don's obvious confidence in Paul. His eyes crossed when he was tense, and now they seemed to be focusing inward, almost on top of his nose. Diego was in the process of formulating an excuse when a servant entered the dining room to announce that Gabriella was on the telephone.

Don Alverez's face beamed with pleasure, giving color to his pale cheeks and new life to a body that was slowly dying. He stood up and gingerly took the phone. "Gabriella, where have you been? I missed your call!"

Paul Xavier watched as the Don's demeanor changed from warmth to concern and then anger. "Do you know who I am?" the Don said very calmly but in a manner that implied threat nonetheless.

"Do I know? Do I know? Am I stupid? Be sure I know!" the voice on the other end replied. "But you don't know me; you don't respect me.

You make a big mistake in yo' ge . . . og . . . graphy. This's the District of Columbia, not Colombia!"

"Is my daughter safe?"

"She fine, mighty fine, gettin' the royal treatment, like a queen, an' she gonna be fine, providin' you cooperate. You gonna cooperate now, ain't you? You a very smart man."

Don Alverez spoke in a clear, deliberate voice. "What do you want, and when do you want it?" His hands began to shake slightly, but his composure remained rock solid.

"Good, good, we gettin' somewhere. Makin' progress. We be reasonable. Business is business. We got two issues. First, you got to o . . . ficially recognize that this is our territory. Unnerstan' we got too much investment to allow competition, an' maybe we want to go into Richmond, maybe Baltimore. You got a problem with that?"

The Don frowned, not sure what the voice was talking about, but prepared to agree with anything. Using hand gestures, he asked Paul for a glass of water.

Paul Xavier put the glass in the Don's hand and stood close, awaiting the next request. Diego was on his feet as well, on full alert, watching Don Alverez.

"When can I get my daughter back?" the Don asked.

Paul brought a chair to Don Alverez, who looked as if he might collapse. Sitting down, the Don listened to the request. When the Don referred to the issue as a "ransom," there was instant, violent disagreement from the man on the line, who insisted the monetary condition was a "reimbursement." The Don smartly chose not to argue. "It will take me three days to put it all together. Would you agree to work with a colleague of mine up there who would act as intermediary?"

Each of the Don's subordinates maintained absolute silence, knowing that something terrible had happened. Finally, the Don nodded agreement, and he asked to speak with his daughter again. He heard, "No way, Jose!" and the phone went dead.

Chapter 5

Outside Clyde's, rush hour was in full stall when the taxi carrying Champ Lewis and Steve Beinhorn to Union Station pulled away. Will MacKenzie watched as his closest friends gave him the finger from inside the cab, each mouthing the word "asshole". That brought a smile to his face and he began to feel good. Their teasing was confirmation of his recovery.

He paid the bill and grinned at the waitress saying, "Keep the change." She blew him a kiss as he left the restaurant.

It was almost dark, and a cold moist breeze over the Potomac brought sudden bursts of snowflakes that stung his cheeks. Even though he'd been in a restaurant for almost six hours, Will was hungry. He turned up a side street to a familiar place.

His destination was an old Georgetown haunt, the 1789 Bar and Grille on Twenty-ninth Street. He was going to eat a steak and further test his will power.

It was early, but the place was already half-full of a well-dressed mixture of business and government executives plus a sprinkling of college students. All of them seemed young to Will. Happy hour, underway since 5:00 p.m., offered one free drink for every one bought. The booze, coupled with an array of delicious hors d'oeuvres, had livened up the conversations. A black piano player, old and grizzled, played and sang the blues with conviction. The tune was sad, and the tale was sadder.

Will walked directly to the long mahogany bar, full of drinkers and smokers. He sat next to a woman who seemed more elegantly dressed and refined than the usual college and yuppie crowd. Expensive pearl earrings matched the triple-string of pearls around her long neck. She had no band on her ring finger, though Will noticed a white mark where one had recently been. Her hands were wrapped around her drink with a death grip. Immaculately manicured fingernails, tipped with a clear nail polish, vibrated with tension.

Will ordered a glass of sparkling water with lime and looked straight ahead at the mirror behind the bar. His face looked healthy with color, and the dark lines under his eyes had almost disappeared. The man on his left was engaged in conversation with a slightly drunk woman who had difficulty enunciating. The woman spoke English with a German accent. Neither of these two strangers was aware of anyone else in the bar. Other couples and groups were also engaged in conversation, their smiles and laughter contradicting the piano player's mournful dirge.

Will blinked from the cigarette smoke and again looked at the reflection of the woman on his right. She was seated cockeyed on the side of her bar stool and appeared to want solitude. She kept looking down at her glass. She wore little makeup and, except for her expensive outfit, would not have stood out in a crowd.

The clothes and jewelry spoke of wealth, but nothing ostentatious. She wore a brown jacket that was tailored to hide rather than flaunt her figure. Her shoulders were rounded and her bearing stooped as if looking for something she'd dropped. Her brown hair was tied in a bun. Dark glasses, horn-rimmed but fashionable, framed a pretty face and hid the tears in her eyes. Will found her attractive.

She stood up, and Will watched her select a table in the farthest corner of the bar. Her presence was so unassuming that she went unnoticed for almost ten minutes before a waiter called at her table.

Will was lonely. She seemed lonely too. So Will did something he hadn't done in twenty years: he walked to her table. He needed someone to talk to other than his dog and a couple of army friends.

He stood, awkwardly at first, hands on the chair facing her. "I've been trying to think of something clever to say, but if you're not waiting to meet someone, I'd like to join you."

She seemed uncomfortable and hesitated for a moment before looking up. "No, thank you. I'd rather not." She cast her eyes down, not wanting to face this stranger.

Dejected, Will turned and started to walk away.

"Wait! I'm sorry. I don't mean to be rude."

He turned around, and she stood up.

She pointed to the chair he had been leaning on, giving him the okay to sit.

He smiled, his heart pumped faster, and nervous as a teenager, he said, "My name is Will."

"Magdalyn. But friends call me Maggie." She offered her hand to him. He shook it gently, delighting in its warmth.

"What are you drinking?"

"Vodka. Absolut on the rocks."

"Waiter!" The waiter jerked around and ran to their table. "Absolut on the rocks for the lady and a ginger ale for me."

"Ginger ale?" She was surprised at his choice. "What's with the ginger ale?"

"I'm an alcoholic," he told her, "so ginger ale it has to be. I came in here to test my will power."

"Am I part of the test?" She finally broke into a smile.

"My will power is not that strong," he flirted back.

There was a moment of silence followed by small talk. When the waiter returned with their drinks, they clinked glasses.

"To the future," he said with a twinkle in his eye.

"To a better life," she replied, forcing a smile.

"I'll drink to that." His eyes never left hers as he took a swallow. "Thank you for allowing me to sit with you."

"You want to know something? I actually came in here hoping to meet a man. That is, hoping to meet a *decent* man, but I chickened out. I just couldn't do it." She broke down crying, took off her glasses, and looked down at the table.

"You're married, aren't you?" Will asked as he reached for her hand, the one with the ring mark.

She didn't pull her hand away. "Yes, but apparently, in his mind, he isn't . . . at least that's the way he makes me feel." Tears now streamed down her cheeks. She made no effort to hide them, being somewhat comfortable with his concern for her. "I'm sorry; I don't want to burden you with my problems."

Will looked from her face to the untouched plate of hors d'oeuvres, saying, "I'd like to cheer you up. Here, have a shrimp." He lifted one up and offered it to her.

"Sorry. I'm just not in a hungry mood."

"Well, I'm starved. It's not good to drink on an empty stomach, you know."

"I don't care. I don't care about anything anymore." And she started to cry again.

Will handed her his handkerchief. She seemed so lonely, so depressed. He wanted to comfort this woman. Without thinking, he opened up to this woman, this stranger.

"We both have relationship issues, Maggie. I caused mine. My wife divorced me and took the kids after two years of my constant drinking, yelling, and screaming. I drove away every friend, ruined a good job, and destroyed a great marriage. It's taken me almost a year to come back from the dead."

She started to answer but stopped as a young couple brushed against their table and then quickly bounced back to the dance floor. "Can't you rekindle your marriage now that you've recovered?"

"You never recover from alcoholism. As for the marriage, I've tried, but she keeps hanging up. I can't even visit my son and daughter. I screwed things up pretty bad. It's been two years."

"Don't you have a girlfriend?" She surprised herself, blurting out what she'd been thinking. "My god, you're attractive enough."

Embarrassed and self-conscious, Will said, "Thanks, but I've spent the last year almost as a hermit. I've been afraid to reestablish old contacts. I burned a lot of bridges, Maggie. Most of the time I've spent with my dog."

She recovered her composure, dabbed her lips with her napkin, and changed the subject. "What kind of dog do you have?"

"Chocolate Lab. Big, faithful, slobbering bundle of love. He saved me from hell."

Maggie smiled when Will showed her a picture of his faithful companion. Then she frowned. "My husband is a big, unfaithful, unloving, slobbering son-of-a-bitch who saves his bundle for an unending supply of young, money-grubbing, wannabe trophy wives. Only, he's too smart to go that route when he can get it for free."

Will tried again. "Well, let's drink to a better future. You certainly deserve it, and I will try like hell to stay off the booze." Once more, they clinked glasses.

"Where's home for you, Maggie?"

"Alexandria. You?"

"Winchester. Out in the country." Will was momentarily distracted as the waiter, very attentive now, returned with another round of drinks.

She finally relaxed. He felt comfortable too. They both needed conversation and began talking about the weather, favorite travel destinations, restaurants, food, and the weather again. She was obviously well read, up-to-date on all the issues of the day. Starved for attention, they both began talking, interrupting each other, stopping, apologizing, and then finally smiling.

Her smile was perfect, the result of thousands of dollars worth of orthodontia. It was a wide grin, framed between two small dimples, and it immediately brightened up her long face. She was prettier than he first realized. She had not smiled much recently. She told him her husband of twenty years had finally admitted his infidelity. She had suspected the worst for some time.

"I knew, but I didn't want to know. It's something you don't want to believe, so you don't believe it." Her husband had not made love to her in several months and showed no interest in her feelings, her wants, and her needs.

"I've always had difficulty talking about sex. Maybe I seemed frigid, but I couldn't just bring up the subject of sex, could I?" She looked at Will and opened up with her most personal thoughts and feelings. In desperation, she had gone to Victoria's Secret. "You should have seen me in the lingerie store trying to buy something sexy. I thought I was on another planet!" She laughed at herself and blushed scarlet.

Will imagined what she would look like in one of those skimpy outfits, thinking of her in a much different way. She didn't notice his lusty grin.

"Nothing I wore, even when it was embarrassing for me to put it on, seemed to have any impact on my husband. He chose to ignore me."

She told Will that when she finally understood her husband's unstated message, she decided to fight fire with fire. Her single motive upon entering the bar today had been revenge. She was looking for an affair but had lost her courage. Now, she was just glad to be able to talk to someone about it.

"How could he not want you?" Will looked directly into her teary eyes. "You're so incredibly attractive. I've only just met you, but it's obvious to me, and anyone who can see, that you're desirable. You have a presence about you, a way of holding your head high, proud, regal looking." *Almost unobtainable,* he thought to himself. "Oh, by the way, you don't need Victoria's Secret. You're plenty sexy on your own!"

"Wow. Thank you. I think you've been spending way too much time with your dog." Her eyes softened. "Even if you don't mean it, I appreciate your saying it. I know I'm not sexy."

"You are too."

He stared at her, working up the courage to ask her to dance. The piano player was playing a slow tune, and a few couples were welded together on the small dance floor. He was surprised when she asked him to take her home.

They left the bar quickly. Will expected to take her to Alexandria, but "home" turned out to be her husband's secret Georgetown apartment that he had been using for his affairs over the past three years. She told him that this would be her first visit.

She had recently received an incriminating note, which included an address and an apartment key from one of her husband's former love interests who had been unceremoniously dumped for a new conquest.

Their walk to the apartment was short and brisk. Neither said a word, not sure of what was going to happen. They did not hold hands. They passed strangers with happy faces, who seemed to have places to go and people to see.

The large apartment was one of four expensive units, divided out of a seventy-year-old Georgetown mansion. The exterior of the tree-lined, Federal-style house was old, oversized, peeling white brick, covered in ivy that needed a trim. The wood shutters and moldings matched the elegance of the thick-paneled doors. Each entrance was cleverly arranged to be private. Four different routes led to the four private doors. Tall hemlock hedges masked each of the four brick walkways.

As Will closed the door behind them, she turned, pressed against him, and engaged the dead bolt. In his arms, she looked at the apartment for the first time.

She stayed so close that he felt her heavy breathing. He pulled her closer, and she was all over him in an instant. She bit his lip. She dug her fingernails into his neck. She mashed his body against the heavy oak door. He returned her passion. Their tongues were in constant movement, darting back and forth as if in a duel. Her actions were overpowering; no longer self-conscious and shy, she became the aggressor. He followed her lead.

She managed to remove his trousers, groping at his hardening crotch, unbuckling his belt and almost ripping the zipper. Will, in turn, tore off her pantyhose and underwear. Then the rest came off. Both were animals now, lost in lust, adrenaline pumping, organs throbbing, hands everywhere, lips locked.

For a moment, they stopped, as if to check that what they were doing was not some dream. Then they held on to each other, their breathing heavier. They were on an Oriental rug in the front hall, like two dogs in heat. He held back, but she had lost all reason, hands cupped between his buttocks and thighs, fingernails digging in, moaning and moving. She wanted hard, fast, driving thrusts; he wanted to slow down. She groaned and begged him not to stop as if he could stop or wanted to stop. He was more concerned for her, trying to hold out. His finger found her, and he massaged her softly, trying to slow her down. Then he rubbed it sideways, then up and down, then very hard as he pressed his pelvis into her groin, humping with increasing intensity.

The effect was electrifying. She screamed, a voice coming from long-neglected depths. "Oh my god, oh my god!" She kept saying it over and over, and he took pleasure for himself finally. Perspiration from his forehead mixed with hers, and for a long time, neither one moved nor spoke.

At last, she got up and looked around, not the least embarrassed with her nakedness. He watched her from the floor staring at her quivering chest, glistening with sweat, as she contemplated what to do next. She hurriedly gathered up her glasses, shoes, panties, jacket, and the remains of her shredded pantyhose, her eyes searching for the bathroom.

He could not remember her name. Maggiebeth or Maggie, something.

In her absence, he pulled on his trousers, removed his ruined tie, and headed for the kitchen to make coffee. It looked to be a challenging night. *Wow!* he thought, *it's been a long time. How much luckier could I get?* He found the sink, washed his hands, and filled a pot with water to boil. Folgers instant coffee was on the counter next to the refrigerator, but milk and sugar were not to be found. Apparently, her husband and his girlfriends drank their coffee black. Will helped himself to a large cup.

After what seemed an eternity, she came into the kitchen with fresh tears in her eyes. She had taken a tour of her husband's apartment, and every discovery had opened old wounds. She came up to Will and kissed him gently on the cheek. "Thank you, thank you, thank you, but I'm going to have to ask you to leave. The closets are filled with another woman's clothes; there are two toothbrushes and makeup in the bathroom and someone else's expensive jewelry in the drawers. I want to burn it all, but the Salvation Army is going to get a nice fat donation instead."

After being walked to the door and kissed softly again, Will said goodbye. Outside, he paused in the walkway and looked back. She was standing in the doorway looking at him with a smile on her face. She had wiped away the tears.

Chapter 6

Don Alverez had moved his entourage to the old library of the main house. The library was an immense room with high ceilings, thickly paneled walls and floor-to-ceiling bookcases. Tall casement windows opened onto a wide terrace that overlooked a lush countryside, and several miles away, the sails of boats that were cruising in the Caribbean Sea.

Normally, they would light up the finest Cuban cigars and relax luxuriously in deep leather chairs. Today, the decanters of whiskey and matching crystal glasses sat untouched on the sideboard. Shaking with anger and emotion, Don Alverez stood behind his massive wooden desk and looked from one to the other. "We have much work to do, and it must be done quickly, without a single mistake. Each of you must do exactly as I say."

He turned to Paul. "You will handle this on the scene. Your every move must be careful, like your life depends on it. Make no demands. Treat their representative with the highest respect. Take Michael in the *Falcon*. It's the fastest jet, and go immediately. This is the man you will meet." He handed Paul a note with a name and a phone number.

Then he turned to Diego, who was under such strain that the veins on his neck and arms were bulging like a dog on a leash, "My boy, you have too much emotion, too much attachment to Gabriella to go. Do you think I've been blind all these years? But you have important work too. You have to gather the money. A great deal of money. They claim to have 'incurred considerable costs.'"

Frustrated that he was not the one chosen to go, Diego was nonetheless pleased that the Don had an important role for him.

"Put it all together and package it. No tricks. Real money, no fakes, no powder, no schemes to trace it. No deviation from my instructions. You must have it ready in twenty-four hours. All of it! Stump will take it in the big plane and go when he gets instructions from Paul." He handed Diego a slip of paper with a number on it.

Stunned at the amount, Diego looked at the Don, his eyes questioning.

"It's nothing, nothing at all . . . pocket change really. All in one-hundred-dollar bills, Diego. One-hundred-dollar bills! Go . . . GO NOW!"

Will MacKenzie was speeding, the jeep doing eighty and ninety miles per hour as he drove down the west side of Ashby Gap on Route 50.

Just before he crossed the bridge over the Shenandoah, he saw the glow of lights from River View Farm. *Joe Arthur must be having a big party,* he thought, saddened that he no longer received invitations to River View.

As he entered Clarke County, Virginia, and passed the main entrance to the farm, he saw state police cars and a couple of county sheriff's cars. He recognized an old friend, Roscoe Harris, in his deputy sheriff's uniform, talking it up with the state police just outside the main gate.

Roscoe was a former high school classmate who had gone into law enforcement and had distinguished himself many times. *He should be sheriff by now,* thought Will.

Continuing his drive toward Winchester, Will wondered who was there, who was worthy enough to be invited to a Joe Arthur party?

Everybody who's anybody, that's who. He thought of his last invite, almost three year's ago.

It had been a beautiful summer evening, and every important person in the tricounty area had been there. People returned early from vacations just to attend a Joe Arthur party.

That party was fun even though he and his wife were having problems. Back then, he had begun drinking way too much. He tried to block out the sad memories, visualize that last party in his mind, and think about the good times there. He smiled as he remembered.

A doctor spilling a drink on a well-dressed woman who, in retaliation, mashed her high heel into his foot so he couldn't dance.

Two women who showed up wearing the same dress and then doing everything possible not to be seen in the same room.

A rich Clarke County politician wearing a bow tie and an outlandish colored pair of pants that didn't match his tuxedo coat.

One bald-headed man dancing every dance all night and sweating on three quarters of the women there as his wife pretended not to know him.

A dark-haired schoolteacher who was married to a judge, getting up and singing with the band. Her husband was always recommending books for Will to read.

A tall man who had made a fortune in the beer business and yet always drank bourbon, never beer, telling one joke after another, his audience loving them even though they were the same stories he had told before at other parties. He'd stay in the middle of a group until his wife, almost as tall as he was, would break through the crowd, blow cigarillo smoke in his face and say, "Honey, it's time to go."

A banker's wife who had downed too many white wines, lifting her skirt and boogying down to the floor in a series of suggestive, sensual moves as her husband tried to become invisible.

Will's golf, tennis, and poker playing pals were usually there, all hanging out together, each wondering why the other had been invited. He hadn't heard much from them since his divorce.

He remembered a group of antisocial types. They always huddled in a corner, complained about having to be there, yet they always came. They were the first to arrive, and the last to leave.

They had all been there: bankers, lawyers, doctors, car dealers, apple growers, big-business owners, small-business owners, actors, politicians, landowners, and heirs to various fortunes.

Crossing Interstate 81, Will thought about Joe Arthur and how much he was admired. Just last week, Joe had been named Citizen of the Year. His picture was in both area newspapers, the *Star* and the *Northern Virginia Daily*, with long articles about his involvement in area charities. Often, he took part in challenge programs, where he would personally match all the money collected from others. It didn't seem to matter what charitable cause was in need; he gave to them all. He had given millions of dollars over a twenty-year period. It was rumored that he was heir to a mining fortune. Some said it was old money, inherited from investments in banks and railroads. Whatever the source, there was no doubt that there was plenty of it, and he was overly generous when it came to community needs.

Joe Arthur wasn't married, but he always had a much younger woman as his unofficial hostess at these parties. Joe was unattractive, even in a tuxedo. His nose had been broken several times, and he had an ugly scar from his lip to his chin. But his "hostess," whom he usually introduced as his niece, would always be at his side, looking up at him in an adoring way. He had a lot of attractive nieces.

Joe's formally dressed waiters and waitresses were routinely busy, serving drinks and passing trays of fancy bite-sized treats. The food was always delicious. Joe had seafood flown in from the Chesapeake Bay, beef tenderloin aged from his own cattle, the finest wines from his vast cellar, and liquor flowing like water. Even the best Havana cigars were always plentiful, and no one asked how he had acquired them.

Guests danced past midnight to a talented band from DC after rocking to a really special orchestra from Shenandoah University. Shuttle vans would take each guest to their cars and limos parked on row after row of Joe's manicured pastureland.

Of course, Will remembered the politicians. They were regulars at a Joe Arthur party. Both of Virginia's United States senators came. The governor too, arriving late on purpose in a jet helicopter provided by a Southwest Virginia Coal Company. Will had heard that these politicians received guest lists and pictures of guests prior to attending any Arthur function to remind the politicians just who their big contributors were.

Politicians flocked to Winchester for a reason. Many came to visit the Byrd family that had produced generations of public servants. Winchester was more an area than a town. Its residents were proud of its history, its influence in power politics, and its diverse economy. For over two hundred years, the town had claimed a role in shaping the country. Colonel James Wood, Winchester's founder, had influenced George Washington's career as a surveyor, a military commander, and a politician.

Winchester had been a major battleground in the Indian Wars and in the Revolutionary War. During the Civil War, Winchester had changed hands scores of times.

For many years, its economy had depended on farming, apple growing, and textile mills. Most of the area's early wealthy were heirs to the founders of these businesses.

One of its most famous residents had been Patsy Cline.

By the 1980s, Winchester's economy was booming as a regional medical center, a widely diversified manufacturing center, and a quality place to live. Jobs were plentiful and the major government worry was controlling growth. New businesses were developing, old businesses expanding, and the American dream had become a reality for many in the area.

New money and old money congregated in Clarke County, just east of Winchester. The moneyed class enjoyed a place to let go and have fun, to see and be seen, and there was no place better than Joe Arthur's fabulous showplace.

What a party that was, Will thought. Those were fun people, and he missed them. It was just one more reason he wished he'd never tried to drown himself in a bottle of whiskey. Maybe people would start to socialize with him again when they knew he had recovered from the booze.

As Will was turning off Merriman's Lane, west of Winchester, alert for deer that had a habit of running in front of cars late at night, he thought he saw a dog flash by with a tennis racquet in its mouth.

Coming into his driveway, he saw another dog sitting in the middle of a pile of trash and junk in front of his garage. It was Watson, his chocolate Lab, who stood up at the sight of the familiar jeep, wagging his tail into a blur. Will had to stop short to avoid the dog and the mess, and when he opened the driver's side door, Watson rushed up and lavished him with kisses. He'd been away all day, and his dog smothered him with love. Will patted his head, gave him a hug, wiped his face of slobber, and managed to get out. The dog kept licking his hand, and MacKenzie pulled it away, realizing where the hand had been earlier in the evening.

He surveyed the scene. Usually when he had to leave Watson home, even for an away trip overnight, he would raise the garage door so the dog could go outside whenever he wished. That morning, before going to Georgetown to meet his friends, he had filled several large bowls with water and dog food and left them in the garage.

The garage door was partially raised, just as he had left it.

Now it appeared that everything that had been in the garage, at least everything that a dog could reach, was now strewn outside the garage. There were plastic bags full of clothes, and boxes of plates, glasses, appliances, and household articles that he'd planned to donate to a local charity, all in shreds, all carried out over a half acre of his property. It looked as if a bomb had exploded. Will spotted a golf bag and a few of the clubs that were once in it. A Ben Hogan driver with the grip chewed off lay next to a towel that read, "Shenandoah College Golf Benefit."

He saw one tennis racquet with the strings chewed out and realized that the other dog decided to take the good racquet home.

Watson was fine by himself, but not a good boy when he joined with other dogs. "Look at this mess!" Will shouted at the dog.

Watson didn't look at the mess as ordered, just sat there looking into his master's face, tail wagging, so happy that Will had come home.

Will could not punish this dog, not with his faithful, loving look. He bent over, put his arms around him, and returned the love.

"Let's go to bed." Leaving the mess where it was, the two walked in the house and went straight for the bedroom.

At River View Farm, the last guests knew it was time to go when the band stopped playing, the bar closed, and lights started to flicker. Joe's bartenders would mix the last drinks and distribute them with napkins that read, "Please go home."

Joe Arthur's household help cleaned up, paid off the band, and turned out the rest of the lights.

Another successful party to his credit, Joe Arthur was just beginning to fall asleep at 2:00 a.m. when the telephone rang. A man with a Spanish accent needed a favor.

Chapter 7

Two DC Police officers sitting in a patrol car in front of the FU Club at Fourth and U streets in Washington DC, were arguing over who's basketball team was better, Georgetown's or Maryland's, when a tap at the driver side window diverted their attention. Officer Marvin Perry looked up at the intruder and rolled down the window. "Why, look who's come to pay us a visit. LD, you are a sight for so' eyes. What you got there?"

"Marvin, my man. Thank God for the law. Don't want you white asses freezin' out here. Thought you boys could use some warmin' up." LD passed through a box of hot fried chicken and two more coffees fortified with Grand Marnier.

"This'll definitely keep us warm," said Marvin as he felt for the envelope in the bottom of the box.

"Heat is what you honkies need, but I'm gonna freeze myself yakin' with you two." City police patrol cars were always parked outside, providing a measure of peace to an otherwise violent neighborhood. With a flamboyant goodbye, LD gave them a one-finger salute, turned, and reentered the club. It was packed with people. Permitted to serve 150 but serving at least twice that number every night except Sundays and Mondays, the place rocked. A live band started at ten and closed up at four o'clock in the morning.

LD, whose initials once stood for Long Dick until his friends began calling him Little Dick, and now just LD, worked his way through the crowd. He sauntered past the two guards at the back of the dance floor and came to a door at the end of a dark hallway. The door was made of thick steel and was blocked by another guard. All of the guards wore black turtleneck sweaters under black sport coats, the unofficial winter uniform of the FU

Crew. The guard opened the door for LD, but he didn't go in. Instead, he lightly knocked to get the attention of the two men seated inside. When they looked up, he just nodded, knowing the two would understand its meaning. They looked and returned the nod, indicating they understood, and LD shut the door without a word.

The two men sitting across a metal conference table from each other were deep in conversation, talking low even though their office was swept regularly for wiretaps. The table sat next to a desk that was bare except for two phones: one red, the other black. The walls were painted dark green and featured a framed photo of young Sugar Ray Leonard in the boxing ring with a powerfully built bulldog of a boxer, who looked like one of the men at the table. An old *Playboy* centerfold, stuck up so long ago that it wrinkled, was hanging next to the photo.

Booker "Booger" Bryant and Hamp "Blue" Smith were best friends and business partners who shared a long, troubled history of mutual support. Smith lit up one of Bryant's cigars, only to choke, cough, and frown. "Where do you get this crap?"

"I keep it around for blue-eyed moochers like you! You mainly smoke Luckies 'cause you lucky. Why you want my cigars anyway? You too cheap to buy 'em with your own money?"

"I like a good cigar, Boog, but I keep forgetin' who's cheap around here. You must have given up smoking 'cause these gotta be ten years too stale."

"Yet you the only one in this room that smokes regular, Blue. You get the shakes when you cain't have one. As for me, I mean to avoid the vices."

"That's right. Oh yeah, I suppose that's purified water you sippin' on?"

"Ain't nothin' wrong with a drink now 'n' then. Besides, a drink's supposed t' be good for you."

"I know that's straight gin in your glass, so don't be preachin' t' me. If that piss is good for you, I'll kiss your ass in front of the band out there."

"Not after what you been kissin'. My ass is too good for you."

Booker and Blue had known each other since their early teens when Bryant had been a promising middleweight boxer and football player and Smith a scholar, having been educated in private schools until the eighth grade. After seven years of the best schools, where Blue always excelled at the top of his class, his mother's money dried up, and he dropped out. Blue wound up attending one of the city's worst schools. There, he met Booger, a school bully, who protected him in return for Blue's making sure that Booger's grades were passing. Together, they made an unlikely pair: Booger, ebony black, short, and stocky; Blue, tall and slender but very light skinned with clear blue eyes.

Blue's mother, the Caucasian daughter of a wealthy New England family, had studied at Smith College in Northampton, Massachusetts. His father, a privileged son of a West African diplomat had been a student at nearby Amherst. The Ivy League couple produced a child named Northampton Amherst Smith, but everyone just called him Blue. He'd been in so many fights over that name and those eyes that he'd become hardened and tough at a young age.

After his parents' graduation in New England, they moved to Washington DC to be close to their African embassy relations, expecting support from the black side of the family. But neither family would accept this mixed relationship, and they ignored the existence of a grandson. Blue's father abandoned his white wife and went back to Africa to become a manager in his country's state-owned oil business. Blue's mother turned to prostitution and died of a drug overdose when he was thirteen.

Booger's family, living in the apartment next door, gave the boy a temporary place to stay, and then, as time went on, he never left. The two men knew each other so well each one could almost read the other's mind.

Booger became serious, saying, "We got to move our little princess to the country."

Blue nodded. "She a prime piece. You sure you don't wanna taste o' that before we go?"

"Off limits, Blue, an' you knows that. We cain't damage the goods."

"Gonna be a war anyway, Boog, and by the way, what about your other guests?" he asked.

"They stay with me while you livin' the country squire life. Need to work with these boys some mo'. Maybe I've been too lenient. I cain't unnerstan' but a couple of words those dudes are sayin'—*Di . . . ago* and *Pa . . . drone* an' *Cartagena* an' *kokane* an' *fukin' up wrong tree*—don't ya see ? Why is it none of our crew speaks a foreign language? Those idiots didn't learn shit in school?"

"They don't know English either, Boog, but the sum'bitches sure can count. My man Jeffery swears that the dudes had more money on them than Peacock says was there."

"Peacock got a high standard o' livin' to keep up. Man's got more greed than the rest of the crew combined. That don't help me with the inquisition. My Latino friends talkin', we listenin', but we ain't communicatin', if ya catch my meanin'?"

"I get your point, but it makes no sense to me. None. I swear that Jeffery talked to several guys those spics was entertainin' in Arlington, and they all three spoke English. One of them had a Brooklyn accent. Find Jeffery and see if I'm not dreamin' this up. You'll figure it out Boog, you always do. You stuck my ass with a much bigger mess."

The conversation turned to travel details, what vehicles to take, where to go, whom to see, when to leave, phone numbers, backup, and so on. They decided that only five men would be needed for escort during the trip. They would need a van and a car, and all but Blue would return. Given the plan, he didn't need anyone else, and help was only an hour away.

"Watch Irene for me while I'm gone. She must be on her sixth Dr. Pepper and Crown Royal by now."

"I got more impotan' things t' do than babysit Irene. Don't ya trust her?"

The lady in question was in the big room down the hall, seated at the bar, drinking her favorite drink, but it was only her third. She had one hand on her glass and the other tapping a spoon on the bar, keeping time with the beat.

Colored strobe lights from the bandstand reflected off the big mirror behind the bar. The atmosphere was surreal: dim to dark lights interrupted by flashes of bright light, loud music, cigarette smoke mixed with the heavy scent of marijuana, and the crowd dancing and singing with the band.

Irene was more striking than beautiful. Her flaming red hair and pale green eyes made her stand out in this crowd, one of the few white faces in a sea of black. No one bothered her though; they knew who she belonged to.

What they didn't know was that she had an agenda too, carrying a small .38-caliber pistol inside her knee-high boots. She was environmentally concerned.

She stood up when Blue finally came out of the office, expecting to dance. Instead, he kissed her and said, "Let me take you home, hon. Sorry, but I got a job to do."

After landing at Dulles Airport, renting a car, and making two phone calls, Paul Xavier and his brother-in-law, Michael Rowe, headed west on Route 50 to Winchester, Virginia.

Paul was worried. He normally planned each job down to the smallest detail. He looked at his brother-in-law sitting in the passenger seat and was surprised to find him smiling as if he didn't have a care in the world, oblivious to the importance of their mission. Paul wondered about his friend's state of mind. That smile was just one more thing to worry about. On the flight up from Miami, they hadn't talked much because Michael usually sat in the copilot's seat, anxious to see where he was going. They didn't need much coordination on most jobs because Michael did the same thing every time. He was a parachutist that always jumped at night, and always with a package to deliver.

Most of Michael's discussion with Paul had taken place earlier in the company's Miami flight operations office, where one of Don Alverez's businesses was air transport, coupled with specialty warehousing. This business included a fleet of planes that could fly in and out of small airports at all times, transporting specialty cargo of all types. One of their largest customers was the U.S. government. Another was flying live organs for heart and kidney transplants.

These activities were profitable, but not nearly as much as their main business, which was the subject of Paul's earlier briefing with Michael in the company's back office:

"Tomorrow night is a big job. We'll be delivering an important package."

"What is it? What's so important?" Michael was short, stocky, strong, and didn't like to be kept uninformed. He stayed in shape lifting weights and running several miles every day. He was in better physical condition than when he was an army paratrooper. In high school, where he was an all-state guard on the football team, he'd had a short fuse, but he knew to be careful with Paul.

"Michael, you don't need to know. Just know it will probably require two bags, large ones, maybe three. You got a lot of preparing to do. This job is the most important we've ever done."

"Ever? Paule, we been doin' this for almost fifteen years. Why not tell me everything so I can do my job?"

"You'll see the cargo when you get to Starke tomorrow. Today, you need to focus on the drop zone, but, Mike, I gotta tell you I'm concerned about your attention span. You've been acting strange for several months now, like you haven't been here. Your mind seems to be somewhere else. And you should know something. I'm concerned about you and Isabella. You've been traveling almost nonstop between jobs. You're rarely home, always hunting or something. Isabella's come crying to me several times. I don't know what you have going, but I know something's wrong. You've been married to my sister three years and no children. Where are my nephews, Mikie? Is there another woman?"

"You don't trust me anymore? After all we've been through? Jesus, Paul. Jesus H. Christ!"

Paul was about to reply when the pilot came in and interrupted their conversation with an announcement: "Everything is ready. We take off in ten minutes." Air traffic at Miami International was always busy; private flights had to land and take off on strict schedules, giving them much less flexibility than commercial flights. So onto the plane they went, some questions unanswered.

The flight to Dulles was scheduled to take two hours and forty minutes, but there was room for headwinds in that plan. The two had separate tasks to perform in Winchester. It was a small town, and most of their work was done in small out-of-the-way towns in the United States. Paul and Mike worked well together. Neither had to worry whether the other knew what to do. They did this all the time.

Before they left the private terminal at Dulles, Paul had several calls to make, reporting back to the Don, and checking on the latest news from Winchester. Michael took the long walk to the main terminal to rent their car. On the way, he made sure he wasn't being followed by Paul, then went directly back to the Southwest Airlines ticket counter. Michael quickly reviewed departure schedules and booked seats on several different flights, all going to the same destination.

Only then did he set out to do what he'd come for in the first place—rent a car.

"Where the hell have you been?" Paul asked when he finally picked him up. "How long does it take to rent a car? This is just what I've been talking about, Mike. Your mind is on another planet. You got to get it together. No screw-up's tomorrow night. Do you understand me?" The look he gave Michael was steely, a warning. "Move over brother-in-law, I'm driving."

"I'm sorry, Paul, I'm sorry. Maybe I'm getting old. I'll bring it home, you know I will. I'll make it up to Isabella too, I promise."

"Well, that's more like the old Mike."

Most of the rest of the trip was silent as each worked out in his mind what had to be done. Nothing could be on paper. Even when Michael and Paul talked, they stuck to business, names and phone numbers of contacts, backup plan, and the like. No more discussion about Isabella. Michael was certainly not about to tell Paul about the vasectomy.

Driving west, they saw some of the most beautiful countryside in America even though it was winter. They passed mile after mile of stone and wooden fences, cultivated forests and pastures, ponds and streams, and occasionally, they'd catch a glimpse of the many huge estates that were visible at this time of year.

Paul maintained the speed limit, as was his custom, cruising slowly through Middleburg. The picturesque town had recently decorated all the lampposts that lined the streets. Shoppers were out in full force. All the store windows showed items of unusual quality: antiques, Oriental rugs, saddles, boots, custom-made riding gear, and a variety of paintings from area artists.

When they reached the four lane west of Middleburg, a white van full of black men roared past them, horn blowing, the men shouting obscenities at them. On the van's tail was a green Mercedes sedan with DC license plates. The Mercedes accelerated suddenly into the inside lane and then surged in front of the van.

Everyone else passed them too. All of rural Virginia seemed to be in a hurry and not mindful of the speed limit. They continued to be passed by cars and pickup trucks for the next thirty miles. Their destination was Lamar Sloan Ford in Winchester, where Michael Rowe rented a second car. After a final review of their plans with each other, the two separated.

As soon as he was certain Paul was on his way, however, Michael drove the second car back to Lamar Sloan Ford and asked to exchange the car for a van. "I got to get somethin' larger, and now I find I'm gonna need it for a longer period," he told the rental manager.

Just then, a huge man walked in and threw a set of keys to the clerk. "Hey, Billy, I'm finished with the white Econoline. You can clean it up for rental."

"Who is that guy?" Michael asked. "I've never seen anyone that big. He must be seven feet tall and three hundred pounds."

"He's our general manager, six foot nine and 325, a former defensive end for the Washington Redskins, and he was driving the largest van in our fleet."

"I'll take it," said Michael.

"I have to clean it up first. That man loves his cigars."

"I'll take it as is, smell and all. I'm in a big hurry."

"Suit yourself, but don't complain to me about the smell an' ever'thing."

"Done deal. Can I pay cash to speed things up?"

"No problem, Lamar takes cash too, but it ain't any faster. Ya still gotta sign the forms."

Michael was anxious to be back on the road, but the rental manager wouldn't let the van out before emptying the cigar ashes and hosing down the exterior. Beads of water from the car wash spun off the van when he left the parking lot. He was hungry, and he had much to do before his final coordination with Paul.

Most of Michael's day was spent traveling west of Winchester, rechecking locations where he'd been many times before. He'd already decided on the drop. They'd used the field west of the hospital several times, and it was still vacant and out of the way. Then he deviated from the plan.

Grabbing a Big Mac and some fries to go, eating and driving, he took his time. He checked both sides of the road, all the while looking back in his rearview mirror, making sure he wasn't being followed. He headed toward West Virginia, out Route 50. Then he went south, past Round Hill, and, finally, all the way to Cedar Creek Grade leading back into Winchester.

On Cedar Creek, he found what he wanted. A new building site that seemed abandoned. The builder had flattened all trees, except the two at the front entrance. It looked as if they'd stopped working due to weather because only the entrance and a few blocks leading to a cul-de-sac were paved with asphalt. A construction trailer, several bulldozers, and a host of other rusting construction equipment were parked in haphazard fashion throughout the site. Farms, orchards, woods, and fences surrounded the abandoned development, making it seem like a sore on the landscape.

Michael slowed to a stop on the road and drove onto the site, all the while checking his bearings. He took a map and compass out and made sure where he was, watched to see how much traffic came by, and noted a farmhouse almost a mile to the northeast. Satisfied, he parked the van where it wouldn't be seen from the road, placing the keys in its tailpipe, and walked back to the two-lane road that led back to town.

It wasn't too long before he caught a ride into town with a worker heading for the second shift at Abex. He was driving an old Chevy pickup truck with tobacco juice staining the entire length of the truck below the driver's side window. Michael noticed the license plate framed in chrome, advertising Jim Stutzman Chevrolet-Cadillac.

The driver introduced himself as Johnny Rich. "But you can call me John. Too cold t' be walkin'. Ya must be new around here."

"You're right," Michael said. "I'm lookin' to buy a place up here. Florida's just too damn hot in the summer."

"Florida seems mighty appealing right now. Goin' to snow soon. How come you're walkin'? Car break down?"

"Nah. Me and my fiancé got into an argument. She wants a house in the city. I want a place in the country. She got mad and left me back at that development."

"Don't even think of buying something there. Too expensive! Go another two miles west an' ya can get good land, cheap too. My grandfather has almost three hundred acres."

"Thanks, Johnny . . . er . . . John, you can let me out up there by the Safeway."

Pulling up to the curb, Johnny was almost apologetic. "Sorry, I cain't take you farther. Only got fifteen minutes before my shift starts."

"No problem. I'll be fine. My gal cools off quick. She'll come when I call. Thanks again, I really appreciate the ride and the advice."

Johnny opened the passenger window before leaving. "Hey, maybe we'll be neighbors someday? Tell that girl she'll love the country."

As soon as the pickup was out of sight, Michael entered the pay phone in front of the Safeway. He checked the yellow pages for a limo service and called the first company listed in the book, AES. He asked for an immediate limousine pickup to take him to Dulles Airport. After a short wait, the receptionist apologized and said that, unfortunately, all their limos were in service. However, to Michael's surprise, the owner came on the line and offered to take him in his personal car. Michael agreed and thanked the owner. While he waited for his ride, he considered how different things were in a small town. Maybe he could wind up in such a place.

For almost two years, he had dreamed of getting out. Only a year after marrying Paul's sister, he had come to hate the lazy, good-for-nothing bitch but knew Paul would kill him if he tried to leave. But now, he had an added incentive. The insane kidnapping of the Don's only daughter had created an opportunity.

In planning the ransom delivery, he had planned his escape. Always before, his parachute cargo had been cocaine or heroin or a much smaller amount of money and never once did he consider double-crossing the Don.

This time, however, he guessed the package would be a huge amount of cash. He just didn't know how much. He'd need the van to carry the cargo. Paul said maybe three parachutes. A car wouldn't do. The van from Lamar Sloan Ford, now parked in an abandoned building site near the drop zone, was 180 degrees from where he was expected to land. It would be waiting for him when he jumped.

The lights from Winchester Medical Center were ideal for identifying the drop zone. The nearby Perry Quarry was also lighted at night, and it separated the cornfield, where he was expected to land. Now, after a thorough recon, he felt confident that his secret drop zone, a cow pasture on Fancy Fruit Farm off Cedar Creek Grade, was perfect. The trick was to jump early enough to avoid being seen by Paul who would have the binoculars and would know where to look.

The farm consisted of four fields, each roughly sixty acres in size. Michael Rowe chose to jump into a remote field, which was just south of the quarry. It was mainly pastureland, covered with a thick layer of winter grass, flat and ideal for landing as long as he steered clear of one large very old oak tree, the only tree left standing.

Well, that was that. He'd made his decision; everything was now in place to execute that decision tomorrow night. He made a long-distance call to a number in Boca Raton, Florida, and then he called Paul Xavier. "Hey, I got it all down. Looks perfect."

"Where the hell have you been? I've been waiting for over two hours!"

"Paule, don't tell me how to do my job. I'm the best there is. I don't mean to keep you waiting, but you want this one to be perfect, don't you?"

Paul thought about the importance of their mission. "You're right, Michael, you're right. I'm a little jumpy on this one you know, a little anxious."

Michael gave Paul directions, described the territory, discussed alternative options, answered a few questions, and waited for his limousine.

By early evening, Michael was back at the company's private terminal at Dulles. One of All American Air Cargo's special pilots flew him back to Florida. It had been a long day. He couldn't get the smile off his face. He had finally worked things out.

Chapter 8

Michael Rowe slept fitfully on the two-and-a-half-hour flight to Boca Raton. His friend, a young cocktail waitress he'd known for almost a year, met him at the airport and dropped him at his Florida apartment, surprised when he wouldn't let her come in.

To show he cared, he gave her $2,000 from a fat packet of cash.

"Buy something nice, a little black dress or something. We're going to take a trip when I get back."

He kept a closet full of clothes at his Boca apartment and a variety of tools and equipment he used in his business. An ex-army paratrooper, he kept this home away from home spotless and well organized.

He had a floor safe for bankbooks, cash, a variety of passports in different names, safe deposit keys, and several weapons, including a pistol with silencer attachment.

Michael decided to pack the safe's entire contents for tomorrow night's trip even though he was exhausted. He didn't bother with his closet and dresser drawers full of expensive clothes. They would be too bulky to take and might arouse suspicion. He couldn't mail them to his ultimate destination because he wanted to keep that a secret. His small leather satchel would carry the important items and never leave his side.

Stump Anderson slowly brought the big Gulfstream jet in for a smooth landing at Miami International. Although he knew where he was going, he waited for instructions from the tower, sitting patiently at the end of the runway. Naturally, he was headed for the Customs and Immigration Terminal. Five men on his plane accompanied the shipment, and all five were used to international travel. They'd been through Miami many times.

They stayed in the plane on the tarmac at C&I for approximately fifteen minutes until the uniformed officials arrived by golf cart. The official faces were familiar, and once on the plane, they gave each other high fives, addressing each man by name. "Y'all got anything to declare?" they asked in an almost mocking tone.

"My ass. Your face," someone replied, and Stump handed over completed forms for each man, together with two fat envelopes.

"Where you off to now, Stump? Goin' someplace exotic?"

"Nah, Elrod, erotic. Just up to Starke."

"Y'all keep it in your zippers, ain't nothin' happenin' in Starke, an' ya don't want to stay in their big hotel," Elrod said, referring to the state penitentiary at Starke.

Stump taxied to the executive terminal where he paid his landing fee, gassed up, picked out a meal from the carry-out menu, and was back in the air after only a short delay.

Driving north from Boca, Michael Rowe arrived at the Starke Airport in late afternoon, a half hour after Stump. He pulled into the private hangar, parked in "handicapped parking," and sauntered in. The hangar was full of activity.

Stump looked up from where he was filling out flight log forms. "Nice of you to bless us with your presence. You on Central Standard Time?"

Michael was used to Stump's nagging. He worried about every detail. "What's your hurry, Stumper? We ain't leavin' for another five or six hours."

"You better check out your chute. Got a heavy load. My guess is you'll need a couple o' chutes, jerkoff. The boys're packin' in the back, but you better supervise this one. It requires personal attention. Your personal attention, Mike! By the way, we're goin' in the King Air. I'm doin' a full maintenance check."

"I'm glad my ass is in such good hands, Stump. You're the best, even though you worry too much."

Stump looked up from his work and pointed his pen at Michael. "Everybody involved ought to be worried about this one. Michael, I'm not kiddin'. Do you know the cargo?"

"Yea," Mike said, not wanting to admit he was acting on intuition. "Paul an' I talked about it on the trip to Winchester."

"You better go in the back, see how heavy those duffle bags are. You may need three chutes."

"What's the weather gonna be?"

"Gonna be colder than a witch's tit. Looks to me like long johns and woolies for your balls."

"Gimmie the details Stumper," pretending to be shaking from cold. "I gotta know how thick my woolies need t' be."

This time, Stump stopped what he was doing and gave Michael his full attention.

"Seriously, it's going to be cold, in the twenties, clear, but a front's comin' on strong. Wind's a little hard to forecast. Might be blowin' some. Gonna snow like hell in the morning, but we'll be long gone."

"Well, aren't you lucky, just have to drink coffee, stay in your warm, toasty plane, and come back to the sunshine state while I freeze my ass off." Michael couldn't resist teasing Stump. He was a good friend, and he wanted everything to seem normal.

At the Hampton Inn, the girl behind the counter wondered about the nationality of the strange man with the blue eyes signing the register. Maybe he was from the Middle East. "Where y'all from?" she asked, looking into his exotic pupils.

Blue looked behind, thinking she was talking to someone else. Then he turned to the girl, whose name tag read "Suzy" and asked, "Who?"

"You, I wondered where you're from."

"Washington DC."

"Really? You don't look like you're from DC." She grinned, flirting with a look and a stance that promised good times if he was interested.

Blue wondered what someone from DC looked like, but he was tired from tension, a long day, and the knowledge of a long night ahead. "When I get some time, maybe I'll tell you more about it."

"Have a good evenin'. Do you need a wake-up call?" the clerk asked, wanting to continue the conversation with this handsome man.

Blue picked up his bag as if he hadn't heard and kept on going to the room.

The phone rang at the front desk. It was a man who wanted to know if they had any vacancies. "Sure." Suzy's voice conveyed a smile, goodwill, and a welcome response. "We're not too crowded. Smoking or nonsmoking?"

"I don't care as long as it has a queen size, a TV, and it's on the first floor. Name's Angelo Baldi."

"I got everything but first floor, hon. Ya still want the room?"

"I'll take it," the gruff voice said and hung up before she could ask for a credit card.

The small plane began to bounce around as Stump decreased altitude over the North Carolina-Virginia border. In the copilot's seat, Michael unbuckled his seat belt, saying, "Time to get ready."

Stump checked his watch and verified his position. "Ain't you a little early, Mike?"

"Got to take a leak. As you told me earlier, better check everything twice."

"Hey, it's your call. Who am I to question the man who chooses to leave the plane before landing?" And Stump turned back to flying the plane.

Chapter 9

Ka-Boom! . . . *Ka-Boom!* . . . *Ka-Boom!* . . . The loud blasts came at them in quick succession, exploding out of nowhere, causing each man to duck, jump back in the shadows, and reach for his weapon. For a while, the three remained still, focusing their total attention in the direction of the sound, hoping they would not be discovered.

They waited, crouched down in the dark cornfield, six eyes staring through the darkness. Then they heard it again, not as loud this time, an engine backfiring and the sounds of a large truck decreasing speed, gears grinding down.

When the tractor trailer came in sight, it was still slowing down to meet the steep curve at the far end of the valley, some two miles away. It was a refrigerator truck carrying a load of frozen chicken wings from Romney, West Virginia, heading east. The men seemed mesmerized as the big rig accelerated toward them after it reached the bottom of the hill. No one said a word as they watched it go by. They continued looking for several minutes until its taillights disappeared beyond the Winchester Medical Center. Then, it was quiet again, not a sound from anywhere.

"Holy shit! We didn't need that!" It was all the big man could say while the other two kept quiet. Then, as if on command, they turned their attention back to the sky, watching and listening in total silence.

Aside from the cold, it was a good night for flying. The moon was almost three-quarter's full, and for most of the night, visibility had been fair.

They were at the edge of a large farm, west of Winchester, Virginia. Almost invisible next to their black van, they had parked on a dirt road in the shadows of pine trees where it couldn't be seen. Each man stayed out of the moonlight and tried to stay warm by constant movement, shuffling feet and rubbing hands.

Angelo Baldi, their driver and mediator, had remained calm throughout the meeting with the other two. He was a heavyset man who had already taken two pisses in front of the rented van. He'd drunk five of the beers out of the pack he'd bought for his companions when they stopped for gas. Both of the others had declined to take a drink.

The man with the blue eyes watched the other two out of caution. He kept to their backs. *Maybe the fat fuck was just warming his hands,* he thought, wanting a cigarette, his body craving nicotine, not able to stand still for a minute. He had limited confidence in tonight's affair. Blue Eyes suspected a double cross and needed something stronger than beer. He especially refused to turn his back on the little prick that supposedly had arranged for tonight's delivery.

Wind chill enhanced the cold. Gradually, the brisk, moist early March wind increased in intensity and seeped through their layers of clothing. Blue felt the chill through to the bone. The man he referred to as "the little prick" was cold but was too focused on completing his part of the mission tonight to react. Only the big guy wearing just a suit, who'd taken the leaks, didn't seem to mind the weather.

Though the three men were strangers to one another, they each represented separate factions of a tightly controlled, obscenely profitable, and often violent business: one on the supply side, another in wholesale distribution, and the third was in retail operations. In terms of annual revenue, their combined enterprise would easily qualify for the S&P five hundred list of largest U.S. businesses. But their business was global and not restricted to the United States.

Each man was a senior member of his side of the business. They had become senior members by learning to survive in their violent world and by being more cunning and more ruthless than their competition.

Waiting tonight required a grudging acceptance of one another's unique role. It was different from anything they'd ever done before.

Drug distribution was controlled in the mid-Atlantic states by the Philadelphia Mafia. The Mafia's representative in the cornfield was the mediator, Angelo Baldi, burly and powerful, whose trademark was beating people to death with his bare hands. Even though it was cold, he was sweating and uncomfortable. He was suffering from an upset stomach and a slight case of diarrhea. He badly needed to fart but was afraid to, afraid it wasn't a fart.

For the moment, Angelo was the host, the driver, and the middleman whose job was to keep the other two from killing each other.

The tall blue-eyed mulatto man in the cornfield represented the retail side of the enterprise. The Mafia distributed a variety of drugs to his business: amphetamines, marijuana, cocaine, and heroin. He was constantly shifting from one leg to the other, moving back and forth, almost jogging in place. He was the second-ranking leader in his organization, and his gang controlled drug dealing throughout the Washington DC area.

Handsome, athletic, and immaculately dressed, he walked with a slight limp. Blue's anxiety tonight was unusually high since he and his DC gang had been the catalyst for this unholy get-together. His continuous moving around was mainly due to not trusting either of the others, but it also eased the effects of wind chill. Coupled with the long wait and other frustrations, Blue's need for a cigarette turned ugly. Usually, when he was in this kind of mood, he killed someone. He reached for the pack of Luckies, patted it, and tried to breathe slowly, knowing he'd have to wait.

Sensing the black man's mood, Angelo Baldi faced the nearby hospital and took another leak to break the monotony and refocus. The hospital was silent even though all five stories were lit with bright lights, giving the parking lot and surrounding area a look of false warmth. Soon though, Angelo knew that workers from West Virginia would be making their way east to jobs at the hospital and other places in Winchester and Northern Virginia. Time was running out.

The third man in the cornfield was wondering if the big Italian had a ten-gallon kidney that had to be emptied every few minutes. The guy was constantly unzipping his pants and pissing buckets. Steam rose from the ground when it landed. Smaller than the other two, Paul Xavier was quiet by nature and normally worked with an ice pick, but he was also comfortable with a pistol in either hand. They called him the Colombian. He was not concerned that the plane was late. It was his plane, and delays had happened before. He was distracted with the thought of how soon he would kill the blue-eyed freak, hating him more with each anxious minute in his miserable, whining company. Yet he hid his anger with a disciplined calm. He never showed his intent and was easy to underestimate.

The Colombian alone was confident that the exchange would take place this night as planned.

Yet too many things could go wrong, and too much was at stake. Failure to complete tonight's exchange was not an option that any of the three could afford. Until they heard the plane, the Colombian's companions were beginning to assume the worst.

Regardless of technology, the pilot had to accept the impact of weather. The headwinds, encountered over the Carolina-Virginia border, were whipped up by a major storm system moving up the coast, colliding with a cold front moving south earlier than forecasted.

Over North Carolina, Stump had considered a radio call advising of the delay. The pilot knew the importance of the flight, the packages, and the exchange. But he changed his mind. Even on a special frequency, the radio contact was too risky to chance, and it wasn't the only concern.

Lower and lower they dropped. At last, the lights of the quarry and hospital could be seen. Stump turned back to Michael to tell him that the landing zone was coming up.

But Michael had already jumped.

Air from the open door was flowing through the cabin, and Stump couldn't close it until he gained some altitude.

After the initial shock of the parachute opening, Mike should have seen the oak tree, for he was well aware of its location and size. But he did not see it because he was trying to follow the flight of the moneybag parachutes, especially the one he'd dropped first. All three bags were moving away from his planned drop zone, and unlike his parachute, the moneybag parachutes were subject to wind and weight and could not maneuver. Immediately after the sudden grab of parachute filling with air, floating above Fancy Fruit Farm, he checked where he was relative to the hospital and the quarry. Then he turned south, in the opposite direction, to the cul-de-sac of the deserted housing development to see if his rented van was still there. It was.

Only then did he see the tree, but too late. He was right on top of it.

His right knee struck first, breaking his kneecap. He caught himself on the highest, nearest limb with a major effort but broke two ribs in the process. His hands, grabbing for the branches, only delayed the fall. He was still over eighty feet above the ground and losing his grip. He hit two more limbs on the way down. The first one broke his left ankle, flipping him head over heels when he struck the second and largest limb on the tree. The parachute caught on the limb and held him suspended in air, upside down; legs tangled in the nylon parachute leaders. His bruised and bleeding head dangled just a few feet from the ground.

He thought about the money and what he planned to do once he got to Canada. The false trail he'd left went in several directions: Montana, Idaho, even Mexico. But the Don had too many irons in the Mexico fire, and though the American West was tempting, it would not require too much of the Don's resources to find him there. He could disappear in the north. He could . . . he could . . .

He'd lost his train of thought. His plans seemed to be in slow motion, and his concentration was slipping.

The men on the ground heard the plane clearly now. It was coming in very low, below officially acceptable minimum altitude, but not low enough to catch the attention of the air controllers at Dulles Airport. The Dulles folks were expecting the plane to be on final approach for a landing in Martinsburg, West Virginia, which, technically, it was.

On the ground, the three men followed their ears and strained their eyes against the sky, looking for a parachute.

Angelo Baldi's thoughts turned from the plane to his main job of keeping the other two from killing each other before their mission was complete. After that, he didn't give a shit. If it weren't for business, he would have liked to strangle each of them himself.

Blue was staring up and then down, his strange wide eyes darting from side to side. He had no idea what to look for, but he made sure the other two were in front of him, still suspecting a trap.

He certainly didn't trust the little Latino, and the overweight garlic-smelling Italian was not as dumb as he acted. He patted the Glock automatic in his shoulder holster, and it gave him extra comfort.

The temperature, already cold, was dropping fast, a prelude to the storm coming. A snowstorm coming so fast that they could almost smell it.

Finally, when they actually saw the plane, it was coming in lower and slower than expected. Even the Colombian was surprised at the altitude. Never had they attempted a jump with so little room to maneuver. It seemed to be too low for a night jump.

How the hell can a parachute open in time to land safely at that altitude? thought Angelo, the only one of the three who had jumped out of an airplane.

Angelo Baldi's large frame looked perpetually uncomfortable as his clothes always seemed two sizes too small. When he wore a tie, as he often did, he never could button the collar of his starched shirt. On this night, he was especially uncomfortable, paying the price for too much wine, beer, sausage, and pasta. Gas seemed to come from every opening in his body. His belches broke the silence of the cornfield and his farts, when they accidentally slipped out, were silent and deadly. He tried to stay downwind as a reluctant courtesy to the other two men.

Angelo had last parachuted almost twenty years ago when he was in the Eighty-second Airborne and now, the thought of strapping on a parachute, knowing that he was not going to land with the plane, still made him nervous. He knew how difficult a night jump could be, but a low-level night jump seemed to him impossible. He was glad he'd stopped free-falling out of airplanes years ago.

Now the plane was barely above treetop level, or so it seemed. It banked steeply to the west and, ever so slowly, began to gain altitude.

All three strained to see the parachutist, Michael Rowe, an expert at night jumps, who always delivered his "package." The window for the jump was closing rapidly with the most recent weather forecast calling for snow in the morning with significant accumulations west of Washington DC.

The three men took turns looking with powerful night vision binoculars. They kept looking, blinking, straining their eyes at the sky several minutes after the plane had lost its sound. They looked high and low. North, south, east, and west, they looked and looked and looked.

But nobody saw a parachutist, and nobody heard a parachutist. The man called Blue looked at the other two for a sign. He was thinking this had to be a setup.

Chapter 10

Lying in bed with eyes wide open, Don Alverez stared at the telephone, willing it to ring. He noticed that both of his night nurses had dozed off.

Since the very first call, when he heard Gabriella's strained voice, sounding desperate, Don Alverez had felt frustrated and anxious. But now, Paul was on the job, and soon, it would be over. Paul would bring her home, and then, he would find out what prompted this lunacy.

The money being demanded was substantial, but a small sum to Gabriella's father. The Don's net worth was now in the billions. One of the richest men in the world, he effectively controlled two South American countries. He "owned" politicians, judges, generals, police, and had his own private army. No one would dare challenge him in his territory. He was called many names, and all of them carried respect. Most of the local people knew him as Don Alverez de Cartagena, "the Don."

The Don hated to wait. In the future, he decided he would keep larger sums of cash in several locations. He'd tried to sleep, but he kept thinking of his daughter. His only distraction was plotting what he'd do to the monsters that had dared cross his authority.

Except for the FBI and the DEA, he was not well-known outside of Colombia. Even in his own country, he maintained a low profile and insisted on privacy wherever he went.

As he waited for news from Winchester, he thought about the problem that had led to the kidnapping. The man on the phone had implied that it developed over a territorial dispute in DC, but the Don couldn't remember what was going on there. He had an army of people looking out for his interests. Lobbyists, lawyers, and other Americans were on the payroll, but the drug operations were mainly done through others. He would ask Diego a few more questions in the morning.

Diego, too, was worried. He had mistakenly assumed that his don owned and could therefore dictate the cocaine distribution territory in the Virginia suburbs of Washington DC. Without consulting the Don, but giving orders as if they came from the Don, he'd opened up several new operations, all of which had been going well, until something unexpected had happened in DC.

Normally, this would have caused no problem. What the Don didn't know wouldn't hurt him. Diego could have fixed things, and no one would have known. But then, events had moved beyond his control, ruining all his plans, and Diego had very ambitious plans. *Who the hell would be stupid enough to kidnap the Don's daughter?* he wondered.

After he'd received instructions from the Don and made preparations to gather the cash, Diego made inquiries about this DC gang. Finally, he got some answers from a DC attorney who'd done work for them in the past.

Fourth and U Crew was the name that instantly came up. According to the lawyer, that was the gang's headquarters location, at Fourth and U streets, but most of the street people in DC knew them as FU. When FU discovered a new Colombian drug ring operating in Arlington, Virginia—FU's territory—the DC gang had considered several responses: go to war with the new competitor, reinforce their existing operations in Arlington, or something more drastic. In the end, they chose to go with all three.

Diego could not allow the truth to reach Don Alverez.

Not one of the team he had sent to Washington could be reached, not one. *Where the hell were they?*

In Winchester, something was wrong. You could see it in the Colombian's eyes even though his face and body language remained calm. He tried to give the impression that this happened all the time.

The predawn sky was now a panorama of clouds moving very fast. It seemed as if the moon and the stars were being turned on and then off. The weather was changing. Angelo could almost feel the snowstorm. Even he was getting cold.

After the sound of the plane had died down, the big Italian kept his eyes on the other two, aware that the slightest mistake could set them off. They'd stopped looking up, having neither seen nor heard anything for ten minutes. Then, gradually, a variety of pickup trucks began to appear on Route 50, going east. There was no sign of the parachutist, Michael Rowe. All three men were now on full alert, each thinking the worst. Only the Colombian was still occasionally searching the sky, staring at the fields to the south and listening. All his senses tuned to pick up any signal that would indicate the parachutist's presence.

The blue-eyed black man finally broke the silence. "Where the fuck is yo' man? You pullin' some shit? Goin' to be serious consequences if this don' go down."

Blue's eyes shifted back and forth, expecting a double cross from the other two. The "eye's" weapon of choice was the shotgun. But he didn't go anywhere without at least one pistol. Tonight, he carried a sixteen-shot Glock automatic, which he could handle with either hand. His suit was so perfectly tailored that the Glock remained totally hidden. The shotgun was always nearby. Usually, he kept it fully loaded, safety off, under a Redskins blanket in the trunk of his Mercedes. Tonight, it rested on the floor of Angelo's black van, still wrapped neatly in its blanket. He thought about it and whether he might have to use it.

"Nobody's fokin' with nobody," said Paul, trying his best to mimic Blue Eyes' DC street talk. As he searched the now moonless sky with night vision binoculars, he said, "We have the 'reimbursement.'" He spat the word out in disgust. "We bring it tonight. You saw the plane. You can feel the wind. But he made the jump anyway. The plane door was open. Now he's on the ground, gathering the cargo. We have procedures to cover a missed drop. Michael will contact us at the hotel. Don Alverez de Cartagena is a man of his word. He will keep this agreement no matter the cost."

Yet the Colombian was anxious as he spoke. Michael had made the parachute pickup many times, hundreds of times really, and it always worked. Only twice in fifteen years had it been necessary to follow the backup plan. Their adversaries, including the U.S. Drug Enforcement Agency and the pesky FBI, couldn't track a parachutist at night. Michael Rowe was reliable. On the most important jump of his life, he would not jeopardize their success. Together, they had perfected the night jumps, and they always worked. Only once had a flight been canceled, and it was delayed for just one day.

The jump schedule was flexible. It included a variable time window to allow for wind effect and possibly air-controller rerouting. Most of the jumps were flawless. Normally, Paul could spot Michael within seconds after hearing the plane, but not tonight. He clearly saw that the plane door was open as it cruised directly overhead.

The plane had long since gone, seeking a higher altitude over the Allegheny Mountains, on its way to a meaningless air freight delivery and pickup in Martinsburg, West Virginia.

Several minutes of silence ensued. No one moved. No one spoke. Still, they looked at the sky and, just as quickly, shifted their gazes back to ground level. Finally concluding that they would not be able to make tonight's payment and transfer, the Colombian made a decision.

As Don Alverez's personal representative, he had responsibility to ensure the success of the operation.

He gave no indication of his concern but absentmindedly patted his left boot, checking to see if the ice pick was still there. The Colombian preferred to kill with it, but he was a practical man and never went without an automatic pistol and a submachine gun. Both weapons were in the front seat of Angelo's van. Analyzing the black man's face, he thought he might need all of his weapons.

He was known as the Inquisitor in Colombia for he was an expert torturer and finder of facts for the cartel. The ice pick was his trademark. His phony street-smart accent revealed his dislike for tonight's business and his lack of respect for the blue-eyed maniac. Yet he knew how important it was to keep this psycho calm. He also knew there would be an opportunity to deal with this problem later. He wasn't concerned about Angelo. Angelo was all business, and he could be counted on to act as the mediator that he was.

Paul made his decision after realizing time had run out. The lights from West Virginia commuters heading east signaled the coming of dawn. They could not risk being discovered.

Blue was restless and more irritable with each passing minute, looking around, expecting trouble from all sides.

Angelo squirmed and further loosened the tie that hung from his unbuttoned shirt collar, cursing his bad luck. Surely, these two were going to turn on each other any minute.

Finally, in a cultured Spanish accent not previously evident, Paul said, "Obviously, Mike has drifted with the wind out of our range." Their backup plan was to return to the Hampton Inn and wait for Mike to call. It made no sense to wander aimlessly about the countryside at night looking for something black in the blackness. They couldn't trust the daylight either. It was safer to wait for a call.

Besides, all three had other calls to make, explaining the delay. Mike, the parachutist, would have some explaining to do himself, once he checked in. *Where the hell was he anyway? Was the wind that bad?* wondered Paul again, more worried than he let on. He couldn't call the plane, and the plane couldn't call him. That's why they had a backup plan.

Chapter 11

On Merriman's Lane, energized by his unbelievable erotic experience of the previous evening, a happy Will MacKenzie dragged the dead Christmas tree off his back porch where it had lain for over eight weeks. Then, he methodically picked up the mess the dogs had left outside of the garage. Even when Watson pulled some article back out of the garage, he didn't get upset. He sang to himself as he packed everything in plastic bags, vowing to go through each one later. Next, he went through a strenuous exercise program: sit-ups, pushups, and weightlifting. After a cold shower, he relaxed with a cup of coffee, and read in the *Winchester Star* about Joe Arthur's latest fabulous party at his Clarke County farm. There were pictures of Joe with important people, and he recognized almost all of the party guests in the background.

The only one he didn't recognize was the new girl on Joe's arm. *Another "cousin,"* thought Will. Joe was such a powerful man in the community that his lady relationships were accepted as normal. Obviously, such a caring man, a man dedicated to improving the quality of life in his community, a man who supported every charity, was a man above reproach.

The others pictured never missed a party. They'd go to a Joe Arthur party even if they had the flu. A Joe Arthur invitation was a command, not just an invitation. If you were lucky enough to be invited, you had to go.

Will remembered one of Joe's parties where a guest had died on the dance floor, had actually danced himself to death. There were at least fourteen doctors partying at the time; none were able to save the man. After the ambulance came, the party tried to continue, but only the real drunks were still able to enjoy themselves.

Will had been there that night and was one of those drunks. He was at the height of his depression-driven alcoholism. After he threw up on a former mayor of Winchester, his wife had finally driven him home. Two days later, Will's wife took the children back to Boston and filed for divorce.

Will was about to turn to the sports pages when the dog's wet nose burst through the paper. Watson had ignored a fresh bowl of water on the kitchen floor, preferring instead to drink out of the hall toilet. He dripped toilet water all the way back into the kitchen and whined to go out for their ritual morning walk. Will folded the crumpled paper and looked at Watson, eyeball to eyeball. "Watson, sit!" he yelled at first, then lowered his voice. "It's still dark. We can't go yet! Eat your breakfast."

The bowl of dog food was untouched as was the bowl of water. Watson never ate dog food until he was convinced people food was not going to be available. Grudgingly, the dog plopped down on the kitchen floor, legs splayed; chin flat on the tile, only his eyes following Will's every move. No matter how desperately Watson had to poop or pee, he would not go out alone.

But he was a patient dog, obedient most of the time, so he stayed spread out on the floor and looked up every time his master moved or made a noise. Every now and then, the dog would sigh just to let Will know he was ready to go. Finally, Will rose from his chair and nodded to Watson. The dog immediately jumped up, excited as a puppy, tail wagging, eyes sparkling, and ran to the door.

As usual, Watson burst through the door as soon as it opened and ran to the adjacent orchard where he peed on the first tree that he came to. Then he would follow a scent or a track, whichever was fresher. This morning, there were many tracks: plenty of deer, rabbits, and several fox prints interspersed with the others.

Will was used to Watson roaming back and forth, always returning as if to check on his master's progress. Normally, they would stay in the orchard for the first half mile, then wind through several pastures, veer around through a large stand of woods, eventually completing a wide circle back to the house. The entire trip took over one hour.

Will caught the white flash of a deer tail, then saw several brown blurs quickly moving against the snowy background, and in an instant, the chase was on.

For a longer period than normal, Will walked alone; the dog seemed to be preoccupied with chasing the deer. Will couldn't recall a single trip with his dog where something like this didn't happen. Every one of their jaunts was exciting, an opportunity for Will to commune with nature, his dog on another hunt.

Dawn was just breaking, and a heavy wet snow had begun to cover the ground. Wind gusts came from several directions, sometimes driving the snow in horizontal sheets, rapidly obscuring the dog's tracks. But his loud barking echoed through the fields, making Watson easy to follow. The familiar sound grew louder, telling Will that his dog had stopped. But this bark was different, not the low growl he'd hear when Watson was standing over an animal burrow. It was more aggressive than usual. Will MacKenzie had heard his dog Watson barking this frantically before, and he dreaded what he would find. This bark was one of confrontation. It sounded like Watson had cornered some animal.

"*Please.*" he hoped, "*don't let it be another skunk.*" Watson was a natural-born hunter, and over the years in the country, the dog had done battle with skunks, groundhogs, squirrels, possums, raccoons, foxes, and a host of other creatures. Will prayed it would be in a tree where the dog could not reach it.

He got his wish.

Nothing prepared Will for what he found in the giant oak tree. He blinked, looked away, and blinked again, thinking it was just his imagination playing tricks on him.

But the image was real: a body hanging right before his eyes. The scene raised goose bumps on Will's arms. The body was dressed in black clothes, attached to a black parachute that wound its way up from the body through the tree. Both the clothes and the parachute were ripped to shreds. He could see dark shrouds covered in fresh snow wrapped around several limbs going up almost eighty feet. A former paratrooper himself, Will knew a parachute when he saw one, though he considered the black color odd.

The body was hanging upside down, just out of Watson's reach. Blood was everywhere—on the man, on the tree, on the dog, and especially in the snow. Will could see a large gash on the side of the man's head still dripping. One of the man's arms looked as if it was torn from its socket at the shoulder. A leg was contorted in a grotesque position. The parachutist's face had turned bluish white, a dead man's look MacKenzie had seen before. A black nylon tether led from the man's chest, around the man's neck, and down to a black bag in the snow. Watson was chewing, pulling, and tugging on the blood-stained tether.

Will was surprised by the expression on the parachutist's face.

He was smiling.

Will wanted to check the man's pulse. But first, he had to quiet the dog. Watson's many outdoor escapades had long ago convinced Will to always carry a strong leather leash. He needed it now, and it took him several minutes to attach it to Watson's collar. With great effort, after almost pulling the dog's head from its body, Will tied Watson to a small fence post some fifty yards from the tree. This only served to make his best friend berserk with rage. His barking became more frequent and much more hysterical. And it was also contagious. Dogs from Glaize's Fancy Fruit Farm, almost three-quarters of a mile away, began to add their howling to the chorus.

Finally, Will checked the parachutist's pulse. He felt the man's wrist and neck. He checked for any sign of breathing. But there was none. The man was dead.

Will surmised the dead man must have been up to no good, black camouflage on his face, dressed in black, and arriving in the night via a black parachute. *Had he carried drugs?* Winchester was a well-traveled distribution corridor in the drug trade between Washington, Richmond, Baltimore, and Philadelphia. Will glanced at the black bag hanging down from the man's neck. It was a leather briefcase like the one his wife's lawyer used.

He decided to go for help, subconsciously picking up the bag at his feet. He had to cut it free from the tether, which was wrapped around the parachutist's neck. Concerned with what he might find but thinking it might identify the victim, he tried to open it.

It was locked.

Watson was barking continuously, straining at his leash, and Will was reluctant to draw attention to himself and his location. He really didn't want to get involved. He just wasn't ready to reenter society, especially under these circumstances. People in town would automatically assume that he was involved in some drunken scheme or, even worse, that he'd dropped the booze for drugs. He thought he could call the authorities and not give his name, call from a pay phone so they couldn't trace it.

He shouldered the small bag, surprised at its heavy weight, and headed for his dog. The barking would only stop when they were well clear of the scene. Surely, someone would be coming soon.

Watson had to be forcefully jerked by his leash the first two hundred yards. Will was relieved to notice that the driving snow quickly obscured his trail. Nevertheless, he made a turn back toward the west and went through the woods in an opposite direction from his ultimate destination.

The dog, ears back, teeth bared, fighting his leash every step of the way, was determined to return to the parachutist and made their first quarter mile very difficult.

Gradually, the woods offered other creatures that captured Watson's interest until the parachutist was forgotten. Will was able to remove the leash. Without the resistance of a 120-pound dog, he moved more quickly home. At the extreme edge of his property, more than a mile from the dead parachutist, he came upon a second black parachute. It had come down in an apple orchard and was almost buried in the snow.

He approached slowly, thinking it might be another parachutist, expecting the dog to react any minute. But Watson trotted unhurriedly over to check it out. Then the dog jumped over a pile of brush to investigate something else. Will reached the scene wondering what else had attracted the dog's attention. Coming closer, he realized that there were two parachutes, each attached to large black objects. The first one was a duffle bag . . . a huge black duffle bag . . . packed full and locked! The second was the same. Both bags were locked. Watson kept going back and forth, sniffing each bag, inch by every square inch.

What's in the bags? Got to be drugs. Will rolled the nearest bag over with considerable effort. The bag was bulky, heavy and hard to maneuver. Looking down, he was shocked to find a small treasure underneath. It sat in the middle of broken tree limbs that had torn off when the parachute crashed down. A packet of cash mashed flat by the weight of the bag. Will flipped through the bills in the packet, mentally calculating the total. Every bill was a hundred dollar bill. *Must be ten thousand dollars in this one packet!* He stuck the cash in his windbreaker and frantically swept the surrounding area with his hands and boots, checking to see if other packets had fallen out. Finding none, he tugged on each bag, knowing that somewhere there was a hole, or a tear, or something. Snow was coming down in sheets, covering the bags and hindering his search. He tried the locks again, but they wouldn't budge.

Next, he tried to drag one of the bags, and after making little progress, he gave up. Frustrated, he raced home; tree limbs slapped him in the face, and disrupted his vision. Twice, he almost twisted his ankle. He was in such a hurry that he finally tripped over a stump, dropped the parachutist's briefcase, and slid face-down in the snow.

Thankful that he didn't break his neck, he carefully got up, dusted himself off, grabbed the briefcase, and slowed down the rest of the way home.

Fifteen minutes later, Will was back in the orchard with his jeep. Watson came with him, excited to be going again. At first, Will struggled with the duffle bags' enormity. He could bench-press almost 250 pounds, but each of these bags was hard to grip, let alone lift. It seemed to take forever, but he managed to drag, lift, and pull each bag until they were in the jeep. When finally loaded, both bags completely filled the cargo area.

Will momentarily forgot about the dead man in a tree as he maneuvered through the orchard with his treasure, heading home, Watson began to whine as it was well past the time the two of them usually ate breakfast. Driving back was difficult, but it took his mind off the dilemma of who to call and what to say. Snow was coming down so heavy that his windshield wipers couldn't keep up. He could barely see between the rows of apple trees. Branches from the trees scraped the side of his jeep.

Home, finally, sitting in his kitchen, after watching Watson devour a large bowl of dog food, Will thought about his discovery. He was anxious to open the bags but was concerned about what he really might find. Then he remembered the parachutist. *Damn!* No matter what, he'd have to call the police, and he dreaded making that call. Will made a decision: he would call from a pay phone in Paw Paw, West Virginia, some thirty miles away. He'd already planned to visit his uncle Jim in a West Virginia nursing home, and Paw Paw was on the way. Or if the storm was too bad, he could call, pick up some supplies, spend the night in his nearby West Virginia cabin, and visit Uncle Jim later.

Either way, he was determined not to get involved. Calling from somewhere in West Virginia was the best way he could think of to avoid what was sure to be a messy situation. He had not yet dealt with the other issue: the bags . . . thinking, *They're going to be a problem.*

Will packed a few things in the jeep, and he and Watson headed west on Route 522. They had to creep along, the snowstorm reducing their speed significantly. His main worry was West Virginia drivers. They didn't slow down for anything. The dog was temporarily occupied, chewing on a T-bone from the freezer, choosing not to interfere with the drive.

Will thought about the man in the tree. It would be difficult to keep Watson away from the scene. The dog's hunting sense would continue to call him back to the tree. Every time he went outside, even for a minute, he would surely race back, seeking out the dead parachutist. Will knew from previous experiences that for at least the next several weeks, the big Lab would have to be leashed every time he left the house.

Will considered whether he'd done the right thing. Was he wrong to want to remain anonymous? Intuitively, he knew he had interrupted some kind of illegal activity. What it was, he didn't know; and given his recent troubles, maybe he should not care. His conscience somehow demanded that he go through this process of justification over and over. Getting involved in this, he feared, might bring back the deep depression, which had taken him so long to escape from.

All these thoughts were going through his mind as he drove through the blinding snowstorm. Looking into the rearview mirror, he was reminded of a bigger problem: THE BAGS. *What on earth was in those bags?* He'd found a packet of money, but the bags had to be full of drugs, cocaine most likely. Someone was going to come looking. Two duffle bags full of drugs had to be worth too much money to ignore. Maybe he should be more concerned about the people who were expecting the duffle bags than the authorities. Maybe he should be worrying about the kind of people who would deal in drugs.

He needed more time to think. The cabin was the perfect place to do so. No one knew about his West Virginia "hunting lodge." He didn't hunt much anymore, but his uncle Jim had left it to him three years ago. His uncle always called him his favorite nephew. Of course, Will was the only nephew, and his uncle laughed every time he said it.

When Will was a teenager, his uncle had been the one who taught him the ways of his mountaineer ancestors: how to survive as a hunter and fisherman, what to eat in the woods, how to track, how to shoot with a rifle or a bow, how to make a fire without being detected, how to make shelter, what roots and plants were edible. He learned how to skin and cook and live in the woods. He was the son his uncle never had.

Other than his house and a few thousand dollars in a savings account, the cabin was the only asset that his ex-wife's lawyer had missed in the divorce settlement. He'd inherited the cabin just before he had drunk himself into oblivion. In a way, the cabin contributed to the final breakup of his family. Depressed and needing to be alone, he had spent weeks at the cabin on drinking binges. His wife had no idea where he went, but at that point in the doomed marriage, she didn't care.

On a clear day it was only forty-five minutes from Winchester, deep in the Allegheny Mountains. NO HUNTING OR FISHING was the only sign marking the road entrance to his property. For a couple of miles, the heavily rutted dirt road wound through thick stands of oak, maple, and pine trees.

The cabin was situated in the center of five hundred acres of woods and pasture at the foot of Blackie Mountain. A small pond in front of the cabin was fed by the creek, which meandered all through the lower half of the property. It was a perfect place to kick back, relax, and forget all his problems, but maybe not this time.

Chapter 12

After they had abandoned their wait for the parachutist, Angelo Baldi took his disappointed companions back to the Hampton Inn. According to the contingency plan, Michael would call them there at his first opportunity. The Colombian assured them that this was the only way to handle the situation, and if the problem persisted, they would bring in a second shipment, but it would take at least two days. "Not to worry," he also said.

Three phone calls were made soon after returning from the missed drop zone. Angelo Baldi's call was local, going to a farm in Clarke County, Virginia.

Blue called a regional number in Northeast Washington DC.

Paul Xavier's call was international. He called a number in Puerto Rico, which was patched and rerouted to a safe phone in Cartagena, Colombia.

All three men were glad that the news was not being delivered in person. On the ride back to the inn, the three agreed to convey the same message to their bosses, that receipt of the ransom was delayed due to weather. They'd seen the plane and assumed that the jump was made. Based on Xavier's assurances, they expected to hear from the parachutist, Michael Rowe, within the hour.

The "gentleman farmer" that Angelo Baldi called in Clarke County, Virginia, was a thirty-year transplant from Philadelphia, who still had not learned to say "y'all." Angelo knew the farmer as Anthony Arturo, a man who didn't look like a farmer and didn't sound like a farmer. His principal occupation was distributor of illicit drugs, arms, and prostitutes. He also was an investor in many businesses, especially those that involved large amounts of cash. As far as politicians, countless charities, and the cream of Winchester society were concerned, Anthony Arturo was known as Joe Arthur, a pillar of society, who gave generous amounts of money to both political parties and every single community cause. Arthur owned and operated a large farm in Clarke County, Virginia, consisting of 1,600 picturesque acres of woods, ponds, and fenced pastureland. The hundred-year-old main house was expansive and intensely private. It was situated on a ridge overlooking the Shenandoah River not far from Route 50.

A thick fieldstone exterior covered its old center section. Three newer, succeedingly smaller, matching sections on the north and south sides of the house were built to similar specifications. The last two stone sections on each side turned inward, into a horseshoe shape. This powerful structure, topped with eight tall stone chimneys and covered with a gray slate roof, gave the house a fortress like appearance. It was a fortress, sixteen thousand square feet of fortress, to be exact. The white shutters on every window were actually reinforced steel, secured to the stone by sturdy hinges. These could be closed and locked from the inside. Each of the massive doors was thick steel covered by half-inch-thick wood veneer inside and outside.

Arthur's fortress was a working Black Angus cattle farm that included three tenant houses, a barn, several equipment sheds, a six-car detached garage, a large swimming pool with bathhouse, two tennis courts, and a stone gatehouse at the main entrance that was always manned by an armed guard. Three other gatehouses surrounded the property, but they were wooden structures of more recent vintage. Sometimes, guards occupied these outlying gatehouses, and sometimes, they were vacant. At present, all were occupied around the clock.

Thirty-six full-time employees worked at the farm. These were reinforced by additional, mainly unskilled, part-time employees as needed. All full-time employees were armed even though their duties ranged from butler, to chauffeur, to cook, to gardener, to field hand, and anything else that required attention. Only the armed personnel were allowed inside the main house and tenant houses. It was for this reason that none of the houses were equipped with an alarm system. The gentleman farmer was always tight with a dollar, so he saved money by asking the question "Why would anyone need an alarm if armed guards were on duty twenty-four hours a day?"

The part-time workers lived off property. All of the armed personnel were related directly or by marriage through an extended Mafia family in the United States and Sicily. Of these, nineteen men had all been employed in the business for at least ten years and were known well by the others for most of their lives. All were trusted.

Two of the trusted ones were guarding their female VIP guest in a large, richly appointed bedroom suite on the second floor of the main house. The bedroom was centered above the main foyer and could be reached from either side by identical wide ornate staircases. But as far as the VIP guest was concerned, the majestic home with its twin staircases might as well be in a foreign country; she was confined to her room.

Will's need for gas created an opportunity to develop an alibi. He slowly drove ten miles past the cabin road turnoff and proceeded to Paw Paw, West Virginia. There, he bought a few more supplies at the mini-mart, filled the jeep with gas, and paid by credit card.

The receipt was critical since he wanted people to believe he was returning from visiting his only surviving uncle in a nursing home in Weston, West Virginia. He normally made several visits a year to the home and often went directly to his uncle's room. After the first few visits, he never registered with the front desk. With every visit, he brought flowers and candy for the nurses in hopes his uncle would receive better treatment. Most of the nursing home staff knew him by sight and might be confused as to the exact date, or dates, of his visits.

Returning from the mini-mart, he almost missed the turnoff. Visibility was limited due to blizzard conditions. Snow depths were much higher now, rising to his hubcaps. He managed the crooked, gradually rising, then falling, drive to the cabin by staying between the trees lining both sides of the winding road. Wet snow was so heavy on the drooping tree limbs that the road resembled a tunnel.

As usual, he found the cabin undisturbed. It was made from thick logs on three sides and heavy stone at the rear which framed a huge fireplace. Its roof was tin, turned charcoal brown with age. Both doors were thick oak secured with solid brass dead bolts. It was one big room with two built-in cots on the sides; a rough homemade dining table and chairs in the center; a stove for cooking; pots and pans; necessary kitchenware including knives, forks, plastic plates, and glasses; a wooden rocking chair; and a couple of end tables holding large kerosene lamps. No frills for this place. The well and privy were outside. Uncle Jim's only luxury was a poor man's library built into one wall. The shelves were lined with well-worn classics and several history books dealing with the Roman Empire, the British Empire, and the American Civil War. Only one picture was hanging on the wall. It was of a little boy standing between his father and his uncle Jim, each holding rifles, but looking very much like hunters.

Several signs surrounded the cabin and pond area that read, "GUARD DOGS! PROCEED AT YOUR OWN RISK!"

Will had no illusions that the signs would stop a determined intruder. However, either the signs or the robust structure of the cabin or, most likely, its remoteness discouraged intruders. Not once over the years had someone broken in.

Watson checked the property from one end to the other every time they made the trip. As usual, he peed on snow-covered bushes and trees, marking the territory as his.

Once Will had satisfied himself that the cabin was secure and undisturbed, he built a fire. Watson promptly collapsed on the well-worn carpet that fronted the fireplace.

Only then did Will begin the process of unloading the jeep. The dog raised his head above floor level every time the door opened, just to make sure things were all right. Then he would drop flat on the floor. Will took his time, not hurried now, and saw the black duffle bags in the back. He brought the smaller things in first, tracking snow throughout the cabin. Finally, he half-lifted and half-dragged the two big bags in and left them sitting in the middle of the floor. For some time, he worked around the cabin, attending to the many chores of unpacking, putting things in their proper place, checking to make sure everything was as he left them on his last visit, and putting water on the stove to boil.

He took off his parka, emptied his pockets, and rediscovered his orchard find, the packet of cash. Again, he calculated that the wrapper was holding perhaps a hundred bills. *Were the bags carrying anything else?* He was almost afraid to look, thinking it must be a trick. But a man was dead, obviously connected to the bags.

Curiosity finally got the best of him, and he decided to open the bags. He couldn't expand the small tear in the one bag, and both locks on the bags held tight.

He opened his tool chest and selected a hatchet and a screwdriver. He tried this for fifteen minutes but had no luck with the locks. One of the blows with the hatchet missed its target, and the screwdriver pierced the canvas. The action created another small hole. Will half-expected white powder to come bursting out. When it didn't, he worked the hole with a heavy knife and managed to open the top of the bag. Something tore as he worked, and he discovered that he'd ripped several more packets of hundred-dollar bills. He was more careful after that, gradually cutting and pulling the canvas away from its contents. Packets of money kept falling out, covering the floor. He began to hum, and a smile covered his face from ear to ear.

The bag contained money, lots of it, loads of it, bundles of it. All the bills were hundred-dollar bills. He began to suspect a trick. Surely, he'd discovered a counterfeit operation. But all the bills looked used. The serial numbers were different and not in sequence. These looked real. He was careful not to dump the contents of the bag, afraid that there may be a booby trap or some other nasty surprise.

But the first bag only contained a fortune, which he stacked neatly on the kitchen table. Methodically, he approached the second bag, confident that some disaster lay hidden in its depths. Careful now, not wanting to tear or spill the contents of the second bag, Will proceeded slowly. It, too, was full of money. Will couldn't believe it. He pinched himself to make sure it wasn't a dream. It was another fortune!

Every now and then, Watson would raise one eye as if to satisfy himself that no food was in the bag. The dog couldn't understand the excitement.

All the bills were hundred-dollar bills, $10,000 to a packet. These he stacked neatly on the large pine table that could comfortably seat eight. By the time he'd counted fifteen packets, one bill at a time, he changed tactics. He did not have a luxury of time, even here. He only counted packets, after thumbing through each packet to see if the contents were, in fact, hundred-dollar bills. When he'd removed and stacked every packet, he attempted to count, but he was so excited he lost the count every time! There were hundreds, maybe, thousands of packets. He'd have to restart the count later; the process had given him a headache. For once, he could smile with a headache.

Will's conscience began to nag. Should he give it back to its rightful owner? *What if there is no rightful owner,* he thought. He was so tired that he decided to think about it later.

The refrigerator/freezer-sized storage bin, hidden under the cabin's wide plank floorboards, made a perfect hiding place for safekeeping the money. When it was first built, Uncle Jim had considered the huge bin to serve the dual purpose of safe storage and bomb shelter.

He carefully repacked the cash back into the moneybags and removed the pine floorboards. Before he could lower the money into the bin, he had to remove several boxes of ammunition, a sniper's rifle that he had smuggled back from Vietnam, a box of miscellaneous sized batteries wrapped airtight in cellophane, two boxes of canned food, a five-gallon jug of distilled water, a first aid kit, and a large canvas bag containing outdoor clothing that smelled like mothballs. After loading the bags, he decided to keep a few packets in cash separate. He set aside ten. The bags were cumbersome, so he had to keep flattening and moving things around to fit snugly in the bin. After an effort, there was not enough room left to cover the two bags with his leather suitcase full of clothes. Although there remained enough room for the rifle in the storage bin, he chose to keep it and the ammunition with him. He found space for the rest of his bin-stored items in various nooks and crannies around the cabin.

Then, he remembered the other bag in the jeep, the small black briefcase that had been attached to the parachutist's chest harness. It was so heavy, he remembered, that it must contain gold. When he stood up to open the door, Watson got up too, not wanting to miss anything. After retrieving the bag quickly, they rushed back into the warm cabin. Watson shook his snow-covered back, dropped back down on the floor, and promptly went to sleep.

This bag was locked too. So Will grabbed the screwdriver one more time, and without too much trouble, the bag opened. Inside, he found more cash, a loaded submachine gun with extra ammo clips, a pistol with silencer, some credit cards, airline tickets, passports with different names but the same face, and, of course, three sets of keys to the other two duffle bags.

Watson's whining reminded him that the two of them had not eaten since they found the moneybags. Will took to the kitchen with gusto. After a hearty dinner of fried steak, eggs, potatoes, and sourdough bread washed down with a quart of West Virginia spring water, Will turned on the radio. He had not called the authorities. Given his new discovery, he was not sure he should call at all. He hoped there would be news of the parachutist. There wasn't.

Will considered opening the storage bin and counting the money for the fifth time but instead decided to shave. He needed to take a break. His heart was fueled by adrenaline and was going full speed. After all the pain he'd been through, after all the pain he'd caused, maybe the money would allow him to make things right. At last, he felt good about the future.

His reflection in the mirror told him how far he'd come in the past year. He had thinned out; his cheeks no longer looked like he was storing a mouthful of nuts. His complexion was ruddy from all the outdoor exercise. The short stubble on his face brought back memories of the time when he had decided to finally shave the unkempt full beard he had been too lazy to shave in his earlier depressed state.

Mentally, he could now deal with it, proving to himself as he remembered. He had had the dream almost every night.

In the dream, everything moved as if in slow motion. He was back in Vietnam. He remembered the unbearable heat, the sweat, the bugs crawling on his nose, trying desperately to keep still as the Viet Cong squatted to pee a few feet from his hiding place. It was a young woman. She was carrying a heavy load of American weapons and gear that she'd stripped from dead GIs. She had moved off the trail while the others continued on.

In the dream, Will saw her face clearly. She had been happy, singing with the others. *Probably some victory song,* he thought. She'd placed her AK-

47, along with the rest of her contraband, on the ground at her side when she dropped her trousers. She wore no underwear. Will must have moved. Maybe she smelled him. Whatever, she saw him in midsquirt. Her eyes opened wide. Her mouth formed a scream. She reached for her weapon, peeing on herself at the same time. Will shot her twice through the chest as all hell broke loose. Machine guns and Claymores blazed through the other Viet Cong, and then it was over.

But some of the Viet Cong were still alive. Will heard a moan from the woman he'd shot, and the dream became vivid. As he bent over her, he noticed she had a necklace hanging halfway down her chest, a gory display of human ears and GI dog tags. Tears were in her eyes as she looked into his face, silently pleading for help. She was no longer a soldier, but a young girl, bleeding from the chest. Will gagged as he saw other blood, not hers, dried on the necklace of ears and dripping around her neck. That blood had come from his comrades, their ears cut off as a souvenir by this woman.

She started to open her mouth to ask for help, but MacKenzie shot her in the face before the words could come out. Will emptied a full clip into the woman, all the while crying and screaming obscenities as he fired. They took no prisoners.

It was the screams that Will remembered and the face that disappeared before his eyes.

The dreams started years after he'd left Vietnam. Years after he'd married, after he had been successful in business. The dreams began to drain his energy. They were so terrible that his conscience ached. He could not forgive himself. It was a secret, internal, self-inflicted guilt, which gradually grew like a cancer into a deep depression. He'd survived Vietnam and been honored for it; he was the envy of everyone, and they did not understand why, over a two-year period of self-destruction, he almost drank himself to death.

Now, looking into the mirror, he was at peace with his past. He looked forward to making things right. Maybe his wife would forgive him now. Maybe old friends would forgive him too. All that money falling into his hands would help. It must be fate. For the first time in many months, his optimism was back.

Chapter 13

The bedroom of the estate was spacious and tastefully decorated. Two guards paid extra attention to their captive in the bed because of a sense of duty and because of their attraction to the girl. They both openly lusted after their captive, who was strikingly attractive even in the loose-fitting sweat suit that she'd worn for five days. She reminded the guards of a Spanish princess.

In fact, her ancestry, going back over three hundred years, could be traced to the Spanish ruling family. In many ways, she was a princess. She was bred to aristocracy, educated at all the best schools and spoiled beyond hope.

At first, she paid no attention to her captors, acting as if they were nonexistent. She was certain they would become nonexistent as soon as her father got her out of this mess. For a time after she was kidnapped, she was confident that the idiots who took her would release her once they learned who she was. Then, she discovered they not only knew who she was, they had singled her out with the express intent of kidnapping her. Their knowledge of her habits, her everyday routine, especially her jogging runs, made the task easy.

She was shocked by the ease with which her four bodyguards were killed. She was fairly certain that her captors would not kill her, but she was not sure that she could remain unmolested. The method and intensity of the men who "frisked" her body made her feel dirty and abused.

She was in a large bedroom, with high ceilings, expensive molding, a four-poster bed with a plush quilted cover, and lots of brightly colored pillows. Several expensive oil paintings on the walls depicted English hunting scenes; horses, riders, and hounds were all racing through the countryside after the wily fox.

In total contrast with her luxurious surroundings, two strange white men dressed in dirty blue jeans and scuffed boots were just standing there, looking at her, making her feel naked. They were both armed with pistols carried in shoulder holsters.

She chose to break the silence. "May I talk to my father?"

"Sorry, sweetheart, maybe later. Right now, you just relax, make yourself at home. We're going to look after you, make sure you're comfortable," answered the bigger of the two men.

"I want to speak to my father. Do you know who my father is? Do you?" *Do you know what might happen to you?* That was the real question she was asking.

Again, it was the burly, dark-complexioned, talkative one who answered, "Yes, we know who your father is. That's why we are making sure you're safe."

His companion kept leering, looking her over, up and down.

"I need to go to the bathroom."

The big one, his name was Barone, but they called him Bones, pointed to a door. "Sure. Anytime. There it is, but leave the door open a crack."

Going in, Gabriella noticed that she couldn't close the door even if she'd wanted to. A block of wood had been nailed to the hardwood floor of the bedroom and extended into the marble floor of the bathroom.

When she came out, she noticed a tray of sandwiches, chips, and a pitcher of iced tea on the table next to the bed.

"Thought you might be hungry," Bones said, and he gave her his best smile.

"No, thank you. I would just like to lie down." She looked at the men as she turned the covers down, hoping that they'd leave, but they didn't. They just sat down, one next to the bedroom door, the other next to the bathroom.

Silently, she sobbed, tears coming down her cheeks as she pulled the covers over her head. She needed a bath. She tried to figure out where she was. She knew it was in the country. She'd heard cows, and she knew that the driveway was a long gravel-covered road from the sounds and the rough ride in the van. She knew she'd been in DC, and could guess from the time they traveled it was just over an hour's drive outside of the Capitol.

At least these people didn't frisk her. The ones who'd taken her put their hands all over her again when they hustled her down to the van. The same voice told her things were going to be all right, that she'd see her father soon, that her father was "coo . . . op . . . er . . . at . . . ing."

Now, under the covers in her new surroundings, she thought her father's help seemed to be taking an inordinately long time. The strangers who abducted her were black. Why did they bring her to a new group of white men who spoke Italian half of the time? Why did her captors have the nerve to look at her the way they were looking now? They wouldn't even let her close the door when she went to the bathroom. She didn't dare take a bath, so she tried to wash with her clothes on. She used a hair dryer to dry one spot at a time, and that seemed to do the job. But she was beginning to feel unclean. Every day, her confidence waned, and she was losing track of the time she had been in captivity. For the first time in her life, she was afraid. She even jumped when she heard the phone ring downstairs.

Angelo Baldi's call to River View Farm was answered by his cousin Frank. It took several minutes before he could find Joe Arthur. Arthur, annoyed at being interrupted, was speaking on one of the four private lines to his good friend, the lieutenant governor of Virginia, about hosting a fund-raiser at the farm later that year. The farmer ended the phone call by not only agreeing to act as host, but also agreeing to match the funds raised at the event. The lieutenant governor was quite pleased as he always was whenever he called upon his very good friend to help.

Normally, Arthur would have been pleased too, but other problems were on his mind.

He did not like being forced into the middle of a dispute by two of his most important business partners. Yet he was the only one they both could remotely trust regarding such a delicate matter. He had guaranteed his "guest's" safety, had agreed to manage the transfer of money and hostage, and had further agreed to ensure the safety of all parties.

For his efforts, he was entitled to keep $1,000,000.

Naturally, Joe Arthur was extremely displeased with Baldi's phone call advising that there was going to be a delay. Don Alverez's most dependable deliveryman, Michael Rowe, had not made contact.

Something about this business didn't smell right.

In Washington DC, Booger Bryant answered his private line on the first ring. Blue nervously tapped his fingers on the Gideon Bible next to the phone as he spoke.

"Booger B., you sittin' down? I got some temp . . . o . . . rar . . . ily bad news." Blue called him Booger B. whenever he wanted to be real personal.

Booger's reaction to the news was nasty, just as Blue had expected. "They fuckin' with me, Blue! They fuckin' with you! They gonna pay, they gonna pay big-time! I ain't talkin' money. Talkin' blood. Those spics are gonna die, gonna die! They don't respect me! Colombians can fo'get DC, can fo'get Richmond too. We talkin' my territory. My territory!"

"Hey, Booger! Calm down, it's gonna be all right. I think they mean to pay. They were upset too. The Don's man, he ought to get an Oscar if he was tryin' to fake it. He was shook. My blue eyes ache from lookin'. I had to keep one of 'em focused on the sky, the other keepin' a lookout for somethin' fishy. It seemed like forever."

"Finally, we heard the plane. Next thing you know, we see the plane. It was a little late, but it was close, Booger. It came down at treetop level. The Don's man says he'll replace the money if the parachute man don't make contact soon. Big Italian fuck named Baldi, works for Arthur, says stay cool, they won't release the bitch without the money."

As he listened, Booker "Booger" Bryant glared at the scared faces of two Hispanic men sitting so close he could spit in their eyes. The two were hog-tied tightly to their chairs. They had been bound and beaten ever since they'd been surprised in their sleep at an Alexandria motel two days earlier. The one with the scar on his cheek, named Julio, kept blinking as if his eyes were drying up.

Booger had planned to ask a lot of questions of the two, but the phone call changed the plan. It didn't matter much. They couldn't speak English except for a few words, and Booker was too impatient to wait long enough for them to answer.

Rat . . . a . . . tat . . . tat . . . tat . . . tat! was Booger's reply as he emptied a sixteen-round clip into the two. Their blood poured onto the basement floor of the old townhouse adjacent to the FU Club. No one could hear their screams since they'd been gagged so tight their lips were beginning to tear.

For a moment, the conversation was silent after Booger had emptied his gun.

"Hear that! Tell the Don to suck on that!" He shouted into the phone at his closest childhood friend. "Tell the Don's man we got five now, and every other Colombian spic fuck within three hundred miles of DC gonna bleed shit 'til I gets my money and 'til the Don lay off my territory. Call me soon's the money comes in. Let 'em know Booker Bryant not t' be fucked with."

Just before he hung up, Booger shouted, "If I don't see that cash in forty-eight hours, bring that bitch back here. She gonna wish her daddy never mounted her mother."

"Money's comin', Boog, I know it for sure. I'm on it, locked on tight! Nobody mess with our crew. I'm on it, man." Blue hung up, wondering for the first time whether this had been a good idea.

Diego Estrada was worried. He had just hung up from a call to his friend in the Colombian embassy in Washington DC. The embassy man regretfully reported that his people had not been able to locate a single one of his five missing men. They had disappeared without a trace. However, the embassy did confirm what Diego had learned from another source, that Gabriella's kidnappers were part of a DC street gang known as the FU Crew.

Another phone call interrupted his thoughts. He tried to ignore it and focus on his options.

The phone kept ringing.

Diego forced himself to concentrate, thinking Don Alverez was sure to discover the truth. So far, the Don had avoided trying to find out why the kidnapping had taken place. But Diego now was certain that it had to do with his Arlington operation and his missing men. He may have to act on his succession plan sooner, rather than later. One man stood in his way, Paul Xavier. Don Alverez had always favored his bastard son Paul. *The bastard!*

"Why don't they pick up that phone?" Diego wondered as his eyes turned to the sound. "JESUS! It's Don Alverez's private line!" he suddenly realized as he grabbed the receiver. He was surprised to hear Paul's voice, the bastard's voice. Paul and those loyal to him would have to be taken down as soon as Gabriella was safe.

But now, he had to know what Paul knew. "What the hell is going on up there?" Diego asked as he rudely announced that Don Alverez was sleeping upstairs and didn't want to be disturbed.

"Tell me it's over Paule? May I tell him it's over?"

"No, Diego, it is close, but not over. That's why I must speak to the Don."

"Tell me, and I will advise him when he wakes up."

"Diego," Paul's voice was cold, "let me speak to the Don. These were his instructions to me. I follow instructions, Diego. Do you?"

He knows, thought Diego. A shiver went up his spine as he considered the consequences of the Don learning of his involvement. "One moment!" he almost shouted, his tone becoming abrupt and formal.

He will regret speaking to me this way, Diego thought as he walked up the stairs to the Don's bedroom. *I will kill him myself.* Gently, he awoke Don Alverez, whispering that Paul was on the line. He sat close, hoping to hear both sides of the conversation.

The Don's reaction to Paul's news was subdued disappointment, an unfamiliar experience in a lifetime of controlling everything. He stared at the high ceiling of his spacious bedroom, almost lost in his massive four-poster bed, his eyes moist with sadness.

The room radiated power and riches. It was his room, and all his choices were masculine. The oversized ornately carved dark mahogany furniture—tables, chairs, armoires, and gun rack were all antiques from the Mediterranean and Middle East. Some of the wood pieces were Roman, some fifteenth-century Spanish. Three large Oriental carpets added color and contrasted nicely with the parquet floors. The walls were covered with murals depicting battle scenes from the Crusades.

Only the drapes and cushions hinted at a feminine touch. His daughter had insisted on yellow silk to offset the darkness of the furniture. The Don gave in to his daughter even though he thought the oversized windows gave the room plenty of light. The cushions and curtains reminded him of his daughter in happier times. But his two nurses, who were always on bedroom duty, brought him back to reality. He was dying; the lung cancer continued to spread. Chemotherapy was not working, nor was radiation. His daughter's kidnapping was the last straw. His will to live was fading. Only his preoccupation with her safe return was keeping him going. All he had fought for and achieved was meaningless if he could not protect the only thing he loved. "Double the money, Paul. Double it if you have to. I want my daughter back safe," cried the Don. "What time does Stump arrive back in Starke?"

"About one hour and fifteen minutes from now, assuming he refueled in Martinsburg and immediately took off," Paul sighed. "I have people in his Gainesville house right now, and I have Michael's apartment in Boca being checked too. However, Padrone, I am sure Michael will call in as soon as he can. We have covered every contingency. We will have Gabriella on her way to you in a few hours. I'm certain."

Paul was anxious to cheer the man he revered as his own father. But Paul had doubts, big doubts. Nothing like this had ever happened before. His suspicions centered on Diego. Could he be responsible for all this mess? Paul knew from his informants that Diego had been planning something. He knew that Diego was attached to Gabriella, that he was devastated when she left for Georgetown. Could he have had her kidnapped? Was he involved with this DC gang?

One thing was certain. When the Don dies, Diego will make his move. *I'll be ready,* he thought. *I'll be ready.*

"Paul?"

"Yes, Padrone?"

"Where do you go after the money is transferred?"

"As soon as Gabriella is on the plane, my men will be gathering. I've not planned anything as you instructed, but it won't take long. These people are fools to insult you, Padrone." Paul assured the Don that Bryant and the blue-eyed freak would die slowly and painfully.

This brought a smile to the Don's face as he lapsed back into sleep.

Chapter 14

A caretaker manager on the Fancy Fruit Farm, Moses Keene, called old Mose by all who knew him, was putting out feed for the cattle in the snowstorm when he heard the dogs' continuous barking. The barking continued without stop for several hours.

Something had to be wrong. The dogs, two German shepherds and a mongrel hound, did not miss a meal. In fact, they generally were not too far from Mose whenever he was out on farm business. Even when he had to go into town, they were always in his pickup. Sometimes they even joined him on the tractor. Mose was sure the dogs had trapped an animal. Maybe they'd treed a possum; the sounds seemed to be coming from near the big oak in the southeast field. *Dammit,* he thought, he was going to have to get them before he got lost in a whiteout. Snow was really coming down.

Mose followed the barking sounds. Sure enough, the dogs were jumping at something in the big oak tree, but this was no possum. It was a man clothed in black streaks and covered in white. He was obviously dead, stiff as a frozen dick. His face was bluish white. He hung upside down with a grotesque, surprised smile of a look on his face. Mose started to cut the man down but realized he couldn't with the dogs going crazy.

"Down, Missy, sit! Sit! Red, sit! No! Curly, no!" But it didn't work. They wouldn't listen. The dogs had trampled the snow and the blood all around the big tree into a purple-white mess. It looked like a psychedelic milk shake. Something animalistic was taking over. Mose knew they'd have to be tied.

Mose didn't have a leash but found a black tether line sticking out of the snow, conveniently lying on the ground, but it was tied to the dead man, wrapped around his neck, attached to his chest. He cut the line into three lengths and, with great effort, leashed the dogs. Roughly jerking their heads from side to side, he dragged them back to the farm, each one fighting him all the way.

"Frederick County Emergency Service, hello."

"Hello, hello, can you hear me?" Mose was hard of hearing, and he always shouted.

"Yes, sir, I can hear you. Do you have an emergency?"

"Who's this? Speak up, I can't hear you!"

"Betty May Benham, sir. Do you have an emergency to report?" she said, speaking much louder.

"They's a man in a tree. I think he's dead. You need to hurry."

"Yes, sir, calm down. I need your name and address."

"The man's still bleedin'. He might be alive. You got to come NOW!"

"Calm down, sir. Where are you? I need an address."

"The farm, goddammit! I'm at the farm!"

"Yes, sir. Thank you. Please, may I have your name? Sir? I need your name."

"What the hell?" Mose turned to his wife, Inez. "I cain't hear a goddamn word she's a sayin'. You talk to her. She won't let me finish."

"Hello, my husband cain't hear too good. He's too stubborn to get a hearin' aid."

"Ma'am, please, I need to know who you are and where you are. Please give me your name."

"My name is Inez Keene, but I didn't see the man. My husband did."

"Thank you. Where are you? I need to know your location."

"At Fancy Fruit Farm off Cedar Creek. You know, the Glaizes farm."

"May I speak to Mr. Glaize?"

"No. He's not here. Just my husband an' me're here."

"The man in the tree, is he there at the farm?"

"I don't know. I just told you my husband found him." Turning to Mose, Inez asked, "Where was the man?"

"In a tree, goddammit! Hangin' upside down in a tree! Gimme that phone."

"No, I'm doin' the talkin'. You cain't hear nothin'! Besides, your goin' t' hell with all that cussin'."

The Frederick County Emergency Services dispatcher, Betty May Benham, heard the old couple arguing, and the line went dead. But she was able to absorb some key facts before the conversation ended. Betty May tried calling back, but the line was busy. She then called the open line for any deputy sheriff in the area to respond.

"Attention, attention, we have an emergency in western Frederick County. A man in a tree at Glaize's Fancy Fruit Farm off Cedar Creek. I repeat. A man in a tree at Fancy Fruit Farm off Cedar Creek. We need an ambulance and a fire truck. They probably need a ladder. The man is bleeding, may be dead, don't know. I am trying to get more information and will advise on route."

Within minutes, a surprising number of people in the area who routinely listened in on the police radio frequency were aware of a report that a body was found hanging in a tree at Glaize's orchard and cattle farm. One woman, a busybody named Vicki Hansel, called WINC Radio with the information she'd heard.

At the farm, Mose and Inez Keene were having another one of their classic arguments.

"Inez, give me the goddamn phone. You're a doddering old fart."

"Don't you cuss around me. You're goin' t' hell for sure. You cain't hear a thing."

"Give me the phone, Inez. You don't know a goddamn thing. What're ya goin' ta tell 'em?"

"There you go again, Mose, you're goin' ta hell."

"Maybe I'll enjoy it if you're not there to nag me."

"Mose, don't talk like that. The devil is listenin'."

"To hell with the devil. I don't give a pile o' cow shit if he's listenin'! Give me back the phone!"

"Take it! Take it! You old fool! Okay, big shot, you do it! Let's just see if you can do it."

And Mose took the phone, but he was so excited he couldn't even dial 911.

Finally, Mose agreed to let her deal with the dispatcher, and shortly afterward, a second 911 emergency call came in to the Winchester—Frederick County—Clarke County emergency services dispatcher's office.

Inez was still excited, even more so as she began to speak. The dispatcher on duty again did her best to calm the hysterical woman on the other end of the line. "Hold on there, ma'am. Slow down. Help is already on the way, but I need your name, your address, and a clear understanding of the problem!"

The quivering voice said, "My name is Inez Keene, I already tol' you that. I work for Mr. Glaize at Fancy Fruit Farm. My husband keeps grabbing the phone."

Another voice in the background, "Goddammit, Inez, let me have the phone. You don't even know where he's at!"

"My husband just found a man hanging in the big oak tree. We think he's dead!"

"Ma'am, please calm down. Help is on the way, but first I need your address please. Is it the Glaize farm or Fancy Fruit Farm?"

Inez turned to Mose and said, "They don't even know where we are."

Grabbing the phone from his hysterical wife, old Mose said, "its west of town, off Cedar Creek, just past Merriman's Lane, we need an ambulance right away! Oh . . . oh . . . I'll meet 'em at the farmhouse and lead the way to the lower pasture where he's at."

"Stay on the line, sir. Don't worry. Help is coming right now. But I need more information from you. Let's start with your name."

One Frederick County deputy sheriff had been unofficially looking for the parachutist since dawn. He knew about the drop, had earlier been on standby during the night, driving around within a mile of the cornfield ready to step in if the three men were discovered. Angelo Baldi, the deputy's friend and sometimes accomplice, had called him at home after the parachutist failed to show up and instructed him to check the area for their man.

As a result, Deputy Roscoe Harris was on full alert when the call came in on his police radio mentioning the Fancy Fruit Farm. He was taking a short break, having a cup of coffee and a biscuit with sausage gravy at the Papermill Place Restaurant.

Before Deputy Harris left to investigate, he made a call to Angelo Baldi's boss in Clarke County, Anthony Arturo, a.k.a. Joe Arthur.

"Mr. Arthur, our missing man might be hanging in a Frederick County tree. The call just came in over the radio. I'm on the way there now."

"Roscoe, you're a good man. I've been unable to sleep wondering where the hell he is."

"If he's alive, I know he'll keep his mouth shut."

"Where is he located, Roscoe?"

"At Glaize's farm. It's actually Fancy Fruit Farm, but I know it. Used t' do some security work for Mr. Glaize."

"Yeah, I know it too. Been there many times. The Glaizes are probably in Florida. Why would the parachutist be at Glaize's farm? That's four or five miles south of where he was supposed to be."

"Well, who else could it be?"

"You're right, it has to be Michael. You're going to have to move fast."

"I'm on it now. Don't worry, I'll get things under control out there."

"Roscoe, the important thing is the cargo. He was bringing in three bags. You got to get to them first, Roscoe. Understand that this is the highest priority. Alive or dead, Michael is not important. The bags are."

"Yes, sir! On my way."

As he sped out Cedar Creek, Roscoe did not report back to the emergency dispatcher, saying he was on the way. He needed all the head start he could muster.

Joe Arthur then called his man Angelo Baldi. "Angelo, I've just heard from Roscoe. Michael may be in a tree at a farm west of town. You remember the Fancy Fruit Farm? You've driven me there several times."

"Oh yes, sir. It's out Cedar Creek, past Merriman's . . . the Glaize's place."

"That's the place."

"Do you want us to go there?"

"No. Sit tight until we hear from Roscoe. He's our man. He'll take care of it. The other dumb-ass deputies will do what he says."

"Does he know what to look for?"

"He knows it's three bags. And he knows not to open them. Stay there. I have a couple more calls to make. How are our two friends getting along?"

"Like a snake and a mongoose. I'll be lucky if they don't kill each other in the next hour."

"Let them know where we are. Maybe they'll stay put a while longer."

"OK, I'm standin' by."

Arthur's next call was to Washington DC.

"Booker?"

"Mr. Bryant ain't here. Who's this?"

"His friend in Winchester, may I speak to him please?"

"He ain't got no friends. Where the fuck is Winchester?"

"May I speak to him please? It's very important."

At this point, Booger Bryant walked into his office. "Peacock, what the fuck you doin' on my phone?"

"Man says he's your frien', callin' from Winchester."

Bryant grabbed the phone. "Who the fuck is this? This's a private number!"

"I'm calling Mr. Booker Bryant with important information. Is this Mr. Bryant?"

"Speakin'. This better be good."

"Mr. Bryant, I choose not to give my name. Just know that I am holding a valuable possession you put in my care. Do you know who I am now?"

"Yeah, yeah, I know. Whassa problem? My man tol' me about a delay?"

"No problem, we've found what we were looking for, and things will finalize soon."

"About time. This performance is wors'n the gov'ment. Better not be a cross, or all hell gonna break loose."

"I knew you would be anxious. Just keeping you up-to-date. Your man knows too. Bye."

Chapter 15

Arthur hung up the phone furious. *Who the hell does that son-of-a-bitch think he is? He needs to be taught some respect,* he said to himself while dialing the secret number to Colombia via Puerto Rico. "May I speak to the Padrone, please?" he said when someone picked up.

"This is his nephew, Diego. I am afraid the Don is sleeping. He's given instructions for me to take all his calls. He is not to be disturbed."

"I'm sorry. This call is for Don Alverez personally. I must speak to him."

"I'm sorry too, but I cannot violate his instructions. Either tell me, or I will tell him of the call when he wakes up."

"OK. Tell him that the delay in Winchester may soon be over. We have found what was missing. At least we think we've found it. We will confirm soon. Please do not be concerned. Everything will be completed as planned."

Diego walked up the stairs to tell the Don. *Maybe it was time for Don Alverez to take his place in heaven,* he thought.

Joe Arthur's last call was to the hangar in Starke. Normally, he would not make this call. The hangar operation was under Don Alverez's control. However, he had the number, and he knew what might happen if he didn't make the call. He wanted to advise that it wouldn't be necessary to hold the pilot, Stump Anderson, since they'd obviously found their missing man.

But the telephone just rang and rang. No one answered.

Within minutes of the second 911 call, five emergency vehicles were en route with sirens blaring: one ambulance, two county patrol cars, a fire engine from Round Hill Fire Department, and a senior deputy sheriff in his souped-up Dodge Durango.

But Deputy Roscoe Harris had already arrived. He was looking for the man who was delivering an important cargo. The man, Michael Rowe, he knew from many previous deliveries. Until he had received the first emergency call, all he had noticed out of the ordinary was a lone late-model white Ford Econoline van parked on a deserted cul-de-sac in the new housing development adjacent to the Glaize farm. This was odd because no work had been done in the development since the first week of January.

Normally, Deputy Harris was paid for not looking, or more specifically, "looking the other way" whenever a drop was to take place in Frederick County. He had been looking the other way for ten years ever since Joe Arthur, the don of Clarke County, had paid off Harris's heavy gambling debts and destroyed the nude photographs of him and two West Virginia prostitutes.

In the succeeding years, the deputy had gotten in deeper and deeper so that now, he would do almost anything for Arthur even though he now knew that he had been originally blackmailed.

During this same time, the deputy had become extremely well respected in the law enforcement field because every year, almost like clockwork, he uncovered a new drug ring or criminal enterprise, thanks to the information Anthony Arturo, a.k.a. Joe Arthur, gave the deputy to arrest such criminals.

The results were win-win for all (except for the arrested criminals): Arturo got rid of competition, and Roscoe Harris got the glory and the praise for a job well done. The deputy only accepted minor promotions to corporal and then sergeant, claiming to be well satisfied without the hassle of upper management.

His current unofficial pay from Arturo's operation was $5,000 per month in cash with no deductions for taxes and government-mandated benefits. He expected a big bonus for what he was about to do.

Roscoe Harris beat the other emergency vehicles to the Fancy Fruit Farm by twenty-seven valuable minutes. During this time, he listened to farm manager Moses Keene describe how his dogs found the stranger, who was, from the farmer's common-sense perspective, obviously dead as a doornail. Mose then led the deputy through the continuing snowstorm to the grisly scene.

Harris recognized Michael Rowe immediately even though his face was grayish-purple and he was hanging upside down and disfigured from blood loss, cuts, and scrapes.

What he couldn't figure out was why Michael was three to five miles south of the expected landing zone and why the duffel bags were nowhere in sight. Where were Michael's weapons? Michael always carried a pistol and an automatic rifle when he jumped. A quick check of the body and the pockets revealed no watch, no ring, no wallet, and no identification whatsoever. The deputy did find a couple of keys, however, draped around Michael's neck. Both keys were identical, and the deputy slipped them inside his pocket moments before the others arrived. Asking Mose to stay put at the tree while he looked around, Roscoe drew his gun and started walking in circles, thinking, *where the hell could those bags be?*

Only after the ambulances and other deputy sheriffs had arrived did the deputy notice that a strap on Michael's vest had been torn or cut. The separation area was recent, a different color than the rest of the tether, which told him that the bags Mr. Arturo had described might be near, maybe cut free while he was still in the air. But what had Michael cut them with? There was no sign of a knife.

Snow was falling very hard, and the only tracks visible led from the tall oak in the middle of the pasture to the old Glaize farmhouse. Everywhere Roscoe had walked, the snow covered up the tracks as fast as they were made. Dog tracks were everywhere under the shelter of the tree, but as they led back and forth from the farmhouse, they were fast disappearing. The officers and ambulance personnel could see scratches on the tree and correctly surmised that Mose's dogs did this too. The mess from the dogs' excited jumping made a search of the area difficult, but it was clear that there were no other tracks of anything else. Certainly, no evidence such as a package or bag having been dragged somewhere.

Deputy Harris did not know the size of the bags nor their contents, but he assumed cocaine. Michael "dropped in" at least once a month and it was no secret what he delivered.

After the EM Techs confirmed the parachutist was dead and pictures were taken, Moses and Inez Keene were questioned again by several county deputies, their conversations recorded, and the whole area taped off and secured.

Roscoe Harris, who had assumed command of the scene, broke away for a snack. He was at the Burger King on Valley Avenue having coffee and a bacon burger when he remembered the white van on Cedar Creek.

He decided to check it out. Sure enough, the Ford Econoline was still there, now covered in snow. The van had a Lamar Sloan Ford sticker on it, and the dealer tags indicated that it had been recently rented. The deputy opened the driver's side door with a metal hook he had for helping drivers who'd locked themselves out. He checked the glove compartment and found airline tickets to Denver, Colorado, scheduled to depart Dulles Airport at 11:00 a.m. that day. Other tickets for different airlines scheduled to depart at later times were there too. The tickets were not in Michael's name. They were in the name of Gary Monroe, as were the driver's license, credit cards, and passport, also in the glove compartment. The picture of Gary Monroe looked just like Michael Rowe, except Monroe did not have Michael's long hair and handlebar mustache.

It was now three thirty in the afternoon, and the deputy knew that Michael Rowe/Gary Monroe would not be taking the flight to Denver. A further detailed search yielded $45,000 in cash under the van's front seat. Harris transferred everything to his jeep, pocketed the money, and called Clarke County one more time.

Roscoe Harris's call gave a new urgency to the situation and resulted in a flurry of additional local and long-distance calls. Harris was ordered to search a wider area and do whatever he could to remain in control of the dead parachutist investigation.

At the Hampton Inn, new calls were made to Washington DC and Colombia, South America, with a plea to stand by for at least a couple of days while things were checked out. The Colombians' emphatically renewed their promise of a second larger payment if the search proved futile.

Simultaneously, the phone rang at All American Air Cargo's hangar in Starke, Florida, but no one answered.

Another call went to Denver, Colorado, to trusted friends. They were told about Michael's plane tickets, the tickets that were found in the van in Winchester. They wanted to find out if anyone was waiting in Denver to meet his scheduled flight. Everyone agreed that he must have an accomplice, maybe several. They were specifically interested in a man named Kevin Slaughter, a cousin of Michael's who lived out west.

The money count was repeated in the cabin in the deep woods, near Paw Paw, West Virginia. A slight warming trend blew in after the storm. It brought sun and melting snow to the majestic landscape. Birds, squirrels, foxes, and deer added noise and life to the white blanket of tranquility. Geese fought one another for space at the edge of receding pond ice, which offered an invigorating swim.

Will was stunned by the amount of money, but he just could not complete a count. He kept putting the bags in the storage bin, pulling them out, starting a count, and getting so excited he would lose track every time. The highest number he ever got to was $4,652,000. He couldn't get much past one-quarter of the money in one bag. Even then, he couldn't relate to the amount. There was too much. Every time he started, he fantasized about whose it was, where it came from, where it was supposed to go, and what it was supposed to purchase.

He needed to think about his lucky find and determine what to do very carefully. *Why on earth would anyone bring in that much cash to Frederick County? It had to be a major drug buy, or something like that.* He thought while he walked in the snow watching Watson chase geese and track rabbits. He tried to envision who would come looking. The person, or persons, who lost such a fortune wouldn't give it up without a fight. He thought perhaps "fight" was not strong enough to convey the emotion and intensity of the search, which was sure to come.

Will realized he was hungry; he hadn't eaten since dinner the night before. Watson came quickly to his urgent call, which was emphasized with the word "cookie." Watson loved his cookies. But they didn't have cookies. All they had was bread, several cans of pork and beans, a gallon of low-fat milk, two pounds of day-old sliced roast beef, and a slab of aged cheddar cheese. Will made sandwiches, Dagwood style. He and his dog, each with a ravenous appetite, ate most of their food supply at one sitting.

Then, they both relaxed. Watson was stretched out on the floor, and Will on the bed with his boots still on. The food, the emerging sun, the melting snow, the stillness of the pond, the isolation of the cabin, the absence of the excited geese, and his overall exhaustion led to deep sleep.

Chapter 16

At the Fancy Fruit Farm, Mose Keene could talk of nothing except finding a dead stranger. Mose's wife, Inez, offered fresh apple pie, her specialty, to all the neighbors who had come by to listen. Nothing like this had happened in the neighborhood since the killings over Robert E. Lee's treasure ten years before. Rumor was that the retreating Confederate Army, on its way from Gettysburg through the Shenandoah Valley, buried a chest of gold and silver, west of Winchester. Treasure hunters with old maps were always combing over former Civil War campgrounds with metal detectors and shovels.

Many of Mose's present visitors were reminded of that day ten years ago when circling buzzards led them to a deep, empty grave in one of Cedar Creek's ancient Civil War battlefields. They found three dead bodies; all bound, gagged, and shot, execution style, the back of their heads neatly plugged. The "grave" seemed smaller than normal and held indentation marks on each side that could have been a coffin or a chest.

Whatever had been in the grave was gone, and from the fresh dirt on the boots and clothes of the bodies, the diggers were unpleasantly surprised. No one was ever caught, and the murder investigation, while still technically open, was as cold as the current weather outside.

Now that unsolved case was a mystery, everyone agreed. This latest incident might be related, and they held out hope that the newest find would lead to solving the earlier crime. The local attitude was, collectively, one of excitement, rather than fear. After all, the dead men were strangers, and their neighborhood was peaceful, except for someone getting drunk every now and then. Generally, the drunks just let off a little steam and didn't bother anybody.

The gathering of curious neighbors broke up when Roscoe Harris arrived. He wanted to go over all the details one more time. If anyone could figure it out, Deputy Roscoe Harris could. He was always catching some criminal, to the surprise of the local citizenry who thought all criminals lived somewhere else.

Roscoe was sweating even though it was freezing outside. He had been walking for hours and hours through snow-covered fields and woods in an ever-expanding circle around the farm. The deputy found several sets of tracks; most were deer, many were rabbits, occasionally, he'd noticed the trail of a fox, but most importantly, he'd seen some barely visible dog tracks, all of which led back to Glaize's farmhouse.

Tired and frustrated, Roscoe sat down at a very old but solid pine kitchen table with a fresh cup of hot coffee and homemade pie. A roaring fire in the wood stove warmed the kitchen beyond being comfortable. Roscoe sensed he was close to the answer but needed more information.

He was on his second piece of Inez's pie when he noticed the three makeshift black dog leashes hanging from a peg in the mudroom off the kitchen. The German shepherds were lying next to their empty food bowls on the floor of the alcove, along with boots, rain slickers, and assorted outerwear necessary for farm life. Mose's mongrel hound was also asleep, but far enough away from the other two dogs to show he was a second-class citizen in the dog world.

The deputy got up from the kitchen table, fork in hand, and walked to the mudroom for a closer look. Sure enough, the "leashes" had been recently cut, and there was no doubt that they matched the missing canvas tether that was unhooked from the parachutist's vest. The sewed-on tether was originally attached to something, but whatever it was, Roscoe couldn't tell from the state of the leashes.

But Roscoe now knew that there were three missing bags, that each had an emergency electronic signal sewn into the straps where they were attached to the bag. In case a bag was separated from the parachutist, it could quickly be found with a signal-finding device that Michael Rowe carried. Roscoe also knew the bags were so heavy that Michael had decided to use more than one parachute, perhaps one for each bag. His device could track the parachutes in case they landed beyond his designated landing zone. It should have been on Michael Rowe's body, but the deputies had found nothing on the body, not even a wallet.

Pointing to the straps with his fork, Roscoe asked old Mose, "Where did you get these 'leashes'?"

Mose, in his early seventies and distracted by the rush of activity, looked at the leashes blankly and then shook his head. "Damned if I know, Roscoe. They's all kinds of odds and ends that I pick up around the farm. Don't nothin' go to waste around here."

"Mose, you sure you're not forgetting to tell me something?"

Mose rolled everything around in his old mind. "I may have forgotten something, but I don't think so. You fellers have plumb questioned me to death."

Deputy Roscoe Harris looked at the leashes again, then at Mose, and concluded that he had found the man they were looking for.

Minutes later, the phone rang in Angelo Baldi's room at the Hampton Inn. Joe Arthur suggested Angelo Baldi and his two friends might want to try to improve Mose's memory about the straps hanging in the mudroom.

Baldi called Blue's room and got no answer. After ten rings, he thought to himself, *Where the hell is that crazy son-of-a-bitch? I told him to stand by until we heard from our man on the scene.*

His next call to Paul Xavier's room was answered on the first ring. "Yes?"

"It's me, Angelo. We got a hot tip. We think the old geezer that found the jumper might have somethin' ta say on the subject of the bags. Of course, we need to ask the right questions. I called the blue-eyed freak, and he ain't in his room. Seen 'im?"

"I don't trust him out of spitting distance. He may be up to no good. Could be shacked up with the clerk at the front desk. Did you see the way she looked at him?"

"Well, meet me in the lobby. He can't hide his black-'n'-blue ass in this town."

"I'll be there in five minutes."

Downstairs at the Hampton Inn's front desk, the missing third man, Blue, was just coming through the door, admiring the car parked outside the lobby. He'd been across the street, buying cigarettes from the corner gas station.

A woman named Maggie was checking in.

"How long you all stayin'?" asked the desk clerk.

"I'm not sure. I have several things to research here."

"You must be a Patsy Cline fan."

"How did you know?"

"They come from all over, honey, lookin' just like you. When ya get settled, you need to go to Gaunt's Drugstore, ask for Harold. He can tell you anything you want to know about Patsy. Don't tell him I sent you. He'll think I still have a crush on him, ya heah?"

"Oh, thanks, you've been very helpful."

"Hey, ya didn't give me a license number for your car."

"Do you really need it?"

"No, but we have to ask. Park it out front, an' it'll be OK."

Her blue Mercedes sedan was parked under the canopy outside, engine still running.

She was tall and well-dressed, wearing dark sunglasses and on a mission. She was looking for a man, a man whose first name was Will, whom, she remembered, lived in Winchester, Virginia.

"That your SL outside?" Blue passed by in a hurry, half-flirting with the woman.

"Why thank you, yes, it is."

"That is some kinda hot car, lady, mighty fine wheels," he said, ducking into the elevator before she could reply.

"Is he gorgeous or what?" the clerk at the desk said to no one in particular.

The new arrival didn't answer, just smiled to herself that the Will she'd met in a Georgetown bar was much better-looking than that.

Stump Anderson's flight back to Florida was trouble free once he cleared the bumpy air over the mountains near Charlottesville, Virginia. Landing smoothly at Starke, Stump was smiling as he taxied off the runway. *Another successful delivery,* he thought, and another $25,000 in his bank account. Actually, it was going into one of his safe deposit boxes since he couldn't deposit that much cash in his bank account. He was surprised to see two Lincoln Town cars next to the hangar, then alarmed when he noticed that inside, the hangar lights were on.

As he parked the King Air and scurried down the steps, the company mechanic, Tommy Joe Bevins, was securing the aircraft and preparing it for the next flight. "Hey, Tommy, who's come to visit?"

"Some o' Diego's guys, same ones who packed the bags yesterday."

"They leave somethin' behind?"

"Nah, I think they want to talk to you."

"Well, they're goin' to have' ta wait 'cause I've had to piss since I crossed into South Carolina." And he ran into the hangar.

The leader of this group, Manuel Esteban, stood up when Stump rushed in, crushed his cigar, saying, "Stumpy, did you have a good flight?"

Stump waved as four other men rose from their chairs. "Manny, gotta take a leak, kidney's about to burst." He shut the bathroom door. "Did y'all fo'get somethin'?"

Manuel motioned for two of his men to go outside, check the bathroom window, and make sure Stump didn't leave.

The air cargo hangar was immense, capable of housing six to eight aircraft at a time, depending on their size. Parked inside at present were five planes: a Hawker-Sidley jet; a brand-new Gulfstream; an old Mitsubishi prop jet, a Falcon 10, and another King Air, identical to the one being serviced outside.

Stump's footsteps on the concrete floor echoed throughout the cavernous interior of the hangar as he came out of the bathroom. He headed for the hangar office with his flight log and noticed that Manuel and a man he didn't recognize seemed to be waiting for him. "Hey, Manny, what's goin' on? You want flyin' lessons?"

"Nah, Stump, we have a problem with the jump an' wan' to make sure from you what it is happened," the stranger said.

"Name's Stump Anderson, Manny's forgot his manners in introducin' us." Stump held out his hand, but the stranger didn't take it.

The stranger was short and stocky with pockmarked face and a large mole on his broken nose. His arms were huge and powerful, stretching his short-sleeved shirt, fists bunched as if he were ready to punch.

Stump, too, was a powerfully built man and slightly taller than the stranger. "Okay, scarface, looks like you missin' some social skills."

Manuel ignored the exchange and asked Stump to sit. The other four men, including the stranger, silently pulled up chairs around him.

"Stump, sorry to trouble you," Manuel began, "but we got a big problem. Michael didn't make contact."

"Whadda ya mean didn't make contact? He sure jumped in time."

"We saw the plane. Came in almost on top of the boys on the ground, but no sign of Michael. He has not called either. Standard backup is a call, right, Stump?"

"Yeah, that's the backup, but he only had to do that one time in fifteen years. The drop zone was hot then. We could see it, but the ground crew couldn't. Somebody had word we were comin' then."

"Well, he didn't show and he didn't call. He didn't do nothin'. Not a word for almost four hours."

"The son-of-a-bitch jumped. That's for sure."

"Did he jump with all the bags?"

"Jesus Christ! O' course he did. He's a pro. None better."

"Stump, did you notice anything unusual? Weather OK?"

"The weather was startin' to turn bad. Big snowstorm was brewin'. It's pourin' there now. Winds were shifty and gustin', but nothin' we ain't seen before. Mike coulda handled that."

"Did you have to alter your plan because of that?"

"Nah, we was on target the entire way. I could almost see the whole cornfield. That's the landin' zone, ya know. The quarry lights 'n' the hospital lights were like beacons on an airstrip. Goin' up the flight was perfect. Had some crosswinds landin' at Martinsburg. Had heavy winds comin' back. Slowed me down, tha's all."

"Then why didn't they see him jump? Paul had night vision binoculars and spotted you a mile before you passed over."

"Well, he jumped early. I asked him why so early when he went back 'n' he said it was complicated. You know, he had three chutes to deploy."

Suddenly, the stranger jumped up and said, "Why didn't you say that in the first place?"

Everybody just glared, and Manuel motioned him to sit down and stay quiet.

"Who's this fuckface, Manny? Looks like he's been hit with chicken shit instead of chicken pox. Man thinks he's tough, look at 'im."

"Never mind him, Stump. We got a job to do. We got to find out what happened. You say he jumped early. How early?"

"I said he went back to prepare for the jump early. I didn't see him jump, but the door was open a minute or two before the actual drop zone."

"Now we're getting somewhere. OK, think, what if he jumped the minute you noticed that the door was open? How far off could he be?"

"Jesus, Manny. How the fuck would I know? It could have been a couple o' miles or more, I guess."

Manuel stared at Stump, trying to catch a facial expression, looking for something, anything that might indicate a lie, or support the truth to his answers. He didn't like what he saw.

Chapter 17

In the Allegheny Mountains, near Paw Paw, West Virginia, a surreal peace enveloped the isolated cabin. It had stopped snowing, and the wind finally had calmed. The quiet was a welcome interlude after the frantic pace of the previous day's excitement.

Will MacKenzie remained in an exhausted deep sleep, slouched across the cabin's only stuffed chair, faithful chocolate Lab at his feet, each snoring in loud regular intervals, not a care in the world. Will was fully clothed, hiking boots on and laced tight. His sleep changed from sweet dreams to troubled and confused; he dreamed he was covered in hundred-dollar bills, and every time he counted them, something interfered with the count, and he had to start over. In this dream, he heard a dog barking and whining, fighting him over the money.

He dreamed that every time he hid the money, Watson would find it. He dreamed that he'd buried the money in several secret places, and every time, Watson would find it and dig it up. He dreamed of a sophisticated woman, beautifully dressed at a Georgetown bar, coming to him through a river of money, and he tried to remember her name. A dog kept barking and prevented her from coming to him.

When he awoke, he realized that he was actually hearing a dog. Watson had suddenly come out of his reverie and needed to go out.

The stranger was getting impatient. They had already searched Stump's house in nearby Gainesville and Michael's apartment in Boca Raton. Michael's apartment produced nothing of interest, but the searchers found a receipt for a one-way airline ticket to Idaho in Stump's house. Also, they noticed that Michael had left a floor safe open in his apartment. The safe was empty even though clothes were in his closet and dresser. It looked like the place had been robbed.

According to Stump's airplane ticket, the trip to Idaho was scheduled for the following week, and one of the Colombians remembered Michael Rowe talking earlier about an upcoming fishing trip in Idaho.

"Ask him about the plane ticket," the stranger shouted, looking directly into Stump's eyes, thinking this will shake him up. Manuel, turned from Stump, glared at the loudmouth, willing him to shut up.

Stump had a bad attitude with all these questions. Who the hell were they to be questioning him? He invented the jump delivery. His replies began to get sarcastic.

However, disturbing facts undermined everything he said. There was the airline ticket, the amount of money in the moneybags, the delay in meeting their planned rendezvous, Michael's disappearance, and the importance of the delivery—all of which aroused suspicion.

"Whadda ya mean about a plane ticket? What's a goddamn plane ticket got to do with anything?" Stump shouted in Manuel's face.

"Stump, we found a plane ticket to Idaho in your house. Pedi here"—he pointed to one of the men—"remembers you an' Michael planning a trip to Idaho together after this job."

"You been in my house! You searched my house? What is this shit, Manny? You an' me, we go back fifteen years, FIFTEEN YEARS!"

"Stump, relax, calm down. You know this is just standard procedure. We got a problem. We just want to figure it out, that's all. What about the plane ticket, the trip to Idaho?"

"Fuck, Idaho! You want me to relax? I want to see the Don. I want to see him now!"

"Stumpy, there's no need for that. We're all friends here. All we want are some basic answers. Take your time. Tell us. We can figure it out if you just describe the flight and try to remember everything as it happened."

"That crater-faced asshole is not my friend," he said, pointing to the stranger. "and I don't like these questions. I don't like being accused of this shit."

"Stumpy, please? Tell us. So we can be doing something about it. Please!"

Stump told them about the ticket and explained that the delay in the parachute drop was caused by headwinds over Georgia and North Carolina. Weren't they aware of the storm going up the East Coast? He told them the details of Michael's jump, including his concern that the jump was too early. But they didn't understand or just didn't believe.

He told them when and where the jump was made, the exact time and the exact location. But they doubted everything. The stranger made a point of being tough as if he had to prove himself to the Colombians.

Stump readily admitted that he and Michael Rowe were very good friends. The Colombians reminded him that Michael Rowe had vouched for and helped recruit him. Stump admitted that the two of them had made plans for a hunting and fishing trip to Idaho after this job. He and Michael had served together in Vietnam, but he didn't know why Michael had disappeared. He also swore he did not know how much money was in the bags.

After the second hour of questioning, they broke his thumb. He began crying, partly because of the pain and partly out of disbelief that this was really happening to him. But they wouldn't stop, and question after question followed: *Why was Michael's safe open and empty? Where's the money? Where was Michael going? Where's the money? Who was Michael's girlfriend? Where's the money?*

But every question brought the same answer. "Goddammit, I don't know. I don't know. I want to talk to the Don."

Gradually, Stump's resistance wore down, and he said, "OK, OK, whatever you want. Get it over with. What do you want me to say?"

"Tell us, where is the money? Where is Michael? Michael! Money! That's all we want to know!" The stranger began to strike blow after blow to Stump's head. The beating continued until Stump's head lolled to one side and his eyes closed. The stranger looked at the others in frustration. "This guy's hidin' somethin', I just know it."

Manuel decided to take him to a more remote location, carrying him out of the hangar and into one of the sedans. Tommy Joe Bevins, still servicing the King Air, looked down at the ground as they passed by. Tommy Joe didn't want to get involved.

On the way out, with two of their men carrying an unconscious Stump, the stranger looked at Manuel and nodded toward the flight mechanic, Tommy Joe Bevins. The stranger rolled his eyes, asking without saying, *Was it okay to leave this guy Bevins alive knowing what he knows?* Without missing a step, Manuel whispered, "He's okay. He's a long-time employee. Keeps his mouth shut."

The stranger took Stump's flight logbook and other papers that were in his pilot's briefcase. But all he found were receipts for service, landing fees, and the cost of refueling in Martinsburg. The other men took the entire contents of the file cabinet, a change of clothes Stump kept on hand, and Stump's car, a new Porche that he always drove too fast.

When Stump woke up some two hours later, he didn't recognize his new surroundings. They were at an old fishing camp, in a dirt poor, tar-papered shack on the edge of Swamp Road near Starke, Florida.

Even though he was hurting all over, Stump Anderson lost his cool. The pilot had nothing to hide, and his relationship with Don Alverez was closer than these goons would ever have. In fact, he'd never seen one of these guys, the one with the threats, doing all the talking. The guy thought he was so tough, Stump would show him what tough was, once this nightmare was over, once they realized their misunderstanding.

Thus far, they had been a little rough, but nothing he couldn't handle. Stump did not like the questions or the insinuations. He did not like the location they had picked for his interrogation, and he was too pissed off to be scared. He would never cheat the Don, not even for his closest friend, Michael Rowe. He was well aware of what happened to the Don's enemies. Hell, he wasn't sure of the contents of the package they were delivering. He assumed it was cash, but normally, it was cocaine. That's what they always delivered.

Gradually, the questioning became more vocal, then more violent. Cigarette and cigar smoke swirled in and out of his vision, already blurred from the beating.

Stump was tough, but there were five of them. They were armed, and he wasn't. Just the same, he had answered their questions, and he was tired. He'd been up all night flying to Virginia, West Virginia, and back, and he needed sleep. Exhausted, he finally turned to the big guy with the pockmarked face and the mole on his nose, the one doing most of the talking. "Fuck you! That's all I have to say. I'll deal direct with the Don myself."

That's when the little guy on his left, his so-called friend, hit him across the face with the broom handle and broke his nose. Blood was everywhere. He couldn't see, pain shot through his skull in waves, and he lunged forward. When he started to get up, all five were required to restrain him. He was like a mad bull. In the old days, he might have taken them all. Not now. He struggled, managed to bite one of them on the cheek, and spit into another's face. In return, he received a head butt to his broken nose that ended his resistance. The guy with the bit cheek pummeled Stump with both hands while the others grabbed him and tied his arms and legs to the old ladder-backed chair.

His actions convinced all four that he was lying, that he and Michael had planned to steal the ransom. They took turns hitting him with fists and the broom handle. They struck his head, his neck, his chest, and his groin.

After the furious assault from every direction, Stump lost consciousness. He grudgingly accepted his fate when he awoke a few minutes later.

"I hope he took it. I hope you never find him. I didn't do anything. Manny, put a bullet in me. I can't say anything I don't know."

None of the five interrogators was skilled at getting information. They broke every finger, one at a time. Several times, they grabbed his broken nose and jerked it side to side until he would pass out after a screaming fit. They poked him in his chest with the broomstick handle until his ribs cracked. They poked him in his penis; they poked him in his balls. His screaming finally ceased, but still, he didn't talk—he had nothing to say. He knew nothing. Finally, in a bare whisper of a voice, he begged that they kill him quickly.

And that's when they realized he didn't know. After eight hours of numbing interrogation, the one with the bloody handkerchief held to his bloody cheek ended Stump's misery with two shots between the eyes.

They tied his feet to his chest, almost bending him double, and unceremoniously dumped Stump in the swamp. The last image of Stump was of his left arm bunched in a fist sticking out of the swamp, and on his wrist was a $5,000 Rolex watch that slowly disappeared through bubbles and ripples of muddy water.

On the way back to Starke, Manuel asked to stop at a public phone booth outside an all-night diner. He knew that Paul would be anxious to hear what Stump had been unable to say.

Chapter 18

Stephanie McWharton was on duty at the Hampton Inn when the telephone call came in from Starke. Stephanie had been reading a story in the *Washington Post* about three male bodies being found in the Anacostia River by a mudcat fisherman. The story made the front page of the *Post* because of the gruesome condition of the bodies. They had been in the water about a week and were bloated beyond recognition. Each man had been shot, execution style, in the back of the head. Based on burn marks, bruises, and cuts around their faces, hands, and genital areas, the three men appeared to have been tortured. All means of identification was missing, but police speculated that the three were Latinos in their mid- to late twenties. They were found tied together by their ankles. Metropolitan Police were offering a reward for any information regarding the case.

Stephanie was so absorbed in the story that she put out her cigarette in her coffee cup when the phone rang.

A voice with a Spanish accent asked to speak with Paul Xavier.

At River View Farm, a frustrated Joe Arthur was upset. He'd called the hangar at Starke several times, but no one answered. Things were getting out of hand.

News of the Anacostia River bodies reached the FU Club even before the story appeared in the *Washington Post*. Booger had his sources in the police department. Furious at hearing the news, Booger and several members of the FU Crew were gathered in a back room of the club.

"Peacock! You gotta be the most useless nigga in the District o' Columbia! Guess what's washed up from the Anacostia?"

Peacock and Cueball stood with their heads down in front of Booger Bryant and twenty of his men. "Uh . . . uh . . ."

"Never mind about thinkin' up excuses. You two can try again with disposin' of two more spics. Since you got no brains, use your strong backs t' clean up that mess in the basement next do'."

"Take 'em outta town, down to Fredericksburg. Drop 'em in the Rappahannock, and tie those spics down with sumthin' heavier'n they dicks. They better not bob up in the Chesapeake either. Understand? An' when you gets back here, you got anotha job. Be ready for a pleasure trip to Winchester. I be thinkin' sumthin's wrong at the farm. Blue ain't called for it, but he might needs some mo' hands."

Inside the cabin, the fire still crackled, but it had died to a few smoldering logs. It was now dark outside. Will turned on the radio for the latest news from Winchester.

Winchester radio station WINC confirmed that a body had been found in a tree on a farm in Western Frederick County. This was big news for the entire area, even bigger than the snowstorm. Every half hour, the story was being broadcast as a major news bulletin. According to the station, the body was an unidentified white male who had parachuted out of a plane.

No other details were available. The dead person's name, once it became known, would not be released until the next of kin were notified. The Frederick County sheriff's department was investigating. A caretaker on Fancy Fruit Farm had found the dead parachutist while searching for his three dogs that were barking and howling in a nearby pasture.

Almost every hour, there would be something else to report. The Frederick County sheriff advised that the FBI might be called in since the dead unknown parachutist was not local and, so far, was unidentified. Officially, the death was not a homicide, but circumstances of the "accident" were bizarre, and illegal activity was suspected. The FBI would be able to investigate flight plans and air routes coming into the area. Frederick County simply did not have the resources to conduct a major investigation.

Rumors were circulating that the parachutist had been bringing in drugs and had been killed for his supply. There was evidence supporting this theory since the body was stripped of all identification and some of the parachute straps had apparently been cut and were conspicuously missing.

An abandoned van was discovered near where the body was found, and authorities were not releasing any information pending further investigation. This was the biggest news to hit the Winchester area in years and took the headlines away from the unexpected winter storm, which had dumped over a foot of new snow across a wide section of the upper Shenandoah Valley.

Will fixed a cup of strong black coffee, replenished the wood on the fire, and fixed what remained of their food for the dog. The tension had subsided. He felt safe and secure, thinking he'd escaped detection.

But staring at the dancing flames, he could not relax for long. New concerns began to pop in his mind. *Whose money had he found? Was it drug money? Should he separate the money into a series of hiding places? Should he keep any of the money at his Winchester home? How much would his safe deposit box hold? How many safe deposit boxes would he need? How many banks and how many locations would he dare go to? How could he evade discovery from the IRS?* Surely, the people who had lost the money would come looking for it. They had to be bad news. They must have huge resources, given the amount of money involved. Lots of questions and too few answers.

Finally, he decided to leave most of the money at the cabin, at least for the time being. It was hidden carefully under the floor and would be very difficult to discover by an intruder. The trap door under the false tile and concrete floor in front of the fireplace was fireproof, and the underground vault was protected by a foot of concrete.

The next morning, Will placed $100,000 in hundred-dollar bills and a Glock automatic pistol under a hasty mixture of clean and dirty clothes in his overnight bag. The bag was topped off with his toilet articles and a couple of Wilbur Smith novels. He stuffed his loaded Beretta under the jeep's driver seat and carefully laid his shotgun and an AR-15 automatic rifle under a blanket in the backseat. Will closed and locked the cabin's sturdy front door, stepped off the porch with Watson, and both he and the dog took a leak in the snow.

It took some time to clean the snow off the windshield and heat up the Cherokee. As MacKenzie worked on the jeep, Watson explored a jumble of fresh tracks left by a variety of animals, which had prowled the woods at night. It wasn't long before he killed a large rabbit and brought it to the front porch, guarding it with a hunter's pride. Watson, the hunter/retriever, never ate what he killed, but always returned with his trophy. Eager to chase anything that moved in the woods, he looked like a porpoise bounding through the deep snow. Just as eagerly, Watson abandoned his kill when he realized he couldn't bring it in the jeep and jumped in the passenger seat when it came time to leave.

The going was painfully slow as they made their way back. The jeep crawled through two miles of drifted snow to the road to Paw Paw. Will frequently had to stop to remove fallen tree limbs that had blocked the road. The trip to the main road took almost one hour. Once there, they headed west, through Paw Paw, and on toward Cumberland, Maryland.

His ultimate destination was a nursing home in Weston, West Virginia. His alibi needed to be strengthened and a visit to Uncle Jim might do the trick.

The Glaize farmhouse phone rang at approximately 7:00 p.m. It was promptly answered by old Mose Keene. The caller was Deputy Sheriff Roscoe Harris. Roscoe apologized for calling so late but wanted to let them know that the FBI was coming, that the agents needed to talk with both Mose and Inez right away because FBI required firsthand information on any case they were working on.

Trying their best to look like agents, "the FBI" turned out to be Angelo Baldi, Blue Eyes Smith, and Paul Xavier.

The black Buick's tires crunched as Baldi drove slowly up the long snow-covered curving driveway to the farmhouse. Just beyond, in a grove of huge oak trees, was the stately but darkened main house, whose owners were spending the winter in Vero Beach, Florida. The three knew from Roscoe that no one was home in the big house.

A white picket fence surrounding the farmhouse kept the dogs away from the herd of Black Angus cattle with its twenty prize bulls. The "farmhouse," the original structure on the Glaize property when it was acquired several generations ago, was now the farm manager's house. It was an old wooden clapboard house with four brick chimneys and a wide porch. Although it had been renovated several times during the past 150 years and had all the modern conveniences, it still looked its age. White paint was peeling from the railing around the huge porch, and a couple of gutters had begun to sag from the weight of the recent snows.

The men walked up the porch steps, knocked on the door, and were surprised to find it unlocked.

"Come on in," they heard old Mose say. "I need to shut these dogs up. They make such a fuss every time we have visitors. Don't like strangers coming at night. Matter of fact, they don't like strangers period."

Inez waved to them from the kitchen and motioned for them to come in. A new pot of coffee sat on the large stove and a variety of cakes, pies, and freshly baked muffins were on the kitchen table. As the three men sat down, Mose came in from the mudroom where the dogs were still yapping.

"Normally, they ain't this jumpy. Perhaps, it's been all the company we've had recently."

What Mose didn't know was that the dogs sensed someone outside and that someone was Roscoe Harris, making sure that the meeting inside would be undisturbed.

Chapter 19

In the brightly lit kitchen, Paul Xavier calmly began the interrogation by asking everyone to sit around the table and relax. The men helped themselves to coffee and cake. Paul thanked Mose and Inez for seeing them so late and thanked them for their cooperation and hospitality.

Then he advised the Keenes that there was considerable danger to worry about from persons unknown and that they were especially at risk given the publicity over their having found the body. He asked Angelo and Blue (whom he had earlier introduced as Officers Baldi and Smith) to check out the farmhouse for security purposes. Baldi and Smith left the kitchen and began tearing the house apart looking for the hiding place where the Keenes had hidden the money. Every now and then, those in the kitchen would hear a crash or bang as drawers were flung to the floor or the sound of a knickknack breaking would reverberate through the house. All the while, Paul was asking questions of the two and reassuring them that the FBI knew what they were doing.

After an hour of hearing noises throughout the house and trying to answer the same questions over and over again, Mose had had enough. He insisted on excusing himself to help the two officers. The three dogs in the mudroom continued barking and whining. Inez was alarmed too, wondering what had been broken. It sounded as though the two officers were trashing every room. Paul assured them that the FBI was careful and needed to check everything out. He told the Keenes that the sheriff and his people were inexperienced in these matters and what was being done was normal and necessary.

Then they heard a horrible crash as Smith turned over an armoire full of antique figurines that Inez had been collecting for fifty years. Paul placed his hand on Mose's arm as he tried to rise and advised him that the FBI would pay for any damage. Mose became irritable and mentioned a search warrant for the first time. These were the words that ended all pretense of civility as Paul decided that anyone who would demand a search warrant must have something to hide.

Baldi and Smith flipped a coin to decide who would go up into the old attic. When Baldi lost the flip and started up the creaky ladder, Smith went back to the kitchen where he planned to check out the adjacent mudroom.

Outside, Roscoe was to investigate the detached garage and tool shed and, at the same time, make sure no unwelcome visitors arrived on the scene. The barn search was going to take some time and would require all four men dividing their search into sections. It was being saved for last in the hope that old Mose would give up the money and the men could thus avoid a long night. As he paced the perimeter of the farmhouse, Roscoe could hear the dog's continuous barking and wondered what the hell was happening.

Inside, Paul's normal self control exploded, "These goddamned dogs are driving me insane! I can't hear myself think!"

In the mudroom, the dogs were going crazy, for they had heard their master's shouts. Two dogs were jumping up against the kitchen door, their heads visible, bobbing up and down every few seconds through the glass door panes. Blue did not say a word as he walked to the mudroom, pulled his pistol, flicked the safety off, and started pumping bullets through the glass and into the frantic dogs. Mose and Inez were struck dumb. All together, he fired sixteen shots, loaded another clip, and opened the mudroom door. Unbelievably, the smallest dog, a mixed-breed hound, was still alive. One shot in the back of his skull mercifully ended his whimpering. Satisfied that the dogs would finally "shut the fuck up," Blue turned to old Mose. "Time for you to tell the truth, else you wind up like the dogs."

But Paul took over. The interrogation did not resemble a good cop— bad cop routine; rather, it was more like "bad cop and horror cop." Inez was crying hysterically, her wrinkled face red with worry. Old Mose kept saying, "Wait 'til Roscoe hears about this!"

Paul shoved him back into his chair. "No way can Roscoe help you. Now, tell us where you put the bags you found on the dead jumper."

Mose began crying. "You ain't the FBI, and I didn't find no bags."

Unhappy with the slow persistent questions asked by Paul, Blue grabbed the torn canvas straps and stuck them under old Mose's nose. "What the fuck are these? These're cut from the jumper's bags!"

Inez started to get up, and Blue slammed her back into her chair. "Enough bullshit!" he yelled. "WHERE IS IT?"

Blue slapped her with a broad sweep of his open hand. Paul held old Mose down in his chair, and when blood erupted from Inez's nose, Mose began to cry.

All this time, Angelo Baldi, back from the attic, had stood quietly by the door to the mudroom. Stepping with care, he entered the mudroom, through the broken glass, and removed a folding straight razor he kept strapped to his left leg. Next, he cut a clothes line that Inez had hung from the kitchen to the porch, carefully removing the fresh-smelling shirts and denim overalls that were clipped to the line. He dropped the clothes on the dogs and the bloody floor and began to cut the line into sections. Wiping his feet on a flowered dress that now served as a macabre welcome mat, he eased up to their two victims.

Without asking Paul or Blue for help or permission, he roughly tied Inez and old Mose to their kitchen chairs. The old couple squirmed, cried, and begged to be let go. Angelo tied the ropes so tight that their old wrists and ankles turned white. With their blood circulation restricted, their skin bruised like overripe fruit. "It's time to stop being nice," he announced.

Looking directly into Mose's eyes, he jabbed his right fist into Inez's Adam's apple, causing her to choke and vomit. Her head shot forward almost into her lap. Next, he took his straight razor and flicked it open, all the time looking directly at Mose.

Mose, voice now quaking with fear, pleaded, "No more, no more, you can have all our money. Look in our bedroom, in our bed, in the bedposts, they's all hollow. They's full o' cash. The wooden acorn caps pull out like a cork. It's all there. Inez's mother's ring and Great-grandaddy's gold railroad watch is there too. They's worth a lot, I promise. Go look. Don't hit her no more. I'll show you where it is if you stop. Loosen Inez's ropes. She ain't goin' nowhere. Don't hit her no more. Please, please, I don't care about me, but I beg you to leave her be!"

Paul turned his head to the stairs and, without saying a word, motioned to Angelo and Blue to check it out. As the two men flew up the stairs to the bedroom, he turned to Mose. "It's going to be OK now. Don't worry, we'll get a doctor here quick."

But Mose had stopped believing at this point. "God, help us!" he whispered, looking at Inez and shaking his head.

In the bedroom, each man was fishing the savings of a lifetime out of four fat wooden bedposts. Blue was the first to comment. "Not a hundred-dollar bill in the bunch! Can't be more'n two, three thousand in any o' these posts."

"Maybe the mattress and box springs is holdin' the big stuff," Angelo said and started slashing with his straight razor.

But it wasn't there either. They stuffed the money, rings, brooches, and old silver dollars into a pillowcase and came downstairs. All in all, it took them about fifteen minutes to discover that Mose was still holding out.

Now, Angelo did not bother with theatrics. He took his razor, cut off Inez's ring finger, removed her bloody wedding ring, and flicked the stub into Mose's face.

Inez passed out with shock and fright.

Looking at Mose, Angelo shouted, "Either you tell us where it is, or we take 'em off one at a time. What's it goin' ta be?"

Mose looked like he was going to have a stroke or a heart attack or puke or something.

He puked. He coughed, he gagged, he cried, he screamed, and when he caught his breath, he shakingly said he didn't have what they were looking for. Off came another finger.

Then another and another and another until Paul mumbled, "Jesus, he doesn't know shit. Look at him, he's glassy eyed. He doesn't know shit."

"Yes, he does." And Angelo hit the old man with his balled fist, breaking his nose and bloodying his lip.

"Son-of-a-bitch, you'll kill 'im, an' he'll nevah talk." Blue stepped in, beginning to worry about Angelo's ferocity.

But Mose, tough with years of hard outdoor, all-weather, back-breaking work, never missing a day due to not feeling good, opened his eyes, finally concluding the worst. "Take it all, take everything, looks like we won't be comin' out o' this mess."

That's when they knew. They knew old Mose did not have anything else to give. They knew he did not have the money and didn't know who did. Paul, without mercy, did the merciful thing and put two bullets into the brains of a man and wife who'd lived happily together for fifty-eight years.

The three cleaned up deliberately, not hurried, not really worried that an investigation would lead to them. Their main concern now was what to do next.

Roscoe tried to calm them down. He assured them that he could find their money. He asked them to go back to the Hampton Inn and wait for his call. He needed some time to check records at the Frederick County Courthouse, which would not open until 9:00 the next morning. Roscoe told them not to worry, that whoever had the money had a big dog or several big dogs, and that he knew how to find the dog owners.

At the Hampton Inn, Blue again noticed a dark Mercedes parked in the lot next to his car, also a Mercedes. The sedan had a Virginia vanity plate with the name "Maggie."

Although he'd told the others not to worry, driving back to his house in the country at 3:00 a.m., Roscoe was worried. He hoped that whoever it was, whoever had taken the money, really did have a big dog and, more importantly, had obtained a dog license from Frederick County. Otherwise, a full-scale drug war might erupt in his territory, and he might be the next victim.

By nine o'clock the next morning, Deputy Sheriff Roscoe Harris was already reviewing Frederick County dog license files and beginning to list the dog owners within a two-mile radius of the Fancy Fruit Farm. Edna Cline, the deputy to the clerk of the court, had allowed Roscoe in when she arrived for work. For years, Edna was always asked, "Are you related to Patsy Cline?" and she would politely reply, "No, I'm from another family of Clines."

As usual, when Roscoe saw her, he teased, "Edna Cline? You any kin to Patsy Cline?"

"She's my third cousin, twice removed, blockhead. And compared to me, she couldn't carry a tune." Her big eyes batted at Roscoe. "What are you looking at dog licenses for, Roscoe? Why don't you look up names o' good-lookin' women?"

"Edna, honey, I don't need to look anywhere but right before me, you get better lookin' every day. You find the Fountain of Youth?"

"Dammit, Roscoe, you aged well yo'self, why don't you come over for some home cookin'? I got sump'in' mighty tasty," she said, giving him a look of welcome that left no doubts.

Roscoe looked her up and down, licked his lips, and said, "I'll bet you do."

"Here, Mr. Deputy, let me help you, we'll die of old age before you find the dogs you lookin' for." In between the shelves of files, Edna moved real close to Roscoe, brushing her breast against his arm, all the while looking into his eyes, a seductive invitation written all over her face.

Edna had had a crush on Roscoe ever since high school. She also thought Roscoe must have inherited some money because he seemed to have plenty of it. Edna was a friend of the dispatcher, Betty May Benham, and they were always talking about Roscoe and why he was not married.

At Joe Arthur's lavish estate, Gabriella Alverez attempted her daily series of aerobic exercises, working extra hard to take her mind off her situation. This morning she moved with anger and frustration, having expected her release days ago. She could not figure out why things were taking so long. Her father was a man of action. When her father wanted something, it happened in a heartbeat. She had no illusions of her father's business, and she had seen his temper many times, but never directed at her. She was his baby. She knew her father would pay a ransom, but something was wrong. Although she was treated with respect, even reverence, she was still a prisoner. Nothing bad had ever happened to her that her father could not fix. This unexpected delay added to her concern, and she intensified her exercise.

Her two guards, the morning shift, carried out their duty with unusual interest, lusting after their prisoner, as usual. Only one guard was needed for the job, but extra caution was necessary in this situation, so two were scheduled each eight-hour shift to keep watch on each other as well as the prisoner. Every guard on duty looked forward to the work. She was a pleasure to watch even when she was asleep. Her beauty was stunningly innocent yet sensual. She wore no makeup but still looked like a supermodel or international movie star. She was sexy without pretense, fresh and natural. Her exercise dance was downright erotic. Both guards were watching sweat roll from Gabriella's cheeks all the way down the front of her t-shirt. To her guards, she looked as they might imagine she would look after a night of violent lovemaking.

Downstairs in the mahogany-paneled library of his Clarke County estate, Gabriella's host, Anthony Arturo, a.k.a. Joe Arthur, felt secure knowing that she was safely locked inside the main guest suite. Even if the Colombians and the FU Crew started shooting each other, he would make sure the Don's daughter was safe. He did business with all parties in this dispute. He would keep her safe until the ransom was paid. He could not release her until all terms of the arrangement were met. After this ugly episode, no matter the outcome, he would still be doing business with both groups. Nevertheless, he was worried about the missing money. It was obvious to him that Michael Rowe had an accomplice. Surely, a scheme of this magnitude could not be pulled off without help. At the top of the list of suspects was Stump Anderson, the unfortunate pilot. But he had been ruled out after brutal interrogation. Certainly, it wasn't Michael's wife. She was back in Colombia and oblivious to anything except cooking, cleaning, and trying to have children.

On the other hand, maybe Roscoe Harris was right. Roscoe was convinced that a local hiker or runner with a large dog had stumbled on the money, maybe accidentally. Roscoe based his theory on footprints and other evidence at the scene. Arthur thought about the situation, doubting that it could be that simple. Arthur's mind was in overdrive, thinking, *Michael was up to no good. Michael had hidden a van, big enough to hold all that cash. So obviously, he meant to take it. Who was in it with him? Who else besides Stump was close to Michael? Could it really be some stranger with a big dog?*

Roscoe was so sure of the big dog theory that he asked everyone to back off plans for a second replacement payment. Arthur didn't like it, but he had to wait for Roscoe. It was their only lead.

It did not take the deputy long to search the county dog license files. He was good at computer searches and analyzing files and documents.

Chapter 20

Roscoe had four good leads, all dog owners located within easy walking distance of the Fancy Fruit Farm. All suspects were living on or near Merriman's Lane. He had just returned to his police cruiser when his radio blurted out, "All units west of Interstate 81, suspected multiple homicides at the Glaize farmhouse, Fancy Fruit Farm, corner of Cedar Creek and Merriman's Lane, ambulances on the way."

Roscoe tore out of the Frederick County Courthouse parking lot and headed to the farm. Knowing what they would find, Roscoe had to ensure that this would be his case. There was no question that he should be in charge. It was in his territory. He had done a good deal of investigation on the dead parachutist already. Due to the publicity, though, Sheriff Bill John Killian was sure to get involved. The sheriff was a born politician that loved the limelight. No matter, Roscoe knew he could deal with the sheriff. It just made his work a little more complicated. Maybe, just maybe, he would earn a piece of the ransom money for his efforts in finding the idiot who was stupid enough to think he could get away with it. Roscoe called Frederick County central dispatch, advising that he was five minutes away.

On his return from West Virginia, Will MacKenzie heard sirens just before making the turn off Route 522 onto Route 37 South. Automatically, Will assumed that an ambulance was rushing to the emergency room at the hospital. As he passed the Winchester Medical Center, he realized the sirens, louder now, were going in the opposite direction from the hospital.

The sharp, loud *bleep, bleep, bleep* of the sirens seemed closer to Cedar Creek Grade, another mile or so away, and closer to his home.

Now he was sure that more than one emergency vehicle was involved, and maybe they were not ambulances, but police cars. Will was nervous since he was carrying over $100,000 in cash and several weapons. He hoped that he would not be faced with a roadblock even though both cash and weapons were hidden from view and he could easily show that he lived nearby and was on the way home. Normally, he took the Cedar Creek exit, but this time, to be safe, he pulled off onto Route 50 and approached Merriman's Lane from the north side.

Watson, recognizing familiar territory, immediately perked up and licked Will's ear with a loving affection that only a dog can give. Next, he barked, then he whined, his head turning from side to side, getting more excited with each mile. Will told him to shut up. The oversized chocolate Lab was now sitting up in the front seat of the Cherokee acting more like a human than a dog. The whole scene eased the tension, and Will laughed at himself. He was sure that police at a roadblock would first focus on the dog, then on his driver's license, his address, his story, anything else, rather than checking under the seats and the blankets in the old jeep.

He needn't have worried; there was no roadblock. But something serious was going on close by. The sirens kept up their noise. Many emergency vehicles were going down Cedar Creek, all going one way. Not one had returned with victims headed toward the hospital. Will thought this very odd and wished he had a police scanner.

Had something new been discovered regarding the body and the missing money? Perhaps they had found new tracks leading to his home. Maybe the wind had blown the new snow off the old snow. Maybe this, maybe that, he worried. Maybe he was getting paranoid.

He rehearsed his alibi. He was out of town visiting a sick uncle. His dog, Watson, went with him on the trip to Clarksburg, West Virginia. *No, he meant to say, Weston, West Virginia.* He'd stopped in Clarksburg for gas and breakfast.

If anyone asked, he would say he only heard the news about the parachutist when he got home this morning.

Will's mind was spinning with so many questions and issues that he almost ran over his mailbox pulling up to his driveway. At the last minute, he noticed the mailbox and swerved out of the way. Watson lost his balance for a moment but recovered quickly. Will realized that he had to focus on one thing at a time; otherwise, he risked making a fatal mistake.

Once in the house, he turned his energy into finding a hiding place for the $100,000, the ammunition, and the weapons. He had already disposed of the electronic transponder in Cheat Lake, near Morgantown, West Virginia.

Desperate for a hiding place, he ripped out the stuffing of two pillows and sewed the money inside. But they didn't feel right, and they seemed too heavy for pillows.

Finally, after trying several other hiding possibilities, he opened a rarely used fireplace flue in the dining room and, with some effort, found an area just large enough for the money. He put the ammunition and extra weapons in the locked custom-made gun case with his shotguns, pistols, and rifles, hoping that no one would think to check the caliber of the extra boxes of bullets. In the center of the fireplace, he positioned a stack of logs, as if ready to burn.

All the activity and Watson's continuous whining caused Will to make a frantic search through refrigerator, freezer, food cabinets, under the sink, and everywhere else, but no food was found. So he ordered a pizza from Domino's.

When the pizza delivery boy arrived, bringing two large pepperonis with extra cheese to his door, he asked if Will had heard the news about old Mose Keene and his wife, Inez. It was all over the radio, he said. Television crews were coming in from Washington DC, and Harrisonburg. A truck from channel 9 had passed him on Merriman's Lane just a minute ago.

Will turned on his radio as soon as the boy left.

Tammy Glass, an overexcited WINC reporter on the scene at the Glaize farm in Western Frederick County, repeated the shocking story of a mysterious parachutist dressed entirely in black who had apparently tried a hazardous night jump, landed in a lone oak tree on a remote pasture of the farm, and bled to death from multiple injuries. The breaking news: just forty-eight hours after finding a mysterious parachutist, several new, possibly related, deaths had just occurred. These new deaths involved the farmer who had discovered the body. The newscaster quoted Kelly Robinski, a worker on the farm who had been interrogated by a host of Frederick County authorities and was now being treated by medical personnel for psychological trauma. Robinski revealed that the elderly couple was tortured and murdered and that all the dogs had been shot.

Talking fast and out of breath, the reporter further said that Deputy Sheriff Roscoe Harris had just left the farm, apparently in a hurry, and had refused to comment on anything, indicating that the sheriff would be holding a news conference later on. WINC then broke for a commercial and returned to their regular program of country and bluegrass songs.

Roscoe knew that the situation would soon get beyond anything he could control. The FBI would surely take charge of the case now. Interstate transportation and multiple murders demanded their expertise, not to mention the publicity it would bring to the FBI. He needed to work the list of dog-owning suspects, look the owners in the eye, ask a few questions, and see if anyone acted nervous or scared. Then his unholy inquisition team could begin their method of questioning.

First on his list and closest to the location of the dead parachutist was Frank Scully, a retired druggist who owned three large dogs. Frank was a widower, and the dogs were his life. Roscoe drove slowly up the half-mile driveway to a rambling stone house that fit snugly in a grove of large evergreen trees bent low from the snow. Roscoe noticed first that there were no tracks in the driveway. Next, he noticed that no smoke was coming from any of the four chimneys that framed the center section and two of the wings. Not a dog barked when he got out of his cruiser and walked up the steps of the entrance porch. No one came to the door when he knocked. No one responded when he banged on the windows. He checked the back door and found it unlocked. The man's friends always called him Little Doc because his father was a doctor. Little Doc was a trusting soul and had never bothered to lock any door even when he was away.

Now, Roscoe was concerned. He slowly opened the door and stepped quietly into the kitchen. Not knowing what to expect, he pulled his revolver from its holster and crept from room to room. Nothing looked out of place. Finally, after checking every room, every closet, every place large enough to hold an adult-sized person, it dawned on him that Scully was away. The Scully house was empty. Driving back out to Merriman's Lane, he decided to check the mailbox. It told him that no mail had been picked up for six days.

Doc Scully dropped to the bottom of the list of Roscoe's suspects.

Next on the list was a divorced drunk by the name of Will MacKenzie. Roscoe had known Will in high school but had had little contact with him since. Living on Old Orchard Lane, Mr. Mac, as some called him, had two large dogs, a black Lab and a chocolate Lab. When he was sober, Mr. Mac walked his dogs every day at first light. Roscoe had often seen him over the past few years because he waved at every vehicle that passed down the lane. Roscoe also remembered MacKenzie's name in the paper some years ago associated with Vietnam, but he couldn't recall any specifics. The guy was a jock and a scholar in high school, and Roscoe remembered he'd been voted most likely to succeed. The thought made him laugh. *What's a drunk gonna do?* he asked himself.

This time, passing under a line of huge oak trees, driving up a winding, snow-rutted road, Roscoe was sure someone was home. Parked at the front steps was a freshly salt-stained, mud—and snow-covered Jeep Cherokee. Lights were on in the brick house. Chimney smoke lazily curled upward to a bright blue sky. Heat from the hood of the Cherokee turned snow into steam, alerting Roscoe that the vehicle had recently been in use. He rang the doorbell and immediately heard a dog barking.

Will MacKenzie answered the doorbell after waiting a minute to make sure everything was well hidden and out of sight. Will tried to act calm but could not hide the fact that he was nervous.

He was immediately relieved when he saw Roscoe Harris. "ROSCOE!" He almost shouted as if they were lifelong friends.

"Hey, Will, how you doin'?" The deputy smiled but immediately got down to business. He advised Will that he was investigating multiple homicides in the area and asked if he could come in and talk for a few minutes.

"Of course, come on in," said MacKenzie. "Would you care for a cup of coffee? I just made some fresh."

"I'd love it," replied Roscoe, a twenty-cup-a-day coffee drinker. "Mind if I use your bathroom first?"

Will pointed down a hallway toward the kitchen. "First door on your left, be my guest."

He watched as the deputy sauntered down the hall, the deputy's eyes checking right and left. When the bathroom door closed, Will absentmindedly reached to his shirt pocket for a cigarette. He patted the empty pocket several times before realizing he'd quit months ago.

Jesus, calm down, he said to himself as his heart pumped loudly in his chest.

The deputy peeked into the kitchen and the dining room on his way back to join Will. The big dog followed him everywhere he went. Somehow, Watson sensed that this man was not a friend.

"How have you been, Roscoe? I saw you a while ago, outside of Joe Arthur's gate, talking it up with a bunch of state troopers. He must have had a hell of a party." Will talked louder and faster than normal, anxious to remind the deputy that they had once been classmates.

At the mention of Joe Arthur, Roscoe flinched but quickly regained his composure. "That was several days ago, Will. Were you there? I didn't see all the guests."

"My invitation must have gotten lost in the mail. I was coming back from a visit with my old Vietnam buddies. Saw you when I crossed over the bridge." Will almost said he never got invited anywhere for at least two years but decided Roscoe probably knew. He was a good policeman.

But Roscoe wasn't interested in idle chitchat, and he got back to business.

During the next twenty minutes, Roscoe thought he'd learned all he needed to know. He concluded that Will, even though nervous and too quick with his answers, was not the person they were looking for. Two reasons brought him to this conclusion: (1) that Will had been out of town for at least three days, could prove it, and was genuinely shocked to hear the terrible news of violence and murder, and (2) almost as important, the deputy found out that Will only had one dog, not two, as shown by county dog license records, the black Lab having died almost a year ago.

Roscoe knew from the dog tracks at the scene that there were at least two or three large dogs involved, one dog could not have made all those tracks. Roscoe wrote off Will's nervousness to the terrible news and having to meet with an authority such as himself.

However, he made a mental note to call the nursing home at Weston, West Virginia to verify that Will did visit his uncle as he had claimed. Or maybe it was a Clarksburg nursing home. It seemed that MacKenzie had mentioned two places in West Virginia.

Back on Merriman's Lane now, Roscoe was down to his next to last suspect, a hunter and outdoorsman named Tucker Wilkens, who owned a travel agency in town. Wilkens was also a runner who could be seen on Merriman's Lane nearly every evening with his two black Labs. Both dogs were terrific hunters, and Wilkens spent part of every run in the adjacent orchards and woods where the dogs chased deer and whatever else they could find.

Roscoe convinced himself that Wilkens should have been the main suspect all along. Grinning with anticipation that soon the money would be found, he would earn a huge cash bonus, and his town would be rid of maniacs like Paul Xavier and Blue Eyes Smith.

The deputy sped up, without thinking, and began to skid on the slick road. Gradually, he regained control of his car and peered through his ice-covered windshield, looking for the Wilkens driveway.

Like most of the houses south of the railroad tracks, the Wilkens place sat on several acres of land amidst large oak trees and lovingly luxurious landscaping. Slowly driving up to the front porch, Roscoe couldn't help thinking that the travel agency business must be mighty profitable. Tucker's house was a huge expensive old wood-sided colonial, painted white, with dark green shutters and a matching green tin roof. Off the main section were several wings that looked as if they were added willy-nilly over a period of sixty years, with no master plan in mind. It seemed that each succeeding generation of Wilkenses had added something to the old home.

Coming up the steps to the house's main entrance, Roscoe's eyes were drawn to the shiny door knocker. It was antique brass, in the shape of a fox head, and it echoed through the halls of the old house when he banged on it. An elegant gray-haired black woman answered the door. She advised Roscoe that Mr. Tucker wasn't home. He was downtown at the travel agency. She also said that Mr. Tucker, as she called him, normally came home for lunch and a short nap every day around 1:00 p.m.

Roscoe politely asked if he could make a phone call from the house as he tried to recall the black lady's name that she had given him when she'd answered the door just two minutes earlier. Roscoe couldn't remember; he had too much on his mind. Hearing the phone at the Hampton Inn ring and ring, he longed for a cigarette.

Chapter 21

Robin Coppedge was opening the mail at the Frederick County Youth Center where she volunteered two days a week. She focused on envelopes that held the promise of donations, and she recognized some names of people who always gave. Joe Arthur, bless his heart, had sent $2,500. One envelope did not have a return address, so she saved it for last, thinking it must be full of discount coupons, since it was so fat. Her hands shook when she spilled its contents.

She screamed for the youth director, Carney Lathrop, to come quick. The envelope was full of cash, all in hundred-dollar bills. There was no note.

Only one clerk was on duty at the Hampton Inn, and she was busy. Her name was Karen, but everyone called her Bebe. She could handle three jobs simultaneously. When she wasn't busy, she would make work. She could not sit still, had to be going full speed ahead all the time. Everyone had decided to check out at the same time, so she let the phone ring. Finally, after the twelfth ring, she turned her back on an anxious guest and answered the phone. Apologizing profusely to her lengthening checkout line, she transferred the call to Mr. Baldi in room 201.

One of the guests in line was an elegantly dressed tall woman whom she'd seen going in and out of the inn at various times. The woman had been asking questions about a man she was looking for in Winchester.

Angelo was impatient and irritable—the wait had been unbearable—especially due to Blue, who had been bugging Angelo for a girl. Angelo Baldi knew every prostitute worth knowing between West Virginia and Washington. After all, he was in the business, yet he delighted in telling Blue that he was not a pimp and suggested that he could always play with himself.

What a welcome relief the phone call from Roscoe was. It sounded like this mess could be wrapped up this afternoon. Roscoe wanted all three at the Wilkens house on Merriman's Lane at 1:00 p.m. sharp, dressed in their best FBI suits, ready for a serious interrogation.

In room 203, Paul Xavier crossed himself when he got the message. His word and the word of his patron were at stake. He was also concerned about Gabriella and her impact on the Don's health. Subconsciously too, the treatment of Gabriella was a concern. Throughout his life, Paul had protected Gabriella from men like himself. Since her kidnapping, she had been at the mercy of nothing but such men.

Paul was a rigidly methodical and carefully patient man. He checked his weapons first and then proceeded in an orderly fashion to dress in his dark blue suit, white shirt, and nondescript red-and-white-striped tie. The tie reflected an absence of taste coupled with Paul's inability to match color. He was much more concerned with strapping the ice pick to his ankle and holstering his sixteen-shot semiautomatic black Beretta snugly against his shoulder. In spite of Angelo's plea for urgency, he never hurried.

In room 205, prior to receiving his call from Angelo, Blue Eyes was in a psychopathic state. More and more, he found himself thinking about how to kill Paul and Angelo, thinking about ways to make their last day on earth as painful as possible. The nerve of Angelo to suggest that he, a ladies' man of renown in DC, use his hands for sex. Angelo, that fat Italian slob, would pay, by god. Paul, the little grease ball, would also die a slow death, trying to deceive him.

They both talked down to him, acted like he was a dumb, black-ass street punk. All his life, Blue had suppressed the fact that his mother and father were educated in America's finest Ivy League schools. Blue was much more than street-smart; he had learned to read before he attended kindergarten. Blue had never been charged with a crime; he was so smart. So angry now, he had worked up another headache. Lately, he seemed to get a headache every day. Two Excedrin would fix the headache, and when this fiasco was over, he would fix the two condescending bigots he'd been forced to deal with.

But for now, the call from Angelo broke the psychotic spell. Blue dressed quickly and focused on the job he was sent to do: pick up and deliver the multi-million-dollar ransom and get the respect that he and his FU Crew deserved.

Within fifteen minutes of Roscoe's call, all three had dressed, armed themselves, and were on their way to Merriman's Lane one more time. Angelo drove, with Paul in the front passenger seat. As usual, Blue was in the back, fantasizing about popping the two as they drove west through the town of Winchester. All three wore dark suits, white shirts, and, except for Blue, conservative ties.

Their images of what an FBI agent looked like were all based on what they'd seen on television. Not one had seen an agent up close or in person. Blue's tie was custom-made in Italy and cost more than the entire outfits of the other two men combined.

Taking his time not to speed, not to draw unwanted attention, Angelo was excited and hungry. After all, it was lunchtime, and his belly kept making strange sounds, reminding him of the hour. His hunger interrupted thoughts of finally bringing the ransom home and ending the nightmare these two had brought to his quiet town. Paul was all business, thinking about Gabriella and the healing effect her return would have on his don. Blue wanted to finish this thing too; the sooner he could, he would teach these guys some respect.

It didn't matter. The three men looked like they were going to a funeral.

Deputy Sheriff Roscoe Harris was sitting in his patrol car in the parking lot of James Wood High School facing Amherst Street on Route 50. The well-marked sheriff's vehicle pointed slightly toward town with the motor running. Roscoe was waiting and watching for his worst nightmare, the three men who required his services again. Slowly, he took a last drag on the cigarette. It was deep and satisfying, and he immediately lit another. Good God! How he had missed a smoke. Eight years since he quit. Eight years! Yet the events of the past few days had broken his resolve. He would have killed himself if not for the cigarettes.

During the ten minutes waiting for their car, he had caused traffic in both directions to slow by an average of fifteen miles per hour.

Roscoe flicked his lights on and pulled out in front of the three well-dressed men in their rented black Buick sedan. Slowly, trying not to draw attention to their little convoy, he led the way. Taking a left on Merriman's

Lane, the two cars cautiously approached the turnoff to the Wilkens home. Just a few minutes earlier, Roscoe had seen Tucker Wilkens drive past on his way home for lunch, looking as content as a man could be.

Merriman's Lane was almost deserted. No one saw the cars as they made a slow, deliberate left turn up Tucker's heavily wooded driveway.

With Deputy Harris officially taking the lead, the four men tramped up the front porch steps. Roscoe rang the bell, and after a short wait, the formal ageless black maid, whose name Roscoe had forgotten, answered. She invited them in and immediately called Mr. Tucker, advising him that he had official visitors. Tucker Wilkens, resplendent in striped, buttoned-down shirt, with his customary bow tie, Southern gentleman that he was, invited them all to lunch.

Mary, he called her, was more than his maid; she was his butler, cook, house sitter, and family friend for forty-eight years, doing every task with a motherly touch. Mary subtly expressed her displeasure at the unexpected lunch by slamming the refrigerator door and rattling pots and pans.

Roscoe thanked Tucker but declined the luncheon invitation, much to Angelo's disappointment. He introduced his "FBI" colleagues and, at the same time, asked Mary—thank God he now knew her name—to wait in the kitchen and advised that he would wait outside.

Tucker, ever the gentleman, offered the three "agents" a drink and advised that he normally had a martini every day prior to having lunch. The men said, "No thanks," advising that they could not drink on the job. Angelo said that if a beer was available, he would join Tucker so he would not drink alone. Both Paul and Blue frowned at Angelo but did not say anything. Roscoe excused himself and went outside where snow had begun to fall. As he lit up another cigarette, Roscoe noticed how quiet it was on Merriman's Lane, not even a bird chirping. It must be a nice place to live, very peaceful.

Gently and patiently, Paul took the lead in questioning Tucker, asking him if he knew about the dead parachutist or the Keenes, God rest their souls. Had he been walking his dogs in the neighborhood?

Tucker Wilkens was a fourth-generation heir to a squandered fortune that, over the last one hundred years, had dwindled to a few million, enough to live comfortably in Winchester, Virginia. Tucker carried himself with perfect posture whether sitting or standing, riding a horse or driving a car. He was always well dressed, almost never without a tie. He grew up in a family that "dressed" for dinner, black tie for the men and evening gowns for the ladies. Like his father and grandfather, he was tall, thin, tanned, and fit. His face was angular, with a beaked nose jutting out almost as far as his chin. Sharp blue eyes gave the further impression of intelligence; they darted around and appeared to miss nothing.

He sat upright in his chair, sipping his martini as if he had been the one who had called this meeting. Calmly, he considered Paul's questions as if he were an authority on the subject. Nodding his head yes, Tucker advised, he knew all about the recent killings.

Yes, he had walked his dogs on both days that people had died, but he had seen nothing unusual.

Tucker then observed that while he was walking the dogs yesterday morning, when he heard all that "siren racket," his first thought was that there had been an accident on Cedar Creek where it crossed under the 37 bypass.

He reminded them that he had been against the Route 37 when it was proposed. It was ten, or maybe, eleven years ago, but even back then, he knew that a bypass would just bring more traffic into the neighborhood. "But the damn developers had the clout, don't you see, and they went ahead and built the bypass anyway."

He continued to sound off on the bypass, saying that other neighbors had objected too, but collectively, "They just didn't have the clout!" His fist slamming into a side table as he made his point.

The martini worked into his thoughts, and with eyes turning upward, focusing on the old parquet ceiling tiles, Tucker started to talk about the piddly amount of money the state paid him for taking some of his land. "Damned imminent domain laws for the bypass," he said, but Paul interrupted.

"What do you know about the killings?"

Tucker then proceeded to talk about where he was yesterday and the day before, how often he took his dogs for a walk in the neighborhood, which was "every damned day."

"How strange the Keenes were—never socialized with anybody, just kept to themselves, acted like the farm was theirs," he said and added, "with the Glaizes off to Florida for so long each year, no wonder something bad happened."

After about fifteen minutes of this pleasant conversation, Blue had had enough. Standing up suddenly, Blue shouted in Tucker's face, "Enough of this busybody country shit. Where's the money? We know you got it! You better start talking!"

At this outburst, Mary ran in the living room asking, "Mr. Tucker, Mr. Tucker, wha's the matter? Wha's wrong?"

Blue turned as quick as a cat and grabbed her by a hunk of her stringy gray hair. Cursing her for interfering, he dragged her across the length of the large living room. Her heels marked a trail through an old Oriental carpet that had been in the family for three generations. She bounced over a room divider as Blue turned into the formal dining room where he slammed her into an antique captain's chair. Without a second thought, he shot her in the mouth.

The sudden silence magnified the memory of her screams and Blue's curses.

Outside, Roscoe was sweating even though the temperature remained below freezing, wondering whether any of the neighbors heard the commotion. He lit his twenty-second cigarette of the day. Just when he thought all was quiet, he heard the sound of a truck coming up the long wooded driveway.

Chapter 22

The Safeway was busy. Its parking lot was full of snowbound shoppers who had waited days to get out. Will was there even though he'd been out. He needed eggs, bacon, milk, bread, dog food, and other basics. When Sue Ellen had first left him, all he usually bought was meat, potatoes, and whiskey. Now he was more concerned about nutrition, and he bought salads, pasta, cereal, fruit, and vegetables even though he was still a meat and potatoes guy.

Watson sat patiently in the front seat, and Will left the engine running as he headed for the store entrance. Something out of the corner of his eye caught his attention. A man and woman in shabby clothes were going through the dumpster on the corner of the property. They were filling an old shopping cart with whatever they could find.

When Will returned to his jeep with arms full of groceries, the old couple was still there. He watched as a bagboy from the store came out and shouted at the couple. "Get out of there, or we call the POLICE!" The bag boy stared at the pair until they started moving. "Leave the cart!"

Sadly, the man and the woman, heads down in shame, left the scraps that they had collected and walked away.

Will took one of the grocery bags out of the backseat—the one with bread, milk, eggs, and bacon—and stuffed a packet of cash underneath the food. He ran after the couple. "Hey, maybe you can use this? I have enough." And he gave them the bag.

Sad eyes and dirty faces looked at Will, saying, "Thank you, mister." When they looked inside, they were so excited with the food that they didn't see their benefactor drive off.

Tucker Wilkens was stunned! He was a peaceful man, an usher at the Episcopal Church. Who were these strangers in his house? How could they do such things? He was afraid to face the maniac who had pulled a gun. Drool formed in the corner of Blue's mouth as he turned back to Tucker. "You happy now? You happy now? Look what you made me do! We not playin' no mo' games, no mo' bullshit, ya heah? Where's the money? We know you got it!"

Tucker tried to stand up, but Paul shoved him down roughly. Angelo stepped behind and held Tucker down with one beefy hand. Tucker couldn't see his maid, but her blood was all over the black man called Blue. All three strangers were in his face. All three had lost any pretense of being civil. Blue slapped him hard across the bridge of his nose, causing a massive nosebleed. Angelo pulled out a pistol, stuck it in his eye, and simultaneously, Paul stabbed the chair just an inch from his crotch with an ice pick.

Tucker screamed, pissed in his pants, and began crying hysterically, saying whatever came to his mind. "I have to go to the bathroom. Look at this chair, you've ruined the fabric. Don't hurt me. I'm not playing any game. I don't know any games. I have money, lots of money. No need for any more. I'll do anything you want. I have over a hundred thousand in the bank. I can get it in a matter of hours. I'm a multimillionaire. I inherited it from my grandmother, got more money in investments, but it will take time. You got to give me some time to get it."

"I'm gonna blow your fuckin' brains outta your fuckin' face!" Blue Eyes screamed. "Tell me now. You got no time left!"

Angelo grabbed Blue's gun hand. "Asshole! You crazy? Let Paul do it. Paul will make him talk. Kill 'im an' we got nothin'. Back off!"

Paul pulled his ice pick out of Tucker's damaged chair, ripping the rich fabric from back to front. Paul then pushed Angelo's gun away and looked Tucker dead in the eye. With brutal coldness, he said, "Guess you figured out we're not the FBI"

Tucker nodded but was too scared to say anything. He looked from Blue to Paul to Angelo, eyes darting about like a cornered rat. With a movement so quick, no one saw the ice pick come down on Tucker's hand, nailing it to the arm of the antique chair. Like he was going to be crucified in his most expensive chair. It took a moment for the shock to wear off and the pain to reach Tucker's brain. His scream caused Roscoe to burn his finger lighting another Marlboro outside in the driveway. Roscoe had his eyes totally focused on the Federal Express truck now coming up Wilkens's driveway. He was sure the driver had heard the scream.

Angelo again moved behind Tucker and held him firmly down in the chair, pinning his free arm back and holding his face up by the chin.

Paul moved around Angelo and said, "Now, we ask you, where is the cash you got from the parachutist—you know, the dead man that your dogs found?"

Tucker, tears in his eyes, shook his head in spite of Angelo's grip and denied any knowledge of the dead man and any money. Again, he offered all his money, repeated that he could raise more than $1,000,000 in a day, more than that if they would give him time. He said his gold Visa card had a $75,000 credit limit and at least seventy thousand of that was available. They could take the card too. When he begged to see a doctor, the ice pick came down on his right knee. Tucker's reflex almost pulled him free from Angelo's grip. Blue wanted to shoot the son-of-a-bitch then and there; he paced back and forth behind the others, all the while wildly waving his pistol, intent on showing this rich turd who was boss.

The ice pick quickly moved up Tucker's right nostril, far enough to cause more blood to erupt. Desperately thinking of what he had to give these guys, Tucker remembered the cash box in the dining room liquor cabinet. The two-hundred-year-old cabinet included a hidden compartment that once held scotch whiskey. Sometime, during the early stages of the Civil War, the secret drawer had been converted to a safe. It served as a convenient hiding place when Winchester changed hands scores of times back then, and the family had stored precious items there ever since. But his head ached, and the pain was increasing, growing, coming from several sources at once; and he couldn't get the words out.

Gradually, Paul pressed the pick upward. He raked the pick from side to side, cutting tissue as he went. Between screams, he heard words that sounded like "liquor" or "cabinet" or "dining room." But the man's words were difficult to understand. The pain and fear had finally burst Tucker's genetically weak heart, and he slumped in his chair, limp and no longer feeling the pain. Blood poured out of his nose and mouth, ruining his bow tie, soiling his freshly ironed white shirt, covering his fancy herringbone trousers, moving down to his highly polished leather shoes, and finally mixing into the multicolored patterns of his ancient Oriental carpet.

Paul asked Angelo and Blue to check every cabinet, go through the dining room, check the liquor bottles, ransack the whole house, and see if they could find anything. "Make sure you find his safe deposit box keys."

Angelo said, "If he put the money in banks, he would need several keys and probably several banks."

Then Paul felt Tucker's pulse; although he couldn't detect a sign of one, he tied him up anyway.

At that moment, they heard the crunch of gravel in the driveway as a truck skidded to a stop at the front porch entrance. Federal Express was making a delivery.

Roscoe was frustrated and scared. The truck driver never had a chance. Standing over his body, gun in hand, Blue looked like he was ready to use it again. Angelo and Paul had their guns out. They were ready too. The situation was quickly getting out of control. Roscoe had to do something, so he stepped between them and spoke, all the while looking directly at Blue. "All right, guys, no need to panic. We have two more dog owners that need to be talked to, but it'll wait 'til tomorrow. We all could use some rest."

"I ain't tired, and I ain't panicked. Let's finish it now." Blue's voice was threatening.

"It has to be planned, Blue. This thing has top police attention. We gotta plan for it. Tomorrow, we can finish, but I need the time to plan." He was almost out of options, and he needed time to think about his own hide.

Blue was shaking his head, rejecting this delay, when Paul said, "Tomorrow, if we don't end it tomorrow, we'll replace the money and add another couple of million for your time."

Angelo spoke up in agreement, and that ended the argument. They agreed to return to the Hampton Inn and await Roscoe's call.

Roscoe watched them leave. Looking down at the poor dead truck driver, he realized that he was about to sign someone else's death warrant.

In Clarke County, Virginia, several miles east of Merriman's Lane, lunch was being served to an increasingly depressed Gabriella. Too much time had gone by. *Where was her father?* She considered flirting with the one who brought her food. Maybe she could escape. The man who brought the food introduced himself as Roberto and said he had cooked it. He was younger than Gabriella, trying to act tough and sympathetic at the same time. He came every day at lunch and dinner. While he was with her, the other two guards took their break. His English was rough. He spoke slowly to make sure he was understood. He had come to the United States from Sicily only recently, being a son of Arturo's first cousin. He seemed anxious for Gabriella to like the food. Every day, it was something different—pasta and cheese in a variety of sauces; chicken, fish, veal, salads with Italian dressings; all with homemade garlic bread. Obviously, she was being treated in a special way, not like a normal prisoner.

Her other guards looked at her with open lust. There was no mistaking their intentions. She decided this cook was harmless and thought there may come a time when she needed a friend.

She pretended to like the food he offered. Normally, she would have preferred lighter meals, with fewer calories and more protein. Eating heavier foods had never given her a weight problem due to her passionate pursuit of exercise. But her current incarceration seemed to create an insatiable hunger, and she ate everything put before her with gusto.

Her "friendly cook" thought he was in love with his captive. Gabriella was accustomed to this attraction from men. It's why she left Colombia in the first place: to get away from Diego. *Ugh!* The thought of him made her flesh crawl, and her mood changed. She stopped eating, left half of her food on the plate.

When the young cook left, his sad face reflected a belief that his angel was not pleased with the meal.

As soon as he left, two guards reentered her room. Although both guards fantasized about sex with Gabriella, one was now planning how he could be left alone with her. Five minutes was all he wanted, thinking of nothing else, blocking out any thought of consequences, overcome with lust.

He was the one who reminded her of Diego.

"SPCA SAVED FROM CLOSING!" read the headline in section B of the *Winchester Star*. The article went on to say, "Anonymous donor leaves $20,000 in cash just two days after the charity announced it was going to have to close its doors due to a decrease in funding. 'The cash, coupled with a generous donation from Clarke County philanthropist Joe Arthur, has given us new life,' gushed Director Fran Dearing." Arthur, smiling, was pictured with Ms. Dearing behind a desk covered in hundred-dollar bills.

Chapter 23

Roscoe Harris was tired. Up all night, active duty all day. He needed rest, but the adrenaline pouring through his body wouldn't let him relax. There was just too much going on. He had been home for only a few minutes when he heard a car pull up in his driveway.

He dreaded seeing anyone. The last couple of days had been a nightmare. As a policeman, he had seen his share of killings and violence, but nothing compared to the terrifying brutality so casually dished out by the three strangers he was currently serving. He was in too deep. Maybe he could get his hands on some of that ransom money. Maybe he could leave town and start a new life. He thought, *Shit, maybe bullfrogs could fly too.*

Then the doorbell rang just as he was pouring a second drink and looking in his empty refrigerator for something to eat. His visitor brought him out of his depression. A wonderful, totally unexpected surprise brought forth a long missing smile to his face. It was Edna Cline at his front door, her arms wrapped around a bag and a basket.

She was wearing a full-length fake fur, leather boots, and purple knit gloves that matched her hat and scarf. The devious smile on her face lit up the room.

Her brownish blond hair was cut short in a bob that framed a still pretty face. Even with the extra ten pounds, she looked like the high school cheerleader she once was, with those rosy cheeks indented with dimples, bright white and perfectly matched teeth, and big brown eyes with long lashes. It made Roscoe wonder why her dentist ex-husband had left.

Roscoe had dated Edna in high school when he had been a star football player for Handley. Their romance never got past the heavy petting stage even though both of them wanted to do it. They never resumed their relationship after high school because Roscoe went into the army and Edna went to college where she found her dentist. But working with Roscoe in his search for dog licenses had stirred up an old flame.

Strutting through the door, she handed Roscoe the basket. "I thought you looked worn out the other day and needed a good dose of home cooking."

He set the basket down on a kitchen counter with a smile on his face. "What's for dinner?"

At that, she opened her fake fur, put her hands on her hips, and pushed out her ample chest. "Breast of tit! I hope you're hungry!"

Roscoe's jaw dropped, and for a moment, he just stared at the delicious sight before him. Edna was wearing nothing but a shear "teddy" underneath the fake fur. The outline of her full breasts mesmerized him. Still stunned, he took it all in, lusting at the whole picture, from head to boots. He could see nipples and pubic hair clearly through the delicate garment. His eyes soaked up every curve of her still firm body.

He joined with her in a rush, moving hands to both breasts, and kissed her roughly. The mesh of the "teddy" tore with his touch. She moaned and pressed close against him. "It's been five years since I've been with a man, Roscoe, no need to take your time."

The two of them frantically did their best to undress. Roscoe started with his belt and then his buttons. Edna helped him out, her hands moving as quickly as a short-order cook, unbuckling his belt, unzipping his fly, and pulling down his pants. Roscoe, in his haste, fumbled with the buttons on his shirt, finally managing to rip himself out of it. Edna pulled him down on top of her in the middle of the kitchen floor, losing the shreds of her "teddy" in the process. She guided Roscoe until their bodies joined together and they moved as one.

Up and down, rolling around, they rutted like two animals; she with her boots on, Roscoe with his shoes on, pants around his ankles, limiting his leg movement. Edna was the first to climax, but her release came in a series of spasms that lasted through his, which came in one full, powerful surge.

He screamed her name in her ear as the release built up to an uncontrollable climax. She emitted a deep growl in her own sexual world, not giving anything to him, immersed in her own pleasure. They continued to stay locked to each other, his feet still entangled in his underwear and trousers. She had curled her legs around him so that the heels of her boots jabbed into his buttocks, holding him down and in, maintaining every last ounce of his rigidity.

For a while, they just lay there, not speaking, until he broke the silence. "What happened to foreplay?"

In a husky voice, she said, "We had enough of that twenty-three years ago. Didn't you know that no meant yes, back then?"

He made a face and smiled, held her close, not wanting to break the spell, and then he began to stir again within her. Since they both had had enough of the kitchen floor, they moved into the bedroom, this time with more patience. Roscoe first sat up and removed his shoes and pants and underwear, before helping Edna pull off her boots. The two then stood up, pulled each other close, and felt the urge rising again.

Neither one in a hurry, they took their time, kissing, fondling, touching with fingers and tongues, naked in the middle of Roscoe's austere bedroom. There, except for the bed, the focus was on an oversized wide-screen color television mounted high in an antique armoire. The room needed a woman's touch, but neither was interested in interior decorating. Many long years had passed.

Afterward, they took a long shower together; washing each other's private parts, gingerly now, massaging everything down to slow motion. Out of the shower, drying each other with Roscoe's not-so-soft towels, only then did they remember the dinner that Edna had brought. Roscoe asked Edna to check the refrigerator for a bottle of wine or a beer, whichever she thought would go best with the dinner. She selected a six-pack of Miller Lite, and left the Naked Mountain chardonnay to continue cooling for another time.

She was positive that there would be another time. Roscoe brought the heavy wicker basket of food into the bed and was delighted to see its contents: home-fried chicken, home-baked biscuits, homemade coleslaw, deviled eggs, country-canned tomatoes and beans, and a homemade apple pie.

Wow! Roscoe thought, first dessert, and now dinner.

Chapter 24

Will was awakened by the piercing wails of emergency vehicles on Merriman's Lane. As he was heading toward the bathroom the phone rang. It was Deputy Harris calling.

"Hey, Will, you up? Sorry about the early call, but we gotta move quick. Can I come talk to you one more time? Sumthin' new to tell ya, maybe I can jog your memory?"

"Roscoe, of course I'm up. What's so important that it can't wait 'til daylight?"

The deputy told Will that he was just giving him a heads-up, that it would be at least another hour before he came, and, by the way, had he heard about another murder on Merriman's Lane? "Poor Tucker Wilkens, his maid, and his dog. It leaked out on the radio. Too many people in Frederick County don't have nothin' better to do than listen to the police radio frequency. Seems like they cain't wait to hear bad news. They cain't keep their mouths shut either 'cause somebody called the radio station."

If the police were checking up on him again, Will wondered, then the bad guys must have his name as well. "Dogs" triggered his suspicions too. Why did they kill the dogs? Deputy Sheriff Harris knew he had a dog, a large dog. Harris had been surprised his black Lab had died. Both the Keenes and Wilkens had been killed along with their dogs. Why? Why the dogs?

Dog tracks were all over the parachutist's death scene.

Will thought originally that the snowstorm had covered up Watson's tracks. It must have snowed at least ten inches after he had left the scene. The tracks had been a concern even though he had taken a circuitous route. *Were the tracks now exposed?*

149

No way could they trace the tracks to his house, not after the storm. Otherwise, why hadn't they come direct to his house instead of the Keenes? The Keenes' dogs had found the parachutist well after the storm had begun. They had three or four dogs, and they had destroyed any trace of Watson. Also, their tracks had led directly to the Glaize farmhouse.

A nudge from Watson interrupted his thoughts, first a cold nose, then a few sloppy licks on his cheek. Watson was now whining to go out for his morning jaunt. Once the dog started, he would not stop until distracted by food or until out the door they went. Maybe he should go back to the scene, following his route that day? At least, he could say he was just curious. He could also check for tracks and, at the same time, create some new tracks; say he was just walking his dog?

Nah, I'd better go toward the lane, stay away from that field. No sense in giving anybody ideas, he said to himself.

Dressing for the cold outdoors took a little longer now that he carried two pistols. *Got to be prepared,* he thought. The Glock fit nicely in the parachutist's ankle holster, and the Beretta would remain available and hidden within the hand muffler of his sweat suit. Just to be cautious, he carried an extra clip for the Beretta in his hip pocket and off they went. He felt the killers would come for him soon. These guys would not give up.

With every step, he looked around. He turned left, right, and quickly checked behind, not wanting anyone to sneak up on him. The last time he had this feeling was in Vietnam.

Will had guessed right. Three minutes into their run, he noticed a dark-colored car sitting at the side of the road across from an apple orchard, and then it began to move. Something was unusual about its movement. The car was going very slow for this time of morning. *It could be a police car,* he thought. The black sedan was cruising north on Merriman's Lane toward the hospital, coming his way. At first, Will couldn't see how many were in the car. Gradually, they came into his vision.

There were three of them, two in the front and one in the back. He didn't recognize the car or any of the men.

Angelo was driving, Paul in the front passenger seat, and Blue rode in the back. By now, there was so much distrust among the three that no one wanted to ride in the front. They cruised by Old Orchard Lane a couple of times and then stopped halfway up it, situated where they could watch for anyone, coming or going. All three were fully alert, eyes constantly moving, first focused on the lane leading to MacKenzie's house, then looking from side to side, through the barren apple orchard, past the green packing shed.

Paul spotted him first, rounding the bend on the road coming down toward their car. They waited for the heavily clad jogger to reach them. A flash of chocolate behind the packing shed got their attention. Paul thought it was a deer. "No," Angelo said, "it was a big dog."

Roscoe had told them that this was their man. "He walks every day at dawn with that dog. Watch out for it; it's as big as a bear."

But their collective attention was focused on the man, not the dog. All three stared anxiously as the man approached. Angelo had his hands on the steering wheel; Paul patted the ice pick strapped to his leg just to make sure it was there; Blue noticed that the blanket that covered his shotgun had pulled off slightly, exposing the stock. Blue covered the stock with his foot in case the jogger got too close.

Not one other car could be seen. Not on the lane and not on the Route 37 bypass a quarter-mile away. No joggers in sight either; everything lonely and quiet. Angelo lowered his driver's window. Paul and Blue prepared to open their doors. Not yet though, they didn't want to alarm this guy.

Will was now within fifty yards of the car. He noticed the "H" prefix on the license plate, indicating that it was a rental. The sedan had pulled off Merriman's Lane, and it now faced him head on. The driver's window was down as he could see the steam from the driver's breath coming out and disappearing into the cold air.

Slowing down, both hands covering the Beretta inside the muffler of his sweat suit, Will knew that time was up. *No more cat and mouse, no more hoping that he wouldn't be found out.* He racked the slide back to chamber the first round. His right thumb automatically flicked the safety. It was already off. Sweat broke out on his forehead even though he was only a few minutes into his run. He could see all three men clearly now. They were wearing suits and ties, but all were alert, looking at him. One man was in the back. Two men were in the front, the driver a big beefy man, the other much smaller. They seemed out of place and nervous.

Will was barely running when the driver shouted, "Hey! Can you give us some help with directions? We're lost."

As MacKenzie came up to the driver's window, the driver reached for his pistol. The big man casually gripped the pistol and was swinging it around and up when Will shot him in the face at point-blank range.

Paul was momentarily trapped in the passenger seat. His door was locked. His left hand held his pistol, and his right hand tried to work the door handle. The extra split seconds that it took to unlock the door seemed like an eternity. Paul felt a pain in his left shoulder and arm; his pistol was out. It seemed heavy, and he couldn't hold it, the pain too strong. Something in his neck caused him to turn quickly, and he bumped his head on the window. Blood warmed the front of his neck and chest.

Everything was in slow motion now. He wanted to open the door. He wanted to move quickly. He wanted the gun in position to fire. But his body wouldn't do what his mind was telling it to do. He looked directly at the jogger who had somehow pulled a gun. The jogger wasn't supposed to have a gun. The jogger wasn't supposed to know who they were. *How did the jogger know to expect them?* This was Paul's last thought as the jogger's fourth bullet hit him in the eye and exploded through the back of his head. Brains, blood, and bone plastered the window around the bullet hole on the passenger side.

In the back, Blue had gotten out, shotgun in hand, and at least two bullets from the jogger had missed him. Keeping down, using the sedan as a shield, Blue worked his way around to the front of the car. Will didn't see the shotgun but saw where the tall guy was going. Will wasn't sure but thought he had nine, maybe eight bullets left in the Beretta. Soon he would have to choose between the Glock, or reloading the Beretta using the extra clip. His hand was getting cold until he used it to steady the warm pistol. Then he saw the shotgun and, in the next second, heard its roar. He also heard a growl and a "What the fuck?"

Then he heard more deep growls and a scream.

Watson had come from nowhere. The dog's first leap had struck between the man's shoulder blades. Forelegs fully extended, massive paws like twin hammers, his 120-pound body launched from a dead run, Watson had knocked the man down just as he fired.

The sudden attack was the second surprise of the morning, and it had thrown off the aim of the shotgun. Blue, now on his back, was trying to grab the dog's collar with one hand and bring the shotgun around with the other to blow its head off. Watson bit him on the shoulder, then the ear, and then the neck, tearing with ferocious effort. Will came around quickly and fired at the only target available, the man's right knee. It shattered and jerked, and the man let go of the shotgun to grab his knee. Will kicked the gun away and shot the man again in the same knee, but this time through his hand, which was holding the knee. The scream and the shot were such that Watson stopped for a second to look up. Watson had blood on his nose and down the sides of his jaws. A huge rip in the man's neck was pouring blood. Grabbing his collar with an iron grip, Will used all his strength to pull the dog off the man. The dog's lips were curled back, revealing powerful teeth eager to tear back into this enemy. The growls were deep and continuous, muscles tense, body shaking, total focus on the man now holding his neck with his good hand and crying.

"Help me, you gotta help me. That fuckin' animal ripped a hole in me. I'm bleedin' to death."

Will kept his pistol pointed at the man's head, knowing the man could still be dangerous. Watson wanted to kill, to finish what he had begun, pulling more strongly now at the hold on his collar. But Will needed answers and looked directly into the man's teary eyes. "Who are you?" he said. "Why did you try to kill me? What do you want?"

The man tried to rise up, trying to be tough. "Motherfucker! I need a doctor! Doctor NOW! Goddammed dog . . . it hurts. My neck hurts!"

POP! was the instant reaction as MacKenzie shot him in the other knee, and the new pain caused his head to snap up. Watson almost jerked out of his grip at the sound.

"Answer the question, tough guy, and then I might get you a doctor!" shouted Will.

"Who are you? Why are you after me? Answer now, or I let the dog go!"

"No, no, no more dog, put 'im on a leash, somebody oughta shoot that dog. You got the money. We know you got it. Fuckin' dog found it, that's what . . . fuckin' dog."

"What money? Whose money?" Will was bending low, speaking directly into the man's ear.

Blood was seeping through the man's fingers; both hands on his neck now, forgetting about his shattered knees. "Doctor . . . need to stop the pain!"

"Tell me. Tell me why you came for me!" Will now screaming in the man's face.

"MONEY! The RANSOM! You know . . . parachutist's duffle bags fulla money. Millions . . . our money, you know it's our money. You got it."

Will got between the dog and the man, looked at Watson and ordered, "STAY!"

Miraculously, the dog sat, his whole body shaking, teeth bared, the dog so close its drool fell at the man's feet.

Will let go of Watson's collar and looked directly into the man's eyes.

"What ransom? Who's ransomed? Tell me who, where, and why? Who's got 'im? Answer me. Answer me now or the dog will open so many holes in you that you'll bleed to death!"

"I *am* bleedin' t' death!" Blue finally opened up, no longer fighting to keep secrets, now willing to answer all the man's questions. In a softer voice, speaking slow, trying to answer the man, he said, "We got the bitch. Gabriella, that's her name. He'd pay anything to get her back. Don messed with us. He don't respect us. He got to show respect . . . got to respect. We the Fourth 'n' U Crew, we own DC. That's our town. Nobody mess with us in our town. Don's got to learn. He be a guest in our town. He got to do business with us, or he don't do business at all. Money don't mean shit, don't mean shit. We got more money'n we know what to do with. Fuck it. You get me a doctor now. I tol' you what's goin' down. Get me some help NOW! MOTHERFUCKER! Need a doctor, now . . . please?"

Blue was losing his tough-guy street persona, feeling the strength flowing out of his body, and was now on the brink of begging.

"I got three more questions, and then you get a doctor: Where's the girl? Where's this Gabriella?" Will recognized the man was losing strength, so he also began speaking softly as if caring for his health.

"On the farm, goddammit . . . she's on the farm, Arturo's farm, you know Anthony Arturo? He the big man here, he the man, cocaine man, got all you want . . . At his farm. No wait . . . Anthony Arturo don' go by that name, he ain't no farmer, an' he ain't no country gentleman like he pretend t' be. Calls himself Joe . . . livin' life as a dandy, tha's Joe, only that ain't his real name."

"Joe Arturo, that's his name?"

"No, no, fuck no. He goes by Joe Arthur; only his real name is Joseph Anthony Arturo from Philadelphia . . . Now I need HELP!"

This news was so unbelievable that Will momentarily forgot about the killer at his feet.

Of course, he knew Joe Arthur.

"HELP! DO YOU HEAR ME?"

Will still couldn't believe it. "This Joe Arthur, Joe Arturo," he asked just to make sure he had heard right, "what's the name of his farm?"

"GODDAMMIT, I think it's River Farm . . . no, not that, it's . . . it's . . . it's . . . River View Farm . . . that's it, RIVER VIEW FARM! Now help me. I'm bleedin' all over."

"I got one more question."

"QUESTION . . . You've asked me twenty questions. Jesus H. Christ . . . I've answered every fucking question."

"Who were the guys in the car with you?"

Blue, exasperated now, said, "What fuckin' difference do it make? They ain't a problem no mo'. The fat wop, his name's Angelo, works for Joe, an' he ain't no farmer either. Fat son-of a-bitch farted like a pig. The little spic is the Don's man. Speaks real slow, enunciates every word, like your ass is hard of hearing . . . talks down to you . . . watch out for the ice pick. He be good with it. Maybe not so much anymore" . . .

The man hadn't mentioned his own identity, so Will persisted. "What's your name? Where are you from?"

Blue's voice began to slur and drop in volume.

"Motherfucker! I'm gonna kill you." And Blue tried to sit up to hit his tormenter. "TAKE ME TO A DOCTOR. MY NAME IS NORTHAMPTON AMHERST SMITH, of course I'm from DC, you asshole! I'm in pain! Pain, cain't you see!"

Will pushed Watson back as he put the Beretta in Blue's mouth and pulled the trigger. "There now, doesn't that feel better? Now, I'm gonna take you to the doctor, Mr. Smith, just like I promised."

Chapter 25

MacKenzie looked around to see if anyone had heard or seen anything. Surely, the police would be patrolling the neighborhood more frequently, given all that had happened in the last few days. Not a sound could be heard except for the black sedan's engine running and now a tractor trailer moving south on 37, the tractor at least a mile away. Watson started to whine now, instinctively knowing that the danger had passed. Will reached into the front driver side door and popped the trunk lid. He unloaded all of the weapons in the trunk, including another automatic rifle, a MAC-10 submachine gun, and a variety of pistols and ammunition.

He put these and the wallets, watches, weapons, cash, and other personal items he found on each of the three bodies in an apple bin. The bin was one of many located in the green-roofed apple-packing shed just beyond the car. Will missed the ice pick carried by Paul, but he found a signet ring that belonged to Tucker Wilkens that Blue had ripped off during their last interrogation.

A car drove by on Route 37, and Will looked up, fearful that the car was on Merriman's Lane, but he was lucky. No way could someone see what he was doing from the bypass.

Using the Redskins blanket, he dragged each of the three bodies back to the trunk. Angelo was the most difficult, but MacKenzie managed. He struggled, more to keep blood off rather than having a problem lifting, but worked to get Angelo's torso in before easily swinging the legs up last. He had some stuffing to do, but the trunk of the Buick was huge and held the three bodies with room to spare. Will seemed to notice the tall man for the first time. He looked different. The man's clothes were immaculate . . . soft, leather shoes, designer tie, silk shirt, and custom-tailored suit. Each article was very expensive. Finally Will realized that the man was a mulatto . . . blue-eyed, fair-skinned, and handsome. *What an unusual look.* He thought as he got behind the wheel of the sedan and told Watson to go home.

Driving away, trunk full of bodies, Will saw his dog not going home but sniffing the ground, rooting around in the blood and sweat and debris left at the scene. Watson, moving back and forth, excited as if he were hunting a groundhog.

Will took a left on Merriman's Lane and headed for the hospital. As he turned to check for traffic, he noticed the passenger side window and its mess of blood, the bullet hole, and spattered mud on the glass. He lowered the window and hoped that no one would ever notice. Two minutes later, he was still looking around, trying not to be seen, as he parked in the doctor's parking lot at Winchester Medical Center. He gave a quick last-minute inspection inside of the car, locked it in spite of one window being down, and got out.

Rounding the trunk, he paused, looked down, and said to the man with the blue eyes, "Here we are at the hospital, just like I promised, tough guy."

There were a few shotgun pellet holes in the trunk and a piece of the right rear taillight was chipped, but otherwise, the Buick looked like it belonged in the doctor's parking lot, which was now only half-full. He kept his head down to hide his face as he jogged out of the hospital grounds. Several cars hurriedly passed him on their way to the hospital. He jumped to the side to avoid their spray of muddy snow and slush.

As he crossed Route 50 and headed south on Merriman's Lane, Will pulled the hood of his jacket on, braced against the brisk wind, and picked up his jogging pace. He was headed home but now wondered how many others would come. It wasn't over. He knew that much for sure. He felt that if these three could find him, then so could others. *How did they find him and his dog, determine his involvement? What clues did he leave?* During his interrogation of the wounded killer, he asked a host of questions, but he had been in a hurry. He didn't ask how they had found him. He didn't ask if anyone else knew about him. *Who was the Don, Gabriella's father? What did the Don do?*

The failure to ask these and other questions nagged at him as he jogged home. Thinking about these things led him to conclude that others surely knew and surely would replace those three. He had managed to surprise them. Maybe he wouldn't be able to surprise others so easily. He was right to be concerned. Others knew, and others would be coming. He considered calling the police again but, as before, changed his mind, knowing that he'd just lost that option. He dared not involve the police.

Will saw a car coming in the opposite direction. It was a blue Mercedes sedan with Virginia license plates that said "Maggie" on the rear plate. He hadn't noticed the front but thought he recognized the driver. She was a brown-haired woman, maybe a dirty blonde, wearing sunglasses, with her head held high.

Roscoe was late and frustrated because he couldn't find anyone on Merriman's Lane where they were supposed to be. He didn't see Angelo's car even when he drove around back of Will MacKenzie's house. Both of Will's cars were there, and both were covered with snow, so they hadn't been driven for a while.

Where the hell could they be? He didn't dare call Angelo on his CB radio. Those three were supposed to wrap this thing up this morning. They knew Will was home because Roscoe had called. They knew Will would walk his dog because he did it every morning like clockwork. They also knew that Will had lied about his whereabouts on the morning of the fatal jump. The Weston Nursing Home's records clearly showed that Will had arrived around noon the day after the ransom was missing rather than the day before as Will had declared.

Snow was starting to fall when Roscoe spotted a jogger in the middle of the road coming his way.

"Goddamned joggers! They think they own the road." He turned on his siren. "They ought to pay taxes for running in the middle of the road." He veered toward the center, forcing the jogger off the road, and gave him a glare. The eyes peering out of the hooded ski jacket looked familiar, but the name wouldn't come to him. Looking right and left, he drove all the way to Route 50, near the hospital, and turned around. *Goddamn Edna Cline, it's all her fault,* he thought. But he couldn't stay mad at Edna, knowing he was just as much to blame as her.

Driving hurriedly now, Roscoe wondered again, *Where the hell could those three guys be?* Merriman's Lane was only a few miles long.

Just as he was ready to turn around and retrace his route, a siren close by fired its last blast, and an ambulance tore into the medical center heading for the emergency room. Roscoe decided to investigate. Maybe his missing trio had something to do with the ambulance victim. Speeding to the emergency room, Roscoe stopped outside when he saw the person in the ambulance was a woman ready to deliver a baby.

The deputy was baffled. How could three seasoned killers just vanish? He decided to pay another visit to Will MacKenzie's house. He must be the man who has the money. He thought surely that Will was being interrogated at that very moment. Maybe their car's in MacKenzie's garage?

Driving back to MacKenzie's house, Roscoe noticed a man on Merriman's Lane with two dogs. He stopped and carefully checked them out. The dogs were too small, Scottish terriers, at least he thought that's what they were, and he asked the man their names just to be polite.

The tall, thin man beamed. "Teddy and Paddy," he said, and as he drove away, Roscoe remembered who the man was. Not his name, but the man that sometimes gave the news on the radio. He was also the man that had recently spent eight straight hours directing the area's United Way Telethon on the local cable channel. Roscoe had heard that the telethon had exceeded its goal due to an anonymous donor's gift of $50,000 in the last five minutes of the program. The donor said to look for an envelope, addressed to United Way, in the radio station's mailbox. *Why would anyone give that much money and not give his name?* Roscoe knew human nature, and that just didn't make sense.

Slightly out of breath from the run, Will turned off Merriman's Lane and up the road through the orchard to his house. No sign of Watson. Hopefully, the dog had decided to return home.

Will stopped, looked around to ensure that no one else was near, and peeked behind the packing shed. He was relieved to see that his cache was still there. He checked the road again, satisfied that nothing was moving on Merriman's Lane. A parade of cars behind a lonely tractor trailer rig slowly inched their way north, up Route 37, heading toward Route 50. Apparently, the new snowfall was keeping most people home. It was not safe to drive. Two significant storms in a week were unusual for the Shenandoah Valley.

He picked up the killers' weapons and other personal articles and rolled them up into the bloody Redskins blanket. He made a final check of the neighborhood, turned off the road, into the orchard, and toted them home. Relieved and exhausted when he arrived, he was especially glad to see that Watson was waiting. Like always, when he came home after a trip, Will experienced overwhelming love as his dog rushed up to welcome his best friend. Once the greeting ceremony was over, his dog began to whine, letting him know that he was hungry, and some things wouldn't wait. Will fed the dog a treat, ignored the whining, and hid the guns and other possessions he'd taken from the three men. He stuffed everything but the blanket inside a garage wall that held several water pipes.

Watson's whines turned into urgent barks, and Will moved quickly for the large bag of dog food stored in the garage. He filled the bowl and held it high as the dog jumped, trying to take it out of his hands.

Will was just returning to the kitchen, thinking of the countless tasks he had to do, when the doorbell rang.

It was Deputy Sheriff Harris. He seemed anxious, pushing the ringer again and again.

"Roscoe, what the hell's the matter? I'm coming, I'm coming," yelled Will as he rushed to get the door. Roscoe was surprised to find Will, the last person he'd expected to see. Will's face flushed from his run in the cold; he looked healthy and unconcerned. Roscoe stepped inside even before Will said, "Come in. Come in."

The deputy looked right and left, expecting to see Angelo, Paul, and Blue. But they weren't there, and nothing in Will's demeanor betrayed their presence. The big dog behind Will began to growl. Will told him to hush, noticing the blood on the dog's face and jowls.

"That damned dog killed a rabbit on our run this morning. What a mess! He doesn't like it when I take whatever he's caught from him. Seems like there's something different every day—rabbits, squirrels, groundhogs, you name it, and he hunts it."

MacKenzie's voice sounded uneasy. Roscoe stared at the dog. "He looks like he's been in a hell of a fight."

"Sometimes there's a lot of blood, and sometimes there isn't."

As he'd done before, the deputy looked around, checking everything, walking through the house. "You wouldn't happen to have a fresh pot of coffee would you, Will?" Roscoe asked and peeked in the hall bathroom. "I got some more questions that have to do with all this violence on the lane and something you tol' me earlier has got me confused." Roscoe opened the hall closet, interested in its contents.

"No problem, Roscoe. Got a fresh pot, help yourself while I feed this dog before he eats the both of us." And Will opened the door to the garage.

Roscoe, ignoring the coffee, followed Will into the garage, half-expecting to see a black Buick rental car parked inside and half not trusting to leave Will out of his sight.

But there was no sign of any car having been in that three-car garage in years. The entire garage was stuffed. There were tools, shelving, furniture, boxes, garbage cans, a dead old evergreen tree that Will planned to burn in the fireplace but forgot, and a thousand other odds and ends that Will couldn't remember that he had, much less where he had put them.

A Redskins blanket sat in plain sight on top of a garbage can. Blood was clearly visible on the blanket. Will tried to distract Roscoe, saying he needed to check the microwave. Roscoe said nothing about the blanket; just turned around and went back into the kitchen and helped himself to coffee.

"Care to have some bacon, eggs, and toast, Roscoe? I was just getting ready to cook breakfast when you showed up," said Will.

"No thanks, Will, coffee's enough for me. I got too much to do and not enough time to do it. You can help though if you can explain again where you were on the day they found that dead parachutist." Bluffing, the deputy added, "Some tracks was leadin' in your direction, but the snow covered 'em up, 'n' you said you was over in West Virginia, visitin' your uncle that day."

"Roscoe, this's the first I've heard about any tracks. Watson was with me in West Virginia, of course, and he likes to ride anytime I go anywhere."

"I didn't say they was dog tracks, Will."

"Roscoe, we spent the night in Clarksburg, went over to Weston, and by the time we got back, the news was all over the radio, and the *Winchester Star* had all those pictures and stories about the dead stranger dressed all in black. Check with the nursing home, they know me, they'll tell you I was there."

For the second time, Roscoe noticed that his suspect had mentioned Clarksburg and Weston but thought the two were reversed in his last story. He needed to call the nursing home again just to recheck Will's story.

"That's just it, Will, I checked with the nursing home. They didn't have a record of you until the next day, nothing on the night or day of the discovery," said the deputy.

"Jesus Christ, Roscoe! Half the time I'm up there, I don't sign in. I been goin' there for almost three years, they know me. Every damn one o' them knows me. Only time I sign in is when they have some new nurse squattin' at the front desk."

"Where did you spend the night, Will? Do you have a receipt, anything that shows where you were at that time?"

"Shit, Roscoe, what am I, a suspect? For what, shootin' down a parachute? I spent the night in the jeep . . . with my dog. Most of the motels up there don't take animals, and I'm not going to leave this dog alone in the car. Do you have any idea how much colder it is in West Virginia? I got other receipts. I know I got gas in Cumberland or Paw Paw. I'm pretty sure I paid with a credit card. Will that do?"

"Let me see a copy. Did you keep a copy of the receipt for gas? Receipts, Will, I need receipts."

Will didn't know how much Roscoe knew, and since he had plenty to hide, he was getting nervous. Even so, he was a natural-born poker player and emphatically stuck to his story, pretending to have proof when he had but one receipt from a Paw Paw gas station for some gas and food. True, the receipt showed that he was out of town the day all hell broke loose, but Paw Paw was only a forty-five-minute drive from Winchester. The receipt didn't show whether he was coming or going, yet he had to be convincing. He did his best not to act too concerned.

Will's mind raced, trying to remember what he had said, wanting to make sure his story was consistent.

Nurses at Weston would be able to state that he had visited Uncle Jim even though he had not signed in, and they would also say that he didn't always sign in. So his story was partially credible, even with a few holes. He wished he hadn't even mentioned Clarksburg. That town added too much complexity to his story. God help him if they got a warrant, but he didn't think they had any reason. No news report he had heard mentioned anything about what the parachutist had or that there was something missing.

"Maybe I have the damn receipt, maybe I don't, but I know that I'll have one when the bill comes in. Visa itemizes everything by date, I'm positive they do. And they don't wait thirty days to send the bill either. Seems like I get it right after I charge something. Let's get on the phone right now and call Visa, and while we're at it, let's talk to that nursing home, anyone of several nurses will remember I was there even if I didn't sign in. It hadn't been that long since I was there, Roscoe." MacKenzie began to gain some confidence.

After being certain that Will was the man, Roscoe began to have small doubts. He looked at Will, looked directly in his eyes. If the son-of-a-bitch had something to hide, he was pretty cool about it.

"Come on, Roscoe, are we gonna call or not. I'm not involved in any of this shit."

The deputy apologized, said there was no need to call, said that no one was a suspect, just that he was going crazy with all the killings. He told Will that every person who lived within three miles of the Glaize farmhouse was being talked to. He warned Will to watch himself, that there were some bad people doing bad things and that he would be back if he had other questions. Roscoe walked out the door, thanked Will for the coffee, got in his car, and left.

Will watched as the tracks of the deputy sheriff's vehicle left a path in the snow down his driveway.

The men who had come for him this morning were ruthless. From reports on the radio and his discussions with Roscoe, he knew that they tortured and killed with deliberate purpose. Why kill the Keenes' dogs? Why kill a nice old couple like the Keenes? Why kill Tucker Wilkens's maid or an innocent FedEx deliveryman?

Of course he knew why, they were looking for their money. If he hadn't surprised them totally, he would have been treated the same as the others. *Money is the root of all evil,* he thought to himself. It sure seemed so now.

Because of it, Will found himself second-guessing his hasty decision to keep the money. *Should he have reported finding the dead parachutist? How many people had died as a result of his greed and shortsightedness?*

Driving back to town, Roscoe Harris was thinking about his conversation with Will MacKenzie. "That son-of-a-bitch is hiding something," he said and decided to call the Weston Nursing Home again. He asked county dispatch to look up the number as he stopped for gas at the Handymart in Winchester. In less time than it took to fill up, he had the number. Roscoe couldn't wait to make the call. He parked beside the phone booth next to the air pump and dialed the number.

"Golden Years, good morning, how may I help you?" answered a voice so bright and cheery that he could sense a smile through the receiver.

"Good morning. Is this the Golden Years Retirement Home?" Roscoe's voice was pleasant as he asked the question.

"Yes, it is. This is Rachel. How may I help you?"

"This is Deputy Sheriff Roscoe Harris from Frederick County, Virginia, and I'm trying to verify some information in connection with an investigation. May I speak with your supervisor please?"

"I can help you, honey. No need to bother Mrs. Osborne. Whatcha need to find out?"

"OK, Rachel, can you tell me if a Mr. Will MacKenzie has been there recently? I believe he has an uncle there."

"Oh yeah, everybody knows Will MacKenzie. Most of the nurses get heart palpitations when he comes, and they forget what their supposed to do when he leaves. He always comes to visit his uncle, Jim MacKenzie."

"Can you tell me when he last visited his Uncle Jim? Do you have a registration record?"

"Don't need a record; I know when he was here. It was March 13th."

"Are you sure about the date, March 13th?"

"No doubt about it, hon."

"How can you be sure, Rachel? Could you be wrong? The date is important."

"It was my birthday. When he found out it was my birthday, he gave me a kiss and gave me a one-hundred-dollar bill! The kiss was worth more though. I didn't wash my face for two days . . . I just love him."

"Thank you. Thank you very much, Rachel. You have been very helpful . . . and happy birthday." Roscoe meant every word, and he smiled as he got back into his car, thinking, *Now, what are you hiding . . . hundred dollar bills? Mr. MacKenzie, you are a lyin' bastard?*

Chapter 26

As Will finished eating the scrambled eggs and bacon, he almost broke the plate when he laid it down on the floor for Watson to lick clean. His mind raced, concerned that events had gone way beyond his control. First he'd felt guilty, and now he was in a desperate gamble to keep what he had found. Yes, yes, he thought, someone else will come looking for him, and it won't be long. There was nothing he could do except run. He would have to spend the rest of his life running and hiding. What else could he do? He would never see his children again. He wanted to see them now that he'd straightened his life out.

STRAIGHTENED HIS LIFE OUT? God, how much more screwed up could it be? Even his wife—ex-wife, that is—and the kids might be in danger.

Strange that he was thinking about what he might do and not about what he had just done. Less than twelve hours ago, he had brutally killed three men, and he felt no remorse, no pity, no guilt whatsoever. He too could be labeled a torturer after what he'd done to the last of the three. Deliberately shooting him in the knee. Promising him medical care if he would just answer a few questions. This was different from that time in Vietnam, and this did not cause a relapse into depression like the last time. Could his conscience be hardening? Was it adapting to a darker side? Was the ghost of Vietnam blocking his feelings? Whatever it was, Will had accepted fate. It was his fate to find the money, and it was fate to act in self-preservation, self-defense. No, he would not feel guilt for ridding the world of scum. Perhaps he didn't have to disappear. Maybe he had another choice. Another plan formed in his mind. It would not be easy, but he still had the element of surprise.

There might just be an option where he didn't have to run after all. He knew he could always call on his Vietnam soul mates. Steve Beinhorn had aged a bit, and he had to be careful given his position at the Justice Department, but he would help. Hell, Will knew that Steve would quit his job to help if the problem were serious enough. Champ Lewis may be the one he'd have to call. Yes, Champ would help, and Champ wasn't afraid of combat. Sometimes, the streets of Philadelphia were a form of combat. You could wind up in a body bag without war being declared.

He decided to call them both, but only after he'd done a reconnaissance to find out how serious the situation really was.

He now knew what the money was for and who was involved. Well, maybe a little about the different groups who were now looking for the money. Who had paid it, who was supposed to receive it, a little bit about the kidnapped victim, who was keeping the victim, and where the victim was being held. Steve Beinhorn would know about these people. At the Justice Department, his new job focused on the national drug problem.

MacKenzie knew a great deal about one of the people involved, Joe Arthur or Anthony Arturo, whatever he called himself. Will knew he had to check out the farm, certainly do a recon there before calling Champ or Steve.

It had been three years since he had been to one of Joe's parties. He tried to remember the physical layout of Arthur's estate from the last time he'd been there.

Three roads, each with its own guardhouse, led onto the property. The farm was surrounded by an elaborate series of fences. He especially remembered the fencing. It was the most elaborate, extravagant combination of fencing he'd ever seen. Nothing compared with it in Middleburg, and they had plenty of estates. On the perimeter of the farm, surrounding several hundred acres, was a stone fence that matched the stone of the house and several outbuildings. Directly behind the stone was a higher wooden fence. Behind the wooden fence was a solid row of pine trees that now rose to a height of twenty or thirty feet, and behind that was an imposing chain-link fence topped with a foot of barbed wire that angled out. The cost of the fencing alone was in the hundreds of thousands of dollars. Hell, the cost of maintaining the fence was huge. No one thought about it, except to say that it looked richly tasteful. Certainly, no one considered that the fence was meant to keep people out. Joe had people in every week.

Only now that he thought about Joe's real occupation, his shadowy background, and that a kidnapped victim was somewhere on the property,

Will realized the true purpose of the fencing. It was to keep nosy people out.

Then he started to question his sudden idea to end this nightmare. It was crazy to think he could outsmart some of the people involved. Did he really believe that if the kidnapped victim were rescued, these criminals would stop looking for the money? But he was desperate. It might take a crazy idea to be free. The moneybags he'd found had made him a prisoner too. If he could determine exactly where the girl was being held, maybe he could do something about it. Too many "maybes" in his thinking, he needed to find out more before he could do anything. Perhaps he could reconnoiter the farm, check things out and see what his real options were. Time was running out; he would have to go tonight. He had six hours to prepare. He began to consider several possibilities.

Checking a three-year-old Chamber of Commerce map of Frederick and Clarke counties, Will decided he would approach the farm from the Shenandoah River. He'd best not use the old dirt road that paralleled the river because it was guarded at both the north and south boundaries of the Arthur property. The maps didn't show the guardhouses, and Arthur didn't own the road; it was really a state right-of-way, which, theoretically, anyone could use. Four years earlier, Will had taken his son along with eight others on a father-and-son float trip and camp out on the river. At the time, they had been surprised to see the guardhouses. Not a problem then because the guards cheerfully let them through to the Dunning State Park, several miles, and several farms, south of the property.

Tonight, he would have to go another way, past Long Branch Farm, to get to the park. The park was only a few acres in size, but it included a launching area, a concrete ramp that angled down all the way into the river. The public park was popular for camping, picnicking, and boating. Every week, throughout the summer and fall, boating enthusiasts entered and exited from there.

He would float his canoe down the river until he could spot the main house, which he thought would be clearly visible from the water. Next, he considered what he would need. He had to be prepared; they were probably more alert now that they had something to protect.

Thinking he'd best be prepared for anything, Will chose a dark warm up suit, a black windbreaker, a pair of long underwear, a black ski mask, black gloves, a flashlight, a long hunting knife, a pair of wire cutters, his Beretta pistol, the dead parachutist's night vision binoculars, and the automatic pistol equipped with a silencer. He decided to wear tennis shoes instead of boots, so out came the black shoe polish. Thank God his canoe was dark blue, or he would have had to paint it too.

Will took a look at himself in the mirror before he left the house. Jesus! He looked a lot like the parachutist did before he hit the tree. Now, there was a morbid thought.

Watson interrupted, wanting to go, but Will couldn't take him. Not this time.

Chapter 27

Shortly after leaving Will's house and driving Merriman's Lane two more times without seeing a sign of the black Buick, Roscoe made the call to Joe Arthur. "Have you heard from Angelo?" he said.

"Angelo and the others are supposed to be with you. What the hell are you talkin' about?"

"The sons o' bitches have disappeared, Mr. Arthur. They were on their way to the address I gave them, and they never showed up. I've checked the entire area; I've called the Hampton Inn; I've checked the Amherst Diner, the Papermill, and other diners where they may have stopped for breakfast—you know Angelo's appetite; I've checked with dispatch; I've checked the hospital emergency room; I've driven up and down Merriman's Lane three times; I've even gone to the dog owner's address and talked to the occupant and found nothing. What do you want me to do?"

"Surely they haven't turned on one another? I know Angelo wanted to blow both of them away. Maybe there's been a double cross. Maybe there's been a change of plans from DC or Cartagena. I need to make some calls. You get back out on Merriman's Lane and keep checking. Keep calling downtown, maybe the FBI's doing something we don't know about. Use your best judgment, Roscoe. You know law enforcement tactics better than I do. Call me if you hear anything. Call me every hour on the hour because I can't call you. Okay?"

"Yes, sir, Mr. Arthur, I'm on it," he said as he walked from the phone booth outside the Chevron station over to the Amherst Diner where he saw a few of his old buddies from high school. There they were, having a late breakfast and solving all of the world's problems. These guys were there every day for breakfast and lunch, and every day, they discussed current news and issues. Politics, religion, race, economy—no matter what the subject, they had an answer. Yes, by god, if only the politicians would listen. Only they didn't share their opinions with politicians or anyone else; these gems were restricted to their small group who never tired of talking about it, whatever "it" was.

Today "it" was the recent killings and grisly rumors they had been hearing about. When they saw Roscoe coming in, their conversation stopped. The fattest of them all (and they were all overweight from eating sausage gravy every day), George Butler, said, "Goddammit, Roscoe. Haven't you solved these crimes yet? It's been three days. Pull up a chair. I know we can help you. Me 'n' the boys think it was Mose Keene's nephew, Frank Whitworth. We used to call 'im Whitworthless . . . a name that started a fight every time! How he's stayed outta jail this long is a mystery, a goddamned mystery, Roscoe. You know what I mean?

"Jesus, George. How'd you ever get so fat with your mouth goin' all the time? Where am I gonna sit at? You're takin' up the whole bench."

As usual, Roscoe had to acknowledge the rest, speaking to each.

"Billy, Marty, Pete . . . how's it hangin'?" Nodding to each, he went on, needing to explain something to these idiots, "Frank Whitworth hadn't been around here since he went in the marines two years ago. What the hell're you boys thinkin'?"

George interrupted, ignoring Roscoe's conversation with the others. "Roscoe, I weighed 225 when I blocked ever'body outta your way so's you could impress all those cheerleaders. You're still ungrateful as ever. Sit down, there's plenty o' room."

"George, that was one hundred pounds and many ham biscuits ago." Roscoe grinned, sitting down beside the big man. He turned to the rest of the regulars. "Boys, I only got time for a pancake or two, if they have any left after you guys. This case's drivin' me nuts. The Feds are pushin' us local ignorants aside so's they can ride in here 'n' save our asses from the wicked." Roscoe shook every hand. "I don't know a damn thing 'cept it wasn't Whitworth. You sleuths need to find yourselves another suspect. Don't call me, I'll call you."

Coffee cups were filled and refilled, and the discussion was lively, naming names and offering reasons why there were so many guilty people in the county. Roscoe was amused and encouraged everybody at the table, including George, who was used to being insulted ten times a day. No one could remember a time when there had been so much excitement.

An anxious maid mistakenly routed the international phone call to Don Alverez's bedroom. A gray-haired nurse, one of three in the room, didn't understand English and transferred the call to Diego Estrada, the Don's second in command after Paul Xavier. Diego had left strict instructions that the Don was not to be disturbed.

Based on the previous night's communication, everyone was certain that at last they had, by trial and error, found the person who took the ransom; Diego had expected the exchange to be completed and Gabriella on her way home.

Expecting the safe return of his Don's most precious reason for living, he had prematurely turned to the task of revenge. Diego had studied the list of every specialist killer allied with the Cartagena Cartel who might be in North or Central America. He had spent all morning trying to arrange for a team of at least ten seasoned and reliable triggermen. They needed to prepare for an urgent mission to teach a lesson in Washington DC. The men came from Miami, Cuba, and Panama, and all were experienced assassins. None of the ten would look out of place in the black sections of Washington DC.

Those black bastards are goin' to pay. thought Diego. *Nobody, nobody fucks with Don Alverez. Why attack family? It doesn't make sense. It's insane!* He wanted Blue Eyes alive. He wanted to pry those beautiful blue eyes out of their sockets, one at a time. He wanted those eyes to die painfully, slowly, and aware of what was happening to him. He'd personally do the same to Booger Bryant, that greedy, ungrateful bastard.

Most of all, he wanted the only girl he'd ever loved out of her predicament and home where she would be safe. He hoped that this experience would get the stupid college idea out of her head for good. Coupled with everything he wanted, he prayed that Don Alverez would finally croak once he knew his daughter was safe. He couldn't risk the return of Paul, the Don's favorite, while the Don was still alive. Paul didn't know the surprise that was waiting for him in Colombia. That last thought brought a smile to his face, crinkling the eight-inch scar on his right cheek into a bow. The smile faded quickly when he learned the purpose of the call.

"No, we have not ordered a change in plans. We were informed last night that you knew who took the money and it was just a matter of time when you recovered it. Why haven't you made the exchange? Is that blue-eyed freak pulling another of his tricks? Is Gabriella OK?"

"Gabriella is fine, fine," Joe Arthur repeated with emphasis. "She is with me. She is healthy. She is getting frustrated, like us all. We just need to be patient. Our friends will turn up. I guarantee Gabriella will not be harmed. Let me call Mr. B in Washington and find out where he stands. Make sure he's not getting stupid. How's my friend, Don Alverez? Give him my regards and assure him he will see his daughter safe and sound. I will call back with any new developments; no need for a new delivery. We will find the money; everyone be cool. Goodbye, my friend."

"You not my friend, you greedy wop!" Diego shouted, but only after he had hung up the phone. Maybe he needed to send a message to that smooth-talking Virginia gentleman too. Very condescending, talking to me, he would not speak to the Don like that. Soon, there will be another Don he will have to deal with. Prices are going to go up. Respect has a price. Some pay with everything they have, others pay a little more cash. That's the way business works around the world.

Chapter 28

In Washington DC, business was still going strong, but Booger Bryant was wondering why he hadn't heard from Winchester. To an audience of three of his best prostitutes, two white, one black, he began ranting. "Shit, they tell me last night, 'No problem, got the right guy this time.' Seems t' me like too many guys with dogs out there. It's hard to find the right one. Do all country people have dogs? I thought they had chickens 'n' pigs 'n' shit like that!"

The girls, all wearing panties and silk slips with no bra, were stoned as usual. They could have cared less, except they didn't like it when Booger lost his temper. He seemed to be losing it more and more, but they couldn't keep track of each tantrum. When the red phone rang, he picked it up anxiously, certain it was Blue. "It's about time, you motherfucker! You retired to the country? You fall in love with a sheep?"

Startled, Joe Arthur recovered quickly. "Booker, that you? This is your friend from Clarke County," he said, reluctant to use his name, not trusting Bryant's phone to be clean of wiretaps. "I am still minding your guest, still looking for your package. Have you heard from Blue? Seems like people have gone underground out here. What's goin' on?"

"What's goin' on? What's goin' on? Fuck, if I know what's goin' on! Maybe, I need to come out there and take that girl off your hands. You tol' my man Blue that the money would be here two days ago! You supposed to own everything out there. Do you or not? Shit, I send my best man out there, and he don't even have the courtesy to call me. I'm gonna teach that nigga a lesson when he gets back to Fourth Street. Last time he blessed me with a call was last night. He tol' me you got the man. You know where ever'thing is. Tomorrow, it all be fixed. Well, its tomorrow today, 'n' now you tell me you don' know shit. What am I to do? Sit here in the city? Listen t' the sirens all day? You tell that Colombian fuck if I don't get my money tomorrow night, he got a war on his hands, 'n' I don't take prisoners, you heah me?"

"Booker, Booker, calm down. No need to be doing anything too quickly. I promise you will get your money. Your guest isn't going anywhere without it. I got money coming to me too, you know. Business comes first. That's a rule we all understand. Give it a couple more days. We got to find our three guys. You don't think they teamed up on us for the money, do you?"

"Not unless your man or the Colombian stuck a knife in Blue's back. He got too much money here to fuck up for chump change. He better show up soon 'cause I ain't sendin' someone else, I be comin' myself!"

"Anytime, Booker, anytime, you know you're welcome. Let's give it time to play out. You know they wouldn't stay out of sight except for a good reason. You know that, don't you? My Angelo is blood kin; he can't be bought for any amount of money. He's there to provide all the support needed to complete the transaction. The Colombian is second in command in his organization, and he's been chief of operations for several years. Nothing would tempt him to take the money. Its chump change for him too. What do you say to a few more days? We'll wind it up, and then we can get back to normal, Okay, Booker? Okay?"

"Two days, that's what I'm willin' to do. Two days. We both got a reputation to keep. Otherwise, more money's got to come outta Colombia. Motherfuckers, they've got plenty of it, but after two days, we got interest, as well as principal, to talk about, you heah? Price's gonna go up!" And Bryant hung up.

Joe Arthur now knew what Angelo had been talking about. Who the hell did these idiots think they were? A lot of blood's going to be spilled in DC, no question about it. Maybe, he and the Don could coordinate a Capitol housecleaning.

Absentmindedly, he looked up to the top of the stairs. Gabriella was up there now, in the most comfortable guest bedroom. Every one of his men treated her like an honored guest. She received gourmet meals. Suddenly, he had an urge to check on her himself. He actually got out of the chair of his study to go to her. He felt a need to assure her, make her feel safe in his care. She might someday be his supplier after all. Maybe one of his sons could be her husband, cement a relationship by marriage. It had been an old and honored custom in their ancestral countries.

He stopped before he reached the thick-paneled door, knowing subconsciously that he shouldn't be seen. Twenty-eight years of developing a deep cover reputation of outstanding citizenship was too much to risk. So he had a telephone delivered to her room instead. The guards told her to stand by for an important phone call. Within a minute of its being plugged in, the telephone rang. Even though they were all expecting it, they each jumped when it rang.

Anxiously, Gabriella grabbed the phone. "Father?" she said with a smile of relief as she brought the phone to her ear. The smile faded as quickly as it had come when she heard the strange voice on the other end of the line.

"Sorry, Gabriella, I am not your father, but I have just spoken to him," he lied. "I have assured him of your good health and good treatment and promised that you would return to him soon. He is distressed by your absence and is doing everything in his power to free you. I have been his friend for more than twenty years and will not let him or you down."

"Can you help me? Help me please!" There was desperation in her voice.

"Just a little while longer, I promise. Keep your spirits high. Surely, you know you won't be harmed. It won't be long now. I am in contact with all parties, and they tell me that it is only a matter of time before everything can be worked out. You can do it. You're young and strong. Okay?" And with that said, he hung up.

Instead of being reassured, Gabriella was crushed. How long had it been? She had lost track of time. She thought she could remember where her captors had taken her in DC, but she hadn't a clue where she was now. They wouldn't let her see out the windows. From time to time, she had heard cows and roosters, so she suspected she was in the country, not too far out of Washington. She assessed her surroundings and concluded her captors were wealthy. The ceilings were at least ten feet high. Expensive molding sat atop designer wallpaper. The fixtures in the bathroom were brass, or maybe gold; the tile, sink, and bathtub made of marble; the towels, thick and soft. Whoever owned this place was rich and had good taste.

As nice at it was it was still depressing. Her caller had mistakenly assumed she would be strong. He was wrong. Never before had she had to worry about anything. Her main challenge had been to elude the constant minders and babysitters her father used to keep an eye on her. She was twenty-nine years old and almost a virgin. Her main sexual experience had been with a cousin who her father would have killed had he known. She was never alone unless with family, and certainly not alone outside the country. She had become fond of one of her bodyguards, Joseph, the tall one. He always looked at her with respect and longing. After many months together, he would tease her and laugh with her. But they were never left alone either. Tears formed in her eyes as she thought of Joseph. She also remembered Ashley, thinking, *Poor Ashley, he would do anything for me. Now he's gone.*

Now another guard was looking at her, but not with love, not to tease. He was a brute. He was a violator of women, she was sure. He was always trying to be alone with her, making her keep the bathroom door open while she went to the bathroom. The man was called Marko, a huge powerful man with a swarthy face full of scars from chicken pox or something. He spoke with an Italian accent and was forever asking his companion guard to go down for coffee or supplies. Maybe the other guard was on to him because he never left the room.

Gabriella finally took a shower, but only after wearing her sweat suit into the shower and closing the shower curtain behind her. Even then, she could feel his eyes on her, and she hurried, not quite getting the soap out of her hair.

For the first time in ten years, she did not exercise. She tried to read one of the books on the nightstand, but couldn't get past the second page. Just before she went to sleep, she prayed, for the first time in a long time. She'd quit when her mother died so many years ago. She prayed that she'd be freed, that her father would get better, that she would be a better person, doing things for others and not be so occupied with her own selfish thoughts. She asked God to forgive her for looking the other way while so much misery and poverty were all around her. Her father was going to have to give her some money to do good for others. She felt better after the prayers but could not sleep. She lay in the bed with her two guards in chairs on either side of the bedroom door, one reading something by a lamp, the other scratching himself like he had poison ivy in his crotch. When she finally did go to sleep, she dreamed that the ugly guard had slipped into her room and was going to rape her. Just as she was about to wake up and scream, she felt a hand on her mouth, muffling any sound she tried to make. She realized that this was no dream.

Chapter 29

A light snow was spitting when Will finished strapping his canoe to the top of his jeep. Driving through Winchester, he noticed that in town, the streets were fairly clear with the exception of piles of ice and slush. Heading east on Route 50, with daylight fading fast, he spilled coffee in his lap and almost wrecked the jeep. *Bad omen,* he thought, but he kept going with renewed determination. Crossing Opequon Creek into Clarke County, he had to turn his bright lights on to see. The temperature dropped with every mile. Turning off Route 50, going past Long Branch Farm, he had to slow down due to patches of snow and ice. The side roads in Clarke County had been the last to be plowed and showed it.

It was very dark when he pulled into the river park. He entered from the campground section when he found the chain up. It was blocking the main entrance. The road was bumpy and slick, but the jeep's four-wheel-drive system allowed him to drive around the chain barrier, back in the trees, out of sight. Will checked his watch and was surprised to see that it was only 6:32 p.m. Lack of visibility made it seem much later. By the time he'd unloaded his canoe and checked his weapons, ammunition, and other gear, it was 7:15. Since it was just a recon, he decided to take only one pistol, the one with the silencer. If he were careful, he wouldn't need it. Will figured it would take only thirty minutes to float down to the Arthur farm. He would have to be very quiet. At this hour, everyone would be awake.

Floating down the Shenandoah River had always been a pleasure—usually with friends, a few beers, some fried chicken, hot dogs, hamburgers, potato chips, and soft drinks, laughing and joking all the way. Everyone brought fishing rods and bait with the plan of catching their meals.

MacKenzie could not remember anyone catching any fish. Someone had once caught a turtle, but that was the only live thing that attached to the ends of their lines.

There was no laughing now, no noise at all, and it created an eerie feeling as he launched his canoe.

On the river, Will could hear with acute clarity the water lapping against each bank, even occasional vehicle traffic going across the bridge several miles downstream. He strained to see a landmark, anything on the west bank that would tell him where he was. Time seemed to move slowly as he silently stroked his paddle. He began to doubt his estimate of time to float to his destination. He jumped at every noise on both banks.

Will assumed the noises were deer. Deer were rampant in this area. In this semi wilderness, there were plenty of other animals that were active at night.

After what seemed like an eternity, he heard a cough. Turning his eyes to the sound, he saw a glow. It was one of Arthur's guards, and he was smoking. Then he heard a radio, the guard was listening to a basketball game. Will could hear everything. West Virginia was leading Pittsburgh in the second half. He checked his watch: 8:05. Damn, it had taken longer than he figured! He hoped that the guard was on the south side of the farm; otherwise, he had floated past his target. He waited another two minutes and then saw lights from a house on the ridge that fronted the river. *This must be it,* he thought and silently paddled to the west bank.

The canoe bumped a tree root with a *thunk* as he reached shore. Holding on to the root, Will remained silent and still for five minutes. Nothing moved. Satisfied that his presence was undetected, Will tied up the boat so that it could not be seen, unless someone stumbled on top of it. He crawled up the bank and waited at the road, again perfectly still. He thought back to the ambush in Vietnam. Someone could be waiting anywhere up there. He could see the outline of the main house from his perch. *Here goes!* He crossed the road without a sound. Crouching down behind the stone fence, he checked again, looking left, right, and above. All around him, it was still. He couldn't hear the guard's radio, couldn't hear bridge traffic. Sound radiated and amplified on the river, but not here. He climbed over the four-rail wood fence and stopped again. He crawled through the pine trees and paused at the base of the chain-link fence. He checked the fence for electric fixtures or signs. All along the river, were signs that warned, "Private Property, KEEP OUT!" But at the base of the chain-link fence, there were no signs and no evidence that he would be electrocuted if he touched the fence. *Thank God,* Will thought, and he briefly relaxed.

Four strands of barbed wire added another foot to the height of this fence, and Will decided to cut the barbed wire rather than try to cut the chain links. Grabbing each strand with his gloved left hand, Will snipped each wire and was careful to keep the noise down.

He made sure all gear was secure and climbed the fence. Once over, he dropped down, remained still, and listened. He checked his watch: 9:10. *At this rate, it will be dawn before I get to the house,* he thought to himself. From the inside of the last fence, Will reckoned it was 150 yards to the outside wall of the stone terrace.

Silently, he crept up through a cow pasture that sloped steeply up to the house. Step by step, he made his way up the ridge, trying to stay in the shadows, avoiding patches of snow where he might stand out. Every few feet, he would stop and listen. Once or twice, he heard an owl, but nothing from the house.

When he was within twenty-five yards of the patio, he saw movement above. It was another guard, lighting a cigarette. In the light, he could see that the guard carried a rifle on his shoulder; MacKenzie couldn't make out what kind it was. Then he heard a zipper open. Next, he heard a stream of piss coming over the wall, landing next to his right foot.

Will held perfectly still, and then someone behind the guard spoke. "Maggio, you told me you quit smokin'. You're goin' to die if you keep it up. Just like you, with a cigarette in one hand and your pecker in the other."

A second guard on the terrace came into view. "Why do I want to spend twenty more years in an old people's home rotting away like a fuckin' vegetable? Better to go young," Maggio replied.

To emphasize his point, he continued, "Tony, you . . . you work out every day, you pump your iron, you eat your green shit 'n' everything, then you're goin' t' get hit by a truck. When they put you in the ground, you'll be healthy as a horse."

"We'll see, asshole. HEY, WHAT THE HELL?" The guard pointed at Will crouching down, trying to be invisible.

Maggio, didn't turn, he didn't react, just seemed surprised at Tony, saying,

"Frankly, I . . ."

The bullets from Will's silencer struck. Neither man knew what hit him. Will was at point-blank range when he fired, and later, he could not recall why he fired; he just did it, and that was that. So much for a recon mission.

Both men fell to the stone floor of the patio, and only Tony's rifle made a noise. Will waited, listened if anyone had heard, if anyone else was around. Suddenly, one of the men began to moan; he was not dead. His groaning stopped when Will covered his mouth and slit his throat. Will hopped up and crouched on the terrace, looking, listening, trying to get his bearings.

There was no sign of other guards. Not much had changed since he had last been to the house. Some of the heavy metal furniture, chairs, tables, and a portable bar were put away for the winter. He knew where he was at least relative to the first floor of the main house. Joe's parties were usually large and involved the entire first floor, along with the patio. Sometimes they'd put a large tent over the patio, mainly for winter parties.

There were four doors leading to the terrace from the main house—one from the library, one from the main hallway, one from the dining room, and the last from the kitchen—although it came out of a wing and was a few steps below the main section of the house. Will stayed perfectly still when he sensed movement. Someone was in the library. It was Joe Arthur.

Will kept to the shadows on the terrace and moved closer to the library. Outside, floodlights lit pockets of the property for a few hundred feet around the main house. Lights from several tenant houses, barns, and other outbuildings gave the compound a false security. Joe had not found it necessary to install electric fences, television cameras, and other security measures, feeling comfortable with a small army of armed workers and guards.

Joe was on the phone. Relaxed, with a Cuban cigar smoldering in a crystal ashtray and a glass of single malt scotch in his hand, Joe spoke in hushed tones. He was in deep conversation with his Philadelphia family, alerting them to a possible problem with their DC retail partners. When the conversation ended, he walked to the double glass doors, opened them, and stuck his head outside.

"Maggio, you there? What's all the fuckin' noise?"

At that, Will stepped out of the shadow directly in his front and stuck the muzzle of the silencer in his mouth. Joe leapt back in a reflex action, but Will was right with him. Will was wearing his black ski mask so Joe assumed it was the Colombians or maybe even the gang from DC. As the two backed into the library, Will said, "Quiet!"

Once the man in the mask spoke, Joe tried to figure out who he was. The accent wasn't Spanish, and it surely wasn't downtown DC. Will removed the pistol from his mouth, pressed the muzzle up into Joe's throat, and asked, "Where is she?"

Joe thought he recognized the voice in the mask, hesitated, almost ready to say, "Who's that?" but the gun was shoved roughly back into his mouth.

"You got two seconds to tell me where the girl is!" MacKenzie removed the gun from his mouth and pushed the muzzle back under his chin.

"She's upstairs." Again, Arthur thought he recognized that voice.

"That's better," Will whispered. "Just where upstairs? What room?"

"She's in the guest bedroom, first room to the right on the second floor." came a meek reply, Joe now shaking with fear.

"Now we're getting somewhere," said Will. "Tell me how many guards? What are they armed with? How many men in the house? Where they are? Tell me everything I need to know and all you get outta this is a small bruise."

"You chipped my tooth. You didn't have to do that. What are they paying you? I'll double it. Let's reason this out. I have twenty-six men on the place. They're all expert marksmen. You'll never get away with it. A hundred thousand's in that safe right there. Whadda ya say?" Joe was relaxing now, thinking this guy is a businessman.

Will ignored him, didn't look at the safe when he mentioned it, and said, "You got two more seconds to answer my questions, or I'll start removing your front teeth since they're so precious."

He tapped Joe's front teeth with his gun. Looked him straight in the eye and, very deliberately, enunciating clearly each word, repeated the questions.

"Where are the twenty-six men? How many men in the house? How many men in her room? What are they armed with?"

Joe started shaking again. "Two guards, there are always two guards with her. I want to make sure she's treated right. We've treated her with great respect and care. She's fine. You gotta believe me. Seven men are always on duty."

"Where are they now? The seven?"

"Two with her in the bedroom like I said, two outside, but you must have noticed them, at least one; they couldn't all be taking a break. Oh, and one at each gate. There are four gates."

"That's eight, not seven. Which is it?" Will grabbed the front of Joe's shirt, sticking the gun against his Adam's apple.

"I'm sorry, most of the time there's only one man outside, but at night, we make it two, one of them brings coffee and stuff to the guards at the gates. I forgot about the extra guard at night. Sometimes, one of them goes into the kitchen for something when the cook goes off duty."

"When does the cook go off duty?"

"Between eight and nine. Sometimes I eat late, but I didn't eat late tonight. I think the cook's gone now. I . . . I . . . uh . . . I know he's gone." Joe is talking fast now, giving more information, adding explanation, anything to keep this guy calm, wondering where the hell his other guard was, the library was in full view of anyone on the terrace.

Will glanced at the tall antique grandfather clock next to the safe Joe had earlier pointed out and noted the time. It was 9:45, but it seemed he'd been here forever. "Where does the cook go when he's off? Where do the men go when they're off duty?"

"They're in the three tenant houses, or . . . uh . . . sometimes, they shoot pool or play cards in the game room next to the tennis court and swimming pool. The tenant houses are all scattered around the farm, one's a half mile away."

Will knew where the game room was; about fifty yards back of the main house. He had been to a pool party Joe had hosted for the Millwood Fire Department fund drive. Surely, some of the men were there. They might hear noise from the main house and come running. They damn well would recognize shots if they heard them.

"I got one more question. When do the guards change shifts?"

"I'm sorry, I should have told you, I just didn't think of it, you know. I'm not trying to hide anything, you got to believe me. They change every eight hours. The last change was at four; they'll change again at midnight. Listen, I'll triple what they're paying you. We don't have to argue here. No need to do something stupid. Can't we work this out?" His voice was now pleading.

Will realized his time was limited. He had, at most, two hours before shift change. He moved the gun back from Joe's neck. "I've already done something stupid," he said and shot Joe right between the eyes.

Not much sound from the shot, just a *pfffffft* from the silencer and a sigh from Joe as he let go of his last breath. He was sitting upright in his tall red leather reading chair with a plumped-up pad that rose several inches above his head. Sitting in the front, on the matching leather ottoman, MacKenzie finally released his grip on Joe's shirt. Joe looked totally relaxed, grotesquely comfortable as his head slumped sideways, revealing a bloody mess oozing down the expensive leather.

Quickly, Will moved to the library wall opposite the patio and turned off the lights. Then, he carefully opened the door leading into the main foyer where he had a clear view of the massive oak stairway. There were wide halls on both sides of the stairway allowing access to the main floor of the house. The lighting was dim, coming from several illuminating lamps above a dozen oil paintings hanging on mahogany-paneled walls. He didn't see anyone, and the only sound he heard was the whir of heat pumps augmenting the furnace system. Oriental carpets covered the foyer, and long-matching runners carried up each stairway to the second floor.

Like a cat burglar, he crept up the stairs and saw the guest bedroom door after he had gone halfway. The door was cracked open, and light could be seen coming out. Keeping low, head almost even with the stairs, Will reached the top and stopped. Through the crack, he saw a pair of legs sticking out from a chair to the right of the door.

Inside, the room was dark except for a low-wattage lamp next to the chair. Coming closer, staying on carpet to avoid noise, Will noticed the man in the chair squinting, trying to read a magazine in his lap. One corner of a large bed was visible, but he could not see whether anyone was in it. He'd fired five bullets from the silencer-equipped automatic pistol. That meant he had only ten left. He assumed the other guard was on the opposite side of the door. A slight snore confirmed the general vicinity of his location. Maybe the two took turns staying awake.

Reminding himself subconsciously of the time problem, Will came in low. Two quick shots into the guard in the chair, rolling on the floor, lying on his back with both hands on his pistol, arms extended, he turned in the direction of the snorer.

But the second man was not where Will thought he would be. The man didn't hear either shot but jumped when he heard the intruder hit the floor. He was in a rocking chair next to the bathroom, which tipped over, the sound echoing on the parquet floor as the man jumped up fumbling for his gun.

"What the fuck was that?" he said as he looked toward where his partner was supposed to be. His first thought was that the girl was making a break for the door, trying to escape. He banged his shoulder against the wall and finally got his weapon out of its shoulder holster, but he was too late! Will hit him with at least three shots, and he fell immediately. Will saw someone in the bed roll over. It had to be Gabriella, the girl he'd come for. He put his hand on her face and pushed her down against one of the huge silk pillows.

The girl was terrified, moving, twisting, turning her head, throwing her legs up to escape Will's hold. Gabriella was sure the man she feared was finally going to rape her. She was very strong, and Will, straddling her with all his weight, put the gun down and pulled off his ski mask.

Immediately, on seeing his face and its obvious expression of concern for her, the girl stopped resisting. She looked into his face as he whispered, "Please, keep quiet. Don't worry; I came to get you out. Promise me, you'll be quiet."

Tears in her eyes, the girl nodded affirmatively, and Will released his grip from her mouth, saying, "You okay? We gotta move quick. I don't know whether anyone heard. Let's move."

He quickly scooted off the bed toward the door.

"Who are you?" Gabriella whispered. "Did my father send you? I have to pee."

Then, the first guard stirred. But Will was ready for anything. He slammed the butt of his pistol into the man's head and turned back to the girl. "Put on your shoes, pee in your pants or hold it. We have no time!"

Placing his finger to his lips, he shushed her to be quiet. Silently, he turned to listen at the door while Gabriella dressed in a rush, coming up behind him. He noticed she wore only a sweat suit and tennis shoes and asked, "Where's your coat? It's cold outside."

"This is all I had on when they took me." And she started to cry.

Chapter 30

He held her for a moment to settle her down. Then they rushed for the steps, expecting the other guards at any minute. They stopped at the top, and again at the bottom, in the shadow of the foyer. All the while, they listened for movements, sounds, anything. Maybe the other guards hadn't heard, maybe no one was around, he hoped. Will opened the hall closet, ready to drag Gabriella inside. But it seemed that they were alone except for coats, boots, hats, and umbrellas. He grabbed a cashmere overcoat and a man's mink hat. "Put these on." And he urged her toward the library. The room smelled of cigars. As they rushed through the library to the patio door, she brushed against the feet of the dead Joe Arthur. She screamed and only stopped when Will held his hand in her face. Surely, if anyone is in this house, they certainly heard that! Will agonized, straining to listen for any sound. Hearing none, they bolted for the patio.

Running with abandon, they moved over the patio wall, down the cow pasture, and reached the fence. It took less than two minutes, but it seemed longer.

Will was slowed by her uncertainty, her tripping on the extra-large cashmere overcoat in her attempt to move fast. The two slip-slided on the snow, stumbled over rocks, tripped over clumps of dirt and debris that were impossible to see in the dark.

It took another minute before Will found the place where he had cut the barbed wire and an even longer time to get her over the fence. She kept sliding back and, even when she made progress, kept getting caught on strands of wire, ripping the cashmere. Finally, she took the coat off, threw it over the fence, climbed over, and moved quickly over the rest, into the road, where they stopped.

Will signaled for quiet while he listened for pursuit. None could be heard, except for a pair of owls and an occasional dog bark, both of which seemed far away. Urging her to remain still, Will untied the canoe. He pulled out his silencer-equipped pistol, fired two bullets in the bottom of the canoe, and pushed it out into the river current. Knowing he had only two bullets left in the pistol, he patted the holstered Beretta to satisfy himself it was still there. It wasn't; he'd left it in the jeep. He checked his watch. It read 10:25. *Time to go.*

They headed south along the river road, every now and then stepping on a dry twig, resulting in a sound that advertised their presence. Sounds seemed to echo on the river. Will, very concerned about the guard, just hoped that the basketball game was still being played and that the guard was still listening. He had been lucky so far, surprise on his side. Four or five men were now dead at the farm, and three in a car trunk at the hospital. Too much to think about now, must focus on the roadblock ahead. If they got by the next guard, they just might make it. The emphasis on stealth made the trip longer. He couldn't be sure how far they had to go to reach the southern guardhouse, so he asked Gabriella to hang back and move quietly. Any noise now might ruin everything. It couldn't be more than half a mile around the bend.

He heard the guard's radio just before he rounded the bend, following the river. *Good.* he said to himself, grinning when he heard sounds that confirmed the basketball game was still being played. Turning around the bend, he could see the soft glow of a light in the guardhouse. He made Gabriella stay put, told her if he didn't handle the guard, she should swim across the river and try to reach one of the houses up on Paris Mountain. Closer and closer he came; he could see the guard's face now.

Snap! The sound of a breaking twig was so loud it reverberated across the river. They both froze in their tracks. After a moment, Gabriella snuck up behind her rescuer, afraid he would disappear in the dark. The guard moved. Will saw the beam of a flashlight and the guard's door opening.

"Who's there?" said an unsteady voice with a pistol raised in one hand, flashlight pointing where the sound had come from. Usually deer would be silent unless they were spooked by something, then they might crash through the brush, not concerned about noise. This noise sounded different to the guard. His name was Donte Familiagi, and he was the most junior of the men on the farm. Like all of the new men, he had been assigned to outside guard duty.

Will was twenty-five yards from the guard, standing perfectly still. Gabriella was behind him, almost invisible in the black cashmere coat and the mink hat. She froze too.

The flashlight moved deliberately back and forth. Then the guard relaxed, confident that everything was under control.

Will was determined to bypass the guardhouse when seconds later, Gabriella stepped on a moss-covered rock, slipped, and fell to the ground. She yelped, and the sound gave away their position.

On full alert, the guard opened the door quickly, gun in hand, and fired two shots in their direction.

Will had already dropped down beside Gabriella, covering her body with his. Without checking her for injury, he took careful aim and placed his last two remaining bullets silently through the guard's chest. *Pffftt, pffftt.* The soft sound of the silencer contrasted sharply with the loud blast of shots fired wildly by the guard.

Gabriella started shaking, not knowing who was shot. She'd seen the flashlight go down into the dirt with the beam shooting off toward the farm fence. Will called to hurry, and she was instantly relieved. "Someone must have heard that. We have to move fast now." Reaching out to her, he held her hand as they ran to his jeep.

The shots were heard clearly on the river, and the northernmost guard called his companion on the two-way radio. "Donte, Donte, come in, Donte, come in?" He waited a minute and repeated the question.

Will and Gabriella heard the dead guard's radio clearly and ran faster. For the first time, Will turned his flashlight on briefly so they could see the road ahead. Gabriella, normally a distance runner, proved to be a sprinter as well, easily keeping up with him as they moved as fast as they could. They reached the park in total exhaustion, both sweating even though the temperature was in the teens. No one was chasing them. They could hear shouts down the river, but the noises sounded far away.

Once in the jeep, temporarily safe, they headed west, past Long Branch and onto Route 50. Gabriella started to shake and cry uncontrollably.

Will, speeding on a back road with limited visibility and trying to avoid slick patches of snow and ice, did the best he could to calm her.

It didn't work. Deep, racking, sob after sob, poured from her in a flood. He slowed down, better able to check on her, trying to soothe her. She kept it up, continued that way for nine slow miles until the lights of Winchester came into view. For most of the drive, Will looked at the road ahead and then turned back to check anything coming up the rearview mirror. He tried to stay in the road, but in his haste, he skidded several times. What irony it would be to get killed by running into a tree after all they'd been through.

Once across Interstate 81, he relaxed and slowed down. Gabriella did not. If anything, she was more out of control than before. She had her arms around her knees, crying with abandon, head down in her lap, rocking back and forth, like a child.

Not a light was on when he pulled into his driveway ten minutes later.

Will pulled around back to the garage and got out. Automatically, he again looked back to see if they were followed. Nothing but blackness could be seen all the way to Merriman's Lane. A few cars and trucks were moving on Route 37, farther away, but everything appeared okay.

He went to the passenger side door and opened it for Gabriella. She had to be helped to exit the jeep. Finally, when she was out, she continued to shake uncontrollably, putting her arms around Will, and refusing to let go.

It took eighteen minutes for the guard at the north river gate to reach the south guardhouse. When he heard the two shots, he'd called his colleague on the radio. After hearing no response, he radioed the main house, where no one answered. The two guards on the main gate and the western gate responded, but they had heard nothing and reported that all was normal at their posts.

There were three off-duty guards in the game room playing eight ball at the pool table for $5 a game. Several hundred dollars had already changed hands. Each of the three had consumed a few beers and the atmosphere was loud and animated, every stroke of the cue greeted with a jeer or a cheer. One had heard something outside, down by the river, but didn't connect it with any kind of threat. All were confident that their fellow guards could control any problem.

The alarm was sounded at the farm soon after the south river gate guard was discovered dead. The three gate guards on duty agreed on their radios that the western gate guard would be the one to report to the main house. The guards at first wondered what kind of punishment Maggio and Tony would get for not answering their call. Perhaps they have met a terrible fate, suggested the guard that was kneeling over Donte's body at the river. All other residents of the compound were alerted by the western guard as he tore through the farm blowing his horn. The three pool players arrived at the main house just before the guard in the pickup truck.

Within minutes, the rest of their stunned crew converged on the main house to learn the situation. Six dead, their captive escaped, their patron among the dead, and their second in command, Angelo Baldi, out of touch. Two guards remained outside—one at the main gate, the other at the north river gate. Thomas Parisi, who was the senior man present, took charge.

"We cannot call the authorities," he said. "We must keep this quiet; otherwise, our purpose will be discovered, and we all go to prison. I'll continue to try to find Angelo. We have a friend in the sheriff's department. He'll know where to find Angelo. Wrap the bodies in garbage bags and take them to the smokehouse. Angelo will decide what to do with them."

Parisi then asked Rob, the cook, to cleanup the library after Mr. Arthur was removed and to fix a large breakfast. Everyone was going to be up for a while.

Next, he took two men to the upstairs bedroom to supervise the cleanup there. He decided to man only one gate, the main one, since anyone coming to visit would use that entrance. He left the two river gates unmanned, asked the river guard to bring Donte to the smokehouse after he had cleaned up as best he could. They would spend the night cleaning and looking for any clue that would help explain what happened.

Parisi looked for tracks in the snow, any sign that would tell him about the men who attacked their compound. Only one person's footprint coming in from the river could be distinguished, which was part snow and part mud. Two sets of footprints going back toward the river were also clearly visible. All outside floodlights were illuminated, and they indicated two people had left through the field toward the river. No other sign of someone coming to the house. *Perhaps they came from the west,* thought Parisi.

He thought out loud, saying to no one in particular, "Should I call Philadelphia tonight? They'd have to know sometime. Maybe they'd know what to do."

Chapter 31

After ten rings, Roscoe answered the telephone. Edna Cline, naked and sweating with desire, back for a second night, fought him hard to prevent his answering it. Roscoe was panting for breath and holding Edna off with his free arm. She then probed his crotch area with her tongue. When he said hello, he said it with a high pitch to his voice.

Thomas Parisi thought he had a wrong number. "Roscoe? Is that you?"

"Hold on!" Roscoe shouted, pushing Edna away. He moved out of bed and cleared his throat. "Hello, this is Roscoe. Is that you, Angelo? Where the fuck have you been?"

"Hell, Roscoe, I was calling you, so you could tell me where Angelo was." The voice on the other end said, "This is Thomas, down at the farm. We need to talk to Angelo immediately. We have a problem."

Edna was now lying on the bed with an erotic pose. Her legs spread wide, her tongue moving back and forth, licking her lips, her hands and fingers massaging hard nipples, and then running them through her pubic hair. Roscoe forced himself to look away.

"I'm sorry; who did you say it was? I didn't hear you."

"It's Thomas Parisi, Roscoe!" he said, speaking louder, as if that would help the man hear. "I'm trying to locate Angelo. We got some problems."

"Where's Mr. Arthur? I talked to him earlier and told him I couldn't find Angelo either. The last time I talked to him was this morning, around 6:00 a.m. Angelo's just disappeared. Let me talk to Mr. Arthur. Thomas? Thomas? You still there?"

"Eh . . . Roscoe, that's one of the problems. Mr. Arthur is unable to talk. He's . . . uh . . . gone. That's why we need Angelo."

"Gone. What the fuck do you mean gone? I told you I talked to him today too."

"Well, Roscoe, he was here, but he is . . . uh . . . unavailable. Won't be available. Can you get Angelo? We need Angelo, and we need him now. Please."

"All right, all right, I'll comb this county 'til I find his inconsiderate ass. I'm gonna tell Mr. Arthur what I think about this whole business. It's not runnin' smooth, not like Mr. Arthur's way o' doin' things, ya heah?"

"Thank you, thank you, Roscoe. Please call the minute you find him. Please, it's very important."

Roscoe could not get to the business of finding Angelo just yet. He hung up the phone and headed directly for a leering Edna Cline.

The house was cold. MacKenzie had forgotten to turn the heat up. But they received a warm welcome from the dog. Watson's tail was moving so fast it knocked over a framed picture on the sun porch. He was fascinated by the strange woman who seemed upset, and he did everything he could to show her that he was a loving dog, and he could make things right. He treated her like family, sensing her despair. He licked her face. He sat at her feet. He looked in her eyes with concentrated adoration. Sounds coming from his mouth were a combination whine for attention and a satisfied whimper when he got it.

She sat on a barstool in the kitchen, not saying much, her head hanging down. Her answers to Will's questions were only one or two words: *yes*, *no*, *okay*, *fine*. Will poured two glasses of water for them and left the pitcher on the table. They were both thirsty and exhausted after a two-mile run in the dark. Their bodies and minds were drained from an adrenaline rush and it's post-effect. The dog would not leave her alone. He kept putting his chin on her thigh, drooling on her leg, and looking into her eyes, demanding attention. Finally, she began to stroke his massive head, and the dog literally sighed.

Only after Will prepared a dish of dog food and leftovers from the refrigerator did Watson turn attention away from the beautiful stranger. He would take a few hurried bites, raise his head, look in her direction, and then attack his dish again.

"Are you hungry? I didn't give everything to the dog." He was thankful now that she had stopped crying.

"No, thank you, I ate earlier this evening, before you came." Then she asked the question she had wanted to ask ever since they'd reached the security of the jeep. "May I call my father?" She was sure he would say no, proving to her that she was not safe after all.

"Of course, use that phone at the desk. Would you like privacy?"

"No, no, no, please stay with me. I don't want to be alone." She spoke in a soft, pleading voice with a melodious Spanish accent.

She dialed the private number, waited for what seemed like an eternity, when she heard a familiar voice, a voice that she despised. "Diego, this is Gabriella. May I speak to my father please?"

Diego ignored the formality in her voice. "Gabby, my dear Gabby, it really is you."

Excited with anticipation and joy, he asked question after question. "Where are you? Can you talk? Are you in good health? Did they treat you well? By Mother Mary, I will kill them all if they harmed you. No matter, I will kill them anyway. They made the biggest mistake of their miserable lives. Thank God they found the money. We have been so worried. We have a plane standing by, waiting for you. When were you released? Now you come home where you will be always safe. No more college. I will protect you with a hundred men. You never need to fear again." He was so happy to hear her voice he couldn't stop babbling.

"Diego, my father, I want to speak with my father. Please, may I speak with my father?"

"Your father's very sick. His sickness has worsened worrying about your safety. I will wake him with the phone. Gabriella, I can't tell you how happy I am to hear you and know you are coming home. Hold on, I will wake your father."

Don Alverez was awake when Diego rushed into the room. The old man had some extrasensory expectation that his daughter was free. One of the nurses held the phone to his ear. His hands were shaking. "Gabriella? Is that you?"

"Daddy, oh, Daddy, I've been so afraid that I would not see you again. I'm all right now. It was horrible, horrible. They shot all four of my friends and a wonderful boy I met in school. I hate them! I want to come home."

"You will, my love, you will. The plane is ready to come for you. Now let me speak to Paul." The relief and comfort from hearing his daughter was safe gave strength to the Don's voice.

"Daddy, Paul is not here. I haven't seen Paul. A wonderful man came to me. He had a fierce fight with four or five of them and brought me out. I am at his home now. He is the most wonderful man," cooed Gabriella as she turned to look at her rescuer.

"What's his name? Let me speak to him. Let me thank him," urged the Don who needed more information. Who was this man and what organization did he work for? How did he find out about Gabriella? Obviously, Paul hired him? How much was he paid? *I will pay him ten times more. I want to know why Paul changed the plans,* thought the Don.

For the first time, Gabriella broke into a grin; looking at the man while speaking into the phone, she said, "Uh . . . emm . . . Daddy, I'm embarrassed to say, I don't know his name. Isn't that odd? I haven't had the courtesy to ask him his name."

By the time Gabriella had given the phone to Will, Don Alverez was ready to adopt him.

"Sir, my name is William Mackenzie and your daughter need not apologize for not knowing my name. Your daughter is safe with me at my home in Winchester, Virginia."

With that introduction, Will looked at Gabriella for the first time. She was a mess, but even in this state, she was magnificently beautiful. Her luxurious dark hair was wildly shaped, a piece of bramble bush stuck above her ear. The big green eyes gazing at him were wide and innocent, framed by long seductively dark lashes. Will had never seen someone so unpretentiously gorgeous.

"Mr. Mackenzie, I want to thank you and your team for saving my Gabriella. You will not be sorry. I am in your debt. Let me introduce myself. My name is Miguel Alverez from Cartagena, Colombia. I am so grateful, so very grateful. Do you and Paul have enough men? I have local people that can be there in a matter of minutes. Is there any danger? Are you both safe?"

Will ignored the reference to Paul. "Sir, no one knows we're here. No one followed us. No one could possibly think to come here. I assure you we are safe. No need for any more men. It will only draw attention to us. I have an elaborate alarm system." Will looked down at his dog. "We cannot be surprised, and I am prepared for any eventuality. I will deliver your daughter to the place of your choice."

It was now after midnight, and the Don said, "Where is the nearest airport that can handle a Gulfstream? Are you familiar with such a plane? It requires about five thousand feet of runway to land and take off safely. We have smaller planes if this will not work."

"Yes, sir, I know the plane. I would suggest the Martinsburg, West Virginia airport. Martinsburg is the home of an air force reserve unit. They fly large planes out of there all the time. Their runway is probably more than five thousand feet. No problem with a Gulfstream. I live twenty minutes from that airport. You just tell me when to be there. If you have some associates in the area, they could meet us there at the same time. Your daughter is exhausted and needs rest, but otherwise, she is fine."

"I thank God, and I thank you. May I speak to my daughter please?"

Will smiled as he handed her the phone. "Gabriella, it appears that you are in good hands. If we can clear customs and have no problems with the flight plan, the plane will meet you at 8:00 a.m. tomorrow. It has been fueled and ready for takeoff ever since you were placed in the care of Don Joseph in Virginia. I would be there myself, but you understand why I have to remain here. I am awaiting a call from Paul. It is not like him to be out of touch for so long. Obviously, Paul has engaged Mr. Mackenzie. My hope is that he can join you and accompany you on your return. I would like to reward Mr. Mackenzie and will ask him to come to Colombia as our honored guest."

"Daddy, you will love him. He is the most wonderful man. I will urge him to join us. I feel like I've known him all my life, yet I have many questions to ask him myself. You mentioned Don Joseph? I did not meet him, but he did talk to me on the telephone. What does he look like? I . . . uh . . . I think he may have been . . . uh . . . hurt when Mr. Mackenzie freed me."

"Gabriella, Mr. Arthur, Don Joseph, is a long-time associate of mine, a large man, not fat but robust and powerfully built, black bushy hair, dark skinned, loves the sun and outdoors; I am anxious to hear of his health. May I please speak to Mr. Mackenzie one more time?"

She handed Will the phone, saying, "My father wants to invite you to our home. He is very happy. He will be most generous."

"Hello, sir, I thought I might follow up on one of Gabriella's comments about Joe Arthur. He is dead, most unfortunate, but our team had no choice." MacKenzie thought it best to imply that he was one of a group of rescuers, not necessarily the one who dealt with Joe Arthur.

"Yes, of course, of course, these things happen; he was an associate, not a friend, I understand, and please know that I am most grateful for what you have done. My daughter is the pride of my life. She is precious to me. I . . . I . . ." Don Alverez had to pause, his voice shaken with emotion and gratitude. "You must understand, I am not well, and this means everything in the world to me. Thank you. Thank you. Would you do me the honor of accompanying Gabriella to Colombia and coming to our home? I would like to show you just how thankful we are."

"Thank you, sir, I too am honored, but I have been well paid. I must not reveal my employer, sworn to secrecy; just know that Joe Arthur had many enemies. Your invitation is too kind. Unfortunately, my passport has lapsed, and it will take time to reissue. I cannot come tomorrow, but promise I will come later, if you so wish."

After a few more courteous requests and an equal number of courteous regrets, the two men hung up and each promised to meet in the near future.

Looking at Gabriella, Will said, "Time for some rest. You must be exhausted, and we have to move early in the morning."

Even after speaking with her father, Gabriella's head was down. She was staring blankly at the dog. The dog had already gone sound asleep in the middle of the kitchen floor. His requirements were simple: food and attention. Once he had received these, he was content. Will touched her shoulder, saying, "Gabriella? Are you all right? We need to rest."

She nodded. "Please call me Gabby, my friends call me Gabby."

"Okay . . . Gabby . . . up we go, let's get you settled. By the way, my name is Will." And he offered to shake her hand.

As soon as they moved out of their chairs, the dog's head rose; he saw where they were going, stood up, shook himself out of his stupor, and followed them up the stairs, acting as if he had only been pretending to sleep.

Will held her by the arm, gently guiding her into his daughter's room, which was across the hall from the master bedroom. "I'm sure we can find something for you to wear," he said, going through his daughter's dresser. "You're taller than she is, but we'll find something. There's a new toothbrush in the bathroom. Towels, soap, shampoo, whatever you need."

The dog followed, determined to make them aware that he was there too. Gabby thanked Will and said she would very much like a shower, being that she had never felt clean while she was being constantly watched.

"Don't worry, we are very safe. I've set the alarms, and I am right here. Call me if you need anything. Good night." He smiled, closed her door, and went to take a shower too.

Chapter 32

A short while after he had gone to bed, Will heard a soft tapping on his bedroom door. It was Gabriella. She apologized and said that she was afraid.

Would Mr. MacKenzie mind if she brought a blanket and pillow and slept on the floor in his room?

"Please call me Will. Of course, we can make room."

The interruption woke Watson, who was sleeping in his normal spot under the bed. Even though it took great effort for such a big dog to crawl under, he had been sleeping there ever since he was a puppy. At the end of every day, he would plop down on his haunches, wiggle under the bed, and fall asleep within seconds. However, even in a deep sleep, Watson was alert to strange noises and smells. Both senses woke him, and he crawled to the edge of the bed, just enough to stick his head out, and gaze up at Gabriella.

Will, sleeping in the nude, covered himself while he grabbed his trousers and clumsily pulled them on. Once clothed, he got out of bed and insisted that Gabriella sleep there, and he would go to his daughter's bed.

But then she protested; she would still be alone. She requested that he sleep in his own bed; she would be perfectly fine on the floor. She just couldn't take sleeping alone this night after all they had been through. He continued to insist that she sleep in the bed while he would move to the floor. The dog followed this conversation back and forth as if he were watching a tennis match.

They resolved the situation by his taking the mattress from his daughter's bed and putting it on the floor in the master bedroom where they would all be together. She helped him carry the bulky mattress, and Will couldn't help notice her firm breasts bouncing free under the loose-fitting nightgown he'd found for her.

Once the makeshift bed was in place with the lights out and everyone settled in their own beds, the dog decided that he would join the beautiful stranger next to him. He crawled partially out from under the bed and got close enough to Gabriella by placing his head on the mattress next to hers.

MacKenzie crashed into a deep, deep sleep immediately after his head hit the pillow.

His dreams came in vivid color, as they always did when he was exhausted. He was fighting strangers, one after another, who constantly try to kill him, and then he was regaining the love of his ex-wife. He was moving in slow motion.

His ex-wife's vision was clear and realistic. She came to him from the hallway, and she was wearing a flimsy nightgown that he could see through. Their reunion was a combination of tears and hugs and then turned to lust. They held each other tight and began to kiss. At first, the kisses were light and tender, but they soon turned hard and passionate. They begin to pull each other's clothes off and touch each other in ways that are familiar and yet strange.

The dream begins to seem incredibly real. Will heard a dog barking in the background. But his ex-wife ignored the dog, moving faster, pressing hard against him, digging into his back with her fingernails. She called his name over and over, telling him that she loved him. But he didn't recognize her voice. The accent was different, almost Spanish sounding.

"Thank you!" she said.

He started to moan. "No, THANK YOU!" And he woke up to the sound of his own voice.

Only then realizing that this was not a dream. It was a reality! He woke up in a passionate grip, wrapped tightly in the arms and legs of his rescued victim.

Gabriella had climbed into his bed. She'd had a nightmare and was so afraid. She needed him close to protect her, so she quietly stole beneath the covers. Still half-asleep, she put her arms around him, and he unconsciously embraced her. She had not known that he slept in the nude and became immediately aware that he was having an erotic dream. He was fully aroused. Gabriella was overcome with emotion and long-suppressed desire. The sudden violence and subsequent captivity in her closely protected life had affected her in ways she did not understand.

Her sexual experiences were very limited. Here she was, twenty-nine years old, in the prime of her womanhood. By accident, she found herself in the muscular arms of a mature man.

He was a handsome man, a man who had risked his life for her, a courageous man that had shown no mercy to her captors. Her first reaction to his nakedness was to remove her nightgown and scoot close to him. She pressed her pelvis against his hardness with a powerful urge that overcame her shyness.

Her whole body was aroused. She felt ready as if this were the natural thing to do. For both, it seemed like a dream; his was a dream come true; hers was a dream of being saved by a prince.

When he woke up and realized what was happening, he apologized profusely and begged her forgiveness. She moaned, put her arms around him, and told him with her body that he and she were bound together forever, that she loved him, that nothing could change her feelings for him. He tried to convince her that she was in shock from her captivity and that what they were about to do was an accident. She pushed against him with her nakedness and kissed him violently. She wanted him. The closer she was, the safer she felt. Miraculously, his mind finally overruled his body. He managed to pull the covers around him, moving his lower body away, just holding her in his arms. She was the most beautiful, innocent thing he had ever seen. He just couldn't bring himself to betray her trust.

Resisting her took all the discipline he'd learned in the army and the greater discipline he'd learned recently as he recovered from alcoholism. But resist he did. Finally, the tension relaxed. He held her, stroked her head, and calmed her until she fell into a deep sleep.

When they awoke, slightly embarrassed, they went to separate bathrooms, not saying much, their emotions mixed. She felt safe with him, wondered if finally it was love, but sensed they might never be together again. She was fearful of returning to Colombia and having to deal with Diego.

But she yearned to see her father, help him through his illness, and show her father that her love for him was as great as his for her.

Will's feelings for her were turning into something, but he couldn't distinguish what. It was too soon for love.

Both knew they were out of time. Each minute of further delay meant danger. They dressed quickly. Gabriella had nothing to pack. Will had to decide what weapons he would take to the airport. He didn't want to lose his prize after all they had been through, so he took an Uzi and two pistols.

He went north, taking the Route 37 bypass, and then on to Interstate 81 to the Martinsburg Regional Airport. On their way, they passed a deputy sheriff's car coming in the opposite direction. It was Roscoe

Harris, continuing a frantic search for his lost comrades. Roscoe thought he recognized Will's jeep but changed his mind when he saw someone in the passenger seat. Will had loaned Gabriella an extra ski cap and an old fur collared parka that hid her features from anyone looking in. Roscoe ignored the momentary distraction; he had to find his three missing men.

All the way to Martinsburg, Will checked his rearview mirror to make sure he wasn't being followed. When they pulled into the parking lot of the Martinsburg general aviation lot, Gabriella was surprised to find it empty, thinking, *Where is Paul? Where are the rest of his men?* Last night, things had moved so fast she never got around to asking why Will had done what he did. She never asked how he knew to come for her. How did he know where she was being held? The plane was on the tarmac, engines idling, ready to go. There was a uniformed man at the foot of the stairs leading to the aircraft, but otherwise, no one else could be seen. Will looked through the plate glass window of the private terminal and saw two other men standing inside in what looked to be pilot's uniforms. Gabriella confirmed this as she recognized one of the pilots who worked for her father.

Will searched in every direction before getting out of the jeep. He kept the Uzi under his overcoat, leaving one sleeve dangling empty. Gabriella pulled the top of the parka over her head and joined Will for the short walk to the terminal.

They were temporarily startled when another uniformed man came out of the bathroom just as they were entering the main lounge. Will wrapped his trigger finger around the Uzi, ready for a trap, keeping one eye on the uniformed official and aware of any other movement with his other. The man's uniform was a different color, and from the official patch on his arm, Will quickly realized that he was a customs agent called to the airport just to make sure anyone boarding or departing from the foreign aircraft was checked out. Normally, a customs agent would be joined by someone from immigration to check passports and review declaration statements, travel plans, purpose of visit, and so forth. But it appeared that the customs agent was alone.

When Gabriella entered the room, both pilots broke into broad grins and said excited greetings in Spanish. She switched to English and introduced Will as her good friend. Then, they all turned to the government man who stood by impatiently, looking very important. The customs agent introduced himself and left no doubt that they could do nothing without his approval. His demeanor changed immediately when Gabriella turned to him, looking like a helpless child in need. Only she wasn't a child, she was the most beautiful thing he had ever seen. Her smile and cultured accent charmed him into an apologetic servant.

The name on his tag read "Wysong," and he almost stuttered when he looked into Gabriella's eyes. He melted when she said his name. He begged pardon for the inconvenience of government approvals and reviewed her passport. A passport that conveniently became available from the pilot she had recognized earlier. The agent took his time looking into her face, his hands starting to shake, as he looked at her passport one more time. She was so beautiful; she made him nervous. He checked the forms and information that the pilots had meticulously prepared. After finding everything to be in order, he approved her for travel and left, smiling and talking to himself as he went out the door.

Gabriella asked the pilots if they had seen Paul Xavier or any other men who worked for her father. Had her father given them instructions to contact Paul? Surprised that they had heard nothing and had no such instructions, she decided not to wait for Paul. But first, she asked Will's opinion on what she should do. Will advised her to go, agreeing with her decision. It was too risky for her to remain, and Paul could take care of himself and would schedule another plane.

Before going to the tarmac, Gabriella turned to Will with tears in her eyes, hugged him tightly, and said, "I will never forget you as long as I live. I will love you forever. Promise me you will come."

Will mumbled. He tried to say something, but nothing sensible came from his mouth. She kissed him lightly on the cheek and said goodbye.

The pilots averted the couple and tried to give them a private moment. The clerk at the terminal, a red-headed woman who loved to fly and who had remained in the background, looked on with envy.

Gabriella held him tight one last time, turned abruptly, and went through the door.

Will watched her as she ran all the way to the plane. She cried openly and turned to face him before entering the cabin. He stepped outside and returned her wave, fighting back the tears. Then the plane slowly taxied to the end of the runway and waited for clearance from the tower. The outside air was cold, and he shivered, watching the aircraft gather speed down the runway and take off. He glimpsed Gabriella through the window where she waved one last time.

The nine-passenger Gulfstream luxury jet could easily fly nonstop from West Virginia to her father's private airfield in Colombia. It would land adjacent to her father's main house, a Mediterranean-style private fortress, which was headquarters and home to the Cartagena Cartel. There would be no customs official to interfere with her arrival.

Within minutes of takeoff, after she had refused repeated offers of drinks and refreshments, she quietly dozed off, only to awake when the pilot announced that she should buckle her seatbelt; they were going to be landing soon.

Gabriella would have preferred a customs official to the reception she saw waiting for her in Colombia. Diego Estrada stood at the head of nine bodyguards, all armed with machine guns, shotguns, and rifles. Diego was beaming, standing ramrod straight, black hair slicked back, holding a bouquet of fresh flowers, dressed in his finest suit, wearing his favorite tie, his shoes spit-shined to a point where they were reflecting the sun. He looked like a groom at a Spanish country wedding, anxiously waiting for his bride. The other men stood in front of a range rover and two large SUVs, which were parked next to the hangar.

He bent to give her a hug and a kiss, and Gabriella coldly backed up and instead shook his hand. He looked behind her, expecting Paul to be departing from the same plane, wanting to shame Paul for not reporting on the ransom and needing outside help to rescue their precious Gabriella.

She advised that Paul had stayed behind, implying that she knew where he was and that he still had important work to do back in the States. Though not pleased, she felt obliged to ride alone with Diego in the middle of a convoy taking her to the villa compound. The short ride home took only five minutes, and she was grateful that their conversation was limited to a discussion of her father's health rather than questions about her rescue. She ignored Diego's expressions of concern for her safekeeping and his undying devotion to her.

When she saw her father, who had made a supreme effort to stand and greet her, tears started to flow; she was stunned by his frailty. From the time she was old enough to walk, her father had been an all-powerful figure, full of life and vitality. Whatever her wish, he could make it come true. She could not believe how much he had deteriorated in the year since their last visit.

Her shock contrasted with his elation. He was overcome with joy. All of his wealth and all of his power meant nothing compared to her safety. With much fanfare, he vowed to protect her from harm at all costs. After holding each other for a long, long, time, she helped a nurse lead him to a comfortable chair and plumped a fat pillow behind his head. Both father and daughter started to talk at the same time. After laughing, hugging, and looking into his gray-colored face, Gabriella held both of his hands and let him ask the questions. He had difficulty and needed to pause, taking water frequently, and his voice grew faint. He needed answers to many questions, and he knew that his time was running out. *Where was Paul when he needed him most?* Even though it was uncomfortable for Gabriella, he asked Diego to do some of the questioning so he could save his strength.

They debriefed her regarding both abduction and rescue. They wanted to know about the kidnappers and her treatment. *Had she been harmed, threatened? How was she treated? Had she been fed? Was she hungry? Had she been able to sleep? Who was her rescuer? How did he get involved? How many others were involved in the rescue? Who did he represent? Who had the money? Was there a split in the Philadelphia Mafia? A gang war? Who knew about the money? Where was Paul?*

There were many other questions until in mid-sentence, her father drifted off to sleep. Gabriella was unable to answer most of the questions. While on the telephone with her father, she had told him that she had many questions to ask of Will, but she never got around to it. She couldn't say why but grinned to herself when she thought about it. Diego wanted to continue the inquisition, but she refused, saying she needed rest too.

Gabriella's limited answers convinced Diego to conclude that Gabby's rescuer knew who had the money. Obviously, he was a dangerous man, linked to powerful interests, but he could not guess what group he was associated with.

Diego was very suspicious, thinking, *Maybe it was the CIA? Don Alverez's air cargo planes were used by CIA all the time, especially in South America. Maybe the Don has a secret relationship with the CIA.*

It wasn't the DC gang. They wouldn't release her without getting their money. Maybe the DC gang did get their money. Maybe they had a problem with Joe Arthur. If they did, why did they agree to use Joe's services as mediator? It couldn't be the Mafia unless there was a power struggle in Philadelphia.

Too many ifs, thought Diego. At least some things were going to change. Paul Xavier did not handle this well. He had a lot of explaining to do when he showed up. Diego had plans for his cousin Paul as soon as Don Alverez was out of the picture. Gabriella would not be so high and mighty once her father was gone. She would need his protection, and for that, she had to become more accommodating. For the time being, her father would not allow any harm to come to his daughter's savior. But that guy in Winchester was going to answer questions whether he liked it or not.

One thing for sure was going to happen, and soon, steps would be taken to teach a violent lesson to the idiots who dared kidnap the Don's daughter. Booger Bryant and his FU Crew would pay and pay dearly. This last thought brought a smile to Diego's face.

Chapter 33

In Washington DC, the leaders of the Fourth and U Street drug gang wanted answers. They'd lost contact with their man in Winchester. He hadn't called in for three days. Booger Bryant tried calling Joe Arthur in Clarke County. Every time he called, they said he was "out."

"Could someone else help? Could they take a message?" Booger was seated at his desk in back of the FU Club's bar. He, LD, and Peacock were listening to an answering machine that LD had taken from Blue's house on MacArthur Boulevard.

"Hello, hello, Blue? Where are you? You've been neglectful. Are you avoiding me? Is this your way of dumping me?"

The voice was his new girlfriend, Irene. There were six messages from Irene on the machine. The last one was "Blue, goddamn you, where did you go, China? Call me. Call even if you just want to say goodbye. I love you. There, I said it, I . . . LOVE . . . you! Do you hear? What else do you want from me?"

The three men listened to the messages over and over, trying to learn something.

Finally, Peacock said, "Boog, she don't know shit."

Booger looked at Peacock. "Do you think I'm deaf? Of course, she don't know shit. I gotta pay her a visit. If Blue's flown the coop, then I'm steppin' in."

LD sat there nodding. "Yeah, Boog, she's fine, I mean real fine."

"But that don't solve our problem, do it?" Booger speaking as he turned the issues over in his mind. "How we gonna find Blue? Where the fuck's our money? You don't suppose our princess's still up in the country, do you?"

Peacock had the answer. "Lemme take a trip up there, Boog. I know Angelo and two or three o' Joe's boys. They talk t' me. If they don't, maybe we teach a wop not t' mess wif the FU Crew."

"Peacock, look at me. You got a history of mental illness in yo' family? Any of yo' kin locked up in St. Elizabeth's? You ain't makin' no sense, boy." And he continued with a lecture on culture.

"You go to Winchester, and it's like a foreign country. How many black faces you think you gonna see? You gonna stand out like a black thumb, bro, a big black thumb."

And LD offered his advice. "You think the mob make a deal with the spics, Boog?"

"Ain't nothin' wrong with your head, LD. You ain't as dumb as you look."

"Sooner or later, we gotta go up there. We a big customer, bizness is bizness, somebody gotta talk sometime. Blue mentioned a lawman named Roscoe. Worse comes to worse, we talk to him."

LD said, "Roscoe? What kinda name's Roscoe? Sounds like a clown."

"No, we be the clowns," Booger said. "Look at us. Got no money. Got no girl. Got no idea where we get next month's supply, and you think those spics ain't comin'? They be comin' all right. We better be ready."

Booger Bryant had been calling Blue's beeper every hour on the hour. Blue had to be dead. If the police had been involved, he would have heard something by now. Booger thought about Peacock's suggestion. Maybe he ought to consider taking a hundred brothers out to the country for a little fun. The rednecks in Clarke County had better beware.

At the Kennedy Center Eisenhower Theatre, Irene was coming out of the matinee when a man stepped in front of her and started walking toward the elevator. Automatically, she followed, neither one speaking. The elevator went to the parking garage, but Irene hadn't driven to the show.

She followed the man to his car, each looking around to see who was there. Nothing suspicious was observed, so she got in the backseat.

Steve Beinhorn, in the front, asked the question, "You wanted to see me?"

"Something's up, Steve. I haven't heard from Blue for four days now. I've left messages. I've called his beeper. I just don't know what's happened, and I don't know what to do next. He hasn't called Booker because I tried to reach him there. Could he have smelled a rat?"

"I know you called. We got a tap. Had a tap for months. Nothing we've heard would indicate a leak. Booker's called a couple of people to check Smith's house. Booker also received a call from a farm in Clarke County, Virginia. They talked about money, talked about an exchange, said something was going to happen within forty-eight hours. The man's name was Joe, and the farm's owner is Joe Arthur, a big deal in Virginia political circles." Steve looked in the rearview mirror. "Do you have any idea where he went?

"He said he'd be gone a couple of days. Had to go to Winchester, Virginia, but didn't say why, and I didn't ask. I don't ask, Steve. I never ask. He has to volunteer what info I get."

"Winchester's only ten or twenty miles west of Clarke County. Irene, how close to him are you?"

"Very close, Steve, very close. You don't want to know the details."

"Irene, you know the bureau doesn't expect its agents to go the extra mile. You can get out. There's lots of action I can put you on."

"If you don't have any specific recommendations, Steve, I'd like to see this through, see what happens. I'm also close to Booker. I know he likes me."

"Do it then. Call the special number whenever you need backup, Irene. We're here 24/7."

Walking out of the garage and taking the short stroll to her Watergate apartment, Irene stopped at the front desk when the guard waved her over.

"Flowers for you, Ms. Irene. Two dozen roses."

"Finally," she said to the guard. *Where has that son-of-a-bitch been?* she thought as she opened the card. *It's about time!*

But it wasn't from Blue, it was from Booker, saying he'd "like to come over."

In Philadelphia, Fredrico Arturo's phone rang three times before the maid picked it up. He was just coming down for breakfast, and he took in the foyer.

"Mr. Arturo, It's Thomas Parisi, down in Virginia."

"Hello, yes. Hello, Thomas, I knew your father."

"Sir, I am calling with bad news, really, really bad news. Your brother is dead."

"Dead? How could Joe be dead? He's ten years younger than I am! He's healthy as a horse. I saw him last month, talked to him last week, and he was fine. He kept an abortion clinic in business. Was it his heart, Thomas?"

"No, sir, it was . . . it was . . . it was . . . a gunshot. Someone shot him and five of our men, Donte, an' Vito, Maggio, an'—"

"Hold on. Hold on. Where are you calling from? Is this phone safe?"

"Yes, sir. I'm calling from a pay phone at the Mountain View Motel."

"I can be there in three hours! Don't tell anyone. Do the authorities know? Does anyone else know?"

"No, sir, no one knows but the family here, and we are searching for more information."

"Let me talk to Angelo."

"That's been a problem too, sir. We haven't been able to reach Angelo. He . . . he's just disappeared."

At the doctor's parking lot at the Winchester Medical Center, a beeper kept ringing in the trunk of the black Buick sedan. Mostly, no one heard it, but every now and then, a doctor would check his beeper to see who was calling.

One, an orthopedic surgeon named Wise, took his beeper off and shook it, thinking it was defective.

Another, a surgeon named McCallister, who'd spent thirteen straight hours in surgery with several difficult cases, cursed his beeper and turned back to the hospital, thinking, *Here we go again.*

Chapter 34

In Western Frederick County, Will felt semi secure. He spent every day, hour after hour, figuring ways to convert cash into investments and avoid IRS suspicion. He hid the cash in over twenty safe deposit boxes, each in a different bank in several towns in the Northern Shenandoah Valley. He kept $500,000 in an ash bin underneath the unused fireplace in his den. Over $2,000,000 remained buried in the hidden floor vault in his mountain cabin just across the West Virginia border. He missed Gabriella, but did not dare try to get in touch with her. He was surprised when she called him and more surprised that her father hadn't called. As often as she could, she called him from a secret place that she said was necessary because she feared a man called Diego. She kept talking about one of her father's men named Paul who would straighten things out when he returned. He regretted not being able to tell her the truth, that Paul would never return, but some things just couldn't be told.

MacKenzie's ex-wife had recently fallen in love with a rich New England banker and planned to get married again. Will had scheduled a trip to Boston hoping to talk her out of it, showing her he'd recovered. Maybe, if nothing else, his visit would delay her plans, and maybe, surely, she would allow him to see the kids on a normal basis. He missed the kids; teenagers needed a father.

The long funeral cortege wound through the Cartagena countryside for over a mile. Traffic stopped in all directions. Peasants by the side of the road took off their hats and bowed their heads.

The Bishop of Bogotá was the only other passenger in the black limousine sitting with Gabriella, holding her hand. He'd delivered the homily at the cathedral and presided over the lengthy funeral with a High Mass. The trip to the family grave site was slow. Many thousands of people, dressed in black, lined the city streets and stood in silence outside of the packed service. Throughout the city and country, cars turned on their lights out of respect.

Alone, in the third limousine, Diego Estrada smiled. After years of planning, his dreams were going to come true. He opened an expensive champagne and drank it straight out of the bottle.

He thought, *Paul will never know what hit him if he ever shows up. And Gabriella better get used to it. I am the Don.*

Don Estrada, it had a nice ring. It resonated authority, respect. People would toe the line. There would be many changes. Too many people get money for nothing. Now, everyone will earn his keep or rot in the streets.

He looked at the car ahead with disgust. He'd earlier been embarrassed by Gabriella when she refused his request to ride with her. In twenty-four hours, there would be more funerals. She wouldn't have a choice for those funerals. She would be staying home. His home now, only she didn't know it.

Will had called Champ Lewis several times. Champ always seemed to be out and didn't have an answering machine.

At the Philadelphia jail, a penitent teenager was being roughly hustled back out of the Maximum Security Section, the lockup for the city's most hardened criminals. The guard, a friend of Champ Lewis, opened four different sets of doors on the way out. Thoughts of some of the inmates' conversations stuck in Champ's head. They'd called his nephew "pretty boy." One had asked the kid, "When you comin' in, sweetheart?" Another said, "I be waitin'." Still, another cooed, "I need a new girl, honey, you be just my type."

The boy was the reason for going to the jail. Champ wanted his nephew, Sugar Ray, to know what happened to drug dealers. "You want to wind up like your mother?" he challenged. (Champ's sister, Sugar Ray's mother, had died violently, supposedly of a drug overdose. But the coroner ruled that she'd been murdered.)

The teenager looked up, visibly upset. "No, sir . . . I don't . . . I'm sorry, Uncle Champ, I mean it. You been mighty good to me."

He towered over the boy. "That's what's goin' ta happen to you . . . if you live . . . and the odds ain't good you be livin'. If you want to make a lot of money, you can work for me. I need someone I can trust. But I also need someone with a brain. You have to do well in school. You think you can do it?"

"Oh yeah, I can do it, I promise. I don't want to wind up in there."

Will hung up the phone and smiled. Sue Ellen, his soon-to-be-married ex-wife had agreed to meet with him in Cape Cod. She didn't believe he had sobered up completely but was willing to talk. That was progress. Will was giddy. He decided to shave and shower, pack a few things, and go.

He was almost in the shower when he heard the telephone. He hesitated to answer; fearful Sue Ellen had changed her mind. He let it ring and ring but finally grabbed the phone; it turned out to be Steve Beinhorn.

"Hello, asshole! Did I wake you up?"

"No, I was waiting by the phone, hoping that an asshole would call. My dreams have come true. What's up?"

"Will, maybe I can mix a little business with the pleasure of seeing you. Do you know a guy by the name of Joe Arthur?"

The question was so unexpected that Will hesitated to answer. He couldn't believe that his friend knew what had happened to Arthur.

"Will, Will, you there?"

"Sorry, Steve, Watson was distracting me, he wants to go out, and he's pulling at my leg. What was the question?"

"Joe Arthur, that name mean anything to you?"

"Joe Arthur? Sure, I know him, everybody does. He's a big man in these parts. I used to know him well. We were on several boards together. He's the main fund-raiser for every charity in town, loads of money, filthy rich, very generous. Yeah, I know Joe Arthur, but I haven't seen him since my love affair with the booze."

"Do you know what business he's in?"

"He's old money, Steve. He's into banking, real estate, restaurants, motels, air freight, cattle, imports, and probably a lot more."

"I would appreciate it, Will, if you could jot down everything you know about him and meet me for dinner tonight in Middleburg."

"Why don't you drive a little farther, just past Upperville, and we can have dinner at the Ashby Inn; I guarantee you'll love it."

"Will, you liked army food, remember?"

"You are an ignorant asshole when it comes to gourmet food, Steve. Trust me. You will thank me after dinner although you may be disappointed with how little I know about Joe Arthur."

"I'll be there at six. I can't wait to see your cultured, gourmet ass. Bye."

Champ Lewis tried another call to Will MacKenzie. The line was still busy. *His new muscle-bound self must be asleep with the phone off the hook. He couldn't be talking this long,* thought Champ.

Will stepped out of the shower just in time to hear the phone. Again, he worried it was Sue Ellen calling to say she'd changed her mind about meeting him with the children in Cape Cod. Again, he was wrong.

It was Gabriella, and she was crying. "Will, oh, Will, I'm so sorry, I've put you in great danger."

"Gabriella, Is that really you? What's the matter?"

"My father died. He died last week, and terrible things have been happening ever since."

"I'm so sorry, Gabriella. I know how much he meant to you."

"It was a blessing. That's not the problem. Diego has appointed himself as head of the entire business empire. Many people have died. Associates of Paul Xavier have just disappeared. Paul has vanished too, without a word. No one has heard from him in weeks. He was last seen in Winchester."

"Calm down now, just calm down. Things will work out for the best. Didn't you say Diego was in love with you?"

"He is determined to marry me and is being very aggressive about it. Diego has plans to move into the main house, my father's house. Even now, he's calling it his."

"It's mainly to make his leadership position look official in the eyes of others," she explained, "especially those who might be loyal to Paul Xavier. I'm doing my best to resist him. But oh, Will, I did something terrible. I told Diego that I couldn't marry him because I loved you."

"Gabby, you're too young. I'm too old for you. You don't mean that. You'll find a wonderful young man and live happily ever after."

"Will, that's not all. I told him that I was carrying your child."

Will gulped. "What? Why on earth did you—"

"He became hysterical and slapped me over and over. I told him that he'd better watch it, that Paul was coming back, and he would have plenty to say about who was in charge."

"Gabby, about Paul Xavier, maybe he's not coming back. What if he's dead?"

"Something's wrong, I know. But that's not why I called. You are in great danger. Diego screamed in my face. He said if I was with child, it would be ripped out of my belly after he'd dealt with the father."

"Gabby, you have to be strong. Things will work out."

"No, Will, things are not working out."

"Gabby, he doesn't mean it. He's jealous, that's all. You must tell him the truth about us. He'll calm down."

"It's more than that, Will," Gabriella continued. "Diego also told me that a large ransom was to be paid, but now it's missing. He said that the ransom was so large that it took three parachutes to handle all the money."

"*Three* parachutes?"

"Yes, three. Carrying lots of money. Michael Rowe, Paul's brother-in-law, died trying to deliver the money. The money was never found. Diego thinks you and Paul and Michael were involved in a scheme to steal the money. Diego says that Paul Xavier is going to pay the ultimate price for his treachery." Gabriella paused for breath; she had been talking so fast. "I don't think you understand. Diego is a vengeful man. The money is symbolic. I want you safe. You have to hide. Go someplace where no one can find you."

"Gabby, come on. Surely, he won't hurt you. He doesn't mean it."

And then she dropped the bombshell. "Oh yes, he means it. Diego has already left for the airport with five horrible, evil men."

Will's jovial expression vanished. He plopped down in the nearest chair.

"They are highly trained and heavily armed." She started crying again. "The plane will be in the U.S. soon, very soon . . . within hours. They are going to meet others who have been assembled and are waiting in Miami. The Miami team has been planning for a revenge assault on the gang in DC that took me and killed my friends."

Will's mind began racing. "Jesus, Gabby—"

"Next, they will be coming for you," Gabriella hissed into the telephone. "I know Diego. He won't stop until you and Paul are dead."

Will stared into space, the trip to Cape Cod and his dinner with Beinhorn temporarily forgotten.

"Promise me you will hide." Gabriella's voice began to shake. "I must see you when this nightmare is over. Believe it or not, I am in love with you, Will." Gabriella gave him the name and address of her parish priest, someone she trusted. Will could call the priest and communicate with her without being suspected.

Will gave her Champ Lewis's and Steve Beinhorn's business and home phones. Those two, he told her, would always be able to get in touch with him.

"Someone's coming. I have to go." She sounded scared and hung up without saying goodbye.

He sat still for a long while, staring into space. Faithful Watson was at his feet, looking up. The dog remained quiet, sensing that something was wrong.

Will tried calling Champ Lewis again, but no one picked up the phone. He petted Watson and stood up. After dinner, he would head north for Cape Cod. He had only four hours to prepare. It was enough time.

Watson was excited. The dog had watched Will pack the jeep and go through a complete check of his weapons. He sat patiently while Will loaded a suitcase full of cash and followed him as he went through every room of the house, turning lights on, opening closets and drawers, making sure that he hadn't forgotten something. When Will didn't respond to a whine, the dog barked again, his trusting eyes conveying a need for attention. Will bent down, ruffled his fur, and returned the love. "It's okay, big boy, its okay. I'll be right back."

He gave the dog a big bowl of leftovers.

On his way out the door, Will heard the phone ring. But he didn't have time to answer it. On the other end of the line, listening to a fifth ring, an excited woman named Maggie, hoping to find her man, hung up in frustration.

Chapter 35

Coming over Ashby Gap on Route 50, something Gabriella said finally reached Will's brain. *Three parachutes? She said THREE! With dufflebags, or three counting the parachutist? Where the hell is the other one? Is there another one?* As he pulled into the Ashby Inn parking lot, Will noticed the first blooms of spring. A hedge of forsythia bushes had burst into a sea of yellow. Multicolored tulips were popping up and out in front of the inn.

The view back up to Ashby Gap in the last light of sun was majestic. Little green buds on every tree indicated the coming of new life to the entire mountainside. In the meadows below, Black Angus cattle lolled around picturesque ponds. At the mountain tree line, a herd of deer had ventured out to feed, feeling safe as darkness approached.

He pulled his jeep into a space between a dark green Ford sedan with federal government plates and a black Porsche convertible with a Pennsylvania vanity plate, MR. CLEAN. The government sedan had several radio aerials sticking up, indicating a very important official.

Will stepped into the foyer and immediately smelled the rich aroma of applewood burning in a fireplace to his right. A familiar voice said, "Is that what a redneck looks like?"

"No," another familiar voice replied, "that's what an ignoramus ASSHOLE looks like."

Will turned to see a laughing Champ Lewis towering over a grinning Steve Beinhorn. Both men had their backs turned to the old fireplace and welcomed Will into the warm room.

Back in DC, soft music from a central tape player enhanced the mellow mood of the few early-bird patrons at the FU Club. Drinks were half-price, and fried chicken fingers were free. A popular local band was scheduled to appear later, and the bar was beginning to fill.

Earlier, outside the club, Booger's lookouts had reported several sedans driving past slowly . . . like they were lost. Inside each sedan were at least four occupants checking out both sides of the street, observing every inch of Booger's territory.

One had parked about a block from the club, and after an hour of sitting, two men got out and casually strolled down the sidewalk into the club.

LD pretended not to notice as he walked past them, back through the bar, down the hall, and knocked on the boss's door.

"They're here."

"How many?" asked Booger as he buttoned up his pants from behind his desk. A naked girl scurried from underneath, grabbing her clothes.

"Only two." LD's voice was calm and serious as his eyes followed the girl down the hall.

"Where?"

"Sittin' at the bar. Two black brothers. One is a mountain of a man, about six-eight, 250 or 260 pounds, calm as a funeral director. Both ordered gin 'n' tonics."

"I want 'em alive. Bring 'em here for a little talk."

LD and three of his men came out of the back of the club and headed past the bar, taking their time.

The two strangers, on guard, expecting trouble, watched the men approaching by, following their reflections in the wall mirror behind the bar.

Calmly, the bartender reached down and produced a sawed-off shotgun from underneath the bar.

The strangers didn't see it until they heard the click of the shotgun's hammers being racked back.

"Hands on the bar. I hope you ain't stupid." The bartender's nervous voice got their attention.

LD stuck a pistol against the bigger man's temple.

The other man kept his hands still, both pressed down on the bar, as instructed. His mustache quivered as he looked past the bartender, pointing the gun, assessing the determined eyes of four men, each holding a pistol. "We just came in for a drink. What's goin' on?"

Neither man moved as they were thoroughly frisked. Four automatic pistols, six clips of ammunition, a barber's razor, and two pairs of brass knuckles were removed from their pockets and placed on the bar.

LD looked them in the eye. "Y'all goin' huntin'? Expectin' trouble? Don't ya trust anyone in your nation's capitol?" And before the men could reply, LD said to hold still, he'd be right back.

Instead of going to the back office, he stepped outside the front door. There, as expected, was a DC police car with two patrolmen inside. LD leaned on the door and asked, "Mind if I borrow a couple pair o' handcuffs? I'll bring 'em right back."

At River View Farm, Thomas Parisi and a Mr. Arturo from Philadelphia (Roscoe hadn't heard his first name) waited patiently as Roscoe explained the reason for his urgently called visit. They were in the living room of the main house sitting by the huge fireplace as Roscoe, too nervous to sit still, paced about the room and told them the latest discovery.

"They found our missing guys. In the doctor's parking lot of Winchester Medical Center. All three stuffed in the trunk of Angelo's rented Buick. Wrapped around the spare tire. Nobody noticed until the recent warm spell. Two days of sunny weather in the sixties and two nights above freezing was all it took. God, did they smell! At first, someone thought it was comin' from the viscose plant at Front Royal. Sometimes, when the wind's just so, it stinks to high heaven. But the smell got worse 'n' it centered on the black Buick."

Roscoe now had their full attention. "The hospital's security guard opened the trunk, vomited, and then he fell, dropped flat on his face. They had to ask a doctor, the head of pathology, to look at the bodies. Even he had problems. Their features were bloated and turned into a greenish grey color. No doubt about who they were though. I got there within thirty minutes of the first call. I was on the eighth tee at Carper's Valley. Dicky D., the man who runs the place, came and got me right away."

Mr. Arturo interrupted, "How can you be sure it was them, Roscoe?"

"Oh, I'm sure all right, Mr. Arturo, I'm sure. They was bloated and discolored, but I could tell. No doubt about it."

"Do the authorities know who they are, Roscoe?"

"Not yet, Mr. Arturo, 'cause they didn't have any identification. No wallet, no ring, no weapon, no nothin'. It'll take time, but they'll ID Angelo and Blue from fingerprints and military records, jail records, and the like. If Angelo used his own name to rent the car, they'll know from that. They'll have more trouble with the Colombian unless someone reports him missing, ya' know."

"How long before they're identified?"

"I give 'em a week, now that the FBI has been called in. What do we do, Mr. Arturo?"

"Well, up to now, I thought the Colombians came after the girl. It's what they do. Shoot first and ask questions later. Don't care who they kill. Don't give a damn about business relationships." Arturo paused and stroked his chin thoughtfully. "But they wouldn't execute their number 2 guy. He was the heir apparent, the Don's favorite. Maybe there's a power struggle down there?"

He looked at the two men to see if they understood. "No matter, I've got to call Cartagena, then DC. They need to know what we know. Maybe we can avoid a war, but it's almost certain the war plans are near complete. They both suspect us, of course."

Parisi interrupted, "I tried to tell them, Mr. Arturo. They called every day asking for Mr. Arthur."

Arturo nodded but turned to Roscoe. "What else, Roscoe? What do we have to be ready for?"

"Well, they might be able to tie the three to the Keenes and the Wilkens. Fingerprints maybe, but no weapons, unless they find the weapons. They'll wanna know why we ain't reported Angelo missing. We can say he was supposed to be with Joe Arthur and he never told us where he was going. Lots o' times, he 'n' Angelo just go. Don't tell us a thing, right, Thomas? That's the truth. It won't be hard t' say. Joe hasn't called in either, 'n' we can say this may make Joe a missin' person too."

Arturo finally stood up. "Roscoe, where the hell is all that money? Somebody has it. Who do you think took it?"

"Well, Mr. Arturo, I got one good suspect. A Will MacKenzie, but there may be others. I got to widen my search of dog owners. Maybe there's someone out there that has dogs but no license. Plus, there's a Doc Scully that was out of town. I assumed that let him off the hook, but now, I just don't know. There's also a dog owner, radio station guy, he had small dogs, but I've seen him with at least one large dog too."

"If we can find that money, we may get out of this mess and repair our relations with all parties. Roscoe, double your efforts and you can have 10 percent." He turned to Parisi. "Thomas!"

"Yes, sir?"

"I'm sending my son, Carmine, and a team of good men down here. They'll be my eyes and ears. Give them whatever they need. Be alert for unwanted visitors from DC, or Colombia. They won't be social. Be ready."

"Yes, sir!" And Thomas Parisi stood up too.

Roscoe left by the unpaved river road, not wanting to be seen by anyone. He didn't want people to connect him to River View Farm and Joe Arthur in any way.

10 percent! Roscoe exclaimed to himself, a smile on his face. *Mr. Arturo said he'd pay me 10 percent if I found the money. 10 percent of what?* Roscoe almost hit a four-rail fence as he thought about the money. *God, there must be millions. Nobody told me how much. Mr. Arturo just assumed I knew.*

He drove a little farther and almost missed his turn, thinking, *If there's millions, why should I return it to anyone? Why indeed. What do people do with so much money?* He couldn't imagine. Well, he wouldn't give it to charity, that's for sure! He thought about the article he'd read in the *Star* that morning about an anonymous gift of $10,000 to the free medical clinic. The day before, a similar amount was given to the Salvation Army. Both gifts were cash, all in hundred-dollar bills. The donor had left no note, no indication of where it came from. What kind of idiot gives away all that money and not get credit for it? He shook his head; *it's got to be a nut case.* There had been several stories recently about anonymous cash gifts to area charities. *What are these people, crazy? Giving money away, and it isn't even Christmas!*

Roscoe grunted at their stupidity.

And then his heart began beating faster. What made him think there were a lot of people involved? What if it was just one person? One person giving thousands of dollars away; one person who just started to give money away around the time the ransom was lost. Oh my god! It had to be the person who found the money. It had to be someone with a big dog or dogs. It had to be someone who walked early on Merriman's Lane with his dogs.

Will MacKenzie. That's who it had to be. Roscoe grinned, thinking he had finally figured it out. He knew he should head straight for Will's house on Merriman's Lane, but he decided to call Edna instead.

Some things just couldn't wait.

Chapter 36

Six desk clerks were busy with customers in the crowded lobby of Washington DC's Mayflower Hotel. They had not noticed the various undercover agents of the FBI circulating in the hall, the lobby, and in and out of the first-floor shops and restaurants.

On the top floor, in the penthouse suite, Diego Estrada paced nervously back and forth. This evening would be payback, and he was wishing he could be there personally. Diego kept looking at his watch, anytime now.

He jumped when the phone rang. No calls were expected. His presence in the United States was a risk, and only a few trusted lieutenants knew of his whereabouts. One of his bodyguards answered. A familiar voice asked to speak with Don Estrada, insisting, "It was urgent."

Speaking in Spanish, an irritated Diego Estrada grabbed the phone.

The voice advised that a housekeeper at a Cartagena priest's parish house had called as instructed. Gabriella had gone to the church, slipped out to the parish house, and made a phone call to a man in the United States.

The man's name was Will MacKenzie, and Gabriella had warned him about Diego's coming to the United States.

Slamming the phone down, Diego turned to his men, his face red with anger. "Pack your bags. We're checking out. I want to leave in fifteen minutes." As the men hurried away, he called to one, saying, "Find a map of Virginia. I want the quickest way to Winchester."

The veins on Diego's neck and face bulged with tension as he loaded hollow tipped bullets into a magazine clip. He was talking to himself as he checked his automatic pistols and carefully placed them in holsters. "I want his balls. I want to give a special present to Gabriella when I return."

The anteroom of the Ashby Inn was bright and cozy; warmed by a roaring fire and lit by a huge chandelier which hung down from a twelve-foot ceiling. Around the massive antique fireplace, a large couch and several overstuffed chairs provided an ideal place for cocktails or just relaxing with a good book. One wall of the room was lined, floor to ceiling, with books. Another wall was covered with paintings from local artists.

"I've got great news," Steve announced, motioning for them to sit. "I've finally located Muldoon, Fetler, and Vaugan. They're in Missoula, Montana."

The other two started talking at once. "How are they? What are they doing in Montana? When did they get out of Vietnam? How did you find them? Did you tell 'em about us? When can we get together?" They went on and on until Steve said, "WHOA! Hold on, one at a time. Let me tell you all I know."

The waitress brought MacKenzie a sparkling water and fresh drinks for the other two.

"An FBI analyst friend of mine tracked them down. All three are partners in a ranch outside of Missoula. I called and talked to Fetler. The others were on a fishing trip, working as guides for an outfitter on the Clark Fork River. Fetler told me they came to Montana right after Vietnam. They were all pretty screwed up after the war and all they'd been through. Didn't like the reception they'd received. Got so bitter they didn't want to associate with anyone. They hunted and fished until they ran out of money. Never got married, though Vaugan got pretty close to one girl and almost married her."

Beinhorn paused to take a drink and continued. "Somebody's uncle died and left one of them some money. Enough for them to make a down payment on this ranch. They've been able to scrape through all these years as guides and by selling hunting and fishing gear. They've all gotten expert at making flies."

"Flies? What do you mean 'flies'?" said Champ.

"Fishing flies. Flies for fly fishing."

"I've never been fishing," Champ said.

"Hell, you've never been out of the big city, until Vietnam. Flies are like worms they put on a hook to attract the fish. The fish bite bugs and flies as well as worms. It takes a real talent for making them so the fish will bite." Will explained.

"You're shittin' me. Those guys can make money outta flies?"

"Yes, it's true. But they haven't made enough, and they're in real financial trouble." Steve's body language matched the serious expression on his face. "They couldn't make the last three mortgage payments, and now the whole mortgage is due. A rich guy by the name of D.A. King is in partnership with a banker named Sanders. Those two are working together to take control of every acre out there. It seems they don't care about hunting and fishing, they want the mineral rights!"

"MINERAL RIGHTS? Is it oil? Gas? Coal?" What is it? Said Will.

"I thought they mined copper out there. Said Champ.

"Don't know what IT is, but those two greedy bastards want it. Our guys are about to lose their ranch. It's going to be auctioned off next week. I've asked my wife for a loan. They need $800,000."

"I'll try to help, but my money's tied up some." Champ explained; he'd put up a big chunk of money to start up a savings and loan business in Philadelphia. "It's really for people down on their luck that normally turn to loan sharks. I'm giving them an alternative."

"The mob's not gonna like your new enterprise." Beinhorn knew how they dealt with competition.

"I can help you with that, Champ." MacKenzie grinned. "I have money for the ranch too. I have more than enough, much more. We can put it in the savings and loan. Use it when we need it."

Beinhorn and Lewis both turned and stared at him, dumbfounded. Both thinking, *Didn't he just tell us that his ex-wife got everything?*

The waitress stepped through the doorway, politely interrupted, and asked if they were ready to eat.

Other diners were beginning to crowd into their room, so they considered MacKenzie's surprise offer in silence as the waitress led them down some stairs into a pine-paneled room with a bar and a fireplace. It, too, was cozy, with antique knickknacks on the walls, spotless white tablecloths, comfortable chairs, tasteful china, and Georgian-patterned silverware.

The waitress showed them a table in the corner and offered them menus.

"Are you serious?" Steve hissed at Will after the waitress left.

"You pullin' our leg? Is this a joke?" Champ was not buying it either.

As they ordered and then got their food, Will told them the incredible story of finding the money. "It's several million dollars, all in hundred-dollar bills. Real money, not fake." He did not mention the three men in the trunk, nor the rescue of Gabriella. *Maybe later,* he thought, *but not now.*

"Well, well, it makes more sense to me now. It's all starting to make sense." Beinhorn nodded his head and pointed at Will with his fork while chewing on a Caesar salad. "You see. It's why I wanted to meet you, to talk about Joe Arthur at River View Farm."

Will nodded back and picked at his salad.

"We've had a tap on a drug gang's phone in Washington. A man called Booker Bryant, who goes by the nickname of Booger, has made scores of calls to River View Farm in Clarke County."

Beinhorn paused to make sure they understood the connection. "Based on what we can put together, Arthur is no longer there, although we have what we think is his voice on some earlier calls. There are many references to missing money. Bryant's looking for money owed to the FU gang, a big payment, nothing about how much, but apparently, the amount is huge. There are references to a 'princess,' or a 'queen,' but she seems to be missing too."

Will choked on a piece of bread he'd just dipped into olive oil. Beinhorn waited to see if he was all right and then continued.

"Bryant has made accusations about Arthur being in bed with the Colombians, but it's been denied every time. A mobster named Arturo from Philadelphia has called Booker Bryant from that farm and has pleaded for patience, saying, 'things will still be worked out'. The Arturo family is head of the Philadelphia Mafia, and that's why I asked Champ to come down."

"Champ knows the Arturos, went to parochial school with one of the cousins, Angelo Baldi, who moved to Clarke County twenty-five years ago." Steve Beinhorn turned to Champ, indicating it was his turn to explain.

"I broke the fucker's nose. He was the school bully. He demanded money from all of us. Said it was for our protection. He threatened to kill me, called me a nigger. It took four guys to pull me off him."

"He should have called you anything but that."

"Didn't matter. He wanted to impress the boys, using me as an example."

"Would you two shut up?" Beinhorn broke in. "I'm not finished. Will, you know there've been several unsolved murders in Winchester?"

Will nodded. "It's been all over the papers and TV."

"You also know that a parachutist was found dead in a tree not far from where you live. Did you know that he was planning to leave in a van with a fake passport and phony driver's license?"

"I never heard that. I never heard about a van or a fake passport. But you guys gotta know. I found the dead parachutist, or rather my dog found him. I don't know why, but I took the bag he had attached to a chest harness. It had money, keys, credit cards, and his wallet."

Will spoke softly, with his head down. "Then on the way home through the woods, I found two other parachutes on my property. They happened to be full of cash, but at the time, I wasn't sure. I guess I panicked. I thought the money was drug money, so I kept it."

He looked at the other two, hoping for their support and understanding. "I thought about turning it in later but knew it would cause me trouble. Everyone would think I'd been involved. He's gone from booze to drugs, they'd say. So I kept the money and covered my tracks."

He stopped talking as a young couple walked by to their table.

"But I know they suspect me. It's just a matter of time before they come for me. I'll end up just like the two families that were tortured and murdered. That's why I need your help. What do I do? How can I get out of this mess?" Will looked from buddy to buddy, hoping they could think of something.

Steve's eyes lit up. "Will, You're right. You've found their missing money. They'll be coming, probably sooner rather than later. But another party is apparently involved, a Colombian cartel. These are bad people. They're the 'spics' that Booger was referring to on several of the tapes. The Cartagena Cartel has recently changed leadership."

Beinhorn dropped his voice to a whisper. "The new don is a man by the name of Diego Estrada, a killer well-known by our people in South America. We taped a couple of calls from Booger to the old don some months or weeks ago. Apparently, there is a dispute between the two. The solution is going to be ugly. They don't take prisoners."

"Sounds like you better move, Will. Why not come with me to Philadelphia?"

"Bad idea, Champ. It's Arturo's home base, too much risk. Let's think this through."

They lingered over dessert and after dinner drinks, discussing travel options for Will. They decided to meet in Montana, at the auction, with enough money to buy a ranch. They'd have a reunion with long-lost friends and find a place for Will to vanish for a while.

Champ asked if they would mind if he brought his nephew. "I need to move that kid to the country. He needs a change outta his environment, or he's gonna wind up dead."

Will said no problem. He might bring his children too if his ex-wife accepted his recovery. Hell, maybe he'd bring her too.

Beinhorn and Lewis had booked rooms at the Ashby Inn, and both urged Will to get out of town as soon as possible.

On his way out the door, after hugging and saying goodbye to the other two, Steve said to Will, "You better go tonight. We know that Diego's in DC, staying at the Mayflower Hotel. He has at least four men with him, and no telling what he's going to do."

Taillights from Will's jeep were still visible when Steve's beeper vibrated, indicating an emergency. He called the direct line to Irene's office, and she picked it up before the first ring had finished.

"Steve, all hell's broken loose! There's been a shooting at the FU Club. Two DC police officers are dead, and many more dead and wounded inside the club. It's worse than the OK Corral. A small army came through the front door and blazed away with automatic weapons. They shot at everything they saw."

"How about Booger? Did they get Booger?"

"Not from what I've heard. There was no sign of him or his top lieutenants, LD and Peacock. We're checking emergency rooms all over the city in case they come in wounded. We have a good team at the club. Arrived about thirty minutes after it happened. Working with DC Homicide. I can't be seen there as you know, but I'm trying to monitor things from here."

"Any witnesses. Anybody see anything?"

"We got zilch. Nothing. Most everyone was hit, and everybody in the place was armed. Nobody's talking so far. Our guys have already called twice, looking for you. I said I'd track you down, fill you in, but they don't have much."

"Stay on it. I'll be there in an hour."

"You may want to stay where you are. We got other news. It was just coming in when the FU shootings interrupted. We think we've found Blue. Winchester police reported three men found stuffed in the trunk of a car in the doctor's parking lot at the hospital there. They think the bodies have been there for weeks, mostly frozen. Just thawed out during the recent warm spell."

"Are they positive it's Blue? Have they ID'd everyone?"

"No, we have to wait for forensics, but one of the men was a mulatto with blue eyes. He was wearing a thousand-dollar custom-tailored suit. Sounds like my man, Blue. One thing about the condition of his body was very strange. There were teeth marks and skin tears on his neck. The pathologist thinks it could have been from a large dog."

"No teeth marks on the others?"

"Nope, nothing but bullet holes, one at point-blank range. The sedan they were in also had bullet holes from a shotgun and a pistol. One of the passenger side windows was shattered, and there were shotgun pellets around the trunk and right taillight. There were no guns, no wallets, no rings, no watches, nor any personal effects.

Steve, We think another one of the bodies is Angelo Baldi, you know the one who's been missing from River View Farm, the one Booger's been trying to talk to."

"Was the third man Joe Arthur?"

"No. We don't know much, but he's not Joe Arthur. He's smaller than Arthur. They think he's a Latino. But we don't have a clue who he is. He had an ice pick strapped to his ankle."

"Weren't there ice pick marks on some of the tortured victims in those Winchester murders?"

"You're right."

"I'll get over to Winchester first thing. See what they know. Call me if anything breaks from the FU massacre."

"When you get to Winchester, talk to a Frederick County deputy named Roscoe Harris. He has been working several of the killings up there, and he was first on the scene when they found the parachutist."

"Roscoe Harris. Roscoe. I've heard that name before. Wasn't his name mentioned on one of the Booger tapes?"

"Not that I know of. But I haven't heard the tapes. I got his name from the sheriff up there."

"All right, Irene. I'll meet up with Deputy Roscoe Harris first thing in the morning. Good night, Irene. Get it?"

"Get what?"

"The song, 'Good Night, Irene.' Haven't you heard it?"

"Never heard of it. You'll have to play it for me sometime."

"I can't wait. Good night, Irene."

"Oh, Steve, one more thing. Diego Estrada. He's checked out of the Mayflower. Gone without a trace. We lost him when the FU fiasco went down."

"Great," Beinhorn groaned, "just frigging great."

Chapter 37

When the Potomac Edison van reached a sign that read "Berryville," the driver knew he'd made a mistake. So he made a U-turn, hoping it wouldn't be noticed.

"Peacock. What the hell's goin' on?" Booger was in the back, working with LD, trying to load a belt of ammunition into a .50-caliber machine gun.

"Sorry, Boog. I missed the turnoff into the farm. It's supposed t' be right after we cross the river on Route 50. I didn't see the guardhouse at the gate."

"We're on Route 7, dildo. Don't ya' remember coming through Leesburg." The voice of ridicule belonged to LD. "When we came out here last time, we went through that little town, Middleburg, remember?"

"Get up front an' show his ass the way. It's like the blind leadin' the fuckin' blind. Peacock, you been smokin' too much o' that weed. It fried your brains, but tha's assumin' you had a brain in the first place." Booger sat behind the big gun, aiming the barrel back and forth, testing its swivel range, as LD moved to the passenger seat.

Big Foot, a huge man sitting next to Booger, moved over to let LD by. Big Foot was armed with an M-79 grenade launcher and a bandolier of grenades. Two other men in the back were busy checking automatic rifles and loading extra clips. These men were all Booger could assemble in the confusion following the club shootout.

Once in the front seat, LD looked over at his friend and grinned. "We gonna die o' old age 'fore you gets us there, Peacock. Take a right by the river, it's a dirt road, but it's gotta come out at Route 50."

"Slow down, Peacock, or this 50's gonna explode," Booger yelled. "Gonna need ever' gun we got if Joe Arthur won't talk to us. Somebody's in bed with those spics, and somebody's gonna pay."

It was dark when the van stopped at the guardhouse entrance to River View Farm.

"You guys from the power company?" asked the guard, who strained to see everything in the van.

"Yeah. Got a call from maintenance," Peacock said, trying to be friendly. "Said a transformer was out at River View Farm. This's River View, ain't it?"

"Well, nobody told me about it. Looks like we got plenty of power." And the guard gestured to the main house up on the hill, which was lit up like Christmas.

Peacock smiled. "You must have a bunch of generators. Backup power, ya' know."

"Where are your uniforms? You don't look like you climb poles for a living."

Booger and two others in the back had their pistols out, thinking it was going to get unpleasant. The guard remained in the guardhouse, and they couldn't see below his chest.

"We on double time an' a half. Come here on the run," Peacock explained. "Sometimes we get called out an' we in all kinds o' outfits. You wanta call sumbody, check us out? We can come back later if tha's what you wants."

LD had his hand on his magnum.

"No, no. Go on and fix the problem. Take all night if you want. Make some big money." And the guard waved them through.

"Can you believe how dumb that Italian guy is?" Peacock laughed as they drove down the long gravel road. "He could barely speak English."

"You can barely speak English too, Peacock. Who do you think you are, Wilbur Shakespeare?"

"It's William Shakespeare, you dumb shit." Booger grinned at LD but couldn't take his eyes off their destination. "Would you look at this place, all lit up. Must be a floodlight on every tree. Gotta cost a fortune."

At the main house, the phone rang, and Parisi answered.

"We got visitors in a Potomac Edison van saying they're coming to fix a transformer."

"Any idea how many? Did they give any names?"

"No names. I didn't ask for IDs either. There are two in front and more in the back. Could be four or five. I had the shotgun ready, didn't know how they were going to behave."

"Good job. We'll be ready. Keep your eyes open. There may be more coming. Out."

"Will do. Out."

As the van pulled up in front, all weapons were fully loaded and unlocked. Booger sat behind the .50-caliber machine gun, ready to fire.

To their surprise, the front door opened, and a man emerged, his hands up in the air. He was holding a newspaper high, so the front page could be seen. So many floodlights were on it looked like midday. The man spoke with an Italian accent. "Don't shoot. We gotta talk. Look at this headline." Slowly, he walked toward the van, speaking loudly. "Joe Arthur is dead. Angelo Baldi is dead. Your man Blue is dead. The Colombian is dead. We didn't do it. Please come in. We need to talk."

At that, the man with the newspaper turned back toward the house and yelled to his people. "Come out. Let them see you!"

Several men with rifles stepped out of the shadows.

There were at least fifteen of them, and they lowered their guns in a show of temporary peace.

Coming up to the van window on the driver's side, he continued, "My name is Parisi. Mr. Bryant, is that you? Are you there? Please come in. Bring your weapons if that makes you feel more comfortable. We are your friends, Mr. Bryant."

"What d'ya think Booger?" LD asked. "Should we talk? That newspaper headline said three bodies found in trunk of car at the hospital. There were pictures."

"Aw right. We gettin' out. Make it slow. Me, Peacock, 'n' LD'll go in. Big Foot, you three stay here."

Inside the house, Parisi led them to the library, pointed to the red leather chair, saying, "Here's where they shot Mr. Arthur. Shot him right through the mouth. You can see where the bullet went through the chair. Took us hours to clean up. We lost six men that night."

Thomas Parisi suggested they first read the newspaper article he'd been holding. It was a special edition of the *Winchester Star*, printed hours after the bodies were found. The pictures didn't show the bodies, only the car with an open trunk, and the hospital in the background.

There were interviews with doctors who smelled the bodies and alerted authorities, interviews with the sheriff, interviews with the hospital administrator, and new interviews with people who had something to say about the recent murders in the area.

Then Parisi told them about Deputy Sheriff Roscoe Harris and his positive identification of the three men. Booger Bryant was visibly moved when he asked if they were certain about Blue.

"Absolutely positive, Mr. Bryant. Roscoe worked with him every day they were here." Parisi lowered his voice out of respect for the man's friend. "As of right now, the authorities don't know who the three dead men are. It might take them a few days, but they'll identify them soon enough."

"Who the fuck did it?" Booger wanted to fight, wanted to know who his enemy was.

"Roscoe thinks it was a man that lives on Merriman's Lane, west of Winchester, a guy by the name of MacKenzie. Will MacKenzie. But there are other suspects too."

"You tellin' me one man did this? BULLSHIT!"

"No. No. No. Obviously, he had help. Probably hired them with the money he found. We'll find out who they are."

"You haven't found the guy with the money? How long has it been? Several weeks now. It's been weeks, and no one done shit. Ain't found shit."

"Mr. Bryant. We know now. Soon, we'll know exactly what happened. MacKenzie is the key."

"Where exactly does he live? How do we get there?"

"Please, Mr. Bryant, hold on. We sent Roscoe to question this guy again. And of course, the other three suspects too. We need to make sure who it is. The whole area is going to be buzzing with cops. Roscoe will lead us to the man, or men. He's the best."

The cook brought in several trays of food, and Parisi asked them to relax for a while, think about next steps, and how they could work together, recover the money, and punish their enemies. Finally, Booger believed that Parisi was telling the truth. He agreed to work with their inside man, Roscoe, and sent LD to the van for the three who were still on full alert. They must be mighty hungry by now.

All during the meal, they rehashed old times, discussed problems with competition, complained about the high cost of lawyers, and began to relax, as Parisi had hoped. Afterward, he took them on a tour of the house and grounds, describing, as best he could, what happened that night, when Joe Arthur was killed and the girl got away.

The plan was for Booger to meet with Roscoe the next day, and after some further discussion, he accepted Parisi's offer of beds for the night.

Every half hour, during and after their talks, Parisi tried to reach Roscoe, but he wasn't home. *Where could that son-of-a-bitch be?* He became so frustrated that he slammed the phone into its receiver.

Chapter 38

In Edna Cline's bedroom, Roscoe felt right at home. They'd spent much of the night satisfying their lust. Roscoe woke before dawn and jumped in the shower. He was in a hurry and wanted to be on Merriman's Lane before MacKenzie and his dog went for their morning walk.

Edna came into the bathroom, looking like a used morning glory. She was stark naked, her hair was curly and uncombed. She wore no makeup, her eyes were drowsy, yet she had a grin on her face.

"Where do you think you're going?" Still grinning, she stepped into the shower with Roscoe.

"Edna, I have to go. It's business."

"What business? Monkey business? You got another girlfriend?" She grabbed him by the balls.

"Edna, plcasc. I have to go."

She started washing him down with soap. She lathered the soap all over, slowing down when she touched his crotch and his buttocks.

"Oh, shit. Here we go again."

After getting a couple of hours' sleep, Will MacKenzie and Watson were up before dawn as usual. They ate quickly, and Will loaded a cooler for the road. Even though it was dark, Will took the dog for his morning walk, but this time on a leash. He was in a hurry to leave.

It was still dark when Roscoe reached the lane leading to MacKenzie's house. He hesitated before going on, wanting to make sure of his approach, so he pulled over and stopped. He had to consider the most effective method of interrogation. Also, he had a decision to make about what to do with the money if he found it. *Was 10 percent enough?* Then he thought about Edna. *What the hell am I gonna do? She's too hot to handle, and I can't let her go.*

Will backed out of his driveway, the jeep packed for a long trip. Then, he remembered the possibility of another moneybag and abruptly decided to turn back up into the woods. He took a small trail through one of Glaize's peach orchards, thinking he would take one last look. Maybe he could spot a bag, or another parachute, now that all the snow had melted. As the sun rose, dark shadows disappeared, and birds, squirrels, and other animal life began to move, some just getting up, some, like the family of foxes that lived in the orchard, just going to bed.

Will parked at the wood's edge, making sure that the orchard hid his jeep. He focused on the woods, looking left to right, scanning tree branches, looking for a black parachute, when he heard his house alarm go off.

Whoop . . . whoop . . . whoop . . . whoop. You could hear it for miles. There was no other sound at this time of morning.

Time's up, thought Will. He'd have to go the back way through several orchards to West Virginia. Then he could work his way back to Interstate 81 and head north.

One short whistle and the dog came running.

Then, he saw it!

A black parachute wrapped around a tall maple. The parachute was torn and had turned a faded color in places, but the bag still hung there. It was up against the tree and hidden by its trunk. Will decided to try and bring it down even though he'd have to climb the tree. It was almost twenty feet up, and the alarm siren at his house was still blaring.

After a tough climb, he paused to catch his breath and then considered the best way to salvage the bag. He could see that the bag was still locked, and its contents appeared to be undisturbed. First, he tried to pull the chute down. The heavy bag helped with his efforts, and the parachute ripped, dropping another five feet.

Will then lost his balance and almost fell out of the tree, grabbing at the nearest limb, swinging out and back. He recovered his grip and his footing, and then, he tugged at the chute with all his might. The bag dropped some more, but there it stayed. It wouldn't budge. Will began gathering the chute. His effort was clumsy; he could only cut when he managed to keep his balance. He thought about cutting the tether but doubted he could cut the heavy tether with his dull pocket knife.

His alarm was still sounding.

At last, the alarm stopped, and a peaceful quiet followed. Will continued to cut through the parachute. Progress was slow. *The knife wouldn't cut butter,* Will thought.

Roscoe jumped when the first alarm sounded. He'd been in Will's house less than a minute when it began to wail. He found the alarm pad and tried to punch numbers, hoping to silence the thing. But it kept blaring away. *Enough to wake the dead,* Roscoe said to himself. He was ready to rip the pad out of the wall when another sound interrupted. It was the telephone ringing in Will's kitchen.

Roscoe answered. It was the alarm switchboard operator, advising of the problem and asking if she should call the police.

"I am the police!" Roscoe shouted into the phone. "How do you shut this thing off?"

"I'm sorry, sir, but you'll have to give me the code, or the police will come," she answered, tension in her voice.

"Look, call the police. Keep me on the line. I can't remember who's on duty, but they'll know me. Do it now. This damn alarm can be heard in DC."

Minutes later, everything resolved with the police, Roscoe was given the code to turn the alarm off. He then called the emergency dispatch at 911 and assured them that everything was fine, that he had accidentally set off the alarm. While on the phone, he leaned against the stove and was surprised to find the burner still hot. Then, he noticed the coffee pot. Steam was coming out even though the power had been turned off. He checked a coffee cup in the sink, and it was still warm.

Son-of-a-bitch! MacKenzie must have just left, he said to himself.

The deputy knew that MacKenzie did not come down the lane because he'd been sitting there for twenty minutes thinking about Edna and what he was going to do: take the money, marry Edna, move away, what?

Where had MacKenzie gone? He must have gone out the back road up through the orchard. Roscoe could see the peach orchard from Will's porch.

He could see movement in a tree at the wood line, beyond the orchard, on a ridge. It looked like it might be a black bear.

"Son-of-a-bitch! It's not a bear, its MacKenzie. Gotcha! Gotcha now, Mr. MacKenzie!"

Roscoe flew out the front door and ran toward the orchard, trying to hurry and trying to be quiet at the same time.

He had gone about a hundred yards up the orchard road when he heard a car behind him. "Shit, I told them not to come. Didn't that bitch believe me?" Roscoe had been anticipating the sheriff.

But it wasn't the sheriff, and it wasn't a police car.

Chapter 39

The sedan parked at the front of the house, its occupants on full alert.

Diego was surprised to find the front door wide open. "Everybody outta the car. Something's going on," he yelled as all four doors opened at once.

The five Colombians ran into the house, guns drawn.

Diego had just issued silent orders for his men to split up, pointing at different directions with his gun, when Roscoe appeared in the middle of the still open front door.

The deputy sheriff, out of breath from the hundred-yard run, had his gun drawn, and in a shaking voice, asked, "What's going on? Who are you?"

Without a second thought, Diego shot him three times.

Roscoe was thrown backward over the porch railing and landed in the boxwoods, a look of surprise frozen on his face.

Diego then turned back to his men, a new urgency in his voice. "Check this place from top to bottom. I want MacKenzie's balls. I want them for a present. MacKenzie is more important than the money. You got that!"

They flew in different directions: into the kitchen because the lights were on there, then, in every room upstairs, every room downstairs. They combed the basement, the garage, and climbed up into the attic.

When they didn't find Will, they tore the house to shreds, ripping mattresses, emptying drawers, slashing paintings, smashing walls, breaking mirrors and antique furniture, and tearing every item of clothing. Nothing was spared. Then someone noticed movement outside.

"Padrone! A car is coming up the driveway. It's a van!"

Peacock approached MacKenzie's house, looked over his shoulder and asked, "Shouldn't we wait for that deputy, Boog? They said he's the man."

"They said MacKenzie's the man too." Booger Bryant turned to the others. "That deputy will never get this guy to talk. I don't want him hurt. Not yet. It's gonna be slow and painful. Gonna be an eye fo' 'n eye. We gotta take him alive. Ever'body got that?"

The van drove slowly up MacKenzie's driveway. Up front, LD and Peacock noticed the many trees, the ivy covering the brick, the slate roof, the boxwoods, and the body lying face up in the middle of the shrubbery.

"What the fu—" Peacock started to say something when he turned to see two men step into the open front doorway of Will's house.

The Colombians began firing as soon as the van pulled to a stop at the front door.

Peacock was hit first. He was trapped in his seat belt, left hand on the front door handle, right hand reaching for his pistol, when his face exploded. His head fell onto the steering wheel, causing the horn to blare.

When Peacock slumped forward, two bullets struck LD in the shoulder and side, but he could still move. He managed the passenger door with difficulty, falling out with a MAC-10 submachine gun. He was just rising up over the snub-nosed hood of the van when he was blasted with fire from both Colombians. LD never got off a shot.

Inside the van, Big Foot slid the side door back so that Booger could fire the .50-caliber machine gun. The sliding door opened directly onto the two Colombians at point-blank range. Booger pulled back on the trigger. In seconds, several hundred bullets savagely tore through the two Colombians, shredding the front door of MacKenzie's house and throwing them back against the stairs.

"Out the back! Get out of this van, or they'll have us trapped!" Booger shouted to Big Foot and the other two.

Big Foot grabbed the M-79 grenade launcher, and the other two carried automatic rifles. They almost knocked each other down as they scrambled out of the van's back door.

Before they hit the pavement, Diego was firing from an upstairs window. He killed one and wounded another. He ducked, just as Big Foot fired the grenade launcher. It exploded in the bedroom ceiling and temporarily stunned the new don, covering him in plaster and dust.

One of Diego's men had gone out the back door and circled around the house. He caught Big Foot, looking up at the bedroom windows, and shot him six times.

Inside the van, Booger turned the machine gun around to face Big Foot's killer. His trigger finger unleashed a quick burst of fire, lifting the Colombian off his feet. The pattern of bullets was so close it almost cut the man in two.

All of a sudden, there was quiet. Nothing moved. Only an occasional moan could be heard from someone lying on the pavement. Booger didn't know who it was, but he waited for a few minutes before peeking his head out of the van. He heard and saw nothing, so he stepped out, an automatic rifle in hand. He looked down and saw that Sticky Fingers, one of his men, was under Big Foot's body, still alive. He was looking up at Booger for help.

Just then, another Colombian burst through the shredded front doorway, his pistol aimed, firing a full clip at Booger. One bullet went through Booger's cheekbone, blinding him in his left eye. Another caught him in the ribs before he managed to take cover behind the van.

Knowing he had hit his target, the Colombian quickly moved around the back of the van for the kill. He stepped over two men on the ground, looking for the man he'd just hit. He was right on top of Fingers and didn't see him reach for the M-79 lying beside Big Foot. He didn't notice the grenade launcher as it came up, almost touching his belly, as he steadied his pistol, making sure of his aim as he cornered a wounded Booger Bryant.

The Colombian never pulled the trigger as he felt his insides blow apart. The grenade fired from inches away, blasted his midsection into a million pieces, covering a shocked Sticky Fingers with so much blood that he couldn't see. Thinking he was blinded and bleeding to death, Fingers dropped the M-79 and called for Booger to help him.

Fingers was screaming, begging for help, when bullets from above struck his chest and head, ending his imagined agony.

The shots had come from upstairs. Diego had recovered, had crawled over to the window, pulled himself up, and saw the man who was making all the noise. With hollow point ammunition loaded into his automatic pistol, Diego took careful aim and fired. The first slug killed Sticky Fingers outright, but Diego put two more into him to be sure.

Then Diego saw another man move. He was out of sight, on the other side of the van.

Booger knew that someone was firing from the upstairs windows. He needed a weapon; he'd dropped the rifle when he was first hit. Blood was pouring out of his chest, but he felt no pain. *That's odd,* he thought, as he crawled around to LD's body and cradled the MAC-10 submachine gun, the one that LD had been unable to fire.

Whoever it was that was upstairs would be coming soon. He tried to get ready, but his vision was blurred. He didn't think he could last long.

Movement showed out of the corner of his good eye. He couldn't see who was coming around the van, but he knew it wasn't the cavalry. Booger pointed toward the movement, knowing the Mac would cover a lot of space. He didn't need to aim, so he just pulled the trigger. At the same time, he lost all sight, the light faded into darkness, and his head jerked back on the pavement.

Diego had time to fire only a quick burst, but one of the rounds hit Booger right between the eyes. The hole it made in the back of Booger's head was as big as a grapefruit. Diego's smile turned to alarm as he felt his whole chest explode.

Diego lay on the pavement, eyes open, wanting to get up, but he couldn't move. Blood was pumping out of his chest like a gusher. *Must have hit an artery* was his last thought.

In the woods, Will heard it all. Instinctively, he'd ducked down when the first shots rang out. Then, after a pause to listen, he resumed his cutting. Finally, he freed the missing moneybag, and it came crashing down, out of the tree. He didn't bother to hide the parachute. He wrapped it around the moneybag, and with great effort, managed to lift it into the jeep. He couldn't see out of the rear window but did not have time to rearrange things.

He forced a quick look beyond the orchard, to his house, wondering, *What the hell was happening down there?*

Watson nudged him from the back, and Will nearly jumped out of his skin. The dog smelled like a rotting corpse, and his face was covered in maggots. What the hell! "You've been rolling in some dead animal! Jesus, Watson. Why now? Of all the times!"

Will got in the jeep and started the engine. Watson, moved at an unhurried pace as if he had all the time in the world, jumped in the front seat, and licked his master on the cheek.

The smell lingered on his cheek as he tore through the woods and orchards.

Will avoided trees and outcrops of limestone rock like he was on an obstacle course. He turned left, then right, back and forth, bouncing over the rough terrain, driving as fast as he dared. Tree limbs slapped against the windshield. Watson's head stuck out of the passenger side window, dodging the limbs as if it were a game. Unlike his master, he was happy as could be, with his mouth open, emitting a breath from hell, and his long tongue flapping in the wind.

Lying face up in a boxwood hedge, Roscoe Harris blinked his eyes. He didn't dare try to move. Blood seeped from wounds in his chest and neck. Waves of pain kept coming, and he stifled a moan. He could see the ragged doorway, blown apart by bullets. He could see the hands and arms of somebody who fell in the doorway.

After the initial shock of being hit, he remained conscious during the entire gunfight. *Mr. Arturo was right,* he thought, Arturo had predicted a gang war.

"Why had the shooting stopped?" Roscoe spoke, his lips moved but no sound came from his mouth. "Was MacKenzie caught? MacKenzie had the money for sure. No doubt about it now."

He could feel that his shirt was sticky with blood, but he thanked God that he was still alive, thinking, *I'm going to get you, Will Mackenzie!*

Then he passed out.

Chapter 40

Gabriella picked at her lunch. Normally, her appetite was voracious. Grilled fish, fresh asparagus, wild rice, and a ripe mango sat untouched on her plate. She stared into space, oblivious to the beauty of her surroundings. Out of the corner of her eye, she spotted a hummingbird sipping a drink from one of the many colored flowers that graced her veranda. She smiled at the bird, suspended in air, admiring its freedom. Beyond the veranda, she could see the sun reflecting off the Caribbean, its surface unusually calm and peaceful, hosting a variety of sails and fishing boats that seemed frozen in place.

But she was not at peace. She was worried. Diego had been in the United States long enough to attack Will Mackenzie by now. She hoped Will had heeded her warning. Subconsciously, she placed her hand on the family Bible. It sat on the table next to her iced tea.

Strange, she thought, *I didn't know we had a family Bible until this morning.*

Her parish priest had given it to her when she'd passed the church on her morning run. "Your father wanted you to have this," he'd said.

She felt like praying and picked up the Bible. Inside the front cover was a letter addressed to her. Tears fell from her eyes as she recognized her father's frail handwriting.

"My dearest Gabriella," it read, "by the time you read this, I will be dead. I have instructed Father Ignacio to hand-deliver this to you in secret so that others may not know what I have to say to you alone. I have done many bad things in my lifetime. God will be my judge. But you have been excluded from my business, and you are innocent. It is my wish that you will leave Colombia and start a new life. You will find this difficult to do, especially given Diego's obvious affection for you. His cousin Paul was my choice to succeed me, but he and Diego have long been rivals. Others outside the family may try to take over, such as my long-time associates in Bogotá, or Medellín. You will be caught in the middle of this struggle if you stay. Please honor my wishes and go. There is a secret safe in your mother's closet, behind the false air duct. You will have to remove the false frame to get to the safe. The combination is your birth date. Please follow my instructions.

"After your mother's death, you were my only pleasure, my only reason for living. My love for you is boundless. Now that I am gone, maybe you can partially make up for all the sorrow I have created. You are kind and caring, all the things I never was. May God bless you in your new life. All my love, Father."

The letter moved Gabriella. It brought back so many happy times with her father. She was so young when her mother died; she could only recall her through photographs. Her hands were shaking as she reread the letter when a uniformed maid interrupted. "Gabriella, Gabriella, the telephone, it's for you. It's the pilot, Juan Menendez."

"I'll take it in the library, Maria, thank you." She went in and picked up the phone.

"Ms. Gabriella, is that you?"

"Yes, Juan. What is it?"

"I have terrible news. Don Estrada is dead. He's been shot with four others in Winchester, Virginia!"

"Are you sure?" Gabriella smiled, hoping the news was true.

"Positive. Don Estrada is dead. I'm not sure who else was with him, but at least four others are dead too. It's all over the news. I saw his face on television. Don Estrada is dead!"

"Juan, do not refer to that evil man as DON! That is a title of respect. Diego Estrada was a reptile! Unworthy of any respect! I spit on his grave! Let him rot where he is! How about the others? Were others killed or injured? Do you know?"

"Yes, there were five or six others. One, maybe two, badly wounded, but I don't know their names or who they were associated with."

"Juan, have they mentioned the name of a Will Mackenzie? Any news of him?"

"Yes, MacKenzie, that's the name. The shootings took place at his house, but he is missing. They are searching for him now."

Gabriella smiled again and breathed a sigh of relief. "Juan, where are you now?"

"I'm in Richmond, Virginia, at Byrd Field, with the plane. What do I do now? I don't know about the others that joined Don, er, I mean, Mr. Diego Estrada. They left here and went to Washington DC."

"Juan. I want you to come home now. Do not wait for the others. Do not take instructions from anyone but me. Do you understand?"

"Yes, yes, I understand. The aircraft is ready to go now, but I need to file a flight plan. It will take some time, but I should be home by early evening."

"Remember, Juan, return immediately. Do not listen to anyone but me. I will reward you for your loyalty to Don Alverez." Gabriella speaking as if her father were still alive and in charge.

"I am at your service, my lady, I shall return at once. Goodbye."

"One more thing, Juan. When you return, prepare the plane for an immediate departure. I have an important mission that my father entrusted to me alone."

"I understand. Goodbye."

Gabriella hung up and ran upstairs to her mother's old bedroom. It had been unoccupied since her death over twenty years ago. Yet every day since that time, the maids had cleaned the room and placed fresh flowers in all the places her mother loved. Everything in the room appeared as it was back then, cheery and bright as if its occupant had never left. Gabriella used one of her mother's silver combs to pry open the false grille in the closet.

Hurriedly, she attempted to open the safe. But it took her four tries before she could calm down. Dust flew when the safe finally creaked open. It was dark inside, and she couldn't see the safe's contents. Years ago, a light would come on when the safe opened, but it had long since burned out. So she lit a candle and reached in. The safe was packed with U.S. currency, all in hundred-dollar bills. To Gabriella, it seemed to contain many thousands of dollars.

Then she found a fat legal-sized envelope. Inside was another letter from her father, just as loving, just as personal, but written years earlier with a firm hand. He gave instructions to Gabriella, including codes and account numbers for several Swiss bank accounts. Some of the accounts were in Gabriella's name, but others were in the name of someone else. Then she found a passport with her picture, but the other person's name, the one on the bank accounts, and an address, and other personal information that she didn't recognize. Apparently, her father had created another identity for her. Her picture on the passport was as recent as when she left for graduate business school at Georgetown. There were several credit cards in both names. Finally, there was another note and pieces of rare jewelry—rings, necklaces, bracelets, broaches, and pins. The handwritten note read, "Your mother would want you to have these."

Gabriella packed the entire contents of the safe along with a minimum of clothes and cosmetics. She hid the bags under her bed, not wanting to alert anyone of her plans. Then she ran down to the kitchen; all of a sudden she was starving.

Chapter 41

Steve Beinhorn was late. He and Champ had lingered over breakfast at the Ashby Inn, both excited about their upcoming reunion with Muldoon, Fetler, and Vaugan. They'd also speculated on the incredible luck of Will Mackenzie, finding all that money. Steve had told Champ not to assume that it was good luck, more likely it was bad luck because Will was in extreme danger. He would know more when he talked with that deputy sheriff, Roscoe Harris, in Winchester. Not once did he consider that Will should give up the money.

As he pulled into the Frederick County visitor's parking lot, Steve observed many police cars racing by, sirens blaring, in a hurry to their destination. "Must have been a hell of a wreck on Interstate 81," Steve mumbled to himself as he entered the county sheriff's office. It took a couple of minutes for him to be acknowledged because all of the clerks were rushing around, some on phones, others searching through files.

"What's going on?" he said to the first clerk that whizzed by the front desk.

"Sorry. Can't talk now," she yelled over her shoulder. "Have a seat."

He whipped out his Department of Justice credentials as he followed the clerk. "I have to speak with Deputy Sheriff Roscoe Harris. It's federal government business."

The clerk, a small woman with a quiet voice, apologized. "I'm sorry, sir. They's a lot goin' on here right now. It's another killin'. A bunch of 'em are dead. The sheriff's there now, and we can't find Roscoe."

"Where did it happen? Who got killed? Is it related to the others? Can I call the sheriff on your phone?"

"Whoa, hold on there. Hold on now. These things just happened. Out on Merriman's Lane again. It's the MacKenzie house this time. Don't know the details yet but sounds to me like it's connected. This is the most killings we've had here since the Civil War!"

"Can you connect me to the sheriff?"

"Why don't you just go out there? See for yourself. It'll be just as quick."

Steve didn't reply but turned and ran for his car. He was still receiving directions from the clerk when he went out the door. He drove as fast as he could, but encountered heavy traffic all along the way.

At the intersection of Merriman's Lane and the road leading to MacKenzie's house, two state police cars were blocking all access. Two ambulances careened around the upper bend in the road, coming down from the house. The ambulances, each with their sirens on, roared past Steve and the troopers, turned left, and headed north to Winchester Medical Center's emergency room.

By the time Beinhorn got to Will's house, Sheriff Killian was holding court in front of two television reporters that had somehow gotten through. He'd taken off his hat and made sure the cameras were focused on his most telegenic side, saying, "Roscoe Harris is a genuine hero. A hero! That's what he is. He confronted a vicious gang of killers single-handedly. There are at least ten people dead here. No eleven. Eleven gunmen! And Roscoe all alone, without backup. He's a hero, I tell ya. Ought to get the Medal of Honor. If anybody deserves a medal, it's Roscoe."

"Excuse me! May I get through please?" Steve was shoving and pushing others aside as he tried to reach the sheriff.

"Our prayers are with Roscoe," the sheriff continued. "He's been mortally wounded."

Holding up his Department of Justice credentials with one hand and blocking the cameras with the other, Steve Beinhorn said, "Stop this interview NOW! FBI! I'll be taking over this case! Get rid of these people!" He pointed at the television crews.

Will Mackenzie took his time as he drove up the long driveway to his West Virginia cabin. He looked right and left, wary of intruders. The mountain looked so peaceful after the violent gunfight he had witnessed earlier. His decision to come to the cabin was a sudden change in plans. He had expected to drive all day to Cape Cod, but was concerned that the police would now be looking for him. What would the police say if they found a few million dollars stuffed into the back of his jeep? So he made the decision to take back roads, through Round Hill, across Route 50, up 522, and on to his cabin.

He had to get rid of the black parachute and the contents of the third moneybag. Over the past thirty days, Will had opened new safe deposit boxes at banks in Virginia, West Virginia, Pennsylvania, and Maryland.

He had opened so many checking accounts, savings accounts, and safe deposit boxes that he believed most of the cash was secure. Two of his safe deposit boxes held nothing but extra safe deposit box keys, records, and a list of his many bank accounts.

Will opened the front door of the cabin and was almost knocked down by Watson as he rushed by to enter first. It was the dog's habit to sniff everything in the place, inspecting for intruders, man or animal. Satisfied that the cabin was untouched, the dog whined to go back outside where he would scout the area and mark his territory on every tree and bush.

By midafternoon, MacKenzie was famished. He'd brought dog food and some soft drinks, but nothing else. He was tired too. His mind was racing . . . so many things to be concerned about. More money than he knew what to do with. For a while, he made an effort to stack it and count it, but like the first time, it was just too much. Will knew the total was in the millions. So he packed most of it carefully in the cabin's storage bin. He kept several hundred thousand dollars in a plastic cooler for the trip to Cape Cod.

Satisfied that the bulk of the money was well hidden, he locked up and whistled for the dog. Watson was nowhere to be found. Will called and whistled and waited, listening for his presence. As he walked around the property, he kept calling the dog every few minutes. After an hour or so, the dog came sauntering back, out of breath, and stinking from rolling in the remains of another rotting animal. Acting as if nothing had happened, Watson calmly jumped in the front seat as Will held his nose.

Will rolled all the windows down, let in as much fresh air as possible, and left for the mini-mart in Paw Paw, West Virginia. He needed gas and food. While gulping down some beef jerky, he noticed the outside telephone booth and decided to call Steve Beinhorn. Watson sat obediently in the front seat while Will made his call. The private number at the Department of Justice rang once and a strange voice said, "Hello."

"Hello. Yes, I'm calling for Steve Beinhorn."

"Who's calling please?"

"It's Will Mackenzie."

"Oh, Mr. Mackenzie. I work with Steve. Just call me, Irene. My goodness, are you all right? I know he's worried about you."

"I'm fine. What's the matter? May I speak to Steve?"

"He's in Winchester, with the sheriff and the FBI. They're at your home right now. There's been a terrible shooting at your house. Everyone is looking for you. Thank God you're okay."

"In that case, I really need to speak with Steve. Can you give me his beeper number?"

"Of course," she said and gave him the number. "But you can call him at your own phone number. I just talked to him about another shooting in DC."

Will thanked the lady and hung up. As he was dialing his own home number, a battered old Ford pickup truck skidded to a stop next to his jeep. The truck carried four young men, all laughing and drinking. The truck's loud amplifiers blasted forth at full volume with a so-called acid rock song. Oppressive noise continued from the truck even after the passengers started to get out. The men were wearing identical black leather jackets with a swastika emblem in the back. Underneath the swastika was the name of their gang, "Mountaineer Brotherhood." A dozen or more empty beer cans rolled out onto the ground as both doors opened at once. Will noticed a woman pull in and park between his jeep and the truck just as someone answered the phone at his house.

He had to turn away to hear and raised his voice when he asked to speak to Steve Beinhorn.

"Steve?"

"Will? Is that you? You okay?"

"I'm fine. How bad is the damage?"

"You know, huh? It's bad, Will. Ten dead, two badly wounded; only one might live. Your house is shot to hell. Where were you?"

"I was in the orchard when I heard shots. I waited until they stopped before heading out the back way. It sounded like a war zone, Steve. They were obviously looking for me. Why the hell they started shooting each other is a mystery to me. No matter what, I knew I had to get out of there. I'm on my way to visit my Uncle Jim in Weston, West Virginia."

"A deputy sheriff surprised them, and they started shooting. He must have been a hell of a shot because it seems like no one got away. The deputy is one of the wounded, has a good chance to make it. One of the neighbors is a surgeon, and he was on the scene before the ambulances arrived."

"That'll be Dr. Calvin Chapman, my neighbor. He's a busybody, but a good doctor. I'm not surprised that he came. He has to know everything."

"Will, it's not going to end here. Two or maybe three groups are involved. All are bad news; they have more resources than some governments. I want you to go into the witness protection program."

"But I'm not a witness. I didn't see anything. How can I be in the program?"

"Trust me. I can get you a new name, a new address, a new life, and you are my witness. After you see your uncle, call my number at the Justice Department. My colleague, Irene, will tell you where to go. In the meantime, lay low, stay away from every place you are known to go. Don't talk to anyone."

"Can I let Champ know? I was supposed to call him on my way to Cape Cod."

"You can call Champ, but forget about Cape Cod for now. Call my assistant tonight. Will, please say you agree. Please. These are evil people, and you won't stand a chance on your own. Promise me you'll do it."

"All right. Okay. I'm all yours. What about my kids? Are they in danger?"

"Yes, they are, and we'll have to do something there too."

"Sue Ellen is going to hate me even more than she does already."

"We all hate you. Will, I have to go. The sheriff's talking to a group of newspaper reporters. God only knows how much damage he's doing out there. Promise me you'll call."

"I promise." Deep down, he knew that Steve was right.

Chapter 42

As he hung up and left the phone booth, Will heard Watson barking and growling. He heard a loud bang and saw one of the men hit the top of his jeep with a baseball bat. Watson jumped back from the open window and ducked when the bat struck above his head.

"Hey! What are you doing? That's my jeep!"

The man with the bat turned, temporarily ignoring the dog. He was heavyset and not as tall as Will. He gripped the bat with long dirty fingernails. His angry face was beet red, framed in a scruffy black beard. A ponytail at the back of his head seemed out of place with a burr haircut on top of his head. He'd been drinking.

"Is that your stinking, mangy dog? He should be put to sleep, and I'm going to save you the trouble." He raised the bat to smash the dog whose head and neck were now out the window, striking and growling at him.

Will grabbed him by his ponytail with one hand and pulled him back. The swinging bat missed Watson by inches. The man cocked the bat again and, this time, focused on MacKenzie. Two of the wild man's friends, both with identical haircuts and ponytails, came out of the mini-mart to see what was going on. Will held on to the big man's ponytail and struck upward, hitting him hard in the nose with the heel of his other hand. Blood poured from the man's nose, and he dropped the bat and screamed. Both of his hands moved to cover and protect what was left of his broken, mangled face.

Will whirled him around just as the man's other two friends were rushing to his aid. A final kick to the crotch sent the man down, doubled over in pain. Will reached for the baseball bat, hoping the other two weren't armed.

A warning bark and look from Watson told him that a third man had snuck up from the back. Will ducked, simultaneously swinging the bat backward at the same time. He caught the third man in the knees, and the man dropped a knife as he fell. Will backed up and faced his remaining assailants. They hesitated, not liking the odds. They were more used to fighting people who couldn't fight back.

"Enough," said a man with earrings dangling from each ear.

"We got to get Bull to the hospital. He's bleedin' t' death!" said the other one. The man's eyes seemed on top of his nose; they were so close together.

The third man on the ground was crying. "Help me. My legs is broke. Help me."

A female voice broke in. "They took my money!" She was also crying. "The big one's got it in his pocket." It was the woman in the old Plymouth station wagon who'd parked next to their truck.

"Give the lady her money back! Will raised the baseball bat to back up his demand.

"It's $76. It's all I got!" she said, her voice hysterical.

Finally, the man who'd said "enough" agreed. "Get her money, Reece. Get it now!" And his companion bent down, reached into his friend's pocket, and removed a wad of bills.

"Give it to her!" Will threatened.

"I got to count it first."

"Give her all that money, or you're going to wish you had."

Reece looked up at his friend, who nodded his head, saying, "Give it to her. We gotta go. Bull might die, and Hoyt's legs look like they're broken."

"You got five seconds to lift those two into that truck bed; and don't try anything, or I'll put a load of twelve gauge up your ass. Move it!" Will reached inside his jeep as if to fetch his gun.

The two uninjured Mountaineer Brotherhood members didn't bother to check whether or not there was a shotgun. They hurriedly put their friends in the back of their truck and raced out of the parking lot, heading for Winchester Medical Center's emergency room.

Will watched until their taillights crested the hill over a mile away. Then he heard the woman say, "Thank you, mister. Why did they take all my money? My husband's out of work, an' we got six kids." Her tears were dried on her wrinkled, sun-darkened face. She was a hard-looking woman, with rough, calloused fingers, yellow teeth, and her hair tied back into a bun. "They gave me too much. It's over $200, you know. I only had seventy-six."

"Wait a minute." Will ignored the fact that she'd gotten extra money from the thugs. "I got something for you that might help." Watson licked his face when Will went to his jeep and opened the door. He emptied a paper bag full of junk food he'd just bought and placed a few packets of money inside. Taking the paper bag to the old woman, he said, "Promise me you won't open this until you get back to your apartment and remember me in your prayers."

"Cain't I look now?" she said as MacKenzie got in his jeep, started the engine, waved goodbye, and took off, heading for Cumberland on his way to Weston. "Hey! What's yore name?" she yelled, but Will had gone.

It was dark when Will stopped for takeout at a Cracker Barrel Restaurant in Bridgeport, West Virginia. He'd had a wonderful visit with Uncle Jim. Will had tried to sneak Watson into Uncle Jim's nursing home room. Before he had reached the first set of double doors, the nurses had caught him.

"Of course you can take the dog in," said Betty Bane, one of Uncle Jim's regular nurses. "But why don't you give him a shower first? My god, he smells!" She laughed but then became serious. His uncle had turned for the worse. He hadn't spoken for days and had not eaten much. They had begun feeding him intravenously.

Will stepped quietly into the room and noticed that his uncle was asleep. So he tried to wash the dog in the shower, but Watson kept shaking the soapy water off, covering Will with the mess. But it did do some good, at least for the dog. Will was able to remove most of the dirt and goo that had stayed with Watson since his morning jaunt.

Out of the shower and still wet, Watson went straight for Uncle Jim and sat by his head, whining softly, begging for attention. Uncle Jim's eyes opened when he heard the dog. He sat up and turned to Watson. His eyes teared up, and he patted the dog, calling him by the name of his old dog, Bo.

Then he noticed Will and said, "Will, it's Bo. Look, I thought he was dead," and he started kissing the dog's head and holding him with love. Watson loved it too. He licked Uncle Jim in the face, delighting in the attention.

"Why don't you stay for dinner, Will? I could eat a telephone pole. Where the hell is Betty? She's usually right on time."

Uncle Jim ate a huge meal of meat loaf, mashed potatoes and gravy, green beans, and homemade biscuits, all the while sharing his meal with Watson. "Bo looks like he's growed some, don't he, Will?" His eyes beaming as he admired the dog.

Will laughed. "Maybe Betty's giving him your food instead of bringing it back here."

After the meal, Uncle Jim fell asleep with a smile on his face. Will stood for a while, just looking down at his uncle sleeping peacefully. Then, he and Watson left, content that they didn't have to worry about Uncle Jim.

At the Cracker Barrel, Will over ordered since he was the only one in the nursing home that hadn't eaten. He paid for his dinner and then saw the pay phone in the back; he remembered he was supposed to call Steve's number at Justice. Irene answered after the first ring. "There you are," she said, not bothering to say hello, who's calling, or anything else. "I was expecting a call before this, Will. Did you get lost?"

"No, ma'am. I just got distracted. I hope you've had something to eat. I know it's late."

"Never mind about me. It's you we have to get situated. We may be running out of time." She gave him the address of a safe house in the Belle Haven section of Alexandria, Virginia.

Chapter 43

It took Will the better part of three hours to arrive at the address. His gas gauge was on empty when he pulled into the driveway. Although it was dark, several lights were on inside, and there were many floodlights on around the house and at neighboring houses as well. The property included a main house, a separate five-car garage, and a tennis court. A large, well-manicured yard surrounded the main house, which was sited at the top of a rise and somewhat secluded by trees and tall hedges. He could tell by the old brick exterior, the slate roof, and the huge columned white porch that he was going to be pampered.

As soon as the jeep stopped, the massive double front door opened, and a beautiful redhead in a smart suit welcomed him to come in. "Watson too," she said. "Hi, I'm Irene," and she shook his hand and petted the dog in one motion. She introduced them both to three other men who were wearing shoulder holsters with their ties and white shirts. Will noticed heavier weapons stored within easy reach.

"Are you hungry? Steve said you have quite an appetite."

"Naw, I ate. Steve's the one with the appetite. He can out-eat Watson, and Watson's always hungry."

"Yeah, and he never gains a pound. I have to work my ass off to fight every inch of fat."

"Looks like your work's paid off. I don't see an ounce of fat." Will was a natural flirt, and Irene was a beautiful woman. He wondered if she and Steve had anything going. Just as quickly, he dismissed the thought. Beinhorn was the most straight-arrow guy he knew.

"I can tell we're going to get along just fine." Irene flirted right back, thinking this guy was as handsome as they come, and single too. "Let me show you to your room." And she led Will and Watson upstairs to the master bedroom. One of the bodyguards followed with Will's luggage. He'd grabbed everything but the cooler, and the weapons that were wrapped in a blanket in the back of the jeep.

"Steve's still in Winchester. He's waiting for a deputy sheriff to wake up. The guy will have a lot to say about what happened. Looks like one of the bad guys might make it too. They took ten bullets out of him, and so far he's holding on. The back of his head was shot out. Doctor's said it was like trying to put Humpty Dumpty back together again. His name's Booger Bryant, and he's head of a DC street gang called the FU Crew. Steve and I have been after them for a couple of years now."

"I know a deputy named Roscoe Harris. He came to my house several times trying to solve a couple of killings in the neighborhood."

"That's the one. Apparently, he's a hero in all this. We can't wait to hear what he has to say. Now you get some sleep. Steve ought to be here tomorrow night. We have shift changes every twelve hours. Don't be surprised if you see some new faces when you wake up. Night."

"Will I see you tomorrow? I don't give a damn about Beinhorn. He and I've been seeing each other since Vietnam. You are a lot nicer to look at."

"I'll bet you say that to all the girls. We'll be seeing a lot of each other over the next few weeks. You are going to look like someone else when we finish your makeover. Good night." And she left.

After a shower, Will brushed his teeth and fell into bed. As usual, Watson crawled under it like he was at home. Will dozed off and on at first, and then fell into a deep sleep. He dreamed of a beautiful redhead who was always just one step ahead of him. Then she turned into a brunette, and then she looked like his ex-wife. He couldn't seem to reach her. But he didn't wake up. He slept soundly for nine hours and would have stayed in bed longer except for two huge paws on his chest and Watson whining in his face. Even though the dog's tail was wagging, he needed to go out. Will found a heavy white cotton robe in the bathroom, put it on, and hurried down the wide stairway. Watson bolted for the front door and didn't wait for Will to join him as he rushed outside. He must have held it as long as he could because he was peeing as he ran for the first boxwood bush.

Three new guards introduced themselves and led Will into the spacious, modern kitchen for some fresh coffee, orange juice, toast, sausage, bacon, scrambled eggs, and waffles. They left him to read several newspapers and enjoy his breakfast.

The headlines in the *Washington Post* read, "'NO NEW LEADS IN WINCHESTER SHOOTINGS." A picture of the sheriff was in front of his house.

He'd read half the article when he thought he heard something outside. Surprised that Watson hadn't returned, Will opened the kitchen door. It was a beautiful spring day, and the warming sun seemed to urge plants to grow and buds to pop. There it was again, a faint voice, yelling, "Get out! Get out!" He followed the sound as it became louder and louder, coming from a large house next door. He noticed the gate between the two houses was open. He walked through and came upon a luxurious swimming pool complex, and in the middle of the pool was Watson, swimming in all his glory, as if he owned the place. Watson continued to ignore the frantic woman who was screaming for him to get out of the pool. Will looked at her but didn't speak. He was too embarrassed. She hadn't seen him enter her yard; she was so intent on the dog.

She was wearing a yellow bikini and holding a towel as big as a tent around her shoulders. The early morning sun kept her face in shadow as she screamed at the dog. A heavy sweatshirt and a pair of blue jeans were at her feet. She must have come for a morning swim when she encountered the canine intruder. Steam from the heated pool enveloped her long shapely legs. She was standing barefoot on the edge of the pool, and her voice was getting hoarse. Something about her was familiar. He strained to see her face more clearly.

She jumped when she saw Will standing there and shouted, "Who are you? This is private property! Then, she just stood staring at him, her face changing from fear to recognition. Her frown turned into a smile.

"Will? Oh my! Will, is it really you? Oh, Will!" She dropped the towel and ran to him.

At once, he knew. He opened his arms, his robe falling loose as he embraced her, softly saying her name. "Maggie!"

Agent Dittmer's head was drooping toward his chest as his eyes fought to remain open. He was seated in the living room, next to the front door, facing a large bay window. Before he'd started to doze, he had a clear view of the driveway and the steps leading up to the front porch. A pump action shotgun lay across his lap and teetered in tune with his head.

In the pine-paneled library, just off the kitchen, Agents Sylvester and Nye were playing gin rummy for a penny a point. Their coats were off, hanging on the back of their chairs. Each man wore identical starched white shirts underneath their shoulder holsters. Submachine guns were stacked against the wall within easy reach.

"Gin!" exclaimed Sylvester as he slammed his cards down on the table, grinning from ear to ear.

"You are the luckiest son-of-a-bitch!" yelled Nye as he threw his cards in the air.

Neither man heard the car door slam out front. But Agent Dittmer did. The noise woke him from his slumber, and he caught the shotgun with an automatic reflex as he stood up. He backed behind the curtain as he observed the vehicle, all senses now on alert.

A smile spread across his face as he realized who it was. Irene's red hair was blown in many directions from her Mustang convertible ride, but he had no doubts that it was her. She had a dynamite figure to match her face. Dittmer knew she loved to drive fast with the top down, and she looked like she was still in a hurry. Both arms were filled with groceries, and she had to close the car door with her foot. Dittmer propped the shotgun against the wall and held the front door open as she ran up the steps, teasing her as he said, "Love your new 'do, Irene. It's very becoming."

Irene glanced in the mirror by the front door and yelped, "Holy shit! Hold these while I try to tame this mess." She handed the grocery bags to Dittmer and, after moving two pistols aside, found a brush in her purse.

Agents Sylvester and Nye finally heard the commotion at the front door and moved to help Irene. Every one of them had a crush on her and would have done whatever she asked even if she weren't the boss.

Irene strutted into the kitchen with the other agents in tow. "Where's our guest? Isn't he up?"

"Yep, an early riser. Had to let the dog out," said Nye.

"Already had his breakfast," said Dittmer.

"Already read the paper," said Sylvester. All three wanted to please Irene, showing that they were on top of the situation.

"Where is he? Did he go back to bed?" Irene noticed the kitchen door open as she asked the question.

The three agents looked at one another, hoping that one of them knew the answer, but dreading the silence that followed her question.

"Well, goddammit! Are you just going to stand there? Find him! Now!" Irene pointed to the kitchen door, to the upstairs, and to the basement, and each agent went in these directions, eager to move out of her glare.

She walked to the kitchen table where Will's breakfast dishes remained. He'd eaten everything except a half piece of bacon. His coffee cup was cold. The open newspaper was turned to page 3, where the Winchester massacre story continued from page 1. A picture of Will's house with the blasted front door frame accompanied the story.

Within three minutes, all agents returned to the kitchen and reported no sign of MacKenzie, and no sign of his dog either.

"The back gate was open." Agent Sylvester offered, slightly out of breath from covering the large yard.

"Let's move. Be ready for anything!" Irene grabbed one of her pistols as the others picked up their rifles and flew out the kitchen door. The distance to the back gate was about two hundred yards over wet, freshly cut grass, and they covered it in seconds. Normally, when the arched gate was closed, its green color blended with the tall hemlock hedge. But this morning, bright light poured through the opening, reflecting off the swimming pool. The brightness temporarily blinded them as they fanned out on the other side, weapons at the ready.

Reaching the pool, they stopped and listened, but the only sign of MacKenzie was a crumpled cotton bathrobe, which lay near the diving board. Irene motioned for them to spread out and move quickly but quietly toward the majestic white brick mansion. The huge old house was covered in shadow by massive oak trees, which surrounded the entire structure.

Dittmer was the first to spot the dog. He was sitting patiently outside the house, looking through a set of double sliding glass doors. Every now and then, the dog's tail would wag, and he would emit a soft whine.

Asking the others to cover her, Irene crept through the boxwoods and azaleas. She crawled over the ivy-covered brick wall and across the patio to reach the dog. Watson sensed her coming. His nose twitched, remembering her scent from the night before. He didn't turn until her hand touched his head; he was so focused on what was inside. Even then, he just licked her hand and resumed his gaze.

Irene stared inside, mimicking the dog. All she could see was a high-ceilinged room with oil paintings on the wall, and antiques spread around. The place seemed elegantly comfortable. *Old money*, thought Irene as she surveyed the room.

She motioned to others to come forward after concluding it was safe to do so. This time, Watson stood and growled, turning toward the men, his ears back and fangs bared. Irene held him by his collar and soothed him, saying, "Good boy, down, good boy, it's all right, down, down, good boy." The dog sat back down and relaxed a bit but still kept his eyes on the others. Irene had them each give their hand to the big dog, showing that they were friendly.

"MacKenzie must be inside. The dog hasn't moved; he seems to be looking for his master."

Dittmer tried the door. It was unlocked.

Irene asked Nye to hold the dog, motioned for Sylvester to go around the other side to the front of the house; and with Dittmer behind, she entered the room.

Watson lurched forward when the door opened, but Nye held him firmly by the collar. When Irene shut the door, Nye began petting the dog, saying, "Good dog. That's a good dog."

None of the house lights were on, but Irene noticed a yellow bikini top at the foot of a wide staircase. She and Dittmer worked their way quietly through the house, checking each room, and then they heard a long moan from upstairs.

"What the hell was that?" said Dittmer, and he looked at Irene with his eyes rolled up to the top of the stairs.

"I don't want to guess, but we'd better check it out." Irene motioned for Dittmer to follow quietly up the stairs. They heard a moan again and stopped halfway up, guns drawn.

"Maybe he's being tortured?" Dittmer whispered into Irene's ear.

"I don't think so," she answered and began moving up the stairs again, eyes on the door where the sounds had come from.

Irene pointed to a chest in the hall and indicated that Dittmer wait there while she slowly checked the door. It was unlocked. She opened it a crack. She listened but could hear nothing. She looked into the room as far as the crack would permit. A yellow bikini bottom was lying on the floor just inside the room. She saw a man's slipper lying next to a bedpost. A bedspread was piled in a heap next to the slipper. Then she heard a noise! The noise sounded like running water.

Irene cocked her pistol by racking back the slide and flipped the safety off. She heard different sounds, first a laugh, then a giggle. She opened the door further and waited. Nothing moved, but she still heard the sounds of running water. She assumed that she was observing the master bedroom. Bright wallpaper with Asian designs covered two walls. Tall windows spilled light into the room, outlining a huge canopied four-poster bed. A mirror above a large chest of drawers gave her a clear view of the disorderly bed. Covers and sheets were half off the bed; pillows were askew. The reflection also presented a partial look through an open door to the bathroom. The sounds were coming from the bathroom. Behind her, Dittmer remained on full alert, concerned that she, and not he, was the person facing a very dangerous situation.

Irene stepped into the bedroom and was confused by a familiar odor. The smell didn't match what her other senses were telling her to expect. Carefully, she crept up to the bathroom door. Just to be sure, she peered into the bathroom and saw movement in the shower. Two people were in the shower, and they were both active. Steam clouded their naked bodies, but there was no doubt about the situation. Will MacKenzie with a woman. Will's face was pressed against the woman's breast. Then he started to move lower. She watched for a moment longer than necessary, then holstered her gun and tiptoed out of the room. She almost bumped into Agent Dittmer, who had moved to the doorway, ready to provide backup.

Irene carefully pulled the door shut and, at the same time, placed her finger to her lips, asking Dittmer for silence. "He's okay." She spoke in hushed tones as she moved away from the room. "He appears to be in good hands. We'll wait outside with the dog. He has to come out soon." Her smile widened with each step down the stairs.

Dittmer was confused. "Are you sure he's all right?"

"Positive. Apparently, he's made friends with the neighbor. He was taking a shower."

"A shower? At a neighbor's house? Irene? One minute he was in the kitchen, eating breakfast and reading the paper. Then, he calls the dog, and the next minute he's gone. Now, you tell me he's taking a shower. What the hell does all this mean?"

Irene paused, carefully selecting her words, while brushing the hair back from her face. "It means, Agent Dittmer, it means that you guys need to do a much better job of protecting your witness, or somebody's going to get screwed."